CERES

2525

By

Micheal Lee Nelson

I

First Edition 2016

ISBN: 978-0-9965630-0-0

Gravity Well Press
Franklinton, NC, USA

Notices:

*This book is a work of fiction. Names, characters, places and incidents either are the product of the authors' imagination, or used fictitiously. Any resemblance to actual persons, living or dead, business establishments, events, or locales is coincidental and not intentional by the author.

*This book contains no detailed scenes of intimacy. Characters are depicted within committed monogamous relationships. Those that vary are characterized as the exceptions to in-world societal norms.

* Combat violence enhances the realism of the action. Gore is restrained to a mild level.

*We take extensive liberties related to religious dogma and beliefs. This material is not presented in order to cause offense or schism in the real world of Earth 1.0, but to lay the foundation for our speculative fictional Galactic setting. Future works in the series will expound upon the themes hinted upon in this book.

*Finally, we genuinely hope you enjoy reading "Ceres 2525" as much as we enjoyed writing it for you. At the end of the book, we have included information on our other books and how readers can contact us. We love hearing from readers, so drop us a line!

Dedicated:

To Dad,
My first, toughest superhero. Thank you and God bless you. R.I.P.
Love, Micheal

To my handsome boys,
I love each of you sooo much. I look forward to reading you these stories myself and enjoying the fruits of these labors together. It is for you that I write of a future imagined greater than today. I am so proud of what handsome and wonderful young men you are. I hope you can all share my sense of wonder at what could be.
Love, Dad!

To my own personal hot redhead,
Thank you, Scottie, for helping me make this dream come true. It has been thanks to your positive encouragement that this book is in my hand right now. You gave consistent moral support as I invested the time into this project.
Thank you for your loving understanding as I worked hard over time to fulfill my highest personal dream. I hope to and work to help make your dreams come true as well.
Thank you, my own sweet strawberry.
Love, Micheal

Author's Note:

"Risk something or forever sit with your dreams." –Coach Herb Brooks

After 40$^+$ years of passive Scifi fandom, I finally decided I did not want to sit forever with my greatest dream. I have been blessed of late, to receive positive support, encouragement, and assistance to fulfill my lifetime dream of writing my book.

It is now known: CERES 2525 is my novel. Mine. Now yours, too! The dream too. I pass it on to you: make your dreams come true, whatever they are. Write *your* book. Think BIG, you have to think anyway.

What happened to me is, these "what if" questions about the past and future of mankind have percolated in the back of my head for a long time, questions inspired by the genre, my contrarian nature, and my observations as I simmered through life. I needed to catch fire!

Then along the journey, I conceived of my own kind of heroic character. He is like my imaginary friend, and he tells me these crazy stories! I got excited thinking of him and how he would live in this speculated future of Earth I have imagined! I wrote it down. I told others, showed more still. They caught my enthusiasm for my character, my story. They encouraged me to share it with you, the reader, the sci-fi fan, the world! They got me fired up to write more!

So, my hero is a bit of a daredevil. He lives a fast-paced life of excitement. You should hear all the things he gets himself into and out of in ways I can't even imagine… well, until I am in the middle of a sentence and he tells me how the sentence ends and how the story goes on. I feel like his biographer.

That is the most fun thing about writing, the discovery of fresh new things, unimagined a moment ago, that seem to come out of nowhere.

Like, the time I wrote my imaginary friend here into a duel to save a redhead woman, from a space pirate who was much faster than him. He attacked that problem by… well, I'd better not spoil the surprise for you, but Act 1 is gonna blow you away too!

I bet you catch the fire and have to see how it all ends! …or is that, begins? Yes!

-Micheal Lee Nelson

Table of Contents:

Chapter 1
Apparently, I'm a Prince

Placetime:
Milky Way Galaxy, Periphery Sector, Shambhala System
Planet Nirvana, City of Shangri-La
2525/7/09/1845 (Local evening)

Oh, the joyful rush!

The powerful flush of energy flowing through his arteries, pumping into tensed muscles, ready for release. Nostrils flared, breaths deepened, senses sharpened, as if accelerated beyond the slowed world, stealing extra life between the chrono's sluggish ticks. The primal instinct to hunt always provided a thrill, prepped the mind and body for the animalistic power soon to explode on his prey.

Fight or flight was never a choice for Ceres. He was a fighter. He craved to fight them. Now!

Midnight colored Ravens broke through the orange strato-clouds of dusk. "Space raiders inbound, Ka'ra!" Ceres' baritone voice called out to his contact. "Tight linear formation, about ten black space-fighters," he analyzed their flight pattern, already running intercept scenarios in his head.

Descending into the atmosphere on wide forward-swept atmo-wings, local air-raid sirens blared out the intruder's background theme music. The sirens had drawn his attention to the horizons, the cloud layers, hovering overhead like a roof on the large world.

His eyesight sharpened by military training picked out the incoming ships right away. The aggressors triggered the rush. He relished it. Tightening fists stretched his black flight gloves, creaking with the strain. If they came for blood today, why disappoint them?

"Oh, Ceres," the girl's coy voice called out his name as if he was making a joke. "We're just getting an airshow today." She made one of her own.

His eyebrow raised at Ka'ra's humor, out of place in such a serious situation. He's experiencing the jellied bowels of adrenaline; she's deflecting her fear with humor? Maybe she's a vac? Space between the ears?

"If they attack I'll pop up to the marina," Ceres said. "Jump in my launch, join the defense forces." He thought it a fitting word to recycle from old Earth, orbital platforms for parking or storing private spacecraft were dubbed "marinas," after their waterborne analog.

Flexing his arms to ease their vibrating tension, he admired the cuts in his athletic physique showing through the taught fabric of the Navy-blue flight suit. Daily physical training and vain pride maintained his toned build since his sports-hero days. His public still saw him as the greatest athlete in the galaxy. He would hate to crush their image of him.

To channel adrenaline-jagged nerves into action, Ceres rechecked the adjustments on the multi-pouched military gun belt around his waist. The smooth grey energy pistol comforted him, despite training to consider *himself* the weapon, at the core of his combat systems.

Out of long habit, he confirmed a full charge worth several shots if needed. Not that a pistol would be much use against a space fighter, but one never knew to what the dynamic flow of combat would lead. Be prepared at all times. Like a good Star Scout.

The belt added storage to the many drawstrings, loops and pockets of his trader-style cargo over-pants. Like any good trade ship engineer, he carried a few gadgets and parts, ready for anything. Not an approved duty uniform ensemble, but on leave, officers could wear what they liked.

Ceres liked the trader's utility and comfort combined with his military uni's base layer and all its special features. It also meant he was ready to go kinetic at any time. With his family history as targets for kidnapping, he needed to be prepared like a good Star Scout.

Flexible from years of grav-ball, he touch-checked the thin red leaves layered across his back; his retracted armor plating was ready to extend over the thin space-grade base suit on command. *All locked and loaded.*

Ceres caught Ka'ra's stark white reflection in the window as he straightened up and finished his gear check. *Was I preening? I wonder how she sees me?* To most, well-tanned skin told the story of years crisping under the intense radiation of numerous stars pouring down upon a stellar career. *I bet she'd say I look burnt,* Ceres thought, *next to a sun-phobic like her.*

In a tight military "parade rest" stance, two-meter tall Ceres stood transfixed at the wall-sized crysteel window, eleven kilometers above the fertile green valley floor. Crysteel was the common term for transparent alloys of steel, replacing glass on all but the most retro and low-tech worlds. He knew it would hold up to the vacuum of space from whence these towers had landed, to quick-craft the city. They certainly would keep him from falling to his death below.

Of course, the air was too rare for open windows or patio living up here. From the penthouse suite he looked down on the parklands between the five sharp arcology towers making up the City of Shangri-La. Forget "ant people," from here he could barely make out the shape of a hover bus.

From his travel experience Ceres knew, typical arcologies—arcs, so named during the Modern Exodus when they saved mankind from a freezing Earth—were self-sufficient towers, one and a half kilometers across their square base. Each held housing and manufacturing, food and power production, workspace, and recreation areas "sufficient to nurture one million souls."

His mother had once quoted that passage from the ancient history holos about the dawn of the Galactic Age of Mankind. She was his reason for being out here on the Rim. Where the hell was she? Did these fighters threaten her among the millions of citizens in Shangri-La? The creak of his gloves echoed off the crysteel again.

Traditional arc's—tightly stretched pyramids topping twelve kilometers—upper decks housed their navigational astronomy, weather control, and communications links. In addition, air-car hangers and telepods for "popping" down from orbital platforms or system ships, as Ceres had earlier. Judging by the towers he could see across and below him, these arcs were third-gen—human designed—with floors that extended or opened out into flowery extensions of curvy stepped terraces.

The earliest three arcs landed here had squatted lower, by expanding their bases the now 10 km tall pyramids became much more stable. Towers Four and Five must have arrived from their progenitor worlds recently, the spires had yet to blossom.

"No shots fired." Ceres tracked the Raven ships, flying cleanly between the five arcology towers making up the circular Shangri-La City. "But that is an aggressive move to fly right through the heart of your city. That was a warning pass."

Skycar traffic peeled away from the city's airspace, only too happy to avoid the threatening fast movers. To Ceres they looked like schools of bait fish he'd seen on Aquapolis, swarming away from predatory blowfins trying to have sushi for lunch.

Through the Modem/Transceiver/Router, or MeTR, implanted in his brain, Ceres commanded his small craft, docked in the orbiting marina, to initiate pre-flight warm up routines. He avoided linking to the local network, the WetNet of minds, but monitored the emergency and military feed into it. The network passed on and amplified his transmission so it could reach his distant ship.

"Strange, they're just advising citizens to remain calm. Calling on their 'peace' forces to stand down and maintain order? They're not scrambling fighters, powering up shields or laser batteries? Nothing?" Something didn't add up. This place had a backwards reaction to these intruders.

"Be calm, Ceres." Ka'ra purred. A petite woman with straight ivory hair, she sashayed closer to him, stopping within arm's reach of his side. "This is a natural part of life in this Rimward sector. Once in a while we have these raids." Her pale hand waved slowly as if it was too much effort to bother. "If everybody pays their tributes, they have nothing to fear."

He turned towards her, mouth agape. "Are you downed on cannahol?" he accused her with a slight chuckle, then turned back to analyze the intruding spacecraft. Cannahol, the latest street depressant, was renowned for its daylong downer effect, a mellow vacation from the real-world's life of hard work. He had heard rumors that out here in the Periphery Sector it was commonplace, the product of pirate gangs. They didn't care that the drug's effect came from slowly disabling nerves within the brain. He had never done drugs.

Lord God, your warrior is ready. Faced with this, what would you have me do? faithful Ceres prayed for guidance.

From the bodice of her white, skirted, lace top, Ka'ra retrieved a slim atomizer and sprayed a mist under her tongue. She wound around between Ceres' body and the immense crysteel pane. Making eye contact with his sapphire blues, she walked her white-tipped fingers lazily up his chest. "Aren't you enjoying meeting me here? Take a deep breath and relax."

4

"Look we both just popped in," he reasoned, stepping to the side half a stride, "I'm following my family's connections which led me to you." He observed the fighters' maneuvers, glancing for eye contact with Ka'ra.

Her reddish irises stood out on her petite albino body, decorated in theme by her all white wardrobe. She went all the way with the style God and nature had given her. It was hard to follow the action with such a lovely distraction.

"You're supposed to be watching my father for us? I've just met you up here, Ka'ra. You seem to be a nice girl but, I'm not as… hmmm, 'socially active'? …anymore, as the news holos made it seem." Damn, her perfume smells great. What is that? Amber musk, mixed with her pheromones?

His eyes blinked, quickening, as did his breathing. Control your body, smart guy, he thought to himself. She's just a regular gal with a nice color theme, not one to introduce to your mother. He winced. Good time to change the subject.

"Besides, aren't you supposed to be leading me out to my long lost father? That's why my family employs you, to watch him."

Bursts of red and orange light flashed up the mirror surfaces of the five stretched-pyramid buildings. Seeing it light up Tower Five in front of him, Ceres looked back past Ka'ra, to see Ravens below, streaking away from an exploding and falling skybridge.

Links between neighboring towers, at one and five kilometer heights, the ten skybridges ringed the city, filled with popular shops and parks, and therefore people. The excuse he was waiting for. When the trigger is pulled the charge explodes, launching the projectile into action.

"Ditch! They shot out one of the bridges. That's it. I'm going out there." He turned towards the back of the room, meaning to jump into the luxury suite's own three meter spherical telepod and pop up to the marina. But why did his legs wobble like jelly, and a sudden chill flow through his veins as if he were standing on frozen old Earth?

Not exactly the heroic leap into action I envisioned. He put out his hands to steady his balance, turned and put one back on the window. "Woah. Must be shockwaves in the building, from the fighter's missiles? High explosive warheads," his brow wrinkled.

More small black attack ships rolled over the edge of the nearest valley ridge and joined the formations of flocking space fighters, rated for both space and atmospheric flight. Some—too many—looped around to make a run at another skybridge, while others climbed for altitude.

Ka'ra stepped closer to Ceres. "Here, let me help you. Sit down here."

She pushed him towards the plush grav lounge, a chaise-style floating half a meter above the polished real wood floor with soft area rugs underfoot. The faux animal furs reminded him of his famous aunt Claudia, her private island on planet Ceres, and her decorating style that allowed her to vacillate between recluse and Wilmingwood socialite as her career, marriages, and moods allowed.

"My legs are failing me?" he questioned aloud. It seemed odd, that he could barely walk, yet somehow she was helping him?

Just a few years out from his academy days, he worked out to maintain his peak physical condition. He had grown more into his manly body as he entered his mid-twenties. She seemed to be in typical slim shape for a young woman, generous curves and prettiness, and a sexy attitude. Yet she's handling this building-quake better than him. How?

A whooshing sound, like "wwwhhrrooOO" reverberated from outside, rising in volume from a whisper to a roar until the window flashed like a strobe. A score of Ravens whooshed by up the length of the building, blocking and releasing the sunlight in staccato bursts. Still, Ka'ra stood motionless over Ceres.

"I see you are feeling fine." he said with a question implied in his tone, watching her with growing suspicion. "I'll just get to the popper. In my ship I should be fine." Losing his equilibrium alarmed him, hampering his progress around the furniture.

"You have space legs, good for floating. Maybe you're not so used to land?" she asked, smiling sweetly. "People react to ground quakes in different ways. I'm from here, for example. That's why I'm meeting you here, for your father." She settled Ceres back onto the chaise. "There we are. Now let's work on the view."

'For your father?' he thought, That's backwards, isn't it? Her bubbly flirtatious manner seemed to become forced. She was acting overly perky considering her city was under attack and the building she stood in at over ten kilometers high wobbled from the blasts of missiles next door. This was getting weirder by the moment.

"TriMaX activate." Ka'ra commanded. The central portion of the room around the luxury nauga-suede furniture cluster flared with light as the standard TMX opening sequence announced the start of the home holovideos display. Ceres turned his head to the window, where reds and oranges glared so much more brightly the holo washed out.

A heat wave of infrared radiation rolled over the room from one side of the huge window to the other. The hyper-building swayed from the force of a distant concussion wave. Finally, the sound of the explosions reached them, a massive "SHOOBOOOMM!" lagging behind all the light speed radiations. Expecting it, he didn't jump, but Ka'ra did.

"Okay, what's going on?" Now he could not move his legs. They felt like he had slept wrong, pinching off the bloodflow. Sometimes he awoke from a recurring bad dream, unable to move due to the sleep paralysis that kept him from lashing out as he dreamed of movement.

That's how this seemed, familiar. But why now? He craved to go fight off these attackers, defend the city. Why was he falling apart instead?

"Invert display. God's view of the city." Ka'ra called out to the penthouse's environmental controls, "Fifteen kilometer altitude."

Holographic images resolved into a crisp, high-resolution, live action, overhead view. Ceres looked up on the supposed "modern paradise" of Shangri-La, its ground level parklands now depicted on the ceiling. So much for paradise, at least today, huh?

She allowed him, his body now stiff, a perfect overhead view, reversing angles to account for his reclining position. He was like God looking down onto the two meter holo-city spires the ant-like humans had built, but unable to do anything but watch.

The holotank depicted clouds and the occasional flock of black space fighters flashing by. Angry flashes of light beamed between the fighters and the skybridges bracing the damaged arc; its upper floors of public telepods and hangers decapitated. Ceres realized the stump of Tower Five would be directly across from where he sat in the adjacent Tower Four. If only he could turn away from the holo to see it directly.

He watched the live holo, horrified as the tower's top gouted heavenward, a massive pyre of flames. *Magnesium gel?* There would be no escape for the million-odd inhabitants of Tower Five today.

"I godda gobe," he said, his voice slurring. "Sumthinsh wwuh-wong."

A feeling of stasis-freeze wormed its way through his veins like ice snakes. Finally recognizing he too was in danger, Ceres tried to grasp his service issue sidearm, the slim M2500 plasma pistol holstered on his right hip. He could not raise his arm. Not a finger would move. His internal alarms were ringing like Cathedral bells.

Ka'ra leaned her body closely over his reclining form again, pressing her upper chest against his cheek. *She's really coming on to me? Now?* The imminent death of a million people was a definite turn off for him.

She reared up, producing a small bulb-tube and dropper, and dripped a tiny amount of liquid into each of his eyes.

Ceres blinked repeatedly in response, finally realizing what was happening. *Must've released my eyes from the paralysis? Great, now I have to watch whatever she wants. What the hell's the point? We're under attack!*

"Breathe, rich boy," Ka'ra said. To Ceres it sounded like her voice grew more forceful. Her sugary sweet tone and all its charm fell away, revealing a new side of her personality, something more predatory. "Or, should I say, my 'prince'?" Her wicked grin and candied voice, now all business, sent shivers down Ceres' tightening spine.

I can't believe I've fallen into a trap. I know better, considering the history of my family. People are dying out there. This is sick!

The flexible bands of his suit tightened, squeezing his ribs then releasing to fill his lungs. Must've crossed the line on low respiration. Thank you, Navy! Let's hope it doesn't need jumpstart mode for the heart.

Satisfied with his state of paralysis, Ka'ra swung one leg over him and sat on his solid thighs. Her tender skin, pale and smooth, showed through the outer latticework seam that ran down her white leather pants. "Okay, hon. Now that I have captured your attention, it's time to watch the show! Then I will explain and we'll leave."

The holo darkened as dozens of small black starships poured out of the heavens in line formations of ten or more. Bombers, over 100 of them, Ceres estimated. Their Size II hulls were twice as large as their fighter cover. More than twice the payloads.

Must be a special day. Starships rarely slog down into the goo of atmo due to their huge plasma drives and lack of streamlining. These bombers were proof that, given engines powerful enough, even bricks can fly.

They took turns lining up strafing runs, blasting away between the buttresses at the foot of Tower Five. Massive contrails marked their flight paths as star-hot, radio-heated plasma engines forced them through the dense lower atmosphere of the large planet Nirvana.

If you're going to commit Galactic crimes of war, the last laws you're worried about are environmental. He did not connect with Ka'ra's mind despite her continual link requests via the WetNet. He wanted to keep his thoughts private, especially now, especially from her. For some reason he decided he could not trust her. Could it be the kidnapping?

Okay Mr. Brilliant. Assess the situation. He had lost control of his body but his mind seemed perfectly clear. Ka'ra had her full faculties. He bet she had drugged him with a paralytic in her breath spray. Possibly a two-part agent, working with something already dissolved in her bloodstream—if not part of her DNA?—to which she was immune.

Exuded with her sweat, that is why she pressed her chest to his face. Made sure he got a breath full of her pheromones. Sophisticated poison?

And she's supposed to be monitoring my father for my family? All my life I have prepared to find my parents and rescue my mother. The last thing I needed is to be taken hostage for ransom by the pirates he's with? Uncle Manny will never let me hear the end of this. Let alone my Sensei!

"Power up telepod." Ka'ra said. She could have used her MeTR. She must have wanted to show him that her voice was command programed here. This was a setup, a trap. By who?

A glance at the holo, Tower Five burned from the top and the base levels, plus the connecting SkyBridges were down. Their stumps jutted out like decapitated limbs cauterized with too much flame. The million or so survivors now besieged, awaited their fates within their horrible death trap.

From his Academy engineering training, Ceres knew the huge pirate fleet he had seen so far could easily continue bombing the tower support buttresses. With so many ships, it would not take many runs bombing the base to send the whole tower and million residents smashing down to the valley floor below.

In fact, they must have already held back from their full damage potential. A pit formed in Ceres' gut as he thought it through. The huge flocks of vultures broke off and orbited the group of towers, as if waiting for a wounded beast to die, confirming his suspicions.

A new set of black ships pierced down out of the clouds. Longer and fatter, these slower moving Size III ships were tipped with strong, spike-shaped boarding prows. Their powerful forward shields pushed aside the atmosphere like glowing umbrellas as they plowed forward.

Hovering at different levels, the newcomers took their own turns at boarding actions on the hapless tower. Ceres wanted to run to their aid. Forced to watch, he felt as helpless as the tower inhabitants did. First, each of these assault ship's fired a plasma weapon like a flame tongue into the side of the tower before them. Blue energy lattices reached out, clearing a path through the air for the solar prominence-like plasma cannon to erupt.

"Zoom in on Dragon Three." Ka'ra called out to the controls.

She must want to see the carnage on the victims faces? What kind of psycho did his family hire?

The Dragon's aft plasma thrusters fired, stabbing the sturdy ships into the weakened holes they had burned into Tower Five. He knew the folded fingers of the prows blossomed inside the tower levels, securing the pirate ship to the surface of the tower. He could see one of them smashing out through a weak section of the tower.

Between them, passages opened to disgorge their crew of boarders. To Ceres it looked like a brace of giant vampiric squids holding on as they drained the life from a sea whale, a horror he had witnessed on his mother's favorite planet. Great image to bring along to this party.

"Every year our pirate King picks one of these Rimward arcology cities for a little...show of force?" Ka'ra grinned wickedly. "We have to keep them in line." Ceres watched as she moved towards his feet and commanded the chair's controls again. "Detach stabilization."

He felt dizzier as the chaise shifted and bobbed under his sprawled weight. *'Our'? 'We'? Whose side is she on?*

"Magnify on Tower Five. Slow zoom out," she ordered. The WetNet comm chatter shifted to shrieked cries for help as savages flooded through whole floors, killing, stealing, raping, and kidnapping as they went. The twelve, now eleven, kilometer tall arcology known locally as Tower Five suffered plunder and pillaging by vicious men and women.

Ceres saw the holo-depiction of hundreds of people jumping and falling from the upper floors as the liqua-fuel dripped downwards and burned. Smoke drafted up in the lower floors, forcing many to the windows, gasping for precious clean air.

His chest tightened, sympathetic with what he estimated must be thousands of victims. He felt frustrated by his restraints and inability to do no more than observe. Ceres' craving to take action, to fight these invaders made him struggle mentally, but it earned him nothing but more anguish.

His perspective rotated wildly as Ka'ra spun the floating chaise lounge around end-for-end. Looking up now between her breasts, the holo-arc's seemed to pierce down into the room around her smiling face.

Ka'ra pushed Ceres a few meters back and within the stout frame of the telepod. The humming sound grew louder, surrounding him, coming from all around them inside the chamber. Stepping to the side so he could see out, she stood upon the white glowing floor panels. Reaching outside the spherical containment housing, she pressed a small red button placed mid-height on the edge of the hatch frame, then again grabbed ahold of his repulsor chaise.

In response, the crysteel door panel curled around the side and clunked solidly into place. Great, at least he could still see the holographic scene of the tower assault, at a high angle over his forehead. How thoughtful.

The arcology, a grand burning monolith poking down from the ceiling, seemed to impale the feathery white hairs of the cirrus layer. Standard equipment, sensor filters removed the obscuring clouds so the high-resolution image of the plundered burning Tower Five remained pristine.

She said, "It's just so fortunate you wanted to come out this season and meet your father! We decided now was a perfect time to show you the fleet in action." Panels glowed in the sphere, their hum rising in tone and volume.

'We' again? I can't believe my long-lost father is connected to this...atrocity, this holocaust.

"So, in a way, you have your father to thank for this show of force today. Kind of like a victory parade for our armed forces? After all, we control the sector. We're the pirates."

Ceres visualized the machine's operation. Engineer trained, he couldn't help but analyze anything his life depended upon so often. Inside the telepod a small wormhole formed, a pinpoint of bright light hanging over Ceres, captured from the quantum foam by the rings of exotic gravity plates. When the machine forced it open in a surge of harmonic power, they would vanish from here. No telling where she would take him on the other side.

Blinking had to do, replacing the gritting of his teeth, maybe even a gulp. Nah, he was too pro for that. Let it come. Replacing the flexing of fingers too. Getting better by the nanosecond. He would have smirked.

Due to his experience with telepod travel, Ceres had long ago grown used to the strange sensation of a strong gravity field squeezing him. It felt like a ton of weight both crushing down from above and buoying up from below.

She did not look comfortable, though. Ka'ra closed her eyes, shook her head, and stuck out her tongue in an impish expression. Ceres tried to chuckle and smirk, but could not.

No witty vet-to-newbie quips, either. Pity, those were some of his best. He had to sit back and enjoy the sideshow to the main event happening in the room.

"We're modelled loosely after the Viking pirates of ancient times," she continued. "I'm a Valkyrie, a recruiter. I'm sent out to bring in worthy new prospects."

'We?' Ceres thought, *There it is. You are a traitor to my family for kidnapping me. I pity you and your 'pirate king.' Once your poison wears off, I am going to tear you all up!*

She lifted her hands to head height, opened them palm up and looked up dramatically, but sarcastically. "Bring them up into the heavens with us. Your father sent me for you."

Oh my God, help me! Did I hear that right? That means... No! he screamed in his head, unable to speak let alone yell.

Stunned now mentally too, Ceres watched the final few moments of the attack, holofilmed and relayed with only imperceptible breaks in clarity. Dragon ships pulled roughly out of Tower Five's upper floors, tearing portions of the walls out. Contents and inhabitants of broken floors rained across the valley far below. They left behind a malignant mess of smoke, flying dust and burning debris drifting on the breezes. For those citizens celebrating their survival of the pirate's attack, it was a ticker-tape parade for hell.

Emotional towers crashed down on Ceres' soul as he watched, rapt.

The view from the holo-cameras panned out, back, up and up above the clouds, through an array of many more small black ships above the planet. Finally, the feed warping the holo into a virtual fisheye shape, Ceres could make out vast radiator panels glowing red, emitting heat, hanging lengthwise beneath a large Capitol starship overhead.

Ka'ra smiled her predatory smile again, pleased to be the one to reveal to Ceres, "Yes, your father is our king."

Sucked into the wormhole that formed in the telepod, an instant later they were gone, the room empty, save for the echo of the machine's telltale vacuum slamming "POPP!"

Chapter 2
A Star is Born

MWG, Sol System, Earth's LaGrangian Point #4
Planet Ceres, orbital space
2500/7/10/0745

"We're going through hot!" shouted Admiral Tarsis. "Activate arrival beacon! Scan for attendant ships!" In the summer of 2500, Galactic Admiral Tarsis had not yet decided to retire young.

"Yes, sir," responded the dark-skinned man in the central grav-lounge. His tight, jet-black jumpsuit studded with brilliant diamonds scattered like a starfield, matched the uniform on rest of the bridge crew. "We'll take care of her, Admiral. I've successfully calculated a Sol System exit over a dozen times, sir."

"Not with my pregnant sister aboard you haven't, Mr. Nabigante'." Tarsis said. He gave his personal pilot/navigator his famous hard stare, perfected over a decade in the command chair. A moment later, his expression softened, worry lines creasing into his star-tanned forehead.

"I know you are just trying to reassure me, Lieutenant." Admirals do not apologize. Perhaps, some acknowledgement of the gesture? These loyal crewers deserve some explanation, however, of why they are being dragged off on their admiral's emergency personal leave. He nodded his head.

"Look, she told me, that bastard New Vegas husband of hers cheated, then hurt her and tried to cause her to lose the baby. I promised her it would be born at home!" As admirals are wont to do, he began to emphasize his words with volume. "I did *not* tell her, I *then* intend to haul the remains of her ex son-of-a-ditch into custody! *If* he survives. Now hurry *up*!"

Navigator Nabigante' closed his eyes, to more expertly guide the Admiral's Barge via the sensor feed directly into his HUD. The heads up display signals fed directly into his optic nerves behind the eyes. This gave him a secure and flexible interface, allowing him direct mental control of the ship through his MeTR. The Newport-au-Prince born pilot and navigator was the best in Admiral Tarsis' Fifth Fleet, famous in his own right for discovering new line-of-sight wormhole space lanes in two sectors.

Tarsis gazed past Nabigante's shoulder. Each station he monitored could pop up screens in their admiral's HUD, giving him instant access to their area of operations. As acting captain of the ship, the pilot often received those screens. Usually an admiral avoided that distraction, instead letting them report to their ship's captain or pilot while the fleet admiral held the big picture of the battle in mind. Tarsis and his pilot both looked down into the crew pit to monitor the rest of the team he had chosen personally to fly his ship and direct a fleet in battle.

While the merely rich had repulsor-car limousines and chauffeurs. Navy Admirals named Tarsis had a personal launch and their own pilot/navigator to interface with the ship, crew and fleet. Of course calling a Destroyer-type combat vessel with its own gate-drive a "barge" was both ancient naval tradition and Military Intelligence's way of providing misinformation to aid in the security of such an important person. Most admirals had lesser ships.

"Yes, sir." Nabigante' said, "We're here."

Intended to emerge relatively near the planet's gravity well at the satellite planet's own L-2 point, the wormhole's exit mouth opened up, causing a quake deep beneath the island planet's oceans. The quantum string connecting the two distant mouths of a wormhole had the gravitational force of a star, fortunately stretched between the two event horizons. In emergencies, the daring sometimes emerged closer than was prudent.

Tarsis privately mused, his three-sided spike-shaped Galactic Starship *Sentinel* knifing out of the event horizon, to be a skinny dipper diving through a sheet waterfall. Space reverted to normal outside. The relativity effect of time dilation in the intense gravity field made it seem as many as 30 seconds had passed in transit. He knew it was an instantaneous passage from entry to exit, as if stepping through a doorway.

When the wormhole's lag effect snapped back in sync with real-time, the admiral, like all aboard, got that familiar starlag feeling. Frequent flyers like Tarsis eventually got used to it.

He didn't bother looking over at Nabigante' any more, the veteran was one of the few humans who had never gotten space sick. Luckily, his bridge crew, like most professional starfarers, had learned to control their innards over vast experience transiting the galaxy.

"Clear space, sir." Nabigante' said, then into the secure comm channels he transmitted his thoughts via MeTR. *"Space Traffic Control: this is Galactic Starship Sentinel. We have Admiral Tarsis aboard and a family member in maternal labor. Requesting priority landing clearance at the Tarsis private spaceport."* Addressing his admiral aloud, he added "Sir, STC is handshaking with us."

"Standard orbit. Await landing clearance," Tarsis ordered.

"Standard orbit, yes, sir." This was standard operating procedure, SOP. Still, it was the admiral's job to give the orders to follow SOP, and the crew's job to receive and execute them. To allow a crew to simply follow SOP automatically was to invite undisciplined sloppiness, unwanted self-direction, and the loss of efficiency and morale that came with it.

Military details handled, it was finally time for personal matters. Tarsis turned his attention to his viewer, the nurse's eyes in the medibay providing visual feed of the birth room directly to his optic nerve feed. Coming just after transit, his vision took a few seconds to catch up from the lag.

It didn't nauseate *him* anymore, but he called out to warn his young sister due to her relative lack of space experience. It was easy for people to get dizzy while their inner ears struggled to stabilize. "Close your eyes Annemarie!" he spoke to her aloud, transmitted through the family MeTR channel link. "Don't move your head."

"Pilot has the bridge." Tarsis said aloud, not waiting for the crew's replies of "Yes, sir," as he exited the bridge. He also didn't bother to explain to them where he was heading. He dropped quickly down the lift chute, the gravity assisted elevator shaft running down the spine of the sturdy vessel.

"Too late!" Anne grunted out loud, which her brother heard through the doctor's link. Wracked in the grip of a powerful abdominal contraction inconveniently timed with her stomach's upward lurches, the blonde-haired woman hurled up the last of her bile. The nurse stood ready with a fresh pan and towels.

"Ditch!" Tarsis swore, now wishing he had not picked that moment to look in on his sister's progress. Strong as he was, his stomach threatened to join his sister's in emptying its contents. Timing mattered.

When she finished vomiting, for now, her eyes started searching frantically, seemingly unfocused on the scene around her. "We're here? We're home?" she asked.

"Annie, use the pilot as your viewer," Tarsis suggested, having discussed her plans before the transit. "Don't bother flicking about to all the sensors in the ship if you want to see home."

"Honey," the female doctor's voice rose, taking on a more authoritative tone. Tarsis grinned, glad that having a family doctor aboard ship was another executive perk of Navy Admirals named Tarsis. "You've held back as long as anyone I've ever seen. Your baby's been crowning for a while.

"But, if you don't push this baby out now, he's going to die inside you, understand? If you want him to live you must have him *now*! Don't make me use my plasma scalpel to cut him out."

Tarsis switched viewers to his sister, which was a more modest view for a brother of a sister who was giving birth. Seeing the blue-green waterworld she called home, through the same main optical sensors feeding the ship's pilot, Anne relaxed, content.

"All right. We're home. He can come now." The young woman seemed to melt into a more placid state as she stopped fighting nature and began allowing, even working with the muscle contractions inside her body.

"It will be over soon, okay sweetie?" the nurse soothed. "You're doing great! Now, let's have a baby, shall we?"

The young mother nodded and sat forward as coached, a mixture of fear of pain showing on her face, along with determination to bear down.

Perched in the center of the ship's exercise center, in the wet-tub remade into an ad-hoc birthing pool, the doctor waved her hands like a crazy person seeing imaginary friends. Tarsis imagined she must be clearing aside the holographic scanner feeds into her mind's eye HUD, so she could see the crowning babe more clearly with her naked eyes.

"Push, Anne," the doctor repeated, "He's ready. If you want your baby, it's time."

"C'mon honey," cooed the nurse.

From the hatchway, a louder, commanding voice, his fear and concern focused into directing what needed doing: "Annie, we're home. *Now!*"

Annie smiled and looked up to see her big brother marching towards her. She reached her hand towards him. Swiftly he took her hand and gritted his teeth. Crushing the bones in his solid hand, Annemarie bore down hard and groaned. Now that she relaxed and pushed, it did not take long.

"There he is. A boy!" Working right between Anne's legs, the doctor half floated in the warm tub and half floated the baby against her stomach with the nurse's help. "He was just waiting to come at home. He's a good size, your little boy."

The lights dimmed, probably under the doctor's thought control via her MeTR. Tarsis could no longer see what her MeTR enhanced for her, but he didn't want or need to see from her eyes right now anyway. He could tell well enough that the baby looked more dark, more blued than pink. Was that a problem? *Shouldn't he be pink?* Tarsis saw most events as strategic or tactical problems to solve. Why should this be any different?

"Suction," the doctor said. The nurse brought over the portable tool and gently sucked out the airways of the baby's nose then mouth. The doctor stood and turned the pale body, laying it face down along one of her extended arms. She rubbed the baby's back, slightly compressing the chest against her opposite palm, then letting off. He began to breathe, then cry. She rolled the boy over, his breath coming in deep and heavy for such shallow lungs.

"Yeaahh!" Tarsis cheered with relief, the baby sounded good enough to him. "You did it, Annie!" The nurse glanced up at him, flashing a stern look. He consciously calmed his voice, holding back from touching her out of concern, but wanting to hug her as always in happy family moments. "You had him at home, too. Good girl. Now, to the family question of the year," he smiled warmly at his little sister. "What's his name?"

They all saw that the boy was pinking up nicely already, the doctor handing Anne her baby. She pulled open the center of the soft half-gown draping her chest, reached all the way out for him and pulled the naked babe to rest across her chest. They sank part way into the warmth and comfort of the water. The little boy wiggled slightly against her skin and looked up at his mother through dark blue newborn eyes.

Anne sobbed and gasped sounding relieved, smiling through tears, wetting the discolored bags below her young eyes. She took up her son and held him bobbing at arms-length, brother and sister both seeing his beautiful face overlaid by the backdrop of their homeworld in her HUD.

"I'm naming him after home. I'm naming him Ceres."

Chapter 3
A is for Asteroid

Milky Way Galaxy, Periphery Sector, Whisp Nebula
Asteroid Valhalla (A-Valhalla), Landing Airdock
2525/7/10/2015

"It's been a lot of work," said Tyrian Tauri as he guided his son Ceres through the vast airdock. Dozens of small black fighter ships littered the hanger floor, lit red by the nebula shining down through the open bay doors overhead. "When I took over the Void Vikings they were a piss-ant minor annoyance in the Periphery Sector."

A small entourage of his lieutenants and consorts, including Ka'ra, watched and listened as their leader spoke with his newly arrived son. A lithe girl of fourteen Tyrian had introduced as Pearla and bragged over as his youngest consort, observant Ceres caught her gaze shifting back and forth between the two men. She glanced up at his hair then over at his father, likely noticing what Ceres had, the undeniable similarities the two men shared despite the estranged nature of their relationship.

Their hair was the same boyish blonde, their blue eyes close to matching in shade. In Ceres' smooth face was a reflection of the handsome youth Tyrian had once been. Time and combat had taken its toll on Tyrian's face, leaving a weathered but still handsome, though in a different way, mask of wrinkles and scars. Ceres saw his future in his father's face.

After a moment, caught by Ceres, Pearla blushed. He imagined she was just now realizing her danger if Tyrian's rugged face might turn and catch her staring at the wrong man. Ceres raised his eyebrows and rolled his gaze suggestively towards Tyrian, hoping she was smart enough to catch the hint.

Pearla's eyes flicked quickly away from Ceres, and his father turned to catch her smiling, doting on every word of her king. Silly young girl has to know better than to anger him with jealousy?

A moment later, when it was clear his attention would be back on showing off his world to his son, she probably could not help but look back again. Sure enough. Some people are easy to read.

This time she wore a disapproving mask and a slight frown of distain. Ceres smirked and chuckled silently, passing it off to his father as if Ceres was impressed by, whatever it was he had been saying.

"I gave them direction," Tyrian boasted aloud. "I gave them the ancient glory of Viking conquest! Now I actually control the sector." He must mean the city he just bombed? Better pay attention. This could come up again. Always distracted by the ladies, though never that young. A solid 'no.'

There were other differences, too, between father and son. Tyrian's hair was long, straggling down his broad shoulders and chest, while the young Ceres' hair modeled a flat top so neat it looked like it had been sculpted by a military grade barberbot that very morning. In fact it had been.

Arriving early for his expected first meeting with his father, Ceres had splurged on getting extra spiffed up. Only to be snatched away by the siren scent of this albino woman slinking next to him like a snake.

That bot was likely a pile of trash now, fallen to the valley floor with the rest of the skybridge. *Okay, pay attention smart guy*, Ceres thought. Plenty of time to remember the fallen later. Might need to know some tiny detail about this place to break out of here.

The Tauri men's apparel contrasted, too, he noticed. Ceres' tanned skin seemed to glow warmly in the gaps around his skin-tight top, and his military issue boots shined with a reflective gloss.

Tyrian wore his billowing black silk shirt loose. His tight black leather pant legs disappeared down into soft high boots. A long, wide ribbon of satin circled his neck, each end tied to short, fat-barreled pistols that hung conveniently near his hands.

Ceres identified them as a matched set of proton and electron beamers. Nice pairing, get you no matter which way you screened for, the other one would punch right through.

Ceres also noted Tyrian's use of the word "I" instead of "we." His newfound father apparently had the egotistical opinion that he was the essential, indispensable star element of the Void Vikings.

The rest of these three thousand pirates are merely his supporting cast? Crew flitted about the vast hanger, performing various maintenance and resupply jobs on the wide variety of black hulls present.

Nearby floated a Tenublian, a sentient that resembled, to human eyes, a cross between a jellyfish and squid. His skin was shaded blue. Ceres had an old friend named Medusa who had humorously explained his own usual blue shades as an alien concession to "people skills." Adventurous male squids sometimes went all blue to indicate to the humans around them that his sex was currently male, a fact the xenomorphic race had learned was somehow important to the overly sex-obsessed Solmen.

Of course, to them, we are the alien xeno-forms, strange, dangerous and in every way different from them, Ceres thought. Same for each of the species of sentients. Perspective matters.

The squid held himself firmly in place with six thick tentacle arms, while two of his many thin white feathery tendrils draped across the back of the necks of two unlucky humans. Twins? Nah. Clones. Why would they submit themselves to this "line-ape" duty? Being driven by a squid like... drones? Punishment?

Flashes of colorful energy illuminated the Tenublian's bulbous floating body, lighting up the thin tendrils from within as red waves and purple pulses rolled down towards the ends. The clones slid a heavy missile into its internal rack, extended for loading below a D-shaped armored spacecraft, their strong bodies responding stiffly to the mental command of their jelly master.

Ceres broke his gaze away from the spectacle, adding the "clone?" question to his growing list of riddles of how his father's band of pirates worked. Harsh non-judicial punishment was used in the Galactic Navy fleet as well, the captain of a vessel needing to operate as a virtual god to maintain discipline on long voyages away from civilized ports of call.

Ceres felt unnerved. Hard labor was one thing. Child-aged concubines another. Hmm, no, couldn't be slavery.

Could it?

To distract himself, inadvertently showing off his depth of knowledge to his father and entourage, Ceres named out the classes of spacefaring fighters present as the small group walked among them. In his youth as his Uncle Manny's salvager's mate he had fixed and flown all of them at some point or another.

"Needle Class fighters, slender and dart-like, you would use these to penetrate defensive screens and laser battery fields at high speeds. You use that Capitol starship as a carrier to open wormholes for the smaller ships, especially the space fighters.

"These Ravens which led the raid on Shangri La, have wide flat wings angled forward, for amazing maneuverability in an atmo. The excess weight of wings also means they have less speed in trade for greater fuel and missile capacity than most starfighters.

"In trade, they are usually carried through space and through wormholes by Carrier class ships. Then they fly down into planetary atmospheres where their wing-borne maneuverability comes into play."

He stopped short when he recognized something odd. The electromagnetically "painted" wings on the nearest Raven didn't match up with the next, or the last. The feathers lay differently. The electro-pigmentation layers, which could affect any of millions of colors, were slightly altered, one ship to the next.

"Each hull is skinned with a unique work of art!" No one came forward to claim it. "I must meet this artist! Professional courtesy, of course. These are amazing."

Ka'ra chimed in, "These Ravens have been touched up, painted, and etched to look even more like their namesakes. Yes, each one is a unique mural." Her smile beamed with pride.

As if she personally did the work of creating these masterpieces? She's stealing credit. From who?

"These broad limbed ships like the D-shaped Pugilist Class here," Ceres pointed, "the dual-hulled Catamaran Class down there, represent your heavy bombers. They carry extra armor plating and added hard points, which you've fitted with heavy beam weapons of various kinds. Their internal bays and external launcher rack's loadouts are short and long ranged missiles."

Tyrian just grinned in response, so Ceres went on.

"Small freighters of all kinds," he spun around with his arms outstretched, taking in the ships randomly spaced throughout the hangers. "You've gotta haul back the goods you raid, right?

"Looks like most have been refitted with added weapons, so I bet the power systems to run those weapons take up a lot of space in their cargo bays?" He made it a question to his father, who nodded in response.

"So to make up for lost cargo space… you have to steal even more cargo ships. You need more parts, more crews, more fuel, more food…. Oh, logistics! It's a never ending cycle."

Tyrian chuckled, nodded and shook his head, seemingly amused at his son's assessment of his job.

Ceres noticed, of all of these great varieties of ships, most were painted a non-reflective, obsidian black.

Black. Ravens. Vikings. Got it! Ceres thought privately. They are all in on their style! If it were my fleet, I'd install a relay to keep them from bumping into each other. Probably how they flew those bombing formations so tightly.

"Quite an impressive fleet!" Ceres said to his father.

The older man smiled broadly. Ceres saw a self-satisfied predator's smile, the smile of a creature that knew its prey was caught in its traps, its claws. "I know," Tyrian answered. Ceres heard his cockiness mixed with pride. Another thing in common.

Ka'ra pushed herself to the front of the entourage and chimed in jovially, "Yes, your father—by the way, he's like the father of us all here—he is a King now—pirate king, sure, but it counts!" she giggled. Tyrian shot a deadly glare at her, and she shrunk back, her laugh cutting off abruptly. Her smile vanished just as quickly, replaced with a scared but resigned grimace.

The play across her face reminded Ceres of a dog which had been beaten, ever after cowering under the raised hand of a human. Ka'ra stared intently down at her feet, blushing and fidgeting coyly with her hair, pursing her lips. *She has shown four different personalities since I've met her. Abused?*

"We started off grabbing cargo ships near undefended jumpgates." explained Tyrian. "After a while we had enough ships and crew to go after an armory hanger. Then we hopped around gathering more fighters. His voice grew deeper, more authoritarian.

"Before long we came out here where there are no planetary defense forces. Now I take tribute from all the settled worlds in the sector. They pay for peace."

Ceres made deeper eye contact with his father.

Tyrian shrugged and grinned. "None of these rim colonies could hope to resist my huge fleet of fast attack vessels. If they did, I could easily take out one of the arc-cities."

Casually, nonchalantly, he said, "Sometimes I do just that, as I put on an air-show for you earlier, to remind them why they are all so eager to pay up." The pirate "king" grinned and winked at his son.

"Subtle." Ceres joked dryly, but the gravity of it dried his mouth, "One arcology is home to a million innocent people, right?" he questioned his father, playing mild sarcasm into his delivery, then watching for its effects on his father's emotions.

"Yes. Busy little hives of bees. Full of golden honey to feed us all so well!" Again the arrogant smirk.

Tyrian seemed pleased with himself to Ceres' eyes. Probably pleased that his long-lost son had chosen to return to him without force? Gloating over finally winning one small victory in some old competition with Ceres' mother. Why they had resorted to paralyzing him was a question yet unanswered.

Ceres' mouth tightened into a similar smirk. He worked hard to keep his face and posture as relatable as he could, an old trick taught him by his uncle and reinforced by his Sensei. He could not let Tyrian see the anguish in his heart their devastating assault on the city was causing him. His own father violated his Christian values, instilled in him by his family, before his eyes.

This is insane! Ceres screamed in his head. I can see now why Mom left him. What was I thinking coming out to the Rim to meet my father? He's a madman, mocking the killing of twenty thousand people in order to control millions more. This is evil! Exploiting and killing all those colonists. Lord, help me. After I served my tours in the Merchant Marine, I just had to come meet him. Frag it, I'm stuck out here now.

As they walked side by side between the myriad ships Ceres debated explaining to his father that not only was it objectively evil to destroy cities and murder people, it was completely illogical. Since Tyrian's and his thousands of pirates' way of life depended on the arc-cities' output, why did he destroy them without a second thought?

Probably not the best time to bring it up. Doubtful he is up for a family meeting, a lively debate on the ethics and logistics of piracy and mass murder. *Let alone the affront to my faith, to God! How could my mother fall in love with this man in the first place?*

For a moment, Ceres almost wanted to laugh, but then he remembered the sight of the arc's bombing, the people jumping from the SkyBridges to avoid being burned. His laugh freezing in his throat, suddenly the feeling of numbness returned, as with hypothermia, frozen to his core.

Once, out with Uncle Manny, in the cold dark air inside a derelict ship, the heating system in Ceres' space suit had malfunctioned for just a minute. Just long enough for the absolute, incomprehensible cold of space to sink in. Traumatized for a week after that, he stayed in his bed.

The doctors at the nearest space station had said he was lucky it was no worse than just hypothermia. It stood as Ceres' only moment of not loving being in space, where he felt most comfortable. Maturing, it gave Ceres a healthier respect for his home.

Here, standing next to his father for the first time, the old man's atrocity still fresh in his mind, he felt that cold again. Only this was worse. This was an encounter with evil, which smiled upon him with love. How long would it take to recover this time?

That is, if I can even get out of here? It jolted him, and he pushed the numb sick feeling that was spreading through him, pushed it down somewhere it could not affect him, at least not for now. He needed to figure out the situation, find a way out. In the past, Ceres had been on covert ops missions with his uncle....

"Why paralyze me? Kidnap me?" Ceres asked. "That was pretty rough considering I came here and sought you out on my own. You knew I was coming."

"Your father's idea," Ka'ra chimed in, brightening, seeming somewhat recovered from her chastisement. "He wanted a grand display of his power. You wanted to go be the 'big strong hero' and fight our fleet.

"I couldn't let you do that, now could I?" Her hand caressed across Ceres shoulders and snaked down the small of his back. Ka'ra giggled when Ceres gave her a look of disapproval.

"That would have spoiled your introduction to my fleet, huh?" Tyrian said, "I wanted to recruit you into the pack, not let them shoot you down by way of greetings.

"Here's the deal: If you do for me what you did for your uncle, I'll let you work your way up the ranks. I could use one man who can do the work of my whole fleet."

Ceres' mouth opened to ask how they knew about all that, but he stopped.

"We have ways of rewarding victory that the Galactic never dreamed of." Tyrian grinned, reaching over to caress Pearla's chin, giving her a lascivious smile, which she returned.

Jaw still dropped open, Ceres was relieved that a commotion suddenly arose around the tour party. The crews started rearranging the ships in the hanger, lifting them up with the ship's own repulsors, pushing them into tighter storage arrangements like jigsaw puzzles along the sides of the hanger decks.

"They're making space for the arrival of the rear guard." Ka'ra explained. Overhead clamshell doors opened like giant robotic lips.

Hundreds of heads turned up, eyes focused beyond the main energy fields holding the airspace inside the base.

"Rear Guard vessels, incoming fast! Clear the deck!" echoed through the vast hanger. It was the deep voice of a Rokkled, working as the pirate base's air boss. Perfectly suited to asteroid life, the tall silicon-based Rokkleds were living statues. Their ancient visits to Earth had inspired the Easter Island statues.

This one's species-typical gravelly voice inspired some laughter amongst his pirate comrades near Ceres. He sounded commanding and fearsome as his voice boomed out of sound emitters spaced along the rocky walls of the cavern covered by the overhead airdock doors and energy fields.

The crews must have heard that in their MeTR group links? So that was broadcast aloud for us. *For me.* Ceres smirked, *I am still not joining their links. After Ka'ra resorted to poisoning me, I do not trust them.*

Moving aside of the cleared deck, Ceres cut his military straight gait into a parade rest stance, and observed. His amused father turned back with him. A sleek yacht, looking like a curvy spearhead topped with the flat roof of an atrium, sliced its way through the energy field, driven as if aiming to skewer Ceres with its bow. *Wanderlust* showed prominently in glowing red lettering emblazoned along both sides of the bow. The rest of the once gleaming, blue and white hull was faded.

The Size-IV hull—over 50 meters long—spun horizontally on its X-axis as it slowly lowered towards the hanger floor. Once the large aft engine pods finally emerged inside the field, their idling hum and growl suddenly reverberated and echoed throughout the hanger.

Hard clanks of landing struts extending, whirrs of hydro-pistons, and the sshhusshhh's of out-gassing systems accompanied the ship's landing, sounding like an arrangement of music to the young pilot's ears. Finally the landing struts contacted the fuse-hardened deck, the yacht settling onto her supports as the hum of the repulsion lifters subsided.

Other ships popped in noisily and landed down the length of the curved, multi-ported bay, and orbited to other hangers around the asteroid, the parade of the fleet overhead planned and timed to impress Ceres. It might have worked, too, but this one vessel had captured Ceres' attention.

"Halberd Class 2500 F/L. Thrust pods upgraded. Enhanced armor. Reinforced weapon hard points," Ceres assessed it. He walked around and under her, running his eyes and hands along the sleek lines. Tyrian smiled approvingly at his son's accurate appraisal of the enhancements made to what was originally a luxury freightliner.

About twenty percent larger than the popular 2000 series, the "F/L" designated the Freighter/Liner version. The engine pods were spread a bit farther, expanding the hull. Ahead of the added cargo compartment, F/L's were filled with a lesser number of cabins.

The highlight of this unique hull design, the forward view lounge was a large atrium-like area where passengers could enjoy observing the amazing vistas of space and wormhole string-space. Ceres spent a moment staring up at the opaque forward view-pane, feeling as if someone was staring at him from behind its impenetrable sheen.

"Upgraded sensor suite. Shield emission ports are bored oversized. Must be.more power in the— "

"Hey Kid! Get your flikking hide-skinners off my ship!" boomed a deep bass shout.

Turning with a frown, Ceres saw a greenish one and a half meter tall thumb. The heavy-grav human was short and barrel-shaped, thick with massively muscled legs and arms. The green-skinned man's neck was so short and thick as to be almost non-existent. Ceres noted the gun belt constricting his waistline. Down the ship's boarding ramp he stomped, roughly towing a shapely young woman by her flaming red hair.

"That's Trok. I'd be careful how you handle him," Ka'ra sent her private thought one-way to Ceres through the WetNet channel she had used before. Rather than open a two-way link with this Jezebel, Ceres visibly smirked at her in response. More crewmembers disembarked from the sleek ship.

The first, a slender, two-and-a-half meter tall lightworlder, rubbed a fresh bruise on his cheek. His face and limbs were stretched into a caricature of a human body. Scowling at the red-haired girl, he flicked his toe at her in an attempt to kick her when she faltered down the ramp. She moved with a dancer's grace, or as much grace as she could muster while being dragged by the shorter Trok, who was roughly pulling her about.

"Hey, knock it off! Leave her alone," Ceres said to both of the pirates. He'd already witnessed enough today. He could not stop the bombing, but this, he could do… something. He would not stand by and let this woman be abused, not if he could help it. Still on edge from the city bombing, he was itching to help it.

Ceres imagined, being the son of their leader, their king, he'd surely have some weight amongst them. And failing that he was well trained in combat arts and had been an academy athlete. He figured he could beat almost anybody.

Trok glared hotly at the young man standing with his boss. He handed the redhead's mane to his tall ship's mate, who proceeded to bully her down to her knees at the foot of the ramp. Trok then effortlessly leaped the seven meters distance between the ramp and the Tauri men. Landing heavily, he reared up with menace.

His fat finger punching the air, Trok shouted at Ceres, "My ship! My crew! My spoils! My new slave! You have nothing to say about any of them, boy!"

Ceres' breath tightened. His pulse pounded in his ears. His wide eyes met the girl's. *Help,* crossed his mind. *Yeah, help her somehow. How?*

Trok handed Tyrian a datapad as he glared at Ceres. "Here's the haul, boss. I'm going to break this one in myself." He pointed his face and a finger at Ceres and reached up to poke the young man's chest with it. "You're new but I don't cut anyone any slack. You want to say or do anything about it?"

Ka'ra grabbed Ceres' elbow and pulled, trying to drag him away from Trok and back into the tour of the base. Tyrian simply stood by, watching his son and his lieutenant, wearing a curious expression.

Ceres saw Tyrian's face, reflected in the nearest starship's canopy. Ceres' thoughts raced, analyzing the motivations of the two men before him. He thought his father must be wondering how his boy would handle Trok's provocations.

The elder Tauri's half-smile towards the younger made Ceres think an unfamiliar paternal feeling had snuck its way into Tyrian's mind since his son's arrival. Never would have guessed that, with 25 years of disinterested silence hanging between them.

It must have taken struggle, sacrifice, and plenty of violence to become the pirate king, and Ceres would have to earn his place here on his own merits. His father's growing smile revealed a distinct feeling of pride, Tyrian was almost certain Ceres would prevail. That gave Ceres confidence in this power struggle with the short muscular pirate.

As for Trok, well, Trok must be replaceable for Tyrian to allow this conflict to flare up uninterrupted. Having his own son leave a life as a decorated serviceman and star athlete, to stand by his side would certainly bolster his father's reputation. No one could deny he was a true king then, not with his son the prince by his side.

Ceres though, overconfident, was paying too little attention to the green homunculus threatening him. His eyes turned next to the redhead. She said nothing, but looked up into Ceres' blue eyes with a pleading, almost expectant look.

Unsure of what would happen, Ceres looked deeply into the nameless girl's beautiful green eyes, drawn in. It was like gazing into the depths of the emerald whirlpool super storm of the gas-giant planet T-chlohn.

To his family's shame, he had played the field with an abundance of girls at the academy. During his peak days as a sports star, they were virtually throwing their bodies at him, but Ceres had never connected with any woman on a deeper level.

He had certainly never experienced, or even considered as possible, the idea of love at first sight. But looking at this redhead, Ceres felt it. His mouth dried, his stomach churned, his heart felt as if pulled by gravity to her.

He suddenly had a strong protective reaction towards her. Ceres was sure he would do anything to keep the redhead beauty from going off with this green hulk to a life of.... *I do not want to imagine it!* He felt it. He knew it. He believed it. He loved.

Ceres' view of her was suddenly broken off by Trok, his muscled chest flared out, stretching up on his toes directly into Ceres' line of sight.

"You like her?" Trok said. "Too bad. She's mine."

What will they do to her if I don't help? Ceres thought. *I can't just let them continue to do this. You can do it. I can do it. Help me. Yes, I must help her. And then?*

"You are going to let her go." Ceres stated finally, his eyes unblinking as he stared into the face of the short, thick man.

A wicked, twisted smile spreading on his face, Trok leaned forward and quietly said, "I was hoping you were that stupid." He opened his hugely muscular arms as he stepped back and roared, "I challenge you!"

Chapter 4
Family Values

MWG, Patriarch Sector, Epsilon Eridoni System
Inner Asteroid Belt, mining ship wreck/debris field
2509/11/23/0400

"Ceerrr-ees."

"Ceee-reees," the womanly voice sing-songed. Annemarie ran her soft fingers gently over the boy's forehead and through his long platinum-blonde hair.

"Sweee-teee. It's time to wake uuuh-uup"

"Mmm-mm," the boy grumbled. "Sseeep." He turned his head away from his mother's voice. He rocked gently in the sleeping bag-like bed fastened to the wall of the starship mate's quarters he shared with his mother. Zero gravity turned walls into floors depending on one's perspective.

"Honey, I've parked the ship in the asteroid belt. Your uncle wants your help placing magnetic tractor beacons on some salvage parts. You have to get dressed for space-"

"Space? I'm *up*!" The boy's clever hands tore through the ripfast strips before she finished her sentence. Pushing off with his legs he burst out of the bed, rebounded off the wall (the ceiling when the ship's engines were not thrusting and the virtual gravity thrust provided was absent), and shot out of the hatch. It reminded Annemarie of pheasants flushed out of the lush grass by her mother's prized dappled Pointers, in one of the many preserved Earth habitats of their home planet, named Ceres.

"Prayers then drink your fastbreak, young man," she said. "Visit the personal and brush your teeth, before you put on your vac-suit."

"Yes, ma'am," echoed from the corridor as the boy rapidly pin-balled his way down the tubular shaft, already underway.

* * *

"Okay, tag that engine pod!" commanded Emanuel Tarsis. "Stay back. Just shoot it straight at the center of mass." The family usually spoke aloud, transferred over comm channels. This bucked the trend of modern people to communicate directly mentally through the WetNet. A high price for mental and technical integration, some societies were losing their voice.

"Yes, sir." Ceres transmitted his thoughts to the family private WetNet group to respond. He mixed his modes of communication more readily than his elders. Annemarie usually coaxed her son to speak by praising his voice. But right now she had another's speech to correct.

Swinging his arms like a diver in the Olympics executing flips and spins, the boy's soft reflective space suit rotated to an angle facing the spinning wreckage. A small mining ship had apparently broken up in an explosion or collisions, tiny fragments drifting off in myriad vectors amid the random chunks of rock filling the star system. This engine was one of the few remaining intact pieces of wreckage.

"Manny." Annemarie's voice chimed in. "He's nine. He's your nephew. He is *not* one of your Lieutenants."

Ceres stretched a fat-barreled blockish pistol out to arm's length. The gun looked ridiculously oversized for its wielder. Ripfast strips wrapped around it helped keep it attached to gloves or suits. Ceres floated in front of their ship, which looked to him like a gigantic metal slice of Chicago Style Pizza, his favorite.

"Not yet, he isn't. He's in the delayed entry program, sis. Reaallly long-term early poolee."

In the squared off bow, the forward cargo bay gaped open, spilling light into the deep darkness. The salvage ship and space-walking crew drifted, surrounded by the target rich environment of a few million asteroids and random ship debris that made up the Epsilon Eridoni system. StarSys maintained a manufacturing center, and there was an independent trade stop orbiting one of the two dead planets in the system.

"Thoop." Ceres pulled the trigger on the fat gun. It spat a spherical metal projectile that moved just slowly enough to track by eye. In the silent medium of space, only the person holding the device might hear some of its sounds transmitted through solid contact with it.

"Manny!"

"Thoop. Thoop."

"Ah-hem. Yes, ma'am." Tarsis' voice lowered, "I'm a former Galactic fleet Admiral, still a rear Admiral, resigned into reserve duty so I can protect my baby sister and her son, and she reduces me to this? Love, baby, love. God help me love my family in Your example." He finished muttering the prayer unintelligibly under his breath and coughed.

"Okay son. Take it easy. You just want to hit it square so you don't waste the tractor beacons, got it?"

"Meanwhile," Ceres said, "I've gotten three magnetic beacons attached, Uncle Manny." Barely contained mirth came through with the young voice.

"Three?! What are you doing? Wasting them like that? Sheesh!"

"Well, *if* we haul this Starflare Number 1600 Plasma Thruster in at all, we will get all three tags back," Ceres smugly retorted. "And if I do it in the right sequence, I can stop the 3-axis spinning it's doing now and it won't get any more damaged hitting your cargo bay walls. That will help you sell it as a whole working unit instead of a pile of damaged parts. Should make the difference between 3900 to 4500 dollari, versus maybe, hmm, 1250 to 1800 Di? Depending if I can.... "

"Okay, okay. Knock it off, you smart-aft kid." Exasperated, Emanuel Tarsis threw up his hands, accidentally throwing himself into a slow backwards tumble of his entire body. *I don't know how he already knows things like that off the top of his head, but that is the kind of experience and life education we are out here trying to give him.* As he went head over heels his nephew swung his arm in his direction. "Thoop."

"Thwunk." echoed inside Manny's hard-shelled space suit. "I'm hit! I'm HIT!" he shouted, his gravelly voice edged with a deep concern. "Something hit me in the back of the helmet! Do you see it? Is it holed? Is there debris plugging a hole?"

"Uncle MAH-ah-Neee" complained Ceres. "Stop waving your arms so wildly. You're making it hard for me to reel you in." The retrieval controls mounted on one side of the blockish tractor beacon launcher. The kid split his attention between the gyrations of his wayward uncle and the complex spins of the plasma drive.

Ceres' little gloves flitted over the controls quickly and soon the spinning form of Uncle Manny righted and drifted backwards, headfirst in a fetal position, towards the open cargo bay of the nearby ship. One axis of the engine's rotation was erased already, leaving the far less complex task of stopping the remaining two axes of spin. The back of Ceres' space suit jetted briefly, pushing the boy slowly on a vector to intercept the engine's drifting path.

The floating captain entered his angular space tug through the energy field that kept pressurized atmosphere inside and space vacuum out. A robot made up of multi-jointed arms stood magnetized to the deck and helped its master land safely next to it. Quickly, Tarsis moved by spidering along the scramble nets attached to the surfaces across the bay, draped ready to snare a spinning chunk of salvage.

Tarsis wrestled his boxy space suit into his seat in the load operator's booth. "Okay, I've got it." He looked up just in time to see he had wasted his time in hurrying.

"Behind you!" he shouted a warning to his nephew. Ceres was distracted, bursting his own maneuver thrusters and curling up his legs. The engine pod loomed directly behind him.

"No, I've got it." A couple quick moves of Ceres' nimble hands on some toggles and a central joystick on the side of the tag-gun, and the engine ceased rotation in both directions at once. It still drifted towards the ship, pulled evenly now by all three magnetic tractors. An extended coolant duct pipe jutting out from the former engine mount snuck slowly in behind his legs.

He caught it behind the knees, bent into a backwards curve and grabbed his ankles. Momentum from the engine pod carried Ceres along while his arch rotated his body forward. He relaxed his spine and swung around to sit on the spar. The starship now hung over his head from his perspective.

"Okay, little Macac. You are a show off," Tarsis said.

"Nah, this is fun. Planet side kids get to play on something called "Jungle-gyms" in their home netschool activity groups. This is mine."

"Oh, they do, huh?" Tarsis asked, "Have you been downstreaming some news feed? You have not been joining the Galactic WetNet have you? You know the family rules. Family group only!"

"I know, I know," the boy half-sighed. "They get a lot more natural gravity but far less space-going. They have to have special places built for them to play. I get the whole galaxy and every ship imaginable to play with. This is better!"

The old man grinned. "Fair enough, Big Time." He used his favorite nickname for his nephew. "This is why your mother decided to give you this kind of upbringing. To let you learn from experiencing life in the galaxy. Now, how'd you time that last burst? The engine was behind you."

"Well, one, I had figured out the timing of the two axes of spin. Two, I saw it behind me reflected in your faceplate," Ceres answered matter-of-factly.

"What?" Tarsis' was incredulous, "I'm about 30 meters away from you now. You must have been looking at over 70 meters with the convex effect making it seem twice that. Nobody's eyes are that good."

"Better than yours!" Ceres teased. "You explain it then, Unc. I bet you five dollari." Ceres taunted his uncle with the old man's usual betting wager. "Oh and, I can see another engine from here."

He sighted the bulky tractor gun in on the wreckage at long range. "It's drifting about 500 meters straight ahead from me, straight down from *The BARGE*. Got a big dent in the fairing though and the impellers aren't still spinning like this one's are. Not sure you'll want to bother picking it up."

"You men are sure doing a lot of talking instead of washing up for break-fassst." Annemarie sang over the crew comm channel. "Good thing nobody's interested in a home style skillet like Grammy makes? Oh goody! This is aaallll for me and Medusa then, mmMM mmmmm?"

"We'll be right there, Sis. As soon as your macac of a son stops showing off out here, hitching rides on personal plasma engines and the like."

Ceres nimbly stood atop the spar he had been sitting on. Looking up at the ship looming overhead, he balanced, coiled his legs under him, and then leaned just so. His powerful leap propelled him ahead of the floating engine pod but sent it spinning like a bottle in an ancient dating game.

"Hey, you messed it all up just to beat me to chow?" complained Tarsis, loudly.

"Yep. You told me there's no such thing as a fair fight." The boy drifted half the remaining 20 meters. Uncle Manny bent his helmeted head forward to see the controls better. He did not see Ceres raise the gun and sight.

"Thoop."

"Okay, I'll help you a little more." Ceres said. He nimbly swept his arms in little arcs and curls around his body and back, rotating his body in mid-flight while his hands quickly worked the controls.

The engine pod was yanked in little shudders as the various magnetic beacons were individually pulled by the ship's salvage tractor beam units. The new rotation from the boy's strong leap soon stopped and the big engine pointed into the cargo bay, like a metallic lollypop about to become dessert in a gigantic robot's mouth.

Meanwhile the boy drifted inside the ship, pushed off on the wall of the bay, pinballed off three surfaces, and finally alighted near the pressure hatch to the interior of the vessel. The double-doored hatch was a backup safety for the entire vessel, SOP in the Fleet, SOP aboard Tarsis' ships as well. Ceres stuck the tractor gun to the wall's ripfast strips, five green lights showing on its side.

"Hey, Big Time? Are you going to leave me out here while you go pig out?"

"Oh you'll be here a while, Unc. The other engine—," The pressure hatch swung shut like a bank vault. Green lights started climbing up the display pad next to it.

"If its space junk, let's just leave it." He looked over and saw the lights change as air cycled into the lock. "Son, you're not going to wait five minutes and help me finish bringing this one in?" The robotic arms, tractors and free-bodied robots of the cargo bay all opened their appendages, prepared to receive and secure the heavy engine.

"The other one should be drifting along in 30 minutes or so. I'll be back by then to haul it in while you eat. I'd like to get the radio emitters out of it for a project," Ceres said.

"We *all* eat family breakfast together." It was a statement, not a request. A Navy crewman would have heard it as an order. "Besides, I said leave it. Who's in charge here anyway, son? Who owns this ship?"

"Yes, sir, you can pull rank, Admiral Captain Uncle Tarsis, sir! We'll wait for the ship's Captain per standing orders, sir!" Ceres called over the comm as he bounced down the central shaft towards the savory smells of the mess deck. "But after family breakfast, I still think I should reel it in for practice, even if it is just to get back your fifth tractor beacon."

Chapter 5
Testing the Speed of Light

A-Valhalla, Access tunnel
2525/7/10/2130

"That's the way it is here," Ka'ra's rant at Ceres, about how stupid he was, echoed back at him again. Spiraling as they walked down the central corridor carved from the asteroidial obsidian-like surface rock, they passed countless tubes leading off to different areas, domes, and hangers throughout the base. Many times the pair dodged bots, hover-trams, and pirates who stopped to gawk, beaming smiles, as they realized whom they were bumping into.

"They're pirates, like the ancient Vikings. They take what they want by force. Money. Goods. Ships… People." Ka'ra looked forlornly down at the floor and closed her eyes. "They kill anyone who gets in their way or challenges them."

'They.' Ceres thought. *As if I will ever believe you are not one of them?*

"Relax, Ka'ra. In the Academy, I held the high score in "Star Duelist" all three years. That's against the best people in the galaxy—all young Naval cadets." He slipped into a false accent picked up from a friend from a planet once colonized by Texans. "Buhsides, this ain't my furst Row-day-Oh."

"This is entirely different," Ka'ra said, seeming to ignore Ceres' attempt to be cute with the country accent.

"I know you were, what, *the* athlete of the millennium, playing Grav-ball on the Navy team. That won't matter. Neither will being the son of our king. It's a matter of honor. You insulted Trok. He will exact justice, in our way."

'Our'. Caught you, thought Ceres. *If you are not paying attention to your words, I sure am. You have no idea what I am capable of, do you?*

She chided him, "This isn't some hologame where you score points and virtual kills. This is REAL! Real guns on full power. No screens allowed. He will probably—no, definitely—kill you!"

Ceres' face darkened in grim determination, as he realized exactly what he had gotten himself into.

From one side tunnel a distinctive scent wafted out to assault their noses. "Cannahol fields?" Ceres raised his eyebrows at Ka'ra and smiled boyishly. She tried to ignore it but eventually broke open a smile of her own. On they walked.

At the bottom of a long access corridor, Ka'ra spoke with a heavily armed and armored guard posted at a huge round hatch. They seemed to be in just another non-descript hallway, but when the hatch rolled aside like the door of an ancient tomb, Ceres realized where Ka'ra had led him.

Stepping into the armory, a large woman in dirty coveralls greeted them. "Welcome, sweetie!" she said. "You're new here, eh handsome?" Her eyes flitted from Ceres to Ka'ra and back, then up and down Ceres. "My! You're a tall drink of water, aren't you?"

Ceres blushed and grinned.

"Ceres Tauri, this is Hleidi," Ka'ra introduced them. "He's Tyrian's son, just in from the Galactic."

"Well, we'll try not to hold that against you, honey." Hleidi laughed, taking his arm and leading him from the entry room to locker rooms carved from the asteroidial rock. "So you're here to pick yourself out something deadly to carry? Are you officer rank already? Well, I suppose you get privileges being the son of our king, huh?" she smiled broadly.

"Pleased to meet you, miss Hleidi," Ceres finally spoke. "I find myself privileged to be challenged to a duel. I carry my Galactic issued plasma pistol, but I wonder if you have something better than that?"

"You're welcome to whatever we have, cutie," Hleidi said. "I'm going to go see what my husband's broke and help him fix it. Just let me know what you choose so I can update the inventory." Hleidi stopped at a hatch and waved the pair inside a room overfilled with racks and shelves, themselves overflowing with weapons of all description.

Ceres checked out their stolen inventory. His eyes widened, and he whistled low in appreciation. Shotguns, repeaters, pistols, rifles, throwing every beam or projectile in existence. "It's the world's greatest gun show!"

Ceres' HUD nearly blinded him, popping up data screens of info as his gaze panned across the room. There were electron ion stunners, old style slug throwers, mass drivers, sonic shotguns, gyrojets, protonic particle beamers, lasers, shaped forcefield swords and pole arms, gravity projectors, plasma burners, burst-firing auto pistols, disruptors—a black-marketer's dream!

"He's from an H-G world?" Ceres asked. He deadpanned it to conceal his excitement.

"Yes. Very fast," replied Ka'ra, curtly.

"He'll have very thick skin, a gorilla's strength, plus amazing reflexes if he's spent much time in Standard-G," Ceres said.

Ka'ra stared down at the floor and nodded. "I've seen Trok's quick draw in action. I think the only way for you to get out of this alive is to apologize. Even then, your life will be beholden to Trok, forced into sub-servitude. And Trok is a cruel master.

"Other side of the coin: if you duel him, Trok might decide to merely wound you and keep you as his slave. Either way, I'm not ready to say good-bye to you yet."

Ceres ignored her personal comments. *Still not trusting a word you say, Jezabel.* He turned away towards the weapons.

Thoughtfully he caressed a heavy pistol, noting the crafter's [TCON] logo. *I'll have to look this guy up!* From the balance and fit of the plasma-fused parts, he could tell it had been flawlessly designed, printed, and assembled by a master craftsman.

Hmmm. None of these holsters will take the bulky thing, what with double barrels and all. What's this? Now I'm even thinking in the voice of my old pal Iron?

Midnight fast approached.

* * *

A-Valhalla, Airdock
2525/7/10 2355

The pirates all had gathered on the sides of the hanger bay. The fact that the girl in the medic vest, with her fiercely tattooed face and pink hair, stood closer to Ceres' end of the challenge area, spoke volumes. That she held a mop and no medkit said worlds.

Trok stepped out from amongst a handful of slaves. Their faces covered in what looked to Ceres to be false smiles, they cheered for their master hollowly. A few of Trok's crew gave him thumbs-up and backslaps, making a show of betting on him. The green-skinned man eyed the captive redhead hungrily, then glared at Ceres.

Ka'ra, tiny Pearla, and a couple of other women stood with Tyrian, near the center of what Ceres took to be "his" side of the crowd. They were a sparse few. *Probably just my die-hard sports fans and those wishing to show support for the boss' son,* he figured. *The few betting on me. That is it!* He laughed inwardly.

Pearla held out one of Tyrian's linen shirts to Ceres. "Gotta drop the uniform, Son," Tyrian explained. Navy uniforms were famed for the multiple technologies built into their high tech fabrics. They helped absorb starlight and other radiations, especially electron beams.

Ceres popped the seams on the top half of his bodysuit, pulled it down to his waist, and revealed his physique for a moment. While he pulled his father's loose shirt over, female whistles called at him from the crowd on both sides. Ceres shrugged, grinned, and got back to tucking the fabric down into his blue and white camouflaged utility pants.

Unexpectedly, Tyrian grabbed ahold of Ceres' shoulders and hugged his son for the first time. "Good luck, Son," Tyrian said with a smile, seemingly entertained by this show. "You'll be a made man around here if you win this." His face turned stern in warning. "Make me proud."

Ceres replied curtly, "I make my own luck." Then, his jaw tightened and brow furrowed, "I'll be right back."

Lines had been scored ten meters apart in the dark-stained floor, remnants of some long past version of the event about to unfold.

Closing his eyes for a moment, Ceres slowly moved his hands over his chest in the ancient sign of the cross, whispering to himself "In the name of the Father, and of the Son, and of the Holy Spirit." He went on praying quietly as he slowly, purposefully strode the death march to the far line, across from a waiting Trok.

"Praise be to the Lord my Rock," Psalm 144 was one of many he had learned on his home planet from his grandfather, a lifelong member of the Knights of Saint Michael, a fraternal order of armored warriors, ready to defend the Patriarch's Stars as needed.

Ceres did not doubt the faith of his mother's family. They had helped in the Modern Exodus as mankind fled Earth, and the Grand Reunification which followed. Like many young adults, struggling to find his own path once loosed upon the secular world, Ceres had gone through periods of doubt and sinful lifestyle. He felt glad he at least remembered the motions to go through right now.

"Who trains my hands for war," Ceres imagined the Psalmist, the ancient hero David, walking out from the cowering lines of the Army of Judea.

"Who trains my fingers for battle," Out to meet Goliath, the gigantic champion of the Philistine's. *I had better sling my rock pretty hard at that thick head,* he thought, looking aside at his opponent, Trok.

A hush came over the excited crowd, anticipation rising at the coming spectacle of death, allowing Ceres' last few marched boot steps to echo across the duracrete deck and ceiling. He turned around towards the crowd and crossed himself once again in completion of his prayer.

One last time, Ceres adjusted his gun belt and small holster, the massive pistol's fat barrels jammed into it, making sure it balanced just right. Raising his head, he glanced about for a last glimpse of the red-haired girl for whom he risked his life.

Hah, you are such a fool for the love of someone you don't even know! Better to have loved and lost, than never to have loved in this short lifetime.

The hooting crowd near Trok toyed with the red-haired girl. Tethered on a neck strap, she was restrained by Trok's skinny ship's mate, lust and anticipation in his eyes. *One day soon, I am going to kill you too, Slim!* Ceres thought.

Still, she stood proudly, as strong and tall as she could, despite the painful tugs bullied upon her by the mate. Her eyes found Ceres' and they stared, seemingly into each other's souls. He thought anew about his chances.

At least I will die for something I believe in. Can I do this? You can do this. I think I can do this. YOU CAN DO THIS! I can do this. You'll be my hero. I'll be her hero!

Drawing in a deep breath, Ceres tightened his mouth, and faced Trok with a determined stare. He quietly quoted from the Lorica, "Christ to shield me today."

The squat, bulky, green human variant flicked off his holster strap, lifted and gently resettled his huge lightning pistol for the draw.

Ceres enjoyed the familiar feeling of adrenaline flushing through his body. Fingers flexed. Time slowed. Senses seemed both sharper and more selective at once.

The noise of the crowd of human and alien pirates faded as blood pounded in Ceres' ears. The whine of a ship's plasma drives seemed to rise in the back of his head. He drew another deep breath, full of the smell of burnt-hydrogenized engine turbines. His vision tunneled around Trok.

Ceres 2525

Ceres' hand twitched for his pistol's grip.

Trok responded instantly, his hand flashing to the grip of his bolt-gun.

Ceres' hand closed around his double-barreled hand cannon, moved it.

Trok had his pistol half way out of the holster.

Less experienced, Ceres pushed—not pulled—his unwieldy pistol's grip.

Trok's gun swung up, now halfway to aiming at his target.

The nose of Ceres' holster swung upwards.

Trok pointed his huge lightning pistol directly at Ceres, the red laser targeting dot crossing from aiming down at Ceres' legs up to his gun arm.

Ceres' holster melted away as the dual blasts of his disruptor tore through it, streaking across the hanger. At the speed of light, the duelists seemed joined by elongated white and gold beams. The instantaneous flash image burned into everyone's vision.

At the same time, Trok's disarming shot leaped directly at Ceres' gun-arm, a third ray of light, red and glaring. The millisecond pulse of intense laser light ionized a trail of air molecules, through which a stroke of lightning leaped for Ceres, enveloping him in its flares of electrical power. Trok had a brief moment of satisfaction before his mind began to register a queasy feeling of heat that swiftly grew unbearable.

The blast from Ceres' disruptor was unimpressed with Trok's tough hide. The white ionizing beam synchronized the spin of electrons throughout the body into one plane, weakening the molecular bonds; the gold disruption beam of alpha particles knocked the atoms in all directions. The field of energy boiled through Trok's barrel-shaped body, leaving behind melted flesh and empty air where his organs had been.

Ceres' arm was ravaged in the bicep by the lightning bolt from Trok's gun. It felt insanely hot, like a solar flare had erupted into his arm. Frozen at first, his grip failed from the energy coursing through his arm and body. With its holster melted away the heavy disruptor fell to the deck with a dull clang. A pivot pin stuck out from the gun belt.

Ceres' ears filled with a gargling scream—*my own?*—that echoed through the hanger as his vision faded. As he fell, the powerful electrical jolt seemed to overtake him, and he was no longer in the hanger, but screaming, falling into a tunnel of darkness.

Chapter 6
The Woman of My Dreams

MWG, Glistening Range, Transient Quarters
9/11/2509/0800

The chill air was blurry, as though seen through a fizzy bottle's glass, distorted, smeared, dreamy.

Young, and therefore short, Ceres seemed to live among giants. He looked up at the blonde haired woman from below her shoulder. They waggled back and forth next to each other, bouncing down the dark tube that curved up away from them in both directions. Rotation gave the false effect of gravity, from the centripetal force of the station's habitation rings.

Grav, simulated or otherwise, was one of the luxuries sought so highly by spacers tired of always floating and drifting, endlessly drifting, through the expanse of night between stars. Ducts and pipes lined the curved ceiling, a meter above the woman's head. Shadows of little items moved randomly through smaller tubes overhead in the large passage.

"What are those things?" Ceres asked, pointing up, as yet another dark, small, indistinct thing shuttled down a tube overhead. His voice sounded tiny, high, hollow, and distant.

"Vacuum tubes, I think, honey." Ceres' mom had a sweet melodic voice, but it was distorted badly today, like hearing it underwater. "This kind of frontier station uses a lot of simple old reliable tech for moving things from place to place throughout the framework."

"Here is our layover rental. Let's get some rest and enjoy the gravity while we wait for your uncle to flip the cargo. I don't like to be stuck aboard the same ship all the time like he does." A portion of the tube's side slid out of the way, revealing a dark hole.

"Maybe we can set up a comm to Grammy and Papa Joe after a nap?" The boy was excited by that. Grinning, he hopped inside on one foot.

As they moved inside, an autolum filled the refitted shipping container with brightness. The spartan furnishings included a day lounger and holoemitter, an auto-kitchen and sonic shower unit, a thermocaster and personal water closet. Utilitarian dull white monotone, it seemed blurry, seen through the haze of his dream.

Large bodies loudly approached in the tube just as the woman and boy entered the boxy room.

Screaming—high pitched and female—ripped the quiet. Angry men shouted in loud voices that boomed in the small metallic area, hurting Ceres' ears as the sound echoed down the tubes of steel and back. Shoved roughly down, he hit the floor.

The woman's voice barked a string of "kiais" amid bangs and crashes behind him. A table smashed to the deck, flattened by a man's body thrown atop it. He groaned loudly.

A strong hand grabbed Ceres painfully by the shoulder and pulled him up, spun him about. Facing a grinning giant with long straw colored hair, he lashed out with his foot and struck something. The giant's hand released him amid a grunt and groan. His uncle and mother had taught the eager lad some basic self-defense moves. That one was instinctive and effective even though he was young and small.

Hearing his mother's shrieking kiai's, he darted between obstacles, tipped furniture, and fallen men's bodies to reach her side. With a quick aikido move, she grabbed Ceres' reaching arm and easily flipped him aside. His body arced up and then down into a dark hole low in the wall, a small squared hatch she pulled open with the other hand.

The blonde boy clung to the lip of the hatch, one hand clinging to it with all of his strength. A vast flow of air pulled him backward, trying to drag him into the warm dark tube, which smelled of chemicals and linen, sweat and machines. Ceres dreaded falling down that tube. He dreaded leaving his mother's side even more. She grabbed his wrist as a giant hand grabbed hers.

"Ceres, RUN!" Her hand flung off his hold on the hatch. He fell, kicking, gyrating, and screaming as he scrabbled at the smooth sides of the snaking tube, finding no grip.

His mother's voice echoed after him, "Run! I love yooouuu!" It was drowned out by huge vibrating booming sounds that caromed down the tube, deafening his ears.

He cried, "Mom! Nooooo!" Sliding down in slow motion, like the last reluctant grain of sand through an hourglass, Ceres was sucked down into the swallowing throat of blackness, to eventually fall into a vast dark sleep.

Chapter 7
Splashdown

A-Valhalla, Medibay
2525/7/11/2300

The distinctive smell of finely aged Highland Reserve assaulted Ceres' sinuses first. Then its stinging wetness. Ceres' eyes burned. "Frig!" he cursed. He blinked and rubbed the watered scotch away from his face with his left hand. He could not feel his right arm at all.

"What the stars?" He hated waking up in a start. After years of discipline and training under his Sensei, Ceres awoke stealthily daily, listening carefully to his surroundings while moderating and controlling his breathing and body movement.

This forced awakening made him fear an interrogation. Fight or flight? Ceres was a fighter. His fist tightened. Only one? Where's the right arm?

As his vision returned between blinks, Ceres made out his surroundings. The medibay, filled with cabinets full of medical supplies, drugs, and tables of scanners and hand-held equipment, the best of the sector, presumably stolen on various pirate raids.

The medic with the tattooed face sat to his side, perched on a tall chair next to a silvery medibot. The red-haired girl smiled warmly from the corner and raised her eyebrows in acknowledgement as Ceres made eye contact. Standing over him, with a beaming smile and arms crossed in satisfaction, was his father Tyrian.

"I'm proud of you son. Very inventive. You're a crafty one, just like in the Sphere. You've earned your place with the Void Viking's," Tyrian sounded proud. He took a swig of the scotch. Ceres noted the name Highlander on the label.

Ceres was fast catching on to his father's respect system but he did not believe for a millisecond that Tyrian suddenly had real fatherly feelings for him now. The horrible death of his top lieutenant did not seem to faze Tyrian as a loss, but as an upgrade to his crew. Trok had not been a trusted insider or a friend, but a tool. A hammer.

"In our honor system," Tyrian continued, "the spoils go to the vikrant. So you can lay claim to everything that was Trok's."

"Whatever works," Ceres said quickly. He would step into the role of Lieutenant, which his father was laying out for him. Infiltration required fitting in and going with the flow as best he could, while learning the back eddies and angles to exploit for his eventual out.

"Now, if that includes her," Ceres glanced at the fiery beauty, "and that ship, it's a deal! But, you'll have to throw in a case of that Highlander."

The elder Tauri laughed and nodded his agreement. "Let's consider it your birthday present." His large hand slapped his son's left shoulder, gripping it firmly. "I'll leave you in the capable hands of these two lovely ladies. I'm sure they can find ways to inspire healing within you."

In response, the medic pulled Ceres' jaw down and sprayed something from a green vial under his tongue. He resisted at first, wrinkling his brow, but when she smiled at him, he complied.

Tyrian grinned at his son and stood to leave. He winked at the redhead and departed with ringing steps down the corridor carved out of the rock of the asteroid.

"It was yesterday, dearest father of the year," Ceres growled. He reached over and hit the kill-switch on the back of the sensor-head of the medibot. It sagged like a balloon animal with a fast leak.

Privacy achieved, he looked directly into the eyes of the redhead. "Now, I want you to understand, I am not going to be keeping any slaves. I did this to save you from that." Ceres spoke softly to her. He noticed a vanilla scent in the air and assumed it was her fragrance. Up close, he noticed her beauty, her femininity, affected him even more.

"What's your name?"

"I am Serenity O'Share," she said softly, in a voice lightly accented. "Good'to 'ear you say that. I sensed it in ya' when first I laid me eyes upon you, that you are unlike these other blokes." She smiled warmly at him, then her face grew stern, the skin under her eyes crinkling to match her small nose.

"We're in short need of a big plan, to escape from this gang. There are hundreds of girls, men, and other beings enslaved here. Some can be saved, like her." She nodded toward the medic who was quietly rewrapping Ceres' burned arm. "That can be discussed after your nitro stim wears off an' your arm regenerates."

Taken aback by her decisiveness and determination, she intrigued him. Ceres had known few women like this before. He smiled, "Okay. And I *adore* your voice." Satisfied, he closed his eyes and relaxed into the medibed.

"One question, though," she dismissed his flattery, asking, "'Ow ever did ya' think of that pivot-'olster idea?"

While drifting back to sleep to dream of her freckled skin, fiery red hair, and those inescapable emerald eyes that he had risked his life for, Ceres breathlessly whispered, "Desperation is the father of invention."

Chapter 8
Making Old Friends

MWG, Asiana Sector, Hunan System
Hunan IV, Win Tau dojo
2509/9/17 1100

"Sensei Aramada, will you teach me jujitsu?"

"In time, young one," the master replied. "But you must first learn the basic forms of karate, judo and aikido. You have just arrived here, and this is but your first lesson," he continued eyeing the tall boy.

"But why can't you just teach me jujitsu directly?" demanded the boy. His blonde hair fell over his sapphire eyes. Captain Tarsis had brought the boy, his young nephew, to the dojo. Visibly exasperated, the captain made the sullen boy promise to behave. Ceres was left alone, to speak with his prospective Sensei while the old master decided if he would take him.

"You must first learn to crawl, then to walk, before you can run, true?" Of Asiana descent, the wizened master had a strange combination of kind yet stern face. His average height, thin build and gleaming white jujutsugi masked his formidable physical prowess.

"I don't want to just run, I want to fly!" the boy blurted in a slightly spoiled, demanding but wondrous tone. He gave his feet an impetuous little stomp, confirming his attitude. The sharp sound upon the real wood floor echoed in the circular central practice room of the vast dojo complex.

The boy and the master were surrounded by dozens of students, kneeling at rest, backs to the curving white wall. They had just displayed their varied skills in myriad combat arts. Racks on the walls held multiple sets of weapons ranging from ancient through modern designs.

"Then you must first learn to crawl, walk, run, *then* how to fall, then to glide, all *before* you can fly." The master smiled, taunting his prospective pupil to protest. The first lesson was not physical, nor even about martial arts. It was about establishing the proper order of things between them, master and student. It was a secret pass/fail test of the young man that would determine both of their futures.

"Why can't we just upload lessons directly into our brain WetWare through our MeTR?" the boy retorted impatiently with a smirk, a cant of his head.

"We do, young one, we do. The body, however, must be trained over time and repetition, to properly move in ways that the mind has learned so quickly. Everyone has a different strength, endurance, foot/body agility, and hand/eye coordination, correct?"

"Yes," Ceres said, imagining himself the hero of martial arts holofilms, strong and athletic and defeating every opponent.

"Yes, so," Sensei adopted a mild lecturing tone, "each person's body has a different training curve to master what we program into the mind. Many of the moves require muscle memory for proper execution. We cannot program muscle memory even today. So you must practice daily over time."

"How long it takes is determined by you, by your determination, dedication," he paused, turned, eyed the boy dramatically, "your natural athletic talent?" The Sensei's white eyebrow raised. "I hope that what has happened to your mother will," he paused, "properly motivate you?"

Ceres shot the sensei an angry, surprised glare.

Tarsis warned me about this... obsession of his nephew's, the master thought. Of late the boy speaks of nothing but finding and avenging his missing mother. It burns hot within him like a star. It drove him to ask his uncle to train him and drove them here to my door. Can this be used to motivate him, to learn every skill and technique in order to complete his quest?

"You must also learn patience, tyro Ceres, 'beginner,'" he defined the new word. "You want the final mastery 'Now!'" he snapped fingers on his wrinkled old hand. "But you must learn to build your skills and knowledge up to that final goal, and beyond."

"What's beyond jujitsu?" asked the boy, his eyes growing wide. This teasing revelation seemed to snap him out of his dark reverie of imagined retributions.

"I will not even speak of it with you until you have mastered the ancient 'gentle art,' jeja, student. Now, get the mop and clean this floor. It is filthy with your footprints."

Ceres looked down and about, puzzled, seeing nothing but gleaming polish over the warm real wood floor. If there were a mess of footprints surely they were left behind by the dozens of students who had earlier demonstrated various martial arts for Ceres and the Galactic Admiral. His arms opened, palms out, and he inclined his head to the martial arts master before him, opening his mouth to begin his angry protest.

A sharp "slap!" rang out in the room as Sensei's open palm crossed Ceres' cheek. The move was so swift there was barely a blur visible between them. Sensei made a show of slowly re-lacing his fingers together in front of him, a smug expression on his face. The young martial artists surrounding them jumped up from knees to feet, assuming fighting stances.

Ceres' hand rose to his cheek as his jaw dropped open in shock. He felt the sting but almost doubted what had just happened? Ceres and Sensei regarded each other in silence for a moment.

"You are a very smart boy, but rich and spoiled." Sensei punctuated his words with pokes of his bony finger at Ceres. "To learn to protect yourself and your family, you must learn discipline and you must learn to accept and execute my orders without question!"

The arranged students took careful steps forward, as if they were feeling their way closer to an opponent to engage in a fight.

"Your uncle once did the same when he was a Fleet Admiral, correct?" Sensei asked.

"Yes, Sensei Aramada," he replied, nodding, then bowed respectfully, mimicking how the platoon of youth around him had moved after their demonstration. He glanced aside, seeing that the students behind him were moving along the walls to get past him, to the side of the hall behind their master.

Ceres whispered bitterly to himself, voice wobbling on the tightrope between anger and sadness, "Whatever it takes. I will never run away again. Mom deserved better."

"Mmmmm. Perhaps," Sensei growled hoarsely. He had heard the whisper. "Your mother fought as fiercely as a tiger defending her cub from a roomful of bears.

"If you wish to defend your mother's honor, you must dedicate yourself to internalizing everything I will show you." The dozens of students, all roughly Ceres age, arranged themselves in a phalanx behind their master, all facing Ceres. They stood in ready stances with their fists or weapons in strike positions. Ceres smirked.

"I ask you now, young man," the high professorial voice returned. As So'ke, the ultimate master of this exclusive school, the sole facility on this, its own planet, and the pinnacle of this new martial art form he had created, he imperiously looked down the length of his nose at the prospective learner.

"Will you commit yourself fully? To learning everything from me, and in the way I will teach it? To all the work? To all the practice of the many arts of combat? To all the hours and days and months and years of kihon practice, of repetition, that I will surely force you to endure?

Impatient Ceres chimed in, "Yes," to each question as the master continued.

One white and grey eyebrow raised slightly. "Most importantly, do you vow loyalty to this house and all members of this family, my school of Subete no Sento', which means 'All Combat' in Galactic, which you must now vow to defend with your honor and your life? Commit yourself to us now."

Ceres pulled himself up fully erect, shoulders back in a model of the P.O.A. His uncle must have taught him this military "position of attention?" Ceres' eyes raised to glare directly into the old Asianan master's grey eyes.

"I will. I do."

"On your mother's honor?"

Ceres grimaced, showing his flare of anger with his bared teeth. He growled the words through those gritted teeth. "On my mother's honor, Sensei, I will learn everything you know and more. I dedicate myself to do all the work, execute all the practice, to endure everything you throw at me, to master all of the arts of combat."

The old Sensei was impressed with this expression of dedication. He recognized finding the raw nerve, to tactfully tweak when he needed to push the boy to focus himself. He now understood and agreed with the young man's own internal motive, for which Tarsis had suggested this whole arrangement.

"I have my reasons," the lad continued, "And I'd appreciate it if you do not taunt me with the loss of my mother. Master."

The Sensei knew he should punish this veiled impudence from the boy, but he decided the cost would outweigh the benefits. He chose a different tack to gain the full respect of his young charge, further turning this negative emotion into a positive motivation, and to take measure of his new student's moral compass.

"We will come to an understanding, then. I will teach, you will learn and do. You have your motives, and I will try to, not push it in your face? I agree your mother deserves respect." The old master leaned forward so he was nearly eye-to-eye with the blonde boy. His voice dropped to a private, conspiratorial tone.

"You wish to know how to rescue her? How to punish those responsible for taking her from you?"

"Yes."

"Harshly?"

"Harshly," growled out between gritted teeth.

The master stood fully erect, looming over the boy, put one fist into the palm of the other hand in front of himself, and bowed forward, head up. The boy mimicked the move, maintaining eye contact as he held his inclined body still and waiting. When the Sensei returned upright, Ceres did as well.

This one learns quickly. Sensei thought. *He remembers everything he sees.* He smiled, rubbing his weathered hands together.

"Very good, young man. We have begun."

Sensei loudly clapped his hands together. The students behind him all made a practice strike with their hands or weapons, punctuated by their "kiais"

A short young girl brought in a gi for Ceres to wear. He put it on with Sensei's guidance, tying the brown belt of the novitiate. Ceres watched as the blonde girl went behind Sensei, to the head of a line the students had formed when Ceres was dressing and not paying attention.

Sensei moved aside and bowed to Ceres and the girl. When the blonde girl bowed to Sensei, Ceres followed suit. The master put his hand between them and shouted, "Begin!"

The girl moved forward quickly and slugged Ceres right on the shoulder. She pulled the punch, he realized, merely tapping him. She pulled back into her starter stance, bowed to Ceres and then to the Sensei, who dismissed her.

The next student, a boy smaller than Ceres, took her place and rapidly bowed to their master. Ceres quickly caught on and joined him in the show of respect, moving to a ready position in time to defend himself.

One by one, the young students paraded up, bowed, and tried to strike Ceres. The half-hearted mild taps delivered by those who succeeded gave him the hint that this was some kind of initiation ceremony. He showed his comprehension of the difference by restraining his defense to mere blocks. His Uncle Manny had reported previously teaching Ceres some beginner's defensive moves of Judo, on the pretext these were what his mother had used.

When the class of students younger than Ceres tapered off and finished, they all departed through a sliding paper door. Ceres looked to Sensei, who returned the eye contact with a raised eyebrow. The boy seemed to grasp quickly that he was missing something.

Ceres' head swiveled and he discovered a dozen students his age had crept silently in behind him.

Eyes wide he spun into the defensive pose, seeing the first was bowing to Sensei already. Ceres skipped the bow and defended himself from the short staff strike the boy aimed at his head. Ceres spun and stripped the weapon from its wielder, kept turning and swept it to strike lightly at the boy's knee.

Ceres drew the staff back and kept it, bowing to Sensei.

"Next lesson:" the old master growled. "Never let down your guard. Never!" Ceres nodded. To the other boy the master glared, "A lesson repeated for some: There is no such thing as a fair fight." He flicked his hand dismissively at the youth.

"From your pose it appears your uncle taught you, only the most basic defensive stance for a common weapon, the improvised staff?"

"Yes, Sensei," Ceres answered, frozen.

The master stepped forward, moved Ceres' feet slightly, raised his elbows, pulled his head back over his shoulders, shifted his hips forward inside his stance.

"Move fluidly. Lightly. Bounce, even."

Ceres bobbed, shuffled his feet. He remained in the improved stance and waited for further comment or the next attack.

"Found items such as rain deflectors, sticks, gentlemen's ancient style walking canes, even hiking staffs, are handy to use in defense," Sensei said. "You have wisely redirected the opponent's weapons against him. Let us see how you fare against, more capable, opponents?"

After the next round of bows, Ceres presented the short staff at a diagonal towards his next opponent, hands split about one third of the way from each end of the meter-long staff.

"'Fraid to get hurt, are you, pal?" the redhead boy drawled.

"No, just tired of my new bruises when you all say, 'hello."

"Awe, we ain't gonna hurt ya." The boy smiled, swinging his wooden Bokken sword at half speed, in a downward slash at Ceres' neck. Ceres blocked with his staff, taking the blow evenly between his hands. The boy's foot came around and caught Ceres across the knee, causing him to turn. Ceres went with the body motion, raising the hind tip of his staff and striking the underside of his opponent's arm.

"Not this time, anyways," the boy teased.

The boys drew back to their starting stances, grinning at each other. They bowed in respect to each other and the Sensei, and the initiation ritual continued.

Now that Ceres used a weapon in his defense, the older and more skilled students assumed he was better trained than the usual newbie. They pulled their punches a bit less and slowed their movements less.

If he had not taken that staff he would not be getting struck as hard, thought Sensei. He would rather stand up for himself and fight, than just stand here like a punching bag and take it. *We must channel his anger into motivation, a drive to excel.*

Ceres grinned, waving his hand at the next je'ja, egging her on.

Chapter 9
Oh, to Awake in Your Arms

A-Valhalla, Private Dome
2525/7/12/2245

Warm scents of jasmine and vanilla perfumed the air. Ceres felt like he was floating in a pleasant cloud of fragrance, weightless. He soon became aware that he lay in a very comfortable bed in a dimly lit room. The faint sounds of light breathing came from beside him.

Gradually Ceres came to understand that someone was lying softly on his left arm. His pulse quickening, he rolled his head to that side, planting his nose in a head of long, soft, luxurious hair. He inhaled deeply of jasmine.

Venturing to open his eyes, he realized that a wall sconce overhead held a pair of burning tapers, providing the only illumination in the large warm room. Yellowish light fell on soft porcelain shoulders above the dark sheet.

The woman (the shape propping up the dark sheet made that obvious) was laying on her back with her head turned away from his view, shaded in hair. Ceres realized who it must be, the same delicious scent had filled his lungs when he had passed out in the medibay.

Beginning to feel his body respond to his undeniable attraction to the redheaded beauty helped him to realize that he had on no clothing, not even undergarments.

This is sudden, he thought. Careful. He moved his body a bit to the right and tried to extract his arm gently from under her neck.

The woman stirred and rolled toward him, draping her arm across the muscles of his chest. Her leg curled over his and her calf worked its way under his knee. She nuzzled into the muscles of his shoulder and sighed contentedly.

In stages, Ceres became aware of several intriguing facts. The curves the sheet had born witness to, were now pressed against his ribs. They felt bare. She wore no undergarments either. And she was looking at him.

As he drew in a quiet gasp, she sensuously placed a long finger over his lips and whispered, "Shhhhh." Her moonlight colored skin glowed warmly in the soft candlelight.

Ceres could not see her eyes well in the dimness, but he remembered looking deeply into those amazing pools of emerald and feeling drawn in, as if hypnotized. Tingling with excitement, his head lifted, pulled by her hand, and he closed his eyes as they kissed softly, sweetly, then more and more passionately.

* * *

What the heck? Inhaling sharply, Ceres opened his eyes. He gasped again with a start and raised himself up on the bed, rubbing his eyes to ward off the sleep. The aroused tingling sensations in his body began to recede as he saw that he was alone in a large semicircular bed. Surrounded by drapes with an animal stripe print on them, lit by a pair of candles ensconced on the wall above and behind him.

He blinked and rubbed his eyes again, looking about, bewildered. Was that a dream, or a memory? he wondered to himself. *I'm really out of it.*

A wonderful scent filled the air, vanilla with a hint of jasmine. Ceres felt disappointed on some levels, relieved on others, as he crabbed his way to the right side of the huge bed, poking his feet out from the gauzy drapes. He realized he was wearing some kind of silky sarong-style pajama bottoms that he had to arrange carefully for modesty.

His torso was bare, probably due to the thin mediplast encasement glowing green around his muscular right bicep. This helped him realize he had a bicep again. *Last I saw of this, it was a scorched chunk of burger as I fell to the hanger deck.*

Ceres stopped to flex his arm, feeling only a twinge of pain or tightness. The regeneration treatments must have gone well, he considered, swinging his bandaged arm about in all kinds of uncommon ranges of motion and degrees of twist and flex.

Ceres' feet sunk into a plush dark carpet. Moving towards a nearby door to his right, he noticed far less vanilla, far more jasmine in the air. A large walk-in closet tucked behind the bed's wall was not what he sought. The next door counter-clockwise along that sidewall led him to the head.

Minutes later, Ceres paused a moment to allow his eyes to readjust to the candlelight. He reentered the room with its thick black carpet, white curved walls arching overhead in triangular panels of solid material.

Ah. Trok had his own dome on the surface of the asteroid. 'Spoils of the Vikrant.' was it? Got it. Must be crysteel set full opaque, to screen out the red light of the nebula. That would throw a weird scene in here, like hell's bedroom.

The bed faced the lowest part of the crater wall, the attached rooms tucked behind the higher wall behind the bed. Overhead triangles of photo-reactive crysteel were currently set dark to screen out the bright light of the nebula and galaxy beyond.

That's when he heard it. Breathing. He instinctively dropped into a ready stance. What the hell is in here? Crouching like a hunter, following the wall counterclockwise, Ceres easily homed in on the soft sound in the immense quiet. There she was. He stood back up and relaxed.

What? You are afraid she is going to...cute you to death? On a soft divan the leggy redhead—its dark but this has *got* to be her—lay back under a sheet. A mahogany pool rippling with waves and curls, long full hair flowed around her head.

Yes, no other female in the crew nearly that tall, plus that scent. Jasmine wafted from her and filled this part of the room. Inhaling deeply, Ceres smiled. She must bathe in the stuff, and layer it on with all sorts of personal products such sensuous women use.

Satisfied, he concluded that his romantic awakening had to have been a dream, or fantasy? Regardless, it wasn't reality. *Yet,* popped into his mind, and he realized he was tingling again in her presence.

Ceres bent down and softly ran his hands under the slim woman's knees and shoulders. He scooped her up gently, feeling her light weight. *She's a feather! Damn she smells good,* he smiled as he carried her across the room.

She stirred lightly with an "mmmmnnn" into his shoulder, then her head rolled back, and her long hair dangled to swish across his leg. She was like a ragdoll in his arms, limp, helpless, vulnerable. Ceres felt glad he was a strong man. This is one of the perks!

Ceres used Serenity's feet to part the drapes and eased her onto the left side of the bed. She sank onto it with another "mmmnn," her lips pursing and relaxing. Pulling the corner of the bed's sheet over, Ceres grabbed her sheet from the divan and pulled it away. His breath caught at the sight of the sleeping beauty.

"Angelic," he whispered. Her generous curves were evident under the thin fabric of what he thought to be some kind of button up lingerie vest and a thongkini, which highlighted her long legs.

Suddenly embarrassed that he'd been frozen in place for untold moments, all but drooling as he watched her sleep, Ceres finally breathed in deeply and pulled the bed's sheet up over her. Settling in her sleep, she rolled onto her side, facing him, nestled into the bed and pillows, and sighed, content.

"Serenity indeed!" he whispered, whistling low and breathlessly. Finally, Ceres forced himself to turn away from the vision before him, crossed the room again and sank back on the divan Serenity had been sleeping on moments before.

With her scent lingering there and on her sheet he had carried back with him—not just jasmine but her own scents blended in—Ceres had a hard time falling back to sleep. *Heaven help me. Lord, I have a chastity problem.*

He hoped he could recover his dream from earlier. He hoped even more so that he could eventually make it a reality. *God help me with self-control until then.*

After half an hour of turning on the divan, Ceres identified the problem. He got up and quietly searched among the various hatches around the room until he found a bot closet low in the wall cut from the rock of the asteroid. "Come with me" he ordered quietly.

The little turtle followed him across the room until he stopped. "On." he whispered. "Do not move."

Tiny lights atop the little turtle flashed, settling on a small green dot. There was no sound. Ceres lifted the flat body and moved it closer to the couch, tucking it underneath one corner.

He laid down and put his head on the pillow, his body weight settling the luxury grav-couch onto the housing of the vacubot. He smiled, satisfied with the low buzzing sound and vibration transmitted through the shell of the turtle into the frame of the divan. Finally, Ceres drifted back pleasantly into dreamful sleep.

* * *

Serenity sighed on the bed and tried to will herself to relax further. She reveled in the delicious tingling sensations inside her body. *I have never felt myself respond to a man like this. Of course I've never listened to one's thoughts like this before, both noble and sensual, and about me!*

She still felt his body, heat traces of Ceres' arms on her legs and back, on her side where he held her body securely against his. Even the areas where merely his gaze had fallen lightly upon her body. *Lite starshine*, she thought, smiling in the dark.

He passed. I am going to have to work to preserve myself for my wedding day. Lord help us avoid further temptation.

She smiled and drifted asleep, sliding back into what was *her* pleasurable dream, rolling up onto his side, hushing his noble objection, entwining, kissing....

Chapter 10
Fitting in Just Fine

Hunan IV, Win Tao dojo, grounds
2509/09/17/1105

"Hey, leave him alone!" shouted the new boy, Ceres. The tough redhead kid squirmed, held tightly by a trio of older boys. The biggest of the pack had his tattooed, muscular arm around the redhead boy's throat in a tight headlock, while two others controlled his limbs. Crouching, another traced lines between the redhead's freckles with a charcoal stick, her long black hair flowing in the light breeze.

"We're just playing connect the dots with our good ol' buddy, Red, here," With her natural Asianan accent, her rendition of a country drawl was interesting. "I want to see what his freckles say."

The pack of bullies laughed. More of the children outside on the grounds, from their varied looks and clothing styles hailing from a variety of different worlds, either ignored the scene or stood aside unwilling to act.

"Oh, okay. Heh, heh. Let me see?" Ceres asked jovially. With a broad smile and a look of wonder on his face he ambled up besides the artist. "Yeah, nice. Your Kanji writing is artistic, like calligraphy. What does it say?"

"I may tell you in a minute," She dismissed Ceres for a smiling fool. "Stand back or you'll be next."

Ceres stepped back a half step, lifted his right knee up to hip height, and drove his foot forward and down into the back of the girl's right knee. "AAAHHHH!" The teen was driven to kneel on the chipwood path, writhing in pain. She flailed her arms behind her, trying to get ahold of her attacker.

Ceres grabbed her left wrist and twisted, locking her elbow in a painful arm bar. Ignoring her right hand's fingernails digging into his calf behind her, he grit his teeth, resolved to see this through.

"Hey, this Aikido stuff really works," Ceres mocked her. "Thanks for letting me practice on you." He grinned with satisfaction at having turned the tables on the bullies. Unable to handle his anger over losing his mother, something inside him had shifted. Her lessons of New Testament-inspired ways of loving forgiveness had submerged beneath his sudden thirst for Old Testament style justice.

Two of the youth, apparently twins, who were controlling the red haired boy's arms, tossed them aside and reached towards Ceres.

"Nuht, Uhh," Ceres warned them. "Touch me, and I'll crush down harder on her kneecap. She won't walk right again. You thugs downstreamed the same dirty-fighting programs I did, right?"

Ceres leaned forward slightly so his body weight was more directly over his foot. The slightly greater pressure caused the Asianan girl to scream out and release her hand from his leg.

"AARRHHOOOWWWWW! Back off, back off dayton crazy genki!" She called her friends 'idiots' in Japanese, according to Ceres' MeTR translator prog. The pack backed away and blended into the other kids around, all but the one with his arm head-locking "Red." He stepped back and flexed his muscles, causing the boy to gag.

"Okay that's strike two for you," Ceres glowered down into the ear of the girl he now controlled. He warned the huge boy, "Let go of my friend there and leave now or your girlfriend here limps for life. Three. Two…" He leaned forward and increased the weight he pressed down on her pinned knee, eliciting an even louder scream. The strong boy let go of the kid and stood back.

"You're the cavalry! Thanks!" gushed the redhead, rubbing his neck and jaws. "I'm Iron." He stepped carefully around the glowering girl and gripped right forearms with his rescuer. "Why'd ya do that? You know they're gonna wanna get you for this."

"It's a Church thing, Mom says, to protect and help people who need it. I don't know if she'd like this way, but it looked like you needed backup." He bent forward again so their leader could hear him clearly.

"Hear that? Now if you ever pick on my friend here, just know, he's got protection. Next time, I break your knee. Got it?" Tough talk like the holo-vid heroes, but maybe they will buy it and leave them both alone?

The black haired girl, head turned, glared back furiously at Ceres but nodded crisply.

Ceres responded by using his off leg to hop back a meter away from the older girl. As he moved she made a spinning hand-grab for Ceres' foot but missed, nails merely raking across Ceres' pants leg. She rose to a ready stance only to find Ceres and Iron facing her, standing in attack stances of their own.

She cleared her throat, stood erect with her hands clasped to her sides and bowed. "My mistake. You win, this time."

Ceres and Iron returned the bow. Ceres said, "There doesn't have to be another time. I thought kids here learned the concept of honor. How does bullying a young boy bring honor to you? Your family? We're all together here, kept safe from bad people who would use us against our parents, and to learn to be…"

"Save it!" shouted the girl. She left, her shame revealed in how she tilted her head forward, but hatred glowed in her dark almond eyes.

Straightening up, the two boys now saw plenty of other kids strewn about who were paying attention to their little dramatic scene. After Sunday services of all the various kinds let out, the thugs had caught the little redhead boy at the end of the dojo ground's large field, just as he headed into the forest. Now the onlookers wisely avoided the girl's eye contact as she slunk away.

"Oh, man!" shouted Iron through a huge grin. He rubbed his cheek, smearing the rude katakana. "I thought Gorira was going to choke me out before they were done. I can't *believe* you took on Ke'inko Sakiri and her gang of bandits, and won with one move! Cavalry to the rescue. You're my hero, cowboy! What's yer name?"

"Ceres. Ceres Tauri." The two gripped arms again and held on. "Is your name really 'Iron'?"

"Yup. Named by my big brother, Grizz. Someday I'll introduce you," His dark brown eyes lit up at mention of his brother. "I named him Grizzly when he needed to start shaving and didn't. He's HUUUGGE and strong and furry like a grizzly bear." Iron thrust his arms bent overhead, fingers spread and bent like claws. He staggered in imitation of a short legged bear-walk and growled from an open mouth. The boys laughed together.

"I'm just glad for those guys you came along and saved them when you did. I woulda put all of them in the medibay!" He shadowboxed some kickboxing moves.

"Sure, sure, tough guy," Ceres slugged his new friend in the shoulder, feeling solid native muscle under his knuckles. The kid had no baby fat and the kind of layered muscles that only come from years of hard physical daily work. Ceres knew this because he was the same from his years of shipboard work through his childhood. His uncle ran gravity aboard ship as much as possible, wanting Ceres to grow up strong, not thin and weak like low grav natives.

Iron did not flinch at the punch, but rather grinned. "Wow, you sure are made of iron, my friend," Ceres said.

Iron grinned back more broadly at the compliment. He started down the trail into the woods, Ceres walking alongside. Other kids came along with them, interested in knowing this cocky kid who was new to the planet.

"Yup, that's why Grizz called me that. Years of helping around the farmstead. I always tried to do what my big brother was doing, and he tried to keep up with the robots. He says it made me strong.

"How about you? You just got here yesterday, and you're already picking fights with the seniors and winning?"

"Yeah!" shouted a dark-skinned boy. "Where did you learn that move? You haven't started training with us. We just beat you in yesterday," referring to the initiation gauntlet. His big grin told that he approved of Ceres' hidden abilities.

"Oh that was nothing," Ceres said. "I downstreamed it last night along with a bunch of other cool stuff. I over slept. So much interesting combat arts stuff to downstream into my head! Sensei said we had to practice what we dream-streamed so our body could learn to move that way, right? So I was looking for a way to use it, is all."

"Only you were brave enough to intervene," A brunette girl batted her eyelashes at him and grinned. Ceres started to blush and opened his mouth to reply.

"Or stupid enough," Iron jabbed, to the mild laughter of the group. "You don't know the pack order here, outside of class and training times."

"Hang on," Ceres said. "Do they do that all the time?" He looked from face to face. Heads nodded. Feet shuffled. "Who here has been pushed around by those thugs?" Several hands raised. Others nodded sheepishly. Some blushed. A martial arts school full of students unable to defend themselves from some of their own? This didn't make sense to Ceres.

Ceres looked from face to face at his fellow student's. They all had been here longer than he, but they now stared up at him with disbelief or admiration at this new kid who had challenged the top dogs. Somehow they looked up to him as a leader?

"I can't believe it. They're bigger, older, and probably more trained, but you guys outnumber them by a lot!" Most of them hung their heads. The pecking order must have been in place for a while, and they didn't know how to overcome it?

Ceres smirked and shook his head. "Well, look, we don't have to put up with that kind of thing anymore. Here's what we do next time...."

* * *

After a while, the two boys wandered down the Kendor trails chattering on like a pair of little monkeys.

"So, tell me why you're here, farm boy Iron?"

"Last year Mom got elected to the Galactic. Thanks again, pardner. We're pals now. Long as I got a biscuit, you got half."

Pouncing on Iron's shoulder, a meter-tall, feathered monkey of the kind native to this world leapt from hiding on a tree branch. The redhead boy kept on talking like nothing had happened, even as Ceres pulled up, startled by the weird creature jumping out of the woods.

"Hey, what the stars is that?" Ceres asked his new friend.

"Oh sorry, this is 'Peanut," Iron stopped and put his feathered friend on the ground next to him. He formally introduced the monkey to his new human friend.

"Peanut, this is Ceres. Ceres, Peanut. Shake!" Iron commanded his pet.

The creature extended a hand tentatively in Ceres' direction.

Ceres laughed and reached out. Peanut grabbed him by the index finger and gripped hard, bobbing his head and whistling in and out rapidly.

"Hahaha. His feathers tickle between my fingers," Ceres jiggled his hand. Then he went with it and shook his hand erratically, shaking Peanut's hand in the process. "Hey look, I'm shaking his hand both ways, hahaha."

The monkey whistled through his teeth and smiling lips, in a way that seemed like laughter to Ceres.

Iron laughed with his new buddy. He dug in one of his pockets and pulled out a small treat. "Here, toss him one." He flung a peanut to Ceres.

The creature reacted faster than did the humans, though, leaping to catch the flying treat mid-air with his mouth. His arms opened for stability, revealing large glider flaps of skin stretched between his arms, ribs, and knees. He rebounded off Ceres' chest in doing so, and up onto Iron's shoulder.

"Ooofff!" complained Ceres, knocked back off vertical. "Man, he's stronger than he looks for such a little guy."

Peanut made a messy plate out of Iron's buzzcut hair and proceeded to crack open the shell, extract the nutmeats and scarf them down, all within seconds.

"Hey! Darn critter!" Iron protested. "No fair, Peanut. You're making a mess on me!" Try as he might, wherever Iron swept a hand to scrape the offending monkey off his shoulders or back, Peanut scrambled away to another spot atop his human buddy. Both boys laughed while the monkey seemed to whistle-laugh along with them, enjoying the game.

"Here, give me a handful of those nuts," Ceres suggested. Iron hooked a thumb to point out the pocket hiding the treats. He seemed to be a little spare on words when actions would do, Ceres thought.

Ceres dug into his friend's pocket, palming a handful of the nuts. He turned around, and after secreting them in a chest pocket on his blue cargoalls, he turned back. Ceres made a show of obviously putting one peanut on his open palm.

Carefully cracking it in plain sight, looking reminiscent of a magician flourishing an object before the audience, Ceres got Peanut's rapt attention. He opened his mouth wide, made the customary "Aaahhh" sound, leaned back, stretched out his arm and tossed the nut in the air on a high arc.

Peanut responded quickly by climbing atop Iron's head and leaping mightily with both legs. The strong push off caused Iron to lose his balance, and he fell to the leafy forest floor laughing.

Peanut caught the peanut on the rise and soared over Ceres' shoulder, tucking his legs up. One hand caught Ceres by the temple, the other arm extended as a wing, and he swung around behind Ceres' head. Finally, he landed, perching on Ceres' other shoulder just as he had on Iron's.

"Wow! This little monkey's got some moves!" exclaimed the blonde boy. "Where'd you get him?"

"Oh, he's not mine. He kind of adopted me because I like peanuts as snacks and walks in the forest for my do'jo meditation time. My family sends them in care packages. I used to toss them up to his nest trying to tempt him down.

"Now I just bring him some, too. He lives out here in the woods. His family's out there somewhere, I guess, but I haven't seen them, so I adopted him as my little brother."

"Well, he's a pretty cool little brother, then," Ceres agreed. "Looks just like you, too."

Iron grinned, showing good humor at Ceres' teasing.

Ceres knew then that they would enjoy trading teases like old friends.

Peanut's thumbed hand darted down into Ceres' unbuttoned chest pocket and came out with most of the peanuts. He leaped off from Ceres' shoulder and began bounding down the game trail.

"Hey!! Stop, thief!" The two boys ran, laughing, down the trail after the nimble hopping creature. With the local gravity one third lower than one standard "Earth G," they easily adapted to Peanut's bounding gait, imitating his whistling calls.

Chapter 11
Planning the Great Escape

A-Valhalla, Private Dome
2525/7/13/0600

"Ceres. Ceerreees?" *Hmm?* Serenity thought. *He is obviously enjoying a dream,* so she watched him sleep. Serenity waited to wake him until his eyes stopped moving under their lids, and her sense of his mind returned to a blank peacefulness.

"Daylight in the swamps, recruit!" ordered the husky female voice. "Shake a leg! Get UP! Get out of the rack and on the road for chow!"

Ceres' feet hit the deck and he stood, groggy, up into the POA. The dream vanished, and he squinted in the opaque white light from the glowing triangular panels of the dome. The impulse to rub his eyes drowned out under the ingrained understanding that any movement would merit I.T., or incentive training, the formal military term for punishment by exercise.

"Open your eyes recruit! Ha ha hehehe," the voice dissolved into a decidedly girlish laughter.

He forced one pair of his sleepy lids apart, only to laugh himself. At himself. With a sheepish grin Ceres beheld Serenity, then fell back to sit upon the divan. She sat opposite him on a plush chair.

"Heh, heh. You make a pretty cute drill instructor," he observed, causing a slight rose glow to light up her spotted cheeks. "You might inspire extra effort in PT," he said, assuming she understood the military abbreviation for physical training. He looked into her eyes and continued, "but practicum scores would suffer from the inability to concentrate in your presence."

"I haven't been awakened like that in years, since Navy Boot camp was our military indoctrination before I entered the Merchant Marine Academy."

"Thanks. You're distractin', yourself, Master," she returned. Her red lips broadened into a wide smile. She tried teasing him to see how it went, to feel his reaction.

"Huh?" His eyes snapped open and the vestiges of sleep fell away immediately. She was grinning at him and his sheepish feeling returned. "Sleep well?" was the best he could do after a silent moment passed between them.

"Absolutely!" she breathed. "That mattress is soooo luxurious! Best I've slept in my whole life. Thank you. And for bein' such a gentleman last night, too."

"Yeah, well, I'm not used to something so soft. I think that's what woke me. That, or a vivid dream I had," he smiled at her.

Serenity smiled conspiratorially, "That must've been some dream, to wake you. Sure it was no nightmare?"

"Oh, no. Quite," he smiled broadly at her, "pleasant. More of a fantasy actually, probably inspired by this place." He looked about at the loud jungle motif. "Although I'd never consider it consciously, my unconscious mind apparently made a fantasy of the thought of waking up next to some slave-girl." Ceres' grin ceased when he saw her face, her mouth gaping in shock.

"Excuse me," he offered. "I said I'd never!"

"No, it just sounds so much like my own dream last night. Tell me yours exactly," Serenity prompted. "Go on," she added after a few seconds. 00

On her home world, women were usually in the lead in conversations and relationships between the sexes. As the young Solman cautiously recounted his dream of waking up, right through to the passionate kiss, and then actually waking up in this room, his audience of one became more and more intrigued. Serenity's eyes widened in astonishment to match her opened mouth.

Finally, she stammered, "Th-that matches my dream exactly, up until you carried me from here to the bed!"

Now Ceres' jaw dropped. "You were awake?"

"Well, if someone's hands went under your back and knees, I'd bet you'd awaken too, love!" She punctuated her points with her index finger pointer.

Seeing how well they were bantering together, she felt quite at ease with this largely unknown man, quite at ease considering he'd carried her to a bed and briefly checked out her body while she wore this tiny little outfit that had the most fabric of any sleepwear the pirates provided to such concubine slaves as they considered her.

Instead of feeling upset, she felt glad he was attracted to her that way. She remembered her body's tingles where he had touched her.

"Yeah, well. You didn't show it. Hey! You were testing me to see if I, climbed in with you, or whatever?

"Hmm, you passed the chivalry test quite well, Ceres, though you certainly checked me out, too." *Passing the interested test*, she thought.

"How would you, how could you, possibly know if I looked at you in the dark?" he asked incredulously. He stood in shock. "And how did we share the same dream? And why did I feel I could hear your thoughts in the hanger yester—whenever that was? How?" He eyed her suspiciously.

Caught, Serenity looked a bit nervous, but her sense of him was of curious wonder, not fear, not hostility, no agenda, but interest and intrigue towards her. Realizing he had fought for her and considering how he had behaved last night, she decided he would at minimum make a good ally in the galaxy.

Plus, she had strong feelings for him as well. That dream had been *her* fantasy, born of her attraction for this tall man with the deep blue eyes who'd jumped gallantly to her rescue, risked his life for her and been scarred for it, for her freedom, and dark thoughts of what life she would have led if he'd not done so.

She decided to ease into the subject. "I'm a Psion."

Stunned, Ceres sat—fell back, rather. Luckily, an overstuffed chair was behind him, part of a grouping of furniture making a small conversation area of this part of the large room. He sat and stared blankly at the gorgeous redhead, mulling over what she claimed, over the events of the last…he had no idea how long he had been out.

To himself, he thought, *After this, I'll never be surprised about anything ever again. Hmmm. If I could hear her thoughts, she must be reading mine.*

"Bollocks!" he thought forcefully, imagining sending it to her but not using the MeTR. "Now, what did I just think?" he asked.

"The balls of a bull will not keep me from hearin' your thoughts, playboy!" she retorted. It was not her first experience with coarse language, even coming from her own mouth. Her people were known for speaking the truth with brutal frankness. Irish insults were legendary even before leaving

Earth. *Amazon's* insults were renowned to blister the paint off Navy starships.

His mind reeled and the swirl of thoughts spilled out of his mouth. "How could they capture a Psionic? One: They all join the Galactic since hundreds of years ago, since it's the only place they can get training.

"And Two: any Psion worthy of the name would've mind-kicked their butts!" *And Three:* he thought, *Can you use this to help me search for my mother around here?*

She again ignored his lack of refinement of command of the English language. "Yes, I can help you find her."

Ceres mouth opened. His squint of suspicion slid into a look of understanding.

"I have not mastered it; really I'm just a novice, untrained. Well, I played around with it with my brother," she winced, "growin' up."

"During their attack these pirates blockaded all space traffic so they could bombard the city free of movin' obstacles. After attacking that arcology, they turned on the ships they had interdicted, includin' the freightliner I'd booked passage on.

"They spaced the crew, oh, the owners were such nice people. They helped me—" She waved a hand in front of her face to cut off that train of thought and conversation. "But the pirates used a stunner on me." She frowned upon thinking of the probable reasons why.

"Earlier you asked if you'd heard my thoughts in the hanger," she added. "That was projective telepathy—"

Ceres mused aloud, "You and your brother must have had a special way of talking. Without using your voices, without using the MeTR and WetNet system?" She looked down at her feet and pursed her lips, but nodded. "Mind control?" he asked.

"I wasn't controlling your mind, Ceres." She raised up and gave him eye contact. "I am not very experienced at that. Yes, I used to try to *make* my brother do silly things." she grinned.

"But your adult, military trained mind is probably too strong for me to do that. I *was* able to put thoughts into your head, speak into your head." Her voice strengthened in her tale.

"You told me what to think? Made me think what you wanted? How is that not mind control?" *I need to remember the mental exercises my family long ago mastered, to prevent alien minds from controlling them.*

"No," she disagreed, hearing his thoughts effortlessly now. "I was just encouragin' you t'do what you already were thinking of. I knew what you were thinking, just as I knew last night when you looked me over, by reading your thoughts, by a simple readin' of the output of your conscious mind." Serenity smiled beautifully, straight white teeth framed by lush red lips.

"Now, I'm intrigued that you received my dream-" She stopped and blushed as Ceres gasped at that revelation.

"You were dreaming that way about us, about me!?" he asked, pointing double-barreled gunfingers at his chest as his roguish grin returned.

Her cheeks, freckled like the moon, reddened further. Serenity admitted to herself that she, too, had been attracted to him since first seeing him the other day. Watching him sleep as his arm healed from the awful wound, her attraction deepened.

She certainly felt—knew—how he felt about her. Even as his eyes had first met hers, she felt the internal explosion of his love and desire for her and her own for him. She would never forget it. Intimidated by the power of these new memories and her current tingly feelings in his warm presence, she looked down. "Th-there must be some kind of connection between us."

She tried to deflect the conversation away from her feelings. "Were any of your relatives or ancestors Psionic? Do you exhibit any mentalist powers?"

Surprised by these questions, Ceres' grin faded and his brow furrowed in thought of old family stories. "Hmm, someone on my mother's side? My Great-Uncle Eli, I think? Died in the first battle of the last Clone War to the guns of some kind of new war bots."

"As for me, I just feel a bit lucky sometimes, but I heard your voice in my head clear enough yester—when *was* that duel? How long was I out of it?" He had not yet synched his implanted datapad and checked the time in his HUD. *She throws me off my usual balance. I kind of like it though.*

"That was just two days ago. We kept you unconscious for nearly two days. I am also a healer. That's why you're already back to 95% in that arm." Grateful that he followed her lead of the subject away from that too-hot dream, she picked up a datapad.

"So. We need to come up with a plan. There are at least hundreds of innocent slaves who need rescuing. You have a new ship. We have to get to know this place, so we can escape."

Ceres' grin settled in and his love and admiration grew for this gorgeous, intriguing woman. He silently mused, *This Woman! I guess she truly is the woman of my dreams.*

"Look, Ceres, let us be clear." Serenity said. "Between us we will communicate openly about our feelin's. I know you're quite taken with me, but I dun'no yet if I *am* the woman of your dreams or if you are just following the pheromones you might enjoy with any available female."

"We felt something together, and we are fond on each other," she continued, "attracted to each other. All obvious. Am I right, love?" He had never experienced someone so frank and direct, confront him with his own thoughts and feelings before.

"Yes." *What, you were listening to me think? Listening right now?*

"Yes, right now," she said aloud in response to his thoughts.

Okay, I need to practice mind-blocking. He thought.

"As you wish. We need to set our chemistry aside and work on getting out of here." she continued. "If we dwell on these emotions we might just degenerate into these pirate's lifestyle and may never get out of here.

"I sensed something noble about you, so I reached out to you to help me get out of the jam I was in. It was bad enough wakin' up in their clutches aboard that ship, but I could have gotten away from one small ship's crew."

Focusing on tactical issues seemed to help him direct his thoughts. "Bringing you aboard the station," he commiserated, "surrounded by thousands of them, it got pretty bleak for you."

"I could've flitted away from one of 'em, easy." she grimaced in disgust at what thoughts and plans Trok had for her, "but I din'nt know how to get away from all of 'em, out of here. That is why I appealed to you to help me. Your thoughts showed you to be a flyer. I thought you'd as like to 'elp me out."

"Now," she continued, "we *are* going to get away out of here! We'll plan it next. Right now let's get the big questions over so you know, I'm not g'nna just fall over the couch with you."

She could tell from the swirl of his thoughts, he had to discipline his mind to prevent indecent images of them together from forming. The tiny patch of clothing the pirates had provided to cover her curvaceous body made it almost impossible for him to look at her without arousal.

Focus, boy focus! You have to control your mind to have a chance to control your body. Ceres bit the tip of his tongue, both to help him focus his mind and to prevent saying something inappropriate.

This is what Uncle Manny told me about, Ceres thought, to which Serenity listened, *'When the woman is worth it, the 'Worthy wife, her value far beyond pearls.' as in Proverbs, you will do the opposite behavior, you will do all you can to not get her in bed as soon as possible. You know you will lose her for trying.*

"I want you to know," she said, "after we are out of here, we will then discuss our relationship in the big picture. I want to know, what do you want? What are your goals in life? Where are you going? What kind of model of a marriage and family is in your mind when you get to that stage with, whomever it is?"

"My sainted grandparents—" he started.

"Okay, love. Not now. Store those questions on your datapins and let that idea percolate in the back of your mind. If ever you get a wild and sexy idea while we are together, just remember, we are not married. It won't happen and I will...." she paused for a breath, turned softer and put a hand on his stubbled chin.

"I would have to disqualify you as the kind of noble man that *I* am lookin' for. Do y' understand? If I could shut Trok down while captive aboard his stolen ship, I can shut you down too."

The cast of her eyes gave him the hint. *She could do painful things to me if I get overly frisky?*

"Yes, exactly."

"What?" he snapped upright "Oh, Psion." He blushed. *Living a more moral life is going to be hard, especially if she calls me on it for my every stray thought.*

"Look here yourself, lil miss," his affected drawl crept in unconsciously at times. "The degree a man is civilized is the degree to which he controls his impulses."

"Granted."

"Besides that, I would like to be able to talk at least to myself without a monitor." They both laughed.

"Serenity," he coughed and drew himself up, "I would appreciate it if you do not constantly listen to my every thought without permission. This is the reason why my family bans our joining the WetNet links we hear about on non-Galactic planets.

"Same reason why the Galactic bans it outside of marriage and builds blocks for it into the MeTR technology." he went on. "Comm only. Heck, even married partners have to plug in the link to share open thoughts at that level. People need to be able to think freely."

"Agreed," she said, "I will discipline myself too, to give you privacy outside of situations essential to our escape." They looked at each other.

"Well, that was easy. Is every argument with you going to be this agreeable?" he smiled.

"I am not sure this counts as an argument." she retorted. "A 'discussion,' sure. We will share our thoughts and feelings freely. Easy. Why make it harder with dysfunctional emotions?"

"I may have to remind you that you said that." They chuckled together.

"I was named after my temperament. I don't get too 'riled up' as you say." She tried on an old country accent similar to his impersonation of Iron, if Texas were once in Ireland. They both roared with laughter.

"Okay," he clapped his hands together and started their planning, "this space-potato is laid out with a continuous ring of hangers around the long-axis belt-line." Turning to work on their escape kept them busy for the rest of the morning.

Chapter 12
Expelled

Hunan IV, Win Tau Dojo, construction site.
2511/01/21/1610

"Gravity ball is coming soon!" Ceres returned from holiday break with the great news. A StarSys crew arrived shortly after him, and the dojo buzzed. All the students looked forward to their new athletic pastime.

ZG Ball was a rich college and pro sport. Only the wealthiest colleges could afford the StarSys monopolized gravity technology. The humble Tarsis family owned StarSys, so Ceres' casual request for a gravity sphere at his military school was an easy "Yes." for his generous grandfather.

Joseph Tarsis was a giant man in galactic business circles. In Ceres eyes, however, "Papa Joe" was just a warm loving grandfather. As the eldest of his generation, Ceres was favored by most of his elders. Little did he yet understand, his unassuming Papa directed the largest Mega-Corp with the largest Gross Galactic Sales in history, surpassing the Galactic Confederations' capped tax revenues by a couple of percentage points.

Built in space, in orbit around a planet, most gravity ball spheres took advantage of the effective lack of gravity. The spheres built on planets had to be completely contained with gravity plates—ryanite emitters which could negate gravity. It was a special property of ryanite exploited for opening wormholes for FTL travel, gravity plating in the most sensitive starships, and lifting the most luxurious spacecars above their planets.

ZG Ball players moved their bodies and the ball with special electromagnetic boots and gauntlets. Wearing them, his new Christmas presents, Ceres was floating around over the metal frame of the ZG Sphere construction site, chattering like a monkey with the work crew and robots.

Left alone down below, Iron looked up at the framework coming together overhead. To Iron, it looked like a giant globe of an artificial planet, before they fill it in with all the dirt and water and stuff.

"Hey, Red!" the Asianan accented voice chilled Iron's belly. "Ohhh, too bad. You forgot your rich bodyguard for once." The black-haired girl, Ke'inko mocked him. "Bad idea."

Not good. He spun, looking for escape routes away from the frame. Seeing one of the old gang's dark-haired twins to his right, he turned left.

"To Ma Re!" the other twin, the one with messy hair shouted, putting his hand out before Iron in an unmistakable sign to "stop." Covering that angle, his arms then stretched low as if he was catching a chicken strayed from the coop. Ahead of Iron the huge pile of muscles nicknamed Gorira lurched towards him, smacking his meaty fists together menacingly. He could take a beating, and it looked more and more like he was gonna take a beating.

Iron glanced over his shoulder to confirm that the girl was coming up behind him, having slipped around or through the work site to cut him off. Great! Surrounded. Rodeo time.

Nodding his red head in determination, he sucked up his courage. Bouncing lightly on his feet like an old-style boxer, he was ready to give as well as he could, and take what was coming. Then he rushed at the twin to his right, hoping to jink past him groundball style and dash into the forest at the end of the big clearing.

"Gotchya!" the teen crowed. Iron tried to baseball slide under his open armed tackle, but the taller boy was ready. Chopping his hand downward, he snagged the sleeve of Iron's gi as his body passed under. The other three thugs sprinted to catch up and were on him in seconds. Out of the cloud of dust rose the redhead boy, curling his fists.

"What did you do to Sume'?" the girl shouted, eyes wide as she searched the dust cloud for the missing twin.

"Don't you guys ever study and practice?" Iron smirked at her. "I flipped 'im. Judo shoulder roll. Easy as mud pies. Come 'n git it. Ahll show all y'all." he flexed his fingers.

Sume' rose up behind the scrappy kid though and kicked him square in the back, knocking the wind out of Iron. Gorira swung a haymaker at him as he lurched forward, but Iron dropped to his knee under it so only his flat red hair took the fanning blow.

Sume' and his twin, Hayato, sporting his perpetually unkempt hair, untied their sheathed katanas and wound up to begin beating Iron with them. Then, the pack jumped in. The kid's pack, the mass of them.

The fight had distracted the tattoo gang, as the kids had nicknamed them, into focusing on Iron. Meanwhile over twenty kids playing on the field and grounds caught up to the fight and more were running in. Sume' grabbed Iron by the shoulder and arm, spun him about to retaliate face to face but he was tackled by two boys from his left. He held on to Iron's gi, and they all spun down in a tangle of flailing fists and thumping sounds from Sume's sheathed sword.

Snarling, Ke'inko kicked out, repelling multiple attackers before four of the biggest girls, who held her twisting limbs in place, overwhelmed her. Hayato used aikido throws to toss aside kids running at him, and then was mobbed down by several younger kids at once, all shouting, "Get him!"

Gorira lived up to his nickname. Piled on by one after another, he soon had six, then eight kids holding his legs and body. Others clung to his powerful swinging arms like paper lanterns tossed in a windstorm. Still more leaped on his back, and then more, pushing the writhing mass over. The big body of Gorira submerged as a lump beneath the dogpile.

With a great growl the gang-tackle swelled up, the head and shoulders of the big boy held tightly by several smaller youth whose bodies' slid to hang downhill. Gorira's tattooed arm swept down, flinging off three kids who had been desperately holding on. The massive fist swung back up for space to begin pummeling the smaller kids with meaty punches.

"Hold!" Sensei cleared his coarse throat. The entire mass of kids froze, including the big guy. "Everyone stand to!" The commanding voice like a general growling out of their Sensei's throat sent a shiver through the group of struggling kids. "Hands off! Stand up!"

The huge tattooed arm never swung. Over a dozen kids let go of Gorira and stepped away in a gaggle, leaving the giant's other knuckled fist holding one initiate off the ground by the back of her gi. He set the kid down.

Iron and his four assailants all bled from their lips and sported bruises on their faces and bodies. Under the writhing piles, the innermost kids had continued to scratch and throw short punches and knees at the bullies' tangled bodies. They had expressed their years of frustration and pain by returning what they had received.

"If you would like to test your skills on a worthy opponent, today, now, is your final exam! You four can defeat me and leave with that honor, or leave in disgrace." Sensei's angered voice gathered control as he spoke.

"Either way, you will leave this school today." He bowed and assumed a very casual, relaxed ready stance.

The kids who had come to Iron's rescue all peeled off. They joined hands and moved around, making a circular area in the grass for the contest. First hearing the melee at the crescendo of the fight, Ceres finally floated down on his expensive gravity ball gear and ran out of the construction site. He rushed to his friend's side in time to help Iron stand.

"You're late," Iron teased his pal.

Ceres grimaced, red faced. "You could have called out in comms?"

Iron just shrugged. More adults arrived from the buildings and the kids settled down, knowing order was restored. They joined the ring of youth surrounding Sensei and his four opponents. The young adult thugs gave each other silent moody looks.

Iron sent thoughts to Ceres via his MeTR, the best friends always being grouped for communication, *"Too bad 'Gorira' don't play groundball. He'd be a great linebacker. Not as big as my brother Grizz, but close."*

Ceres thought *"Good thing he didn't get ahold of you. He'd mash you into a juicy steerburger."*

After a moment the tattoo gang nodded between themselves and then towards Sensei in the barest of bows. They arranged themselves in a diamond pattern, crouched in their favorite ready stances from the many martial arts learned here.

"They are probably communicating about tactics in a group, the same as us." Ceres thought to Iron. *"Using the Gorira's big body to screen the other's attacks. Not bad."*

"Really? I'm glad you are here to play-by-play the obvious for me, cowboy." Iron smirked then winced, which hurt his split lips and eyebrow.

Gorira bull-rushed his Sensei, a predictable, throwaway move. Sensei stood his ground as the muscular young man leaped forward on thick legs built strong on his higher-grav homeworld. The other two boys followed close behind. Belying his age, the old master leaped up, nimbly stepping on the huge teen's outstretched arm as a second liftoff point.

The slim master soared high, flashing a kick to the back of the big boy's head. The rushing bull's face crashed down and slid on the grass. The old man landed past the feet of his first downed attacker.

Close behind Gorira, the two mid-sized thugs split to flank their master. Both attacked him as Sensei landed, with unsheathed swords sweeping at their master front and back. Sensei moved left, inside the body space of Hayato with his scruffy hair, grasped his tattooed left arm by the wrist and pulled to the right.

Sensei's left hand cupped Hayato's head, guiding it as they pivoted smoothly like a couple executing a dance move. The teen's body swung around into Sume', his twin.

Momentum from the swing threw both boys together. Their heads struck with a solid "klonk," knocking them both unconscious. They landed in a pile atop the back of Gorira. So far in three seconds Sensei made two moves, knocking out the three biggest attackers.

Bright rapid strobing from a pulse laser caught the attention of everyone in the ring. When the boys attacked, Ke'inko had stepped back and pulled a laser pistol. She aimed it at Sensei but missed. Her fat-lensed pistol jerked to the side as she fired, her arm pulled along with it.

The laser leaped out of her hand, her eyes opened wide in wonder. It flew through the air and landed in the grass, halfway across the circle towards Ceres and Iron. Ceres' grav-ball gauntlet glowed blue around his outstretched forearm.

"Never drop your gun to pet a mountain lion," Iron drawled, eliciting raucous laughter from many of the surrounding students.

Ke'inko glowered at him at length before turning back to Sensei. The old master merely looked at her expectantly. "Yield." She bowed forward an inch, not waiting for her master to return it, but stalked off towards the barracks, defiant head held high.

"I wasn't here in time to help you, Iron buddy," Ceres' hands opened in a helpless gesture.

"No, pardner. You were." He nodded towards the other kids, who had started to gather closer, checking on their mutual friend. "When you stood up to them last year, you brought us all together as a 'gang' of our own.

"In the year since, we've changed this place from exclusive little clicks to inviting and accepting everyone into a family again. They gave me the wire brush treatment, but instead of one coming to my rescue, I had 30. 50! Thanks to you." As they gripped forearms he smiled warmly at his friend, splitting his lip open again to show fresh blood.

"Thanks everyone, for coming to mah rescue." They cheered and tousled his red hair. "Now, ifn y'all don't mind, would someone drag my carcass to the medibay." There was no shortage of friendly hands.

Chapter 13
Master Slaver

A-Valhalla, Ceres' private domes
2525/7/13/1042

"Upstream the training modules from this pin to your onboard memory." Ceres held out a tiny datapin.

"Why?" Serenity asked him.

"If they consider you to be a slave, you should spend at least *some* nights in those quarters. They would get suspicious if you had a pin sticking out. Too dangerous. If they pull it and read it, they will throw us both overboard."

She frowned.

"I don't like it either," he added "but we need to start interacting with more people aboard the asteroid."

"At least I can find out which slaves are really on their side," she capitulated, "and which we can ask for help. I'll start to gather information, so we can escape with as many as possible."

Exactly!" he smiled. "I have loaded that pin with a spiral sequence of basic training. Every time you REM sleep it will play the next module, right into your mind. When you are awake and alone, you should practice what you can, even if it is in slow motion."

"As long as it doesn't contradict the training I already have from my home planet," she asserted. "We have a proud history of our own unique martial forms, dating back to the colonization of my planet."

"I understand." he agreed. "I am interested to learn your styles as well. Add them to my own?"

She still seemed hesitant but she took the pin and stuck it into the soft data socket behind her ear.

"Now, let's go over the layout of the asteroid," he started over, "Brainstorm. Speak every crazy idea that comes to mind. You never know when some strange observation will lead to an unexpected approach vector."

"Actually," she tapped her foot, eyes raised to the dome, *"let's take this conversation inside our heads,"* she retorted, switching effortlessly to mental communication. *"You never know when someone may be listening."*

* * *

The co-conspirators were surprised at mid-morning by a chime from the entry hatch. *"Did they give you a heads-up they would be coming today?"* Ceres asked Serenity.

When he moved toward the hatch, the link to its sensor systems popped up in his HUD. He saw a few pirates shuffling up the access tube towards his dome, fed directly into his optic nerves.

"No, love. Visitors?" Serenity asked.

Ceres knew "love" was a common expression of her planet of origin going back to the Irish usage, not a personalized term of endearment. *Not yet,* he thought privately. The hatch beeped.

"Speaking of the devil," he warned, then through his MeTR, thought *"Open."* The hatch double-beeped and slid open at his thought command, transmitted from his MeTR to the linked door.

The first guard marched in, oversized green armor and electro-staff clattering, followed by a line of several people up the tube from inside the base. *What is this? Some kind of parade?* Ceres backed up to the sitting area to make room for his guests.

"Master Ceres, I am Master Dooms." The middle-aged guard identified himself. Long black hair fell over his face like a hood, a weak jaw and a strong grin showing through. Dooms stroked his black beard down over his plasteel shell, bowed at the waist, and moved to Ceres' right.

Ceres could not decide if the man's gait was aided, or impaired, by his use of his electro-stunner as a walking staff. Its power head crackled energy between four electrode tines.

No helmet. Ceres thought to himself. Wants everyone to know exactly who he is. Show of force?

"I discipline the slaves." Dooms gloated. His eyes glinted and a sly smile crossed his thin lips. He seemed to be so slimy that he continuously wiped his own hands on his black beard as if milking livestock.

Ceres felt a knot form in his stomach. He did not like the way Dooms said that. But he just nodded, unsure what to do or say, because next behind Dooms, in strode Ceres' father.

"Ah, a family meeting." Tyrian sneered. "I should have brought my women too." Serenity turned to shoot a look at Ceres but caught herself before she broke out of her role. Ceres' stomach churned noisily. He remembered with regret having been a womanizer in college, up until a particular incident in his second year.

"These lot are your property now," Dooms said to Ceres, his arm sweeping magnanimously as if presenting gifts to a prince. Three women, whom Ceres saw were clad in about as little as Serenity, led the parade.

Ah, I see, thought Ceres.

"Yes, you see too much," Serenity chided to him. Even when he thought he was thinking private thoughts, she was listening.

Dooms continued, "We feed them in the pens but when you bring them out like this, you are responsible for their feeding and *discipline*." He again emphasized the word more than Ceres cared for.

One by one, the female slaves proudly presented themselves before their new owner with a simple dance pirouette, and then kneeled. When Ceres nodded at them in turn, they sat back onto their feet submissively. He carefully held a mild smile on his face, seeming to play along with his father and the apparent culture of the Void Vikings. Inside, he was revolted.

My cousin was attacked in college, thanks in part to the debauchery of frat culture I participated in- I led. Ceres closed his eyes, reliving his taking revenge on her behalf. He had championed against this culture of use of women ever since. And now, here he was being given several women to use as slaves? He breathed out slowly, passing it off as if anticipating the gift.

"Use them as you will." All three were young and sporting bruises in varied stages of recovery. Ceres turned back to Dooms, seeing him stroke his beard as he grinned down at the slave girls.

I want to smash that devilish grin off your face, eel! Armor or no I would give you one breath-span to live. Ceres felt his face turning red with his anger at Doom's "discipline," evident upon the girls' bodies.

He was grateful for the next distraction, allowing him time to slip into a character more fitting with the pirate's culture.

Four young men in utility coveralls filed in, carrying a small portion of Ceres' belongings—his clothes and gear removed after his duel sent him to the medibay. One man held his form-fitting one piece Navy uniform. It was rolled up around the graphene plate armor, attached and collapsed on the back of the futech under-suit.

He also carried Ceres' camouflaged utility cargo pants filled with whatever engineer's gadgetry Ceres had brought along with him. Another held Ceres' plasma sidearm and its pocketed belt, plus the fat disruptor. Ceres knew he would would have to get or make a real holster for that thing.

The last one had Ceres' tractor-pressor bracers and his customized military boots. Little did anyone know the extreme value of these last items, laced with highly pure ryanite gravity projectors.

Ceres belongings were placed with care on the gravcouch away from him, the men then standing in line behind the girls. Finally, two old women shuffled in. Another guard in green armor stopped outside the hatch and posted his electro-staff at order arms. *Former military somewhere?* Ceres thought.

He looked over the three women now kneeling in front of him. A slim girl with dark hair and skin wore a single, wide ribbon wound around her entire body. A blonde proudly wearing nothing but a light tan and dozens of long strands of pearls fidgeted next to a short brunette with colorful appliques of fresh flowers and autumn leaves over her pale skin.

Each of them wore the ubiquitous cupless 'underbra' across their ribs which lifted their breasts without covering them. Fashionable on the outlying sectors, such attire was too immodest for polite Galactic society, let alone the Patriarch's Stars.

"I see." Ceres did not need anyone to explain for him to draw the obvious conclusions. His anger boiled, this atop their bruises, he wanted to rip the heads off all of these slavers. Once again feeling his body prime for a fight, he imagined attack sequences to cut through them quickly.

Ceres felt a dagger of ice slice through his flaming anger when he realized the danger of taking action too early. This was still the slavers' game, played with their home field advantage. There would be no escape if they fought their way out too early. He would have to prepare the field for *his* game.

Curt with restraint, Ceres turned to dismiss the slave master. "Thank you. I will figure them out from here."

Dooms looked at Tyrian, who nodded and tilted his head toward the hatch. Frowning intently at Ceres, Dooms left in a huff, pushing the other guard ahead of him. They muttered between themselves, heard to echo up the corridor until cut off by the automatic hatch.

Eyebrow raised, Tyrian tilted his head and looked below Ceres' grav-lounger. "Trouble with your bot?"

"Oh, I forgot about him." Ceres did not turn nor blush in deference, not within the castle of his own dome, knowing exactly what his father had seen.

"I grew up in space, completely used to the background sounds of starship's engines. So I tucked the vacubot under the divan so the vibrations hummed through the frame." He shrugged, "In quiet places, I do what I have to for a little white noise for the night. Otherwise I can't sleep."

Amused, Tyrian nodded, "I see," grinned and stroked down his beard in the same manner as had Dooms. "Well, maybe your new duties will help exhaust you?" His devilish grin turned Ceres' stomach again."

Oh, I have to keep them away from him! Ceres thought.

"I have much to do myself, son," Tyrian began, his eyes wandering across the line of girls then flitting up to linger on Serenity, sitting apart on the divan. "We should have a talk, father to son, or, man to man?" He caressed his yellow-white beard looking Ceres directly in the eyes.

"Perhaps we can discuss this in a week?" Ceres offered, trying to pattern his voice like his father's. "I would like to get to know my, family, as you called them when you came in. Then I can make wise decisions." He extended his hand to his father to end it, and they traded firm handgrips on their forearms.

Ceres restrained himself from using the proximity for attacking his father. Being a man of action, he desperately wanted to *do* something. His muscles were tense, flush with energy. Crushing his father's hand would be a clue to his emotional struggle. He gripped hard but eased off. Save it for the right time. Deliver a crippling blow.

"A week. I can wait that long." Tyrian's hand caressed one girl's cheek as he slid past their line and backed towards the hatch. "See you again soon, my ladies."

He smiled, waited while everyone in the room bowed or nodded towards him, and then whirled off to the hatch in a rush, clomping his boots down the corridor. The hatch slid shut with a solid boom.

"Whew!" Ceres breathed out a long sigh, swallowing his disgust. He felt slightly sick to the stomach, but knew he had to suck it up and perform the role given him of master, for these slaves too. Never know who is on your side. He looked over at Serenity and took a couple of deep breaths to calm himself down from fight mode.

"He didn' ask about your arm," Serenity's voice whispered in Ceres' head.

"I noticed. My 'long lost, caring' father." he smirked. *"I'm not certain he missed it, that I was not sleeping in that bed, with you."*

"Wait to fit these slaves into our plans until after I've had a chance to get to know them," she ignored his warning and gave her one of her own.

"Right. Now I have to play my part." He sighed, paused, affected a dramatic nod, sat back on the chaise lounge and threw one leg up on it. He spread out as if he was a big man who was used to being in charge of people he owned.

Turning to the elder women, he began, "We will learn names as we go. Which of you sews?" One of them presented a wrinkled hand, curious look on her face.

"These," he paused in thought, "I hesitate to use the word 'clothes' for what the lovely young ladies are wearing here. Is this all they are provided?" He smiled and the old woman nodded grimly. Glancing at the men Ceres saw from their rapid breathing and downward stares that they were fighting to not laugh, and winning.

"Affecting a princely voice?" Serenity had an accusatory look, which Ceres turned and noticed.

"Play along." He stared at her for a moment then motioned with his head towards the end of the line of kneeling women. Serenity moved there and knelt alongside the others. Ceres knew she was sliding into a role she resented, he could see it on her face in the curl of her lip, the way she proudly kept her chin up, the defiant flash of her eyes. From their morning's planning, they both knew she would have to infiltrate the slaves just as Ceres would infiltrate the Viking pirates.

Once Serenity sat on her heels the way the other girls did, he was taken aback. Am I slipping? Why didn't I see it before? Black-haired, brunette, a blonde, and now a redhead? Trok was a collector? —Serenity the final item! That degenerate mushroom. I wish I could shoot him again!

Ceres looked up at the triangular struts of the dome arching overhead, breathed deeply, and then lowered his gaze onto the two old women. "Mother? What is your name, your home world? What do you do here? Cook? Sew?"

"Anastasia, of Nau Saint Petersburg, sir. I have been a housemaid and sometimes seamstress for, your predecessor." Her colorful accent implied an upbringing with Russian as her primary language. Not many planets in and outside the Galactic chose their native Earth language as primary on the colony worlds, but 500 years into the Galactic Era of Man, nostalgia was becoming more popular.

"Galactic" was the common trade language across the human-dominated Milky Way Galaxy, even beyond, learned by the few sentient races encountered as humanity spread. Grown out of old American English, it fattened up on all the trade-words from nearly every major language of Earth. At over 1 million words, when it left the gravity well of Earth 1.0, the Tarsis family and StarSys took to calling it "Galactic," which stuck.

Noting the babushka's grandmotherly white hair Ceres realized it could have once been auburn, most common on planets colonized from Earth's Eastern Europe. He turned sharply to look at the second older woman. Grey was overtaking her chestnut waves. *Million dollari she's down from a French bloodline. Thick-headed bastard had all the flowers in one vase!*

"Anastasia, organize these patient girls into gathering what you need, to make proper clothing for the ladies." Every one of them opened their mouths in surprise. One of the men turned his head with a quizzical look on his face. The spell of waiting for their master was broken after too much silence, broken with such a shock.

"Play along yourself," Serenity thought to him.

"I have it. No worrying women here," he thought humorously in her direction, confident that she was going to continue listening in despite their conversation earlier. He had already forgotten to flex those mental muscles to shield his mind from her.

"Let us just say, my preference is to leave a little more to the imagination, a little more to discover, shall we?" This seemed to be understandable to the women, they tightened or wrinkled their lips. None of them enjoyed this display of their bodies as offerings to their new owner, no matter how handsome they might have found him under different circumstances.

"And I would rather not share, hmm," he said slowly as his eyes drifted down the line of girls, "the sparkle, of all of my jewels with the others around, for free?" The men nodded. Apparently, they understood that, meaning he had covered for himself well enough.

"You're enjoying this too much." Ceres clearly heard Serenity's voice like a second conscience in his head.

"Be careful what you pray for," he answered in his thoughts. *"You just might get it."*

"Sir, may I speak?"

"Yes, Anastasia, please."

She seemed taken aback at his use of "please" with a slave. "Sir, there are not many fine fabrics aboard this asteroid. These pirates tend to burn them in raids or sell off whatever they capture in bulk. They snatch their clothes right off the rack in raids, or off their victims." She did not look away, intrigued to see his reaction.

"Hmm, we will have to be resourceful then." He glanced around the room, as much to avoid the old woman's piercing gaze as for a purpose. "Take these gaudy drapes and see what you can make of them. I don't need more than one top sheet left, either.

"Do what you can with those bedcovers, for a start." He waved her towards the young women and the bed in one expansive sweep of his double-barreled gun-fingered hand. She stood and bade the scantily clad girls to rise from their knees.

Ceres pointed at the greying chestnut haired woman. "Cook?" She nodded and smiled.

"Brunch," he ordered. Both of the old women smiled and nodded, gathered the four barely dressed girls into a group, and herded them safely away from the men.

"Enjoying this far too much!" Serenity thought to him.

"Good!" Ceres said aloud, grinned with satisfaction, and clapped his hands together again. "Whatever works! Now men, what do *you* do around here?"

Chapter 14
Lost Boys

Hunan IV, deep forest
2512/06/13/0937

"WHOOSH-THOKK!" The ironwood blade slashed the empty air, striking a tree trunk. Ceres ducked under the sneak attack between the dense trees of Hunan IV. The kendo bokken vibrated loose from its wielder's hands, fell, but caught, suspended amid strong spikethorn vines woven between the trees.

"Ouwww," whined the redhead boy with the compact body. His hands merely stinging from the vibrations of impact with the solid tree, he cried out from Ceres' foot thrust sharply into his midsection.

"C'mon, weenie," taunted Ceres, reaching and claiming the fallen heavy sword as his own. "In real combat you'd be dead right now. You never cry, and you NEVER drop your weapon! You're getting rusty."

"'Cept if'n it's tah buffalo you whiles I pull another, such lahk THIS!" the boy drawled thickly as he gleefully retorted. Rising, Ceres turned to discover his opponent laying a shorter straight blade across Ceres' neck, above his retracted balaclava. The hood of his fuzzy pullover rippled with the colors of the forest around them. This black Wakizashi sword, not made of wood but nano-sharp diatanium steel, the hardest alloy of diamond and titanium, remained safely sheathed.

"Concession. Good move, Iron," Ceres smiled with respect and admiration at his best friend. "No! Rusty!" Ceres beamed. "Now I have a nickname for *you* too!"

"I reckon that's a fair deal, Cowboy," they both laughed.

"You took that kick pretty well," Ceres complimented his friend. "You really live up to your name. You're the toughest kid I know."

"Naw, you're tough too. And my big brother is way tougher." The two punched fists in an ancient manly gesture of friendship. They did it very hard and solid as if they were punching an enemy, hearing a meaty "smack," yet neither complained of pain.

"You two should be mindful to not injure yourselves with that silliness," The old Asianan voice sang out quietly from overhead. "Though you have been practicing the ancient bone hardening techniques for years, you are yet young men, not grown into your manly bodies."

The boys searched up in the branches and discovered a large example of the feathered monkeys native to the planet perched in a nest in the trees six meters above them. Used to this game by now, the boys addressed it by name.

"What are you, a Sensei bird?" joked Ceres.

"No, a Master Monkey," tried Iron.

"Lame, brother. Your humor is rusty!" Ceres teased his friend. Iron just grinned and shrugged. "I'm not quite as quick and witty as you, my blonde buddy. But I do like being considered your brother."

They had grown as close as two boys coming of age could. Sharing their lonely sheltered lives of the hardships of training on a remote world, separated from their wealthy families in this ancient version of military school, the students clung to each other in fast alliances.

These two boys had spent the last three years as inseparable as conjoined twins. They even took turns going home to family holidays together. They loved each other as most brothers never did. Being boys, though, they still dug at each other as most brothers do.

"I'm sorry. Don't let me down you, Iron," soothed Ceres, "You always come up with the most amazing country wisdom and funny sayings. That is a different form of smarts you have than being fast with a smart-aft joke."

"Thanks, but ya' don't hafftuh' always try tuh make me feel better." The boy's real accent seeped out, revealing his rural planet of origin and its ancient heritage as a colony from the southern USSA, secessionist Texas actually, post Alien Infestation era of Earth 1.0. It was common to hear broad accents in the galaxy due to the facts of the Galactic Homestead Act of the 21st Century, upon which was founded every first gen colony. "My big brother Grizz would'a punched me in the arm for that one."

While the boys wandered down forest trails left by rampaging Kendor deer, part of Ceres' brain roamed through the MeTR training modules of history. He was curious how his tough friend had such a strong Earth accent 500 years past the era of the Modern Exodus.

Soon after most arcs landed upon their planet, the majority of the colonists rushed forth to claim their 10 square kilometer patch of fresh wild new planet. The scale-like pattern of hexagonal land grant plotting made for a rural colony of independent farms, ranches, or mining claimsteads. Sufficient wildland patches between the farmsteads maintained the natural environment and species dependent on them.

It also spread people out to an extreme degree after being crammed so tightly aboard the arcology. A secret part of the StarSys plan, the minimal steerage-sized accommodations necessary aboard the Arcologies were a hidden incentive for moving the masses out of them upon planet fall.

Xardyon assembler systems that had built them in space, now proceeded to cannibalize them from within for resources. They built a network of surrounding family farmsteads and everything the colonists needed to kick-start their new lives.

The Homestead Act had devastated property values Earth wide. With Xardyon assistance to colonize, it was so easy to just find another planet to colonize that people realized the only things of real worth most owned were their own lives, character, and their education. Knowing how to run a successful ranch life and make a living with your own brains and hands was far more valuable than any given patch of dirt out of the unlimited patches of dirt to be had, free for the taking across the galaxy.

Estimates ranged from five million down to one million years of current exponential human birth rates before land and resources became scarce again. And by then the neighboring galaxies of The Local Group should be reachable with whatever new transportation system was in vogue at that time. The claimsteader's independent rural lifestyle of owning one's own means of livelihood lead to a massive trend; most rural colonists adopted an independent, self-reliant, orthodox values mindset.

The central arcology often served as the planet's center of manufacturing, education, and governmental headquarters. Generally owned and operated by entrepreneurs, and staffed predominately by robots rather than human employees, the ancient Earth trend, of urban centers to be hotbeds of dependency upon others for one's livelihood, reversed.

With hourly wages outlawed, commission pay based on productivity became the norm for those few choosing to work for others. The Industrial Age norm of mass employment by factory-modelled companies, of urbanite socialist thinking and feelings, and of entitlement, were upended. The honest pride of being a self-made person took hold as the goal of most adults.

The ancient country of origin accents flourished in the generations of isolation on every new planet. By the time the Galactic trade economy fully took hold and galactic interplanetary travel became commonplace, the isolated colonies were firmly entrenched in their own historical culture, strong local accent included.

Thus, 500 years later, the "Texan" Iron was always making the galactic vagabond Ceres laugh with his quaint sayings in his strong accent. The farm boy was often quoting his big brother, or his father and uncles. Iron seemed to try hard to keep his best friend laughing with new material he said he had gleaned from family gatherings.

Between the forest's tree trunks, the stout Iron shoved taller Ceres hard, both hands square on the pecs. The taller boy fell back hard but nimbly turned the momentum into a roll back onto his feet, crouched at the ready for a fight. His blood boiled up in preparation for counterattacking his friend.

"WHUUMMPPH!" A heavy branch crashed to the leaf-littered floor of the wooded trail between the boys. Iron had wide eyes as he stared at Ceres from two meters away.

"Thanks," Ceres offered as he realized his friend had just saved him from injury. Looking up, eyes wide with belated fear, he saw the clean-cut stump of the branch high on the trunk of a large bole. No Sensei sat smugly on his feathery nest perch. "No joking in the middle of a mission. Got it."

"He's ghosted on us," Iron said in a hushed voice. "Forget this 'assassin and bodyguard' simulation. Let's us both get 'im!"

"Furst to fahnd 'em wins!" Ceres hoarsely replied in imitation of his friend's accent. He bounded up the trees with small leaps back and forth between nearby trunks, just as their master had been teaching them earlier.

By the time he reached the level they had last seen their Sensei, Ceres had transformed his look completely. Setting his infiltrator hologram to depict one of the forest birds, Ceres' slim body took on the appearance of a huge stout bodied owl.

Iron meanwhile followed the animal trails through the forest. The tall and wide ones were usually cut by the four to five meter tall Kendor, giraffe-like herbivores with long antlers. Iron made good time running quietly along their trails, though he had to cut back and forth more often than his friend who skimmed over the underbrush.

While his best friend had searched low, Ceres had gone high, now gliding from tree to tree like the local blue feather-scaled Great Owls. As on Earth, ancient dinosaur scales had adapted into descendants feathers, so here, the scales of the reptiles often had feathery edges. Instead of flapping wings, Ceres held his arms steady, out from his shoulders, which helped preserve the owl illusion.

He glided on his tractor-pressor boots when he wanted to cross a large space. These expensive tools were almost identical to the magnetic Zero Gravity ball boots used inside the metallic game spheres. Rare ryanite rings provided gravity or antigravity thrust or pull, though the power cells drained quickly when overcoming a planet's gravity.

Half-crouched for balance, Ceres surfed across gaps meters above the ground, like the extreme sports stars of Grav-ball, which he enjoyed imitating after watching on the thoughtcast replays. Ceres and Iron organized the school's kids into teams, and they all exercised and played in the local sphere frequently.

Outside Ceres wore these gauntlets and boots almost all the time, extending his practice beyond the limits of the do'jo's few metal buildings. He enjoyed flying through the surrounding primeval forest.

Meanwhile he voice-called the humming sound of the wind sailing between the feathery scales of the owl. There were sound effect settings available in the infiltrator pack, but Ceres did not like the repetition of the canned sounds. Besides, it was yet another unusual and unique ability which most ignored. Ceres enjoyed being the best at something, anything, many things. It fueled his energy to practice longer, harder, better than most tried. It also fueled his ego.

Ceres had made a reputation in the dojo on selecting and mastering such obscure talents the rest often neglected. Ke'inko had often criticized and teased Ceres about learning useless skills irrelevant to his probable future life as a captain of industry. Privately, Ceres enjoyed the payoff coming due now, as he was able to imitate this native wildlife in the most complete way, impossible to anyone else.

"Wow, Ceres. For a second I thought you really were a big ol' wood owl," Iron's youthful boy voice complimented his friend over their private WetNet channel. *"You're getting good at making that sound."*

"You can do it," Ceres answered. *"You just have to practice any skill."*

"What's that whirring sound?" Iron thought.

An elongated tree branch leaped out at Ceres. "Duck!" Iron yelled up at his friend, his vantage from below helping him to see the attack first.

Ceres just folded up his wing/arms, pointing his big toes down to pull down towards the ground with his tractor beam boots. The flattened tree branch was faster, hitting Ceres' left arm and grabbing hold.

"It's a Ryu'u'! Flying snake!" Iron yelled.

Ceres felt the flush of numbness through his arm. His body slapped against the underside of the snake, its ribs flattened, spread wide as it swam through the air. He could see his arm punctured by numerous needle teeth, his blood seeping into the fabric of his sleeve, but he could not feel a thing.

Hunan IV's light gravity helped many creatures adapt through gigantism. By flattening their body and using the same wriggling motions as on the ground, Ryu'u' caught the air and created lift over their body, allowing them to fly horizontally between the trees. The sole predator of the owls Ceres was impersonating, the flying snake' had adapted the coloration of their scales to match the aspen trees' bark.

Iron acted fast to help his best friend. Leaping up the trees, the redhead whipped his katana tip at the snaking body flying overhead. The feathery scales of the snake were strong enough to ward off the laser sharp blade.

Ceres understood he was experiencing the slow time sensation of adrenaline rush, the accelerated thinking effect. He knew adrenaline would only speed the venom coursing through his body. He thought his shoulder should be hurting a lot more than it was, understanding this was due to the flying snake's natural nerve agent, blocking his pain.

Ceres almost casually observed Iron's katana slash across the snake's scales, sliding away with little effect. With his right hand Ceres pulled his laser survival pistol, to shoot up at the underbelly of his attacker, but watched it fall away below. Seeing a branch sweep by he realized his hand should be broken. With a heavy impact to his head, Ceres' world went dark.

Iron almost panicked when the flying snake coiled itself around a tree trunk and started constricting. Ceres' body, lumpy underneath the flattened snake's body, crunched and popped as the snake wrapped tightly around the tree. Iron scrambled up a pair of trees near it. His leap for its head and loud "kiai" shout caught its attention.

Its head snapped forward and spun off, still hissing, to the forest floor.

Iron bounced down to the underbrush, rolled to his feet. "Ceres!" Iron shouted. "Ceres! Hang on buddy! I'll get you outta there!" He ran to the

91

base of the tree, opposite the side where the snake head still gaped its rows of needle teeth, opening its jaws in a futile attempt to strike at him.

Iron still gripped the forcefield sword he used to decapitate the snake. Thumbing the end of the flashlight-shaped hilt, the blade snapped back into being with a pop. The shaped plane of energy was no wider than an atom, the edge thin as an electron. Iron cut carefully into the tree's base; Ceres stuck 5 meters up, smothered under the snake's headless writhing body.

"Hold on, pardner! I'ma comin'!" The tree proved no challenge for the forcefield sword, but Iron took care to cut a wedge out on the right side so the tree would catch on nearby vines. He wanted to lower Ceres more carefully than a deadfall.

With one last mighty hack through the trunk, the tree leaned, finally falling to the forest floor. The upper branches caught on the way down on spikethorn vines, softening the fall. Iron leapt over, easily removing tree limbs to get to his friend, and started cutting up the snake's body. He was immediately joined by his Sensei.

"Good work, Iron," Sensei praised. "We will have him out in a moment."

"Why is it still holding him?" Iron almost cried, "Why don't they die?"

They peeled away the muscular ribbon of snake's body that still constricted, still pressed Ceres to the trunk. "It is already dead," Sensei answered. "This is the rigor mortis, muscle contractions after death. It will soon stop. We must work fast."

Sensei caught Ceres in his arms, laying him on the ground.

"I'll run and get help!" Iron shouted, turning.

Sensei caught Iron's gi and held him back from running off. "No. I have already summoned help in the instructor's group. Stay calm, Iron. Your brother needs our help!" Iron nodded at his master. "We need to help him live. Hold his feet off the ground."

Iron helped Sensei do everything needed. He produced a flare and shot it up in the air, a red firework, which hung overhead. Sensei used a dropper to place medicine inside Ceres' lips for fast absorption. Iron helped lift his friend's rigid body into the popper in the back of the emergency air-car, sending Ceres ahead to the dojo's medibay.

When Ceres awoke, Iron was sleeping atop the bed covers, beside him.

"Hey, Rusty," Ceres whispered, groggily.

"Hey, Cowboy," Iron yawned then grinned. "Okay, bird-brain, promise me: no more bein' snake-bait!"

Chapter 15
Overhauled

A-Valhalla, Main Hanger Strip
2525/7/14/0750

"Thanks for the blood sample!" Ceres shouted in the noisy hanger. The Rokkled airboss turned without a word. Ducking his four-meter high head and shoulders under the aero-wing of the scruffy white ship, he marched away. Ceres noticed the huge engraved "tattoo" covering his back, a carved mural of several triangles. *Maneuvering starships?*

Ceres examined the clear container filled with silver oil, donated to the cause by the huge xenomorph. He thought it looked like goo alright. Pulling a datapin from the back of his head, Ceres dropped it into the oil.

The pin sunk in, submerged under the billions of microscopic nanites. With expanding ripples, the oil turned to a golden shade and the pin rose back to the top as if floating. It seemed to be working.

Ceres picked up his pin, along with a small droplet of the golden goo containing millions of Ceres' newly reprogrammed nanites. He hoped this worked for him instead of against him now. Turning to the bot next to him, he stabbed the pin into the interface socket atop the robot's flatscreen head.

"Okay, Arm Wrestler," he teased the robot for its many arms, "Go find the parts we need. Visit every ship, robot and crew aboard the asteroid. I'll transmit more parts to your list as we identify them. If you have to negotiate, use your 2-D screen, holocam, and link back to me, got it?"

"R-W-33" was stenciled on the sides of what looked like a round trashcan on tracks, with a variety of utility arms that spun into position on its one circular shoulder. Its screen displayed an animated happy face to interact with people.

The robot saluted as Ceres' datapin had programmed it to, then rolled over to the nearby cargobot. This six-wheeled flatbed robot had two loader arms for lifting pallets of cargo aboard then securing it as it moved. Arm Wrestler interfaced with it via a slender data arm extended from its head, transferring a handful of nanites along with Ceres' data packets of worm programming.

The pair of bots rolled off on their mission to gather parts for the overhaul of Ceres' new ship. Out from the access corridor walked the slave medic Ceres remembered.

"No mop this time?" he smiled, hoping he could trust her, hedging his bets each way. After Ka'ra he was hypervigilant.

"Happy Birthday!" she smiled. "Who wants presents?"

Ceres raised his hand and grinned. "Pardon me, I didn't get your name, yet."

"I'm Petalia Duet," she did not offer her hand. Probably mindful of her status as a slave talking to a master? "They call me 'Two' around here. I brought you two doses of vaccine for Cannahol and two of ACH inhibiter," in case you smell any parathion perfume again."

"Oh? Pity. It was a lovely fragrance," he joked along with her mild teasing. "Good thinking, Two." She seemed awfully familiar for a slave. This made him suspicious of her as another possible double-agent.

"Not me, your concubine asked for them."

"Who?" his mouth dropped open. "Oh, her. I'm not used to all this yet. Thank you. I am surprised they had this particular medicine here. It seems like the last thing they would want around." He hoped that was a good enough save if any pirates were listening.

"A doctor's recipe was in the database. I had the medical crafter spit some out. Enough to vaccinate you and one close friend," she raised her eyebrows as if hinting it should be her. "Not enough base ingredients here to craft any more than that. You'll have to choose wisely." Her smile, too, suggested herself as a candidate.

"I will do that. Thank you, Two," he smiled amiably. "I'll call on you when I need you. Thank you." He nodded, turning up the ramp to enter his ship. He hoped she would get the hint.

He did not want to give any details away, despite Serenity's apparent endorsement by speaking about escape in front of her in the medibay. *Even if she is on our side, let's keep secrets secret.*

"Hey, boss!" sang out in the hanger. "Room for one more?" Turning around, Ceres saw Two walking away, shoulders slightly slumped. Her head turned slightly as she smiled at a passing pirate, who walked towards Ceres' ship. The man's long black hair and beard parted in a huge grin. Hand raised to flag down Ceres, his colorful tattoo swirled in a pattern that seemed familiar.

"I am Ceres. You are?" He pressed his hand to his heart then swung his arm out into the introductory gesture to trade grips of greetings.

"Kangee, young prince," he half bowed from the waist. "I am part of Jarl Jaeger's crew."

That word shot Ceres eyebrows up. Maybe they took this "Viking" thing farther than he thought. Not just hijacking part of the myth? "Mechanic or warrior?"

"Neither," Kangee answered, causing Ceres' eyebrow to raise in silent question. "I'm not a pirate, actually I was kidnapped for ransom but they decided I am too valuable to set free.

"Now I'm a—?" he considered for a moment, "trustee, let's say? They give me a lot more liberty than their average slaves.

"I am an artist. I paint the ships. I got bored one day stuck in my cell and started scratching designs on the walls. The captain liked it. Word spread. Eventually I have redone the entire fleet."

"Ah, so you came up with the idea of 'painting' the Raven fighters to actually look like ravens?" Ceres asked.

"That was me, yes," Kangee smiled proudly. "I started out working in my people's native arts—I am from the ancient Raven tribe bloodline—then I studied the great masters of all cultures. This is squigglism, for example," he thrust forth his arms, showing his sworled tattoos.

"You inked yourself?" Ceres asked, impressed. "That must take some special talent, to create art which hurts you as you perform?"

"Yes," Kangee grinned. "Settle into a nice middle place with the peyote, you know? Mello, pain free, and visionary, but still able to create."

"I wouldn't know," Ceres answered. "I have never done illegal chems."

"Never?" Kangee exclaimed. "Peyote is not—"

"I said 'never' and I mean what I say," Ceres interjected. "I don't like to lose control." He shrugged. "My mother told me stories about my father losing control. I don't want to be like that." *I don't want to think about that right now either. I'm here to find mom, not share my biography. Maybe later. This guy is intriguing, at least.*

"So," Ceres changed the subject with a clap of his hands, "what would you like to do for me, my fine artist Kangee, for my new lady here? Would you like to create something unique on her curvy canvas?" He smiled.

95

"That might be fun," Kangee said. "What's her name, this fine lady? How will you make use of her?"

"I'm thinking of a classic name," he stood beside Kangee, waving his arms as if painting an epic story in his mind. "Something ancient. Something heroic. Something special."

Kangee licked his lips in anticipation, eyes alight with curiosity.

"Pegasus," Ceres said.

"Oh, yeah!" Kangee agreed. "That sounds perfect. The beautiful wild horse that flies free! A combination of sleek fast ride, able to carry a load, too. Evokes a timeless legend, which we're still scouring the stars, hoping to find it exists. That's perfect for this kind of spaceship."

"That's what I was thinking, exactly."

"I can adapt my usual winged theme to that really well, too! No raven's black or dragon's bat wings here, more beautiful."

"That's what I was thinking," Ceres repeated with a grin. "Well, that's what your new patron has in mind, Kangee. I'll leave you to do what you do. You're the creative artist."

"Oh, sir?" Kangee asked. "One more question: what's my budget?"

"Unlimited," Ceres answered with an open palms gesture. Kangee's eyes bugged out and he blinked. "Whatever you need, just ask. We'll find a way to get it out here."

"I'll start with some sketches." Head down, Kangee started to wander away, lost in his excitement, his imagination. Turning back, he took in the shape of the ship, her curves.

"I'm thinking a white background. Maybe ivory...." Stroking his chin, his beard, he turned away, mumbling to himself as he walked.

Ceres grinned, then ran up the ramp into his ship, anxious to see who else had volunteered for his repair crew.

"Okay, boys and girls," Ceres looked about at the small group of pirate volunteers, "and other." These few had answered his call to help overhaul the sleek spaceship Ceres had won from Trok in the duel. Gathered in the ship's aft cargo bay, Ceres looked over his work gang. *This is it?*

The four male slaves he had received in his quarters, plus two more men—large muscular ones at that—and two women, completed the Solman contingent. Ceres remembered from his tour through the hanger, the Tenublian owned the two huge men.

The xeno stayed to help as well, though it did not attend the meeting physically. Projected beneath a rotor-drone, a hologram floated near the front of the bay, indicating the alien's virtual presence while it performed other chores bodily. Known to possess multiple brain lobes, each controlling one of their many limbs, Jelly-squids could multi-task in ways other races could not comprehend.

"I thought there would be more," Ceres said, disappointed.

The hologram spoke up, translated into an intellectual but flowery human-like voice. "There were exactly 1,379 volunteers responding to your request transmitted into the crew group—fully half of the eligible pirate crew. I told them we had the core of a starting work gang and would call upon them as needed."

"I see." Ceres said, suddenly grinning with pride. Still got it! "Well, in the future let me make those decisions. I am the captain, after all," he raised his hand and pointed a finger.

"Yes, Captain," the holo said. "As you wish. I am now below, diagnosing your computing systems as we speak."

"Thank you, I—" Ceres was cut off, which annoyed him.

"The ship's weapons control computer is a useless civilian defense model," the xeno cut in. "It must be replaced, or you will have no offensive capability.

"If you need strong men, my Cassius and Yukozune are at your disposal. If they are not completely satisfactory, just inform me with a thought and I will discipline them immediately." It cut off transmitting, leaving the holo in a listening mode, indicated by a change from green to yellow tint over the entire hologram.

Six men and two women all stared back at Ceres. His finger still pointing, he nimbly shifted tacks.

"Gotta pick your battles," he muttered while opening his arms to shrug. "Squid help is better than no help at all." Everyone but Yukozune laughed. "Anyone besides me have any starship engineering training or experience?" Ceres asked, hand raised.

One of his men raised his hand. He was short but solidly built, with weathered brown hands and dark hair just starting to show streaks of white at the temples.

"Name?" Ceres asked.

"Arturo, sir," he answered.

"Good, Arturo," Ceres said. "Go on. Speak freely."

"Thank you, Señor," Arturo continued. "I was Señor Trok's crew chief for maintenance. I grew up around my family's repair shop. By the time I was old enough, I had earned and saved enough to put myself though a top tech school." Ceres was impressed. He looked forward to learning from this hands on mechanic.

"These señoritas are the 'go-fers,' on loan from the base supply chief," Arturo explained, "thanks to your holographic squid friend there. I have worked with them before. Good liaisons—good parts scrounges. They know their ships and components."

The two women waved and smiled, their small bodies engulfed by oversized blue cargoalls designed for men. *Maybe they know where the Hanger Queens are that they can cannibalize?* Ceres thought. *Maybe they are the hanger queens.* No matter, they needed a good parts scrounge or two.

"These men were my helpers here in Valhalla," Arturo pointed to the other three men Ceres had acquired in the duel.

"Are they any good or can we find better among the 1300 volunteers?" Ceres asked bluntly. The three stiffened in response.

"Hmmm," Arturo caressed his black and grey chin beard. "I think, under those terms, their work will earn them their air, Señor." He chuckled, then playfully punched the shoulder of the nearest man, who was paling visibly.

Ceres thought it would be good for morale to have another joker among them. Clearly these men did not want to be put off the work crew into unknown assignments by the pirates. He had the chilling feeling these Vikings did not suffer useless or unwanted mouths aboard the asteroid.

"Hmm, okay," Ceres said, then broke into a grin and laughed. "I appreciate loyalty. I won't trade you out, men. Relax." They returned his grin meekly. Clearly unsure of his humor, they stayed tense. *Tactical error?* Ceres wondered. *Won't hurt the long game. Probably make them work harder to prove themselves, which was the intended point.*

"You're a pretty handy guy, Arturo. We haven't even started yet, and you've organized the crew?"

"We worked together under the last Capitan, Jefe." He pronounced the titles he assigned to Ceres with an authentic Spanish accent.

Must be smart to be fluent in both languages? Ceres thought. *So he floats in and out of both in that beautiful 'Spanglish' way. Makes for a rich, colorful accent. Always liked it.*

"Arturo, if you want to keep that job as crew chief," Ceres smiled at him, "why don't you start with briefing us on the systems and features of this fine ship."

"Si, Señor," Arturo nodded, strongly pursing his lips. "This ship is a fine, elegant lady, no?" He did not wait for their favorable answers.

"She is Halberd Class, which gives her the elegant curves of an ancient weapon. But, she is not a warrior, my señorita, she is too sexy!" It was obvious to all that Arturo was fond of this ship.

"Nearly 100 meters, this is a luxury starliner, a refined lady of high quality and elegance. She has the added cargo space to carry a wealthy family on an extended vacation tour, or a wealthy executive and their finest cargo as they do business across the galaxy. This is an F/L version, freighter as well as liner, you see?

"Her aft staterooms were removed in favor of the cargo holds. The spaceframe stretches wider as well, so those forward rooms are much bigger, which is more luxurious, yes? Just wait until you see all the stars from the forward lounge, my amigos. It is so wide thanks to the bigger ship design.

"The engines are spaced all around the hull on extended pods. They flex for vectoring the thrust up, down, left or right as you need it, Señor." Arturo smiled at Ceres, assuming that an Academy pilot would fly his own ship.

Ceres had downstreamed every design schematic for the Halberd Class and most others in his Academy days, but chose to let Arturo go on with his colorful descriptions for some time. *Sounds like, inside a week since Trok stole this ship, Arturo already loves it. I can't blame him. There is some design genius hidden under the skin of this one.*

Ceres summed up Arturo's flowery praise with a quote, "A great designer named Porsche once said, 'Design is not simply art, it is elegance of function.' I think that applies to how we feel about this beauty, eh boys and girls?" He remembered hearing the quote in starship engineering classes while in the Academy. Handy education.

"Thank you, Arturo for sharing your extensive knowledge with us. Now, let's get on to the repairs and improvements, shall we?" He clapped his hands together to punctuate the transition, a gesture he learned from his favorite college coach.

"Okay, the basic game plan here is to update all the systems inside the ship," Ceres began. "The keel for this beauty was laid before I was born. There have been many improvements on the starship market since then. The

Galactic's peaceful interregnum is over. With war development finally returning to scourge all Solmen, technology has come out of the colonial dark ages and started improving exponentially again.

"We're gonna drop in a whole new power core, shield magnetic field coils, and weapon capacitors." He stood among the group, pointing animatedly as he spoke about different aspects of the project.

"We will lay in new networked power conduits to handle the amped up load distribution, and major components all around to use it up. The size four hull has grade two engines, standard, but I want to upgrade the central drive package to grade three."

"We only have one ship with grade three drives, Jefe," Arturo chimed in. "The flagship *Marauder* your Papi uses to open the wormholes for his fleet of little ships."

"Good to know, my friend." Ceres smiled. "I'll have to trade him these little peppers for his big ones. No problem, right?"

The crew grinned back at him. No problem. Right.

"Okay!" Ceres continued. "While I look for bigger drives, we'll overhaul the plasma drives we *do* have one by one. Major tune up. Though I bet the owners of such a fine luxury yacht paid for good maintenance, I doubt they ever cranked the drives up to full military power. If we need to run with this fleet, we will need to make sure we don't melt down.

"Then let's talk weapons: I'm going to remove the pop-top turret and put in a 'Twin-Hammer' Ion Cannon. Bottom turret gets a Phalanx—a ten barreled laser cannon. With so much power to feed, we'll need some weapon-dedicated power-plants, right?" Blank stares. They're not used to thinking big over a long-range plan with an unlimited budget, Ceres thought. Lately they have had to work with all stolen goods, and every ship aboard station fights over the same, looted components. Got it.

The strong man with dark skin and short hair asked, tentatively, "Why an Ion, and why up top? Seems a step down in firepower from old-fashioned chem-laser options. New fashioned plasma-shot launchers?"

"Good question!" Ceres praised. "Are you Cassius?"

Cassius paused, and then gave a thumb up.

"Great," Ceres continued. "I kind of figured our 'sumo' looking friend here was Yuko?" Ceres smiled but the huge man of Asianan descent just glared back at him.

Humor had previously worked well for Ceres among a military crew, and with those who were dazzled by his fame. These slaves probably needed a little more effort to loosen up. They were not yet in the mood to feel like brotherly comrades in arms. Especially with a "master," as they saw him.

He would have to continue working on them, banking on his sports celebrity which always underscored every conversation he had. Ceres grew up with a self-actualized philosophy of assuming 'everybody loves me,' so he usually started out acting as if everyone was a friend. It rarely failed to prove true in the end.

Of course there was another side to that coin. In conflict situations his martial training made him suspicious and hypervigilant, constantly analyzing how to defeat everyone around him on a moment's notice. It was hard to balance these two sides on the knife's edge of reality in his everyday life. There were so few he could truly trust.

His family's fame painted a bullseye on him. That's why he enjoyed being around starships and beings who loved them as he did. He was able to relax his guard and enjoy being an expert in the field and funny among his peers. Now to bring this eclectic crew along into his inner circle of fellow starship loving buddies. Now to make them *his* crew.

"Okay," Ceres went on. "Finally, Cassius here is a local who's neurons aren't all burnt out yet on babes, booze, and blahs, huh?" He used another slang for downers such as the ubiquitous cannahol.

Everyone chuckled. Cassius' stone faced partner Yukozune' looked like he was almost going to smile.

"To answer your question, while dogfighting down in a gravity well," Ceres explained, "frying the enemy's power is often enough for the kill. And for piracy, depowering the target lets us take them and their goods, and their ship too if we want. Got it?"

Nods of enthusiastic agreement bobbled heads all around. He imagined these slaves didn't get off the rock much during combat operations. Piracy tactics were not in their job descriptions. His either if he could avoid it.

"And forward I want to put in a neutral PBC." Arturo's eyebrows lifted while the crew of volunteer mechanics and engineer's eyes grew large as saucers. No one had seen a space-to-ground rated Particle Beam Cannon yet in this sector of the rim. That was Galactic technology reserved for Capitol type starships, so of course these pirates knew all about it.

"How," Arturo asked for the group, "do you hope to get 200-plus meters of accelerator into a spaceframe under 100 meters? Giant Cubano?" He pantomimed drawing a long cigar out of his non-existent breast pocket and lighting it up with an invisible Zippo. The other crew members chuckled amongst themselves.

"Si, my amigos. You go ahead and laugh at Arturo," Arturo said, miming blowing a smoke ring and waving his invisible cigar in a practiced hand. "I have found a way to imagine a normal life, to keep me loco."

The crew all laughed aloud. Cassius said in his deep basso voice, "You mean, to keep you *sane*, right?"

"This is what I have said." Arturo's eyes were animated, his smile amused.

Ceres thought, *He's playing at being crazy. Smart. Probably throws off the masters, too.*

"Coil your Cubano Grande around a central open cylinder," Ceres said nonchalantly, finally answering Arturo's question about how to install a destroyer-rated gun aboard a small freighter. "Then it is a mass driver too. One-two punch."

"Oh no, Señor," Arturo challenged, waving his hands back and forth. "This elegant little señorita, she is not made for orbital bombardment, no."

"Yep," Ceres said. "If it comes to that. We can destroy ground targets in several game-changing ways. But it's even better in space, of course. Less diffusion of the beam."

"Let's see, what else?" Ceres said. "Up-powered gyrotons to inject ions into the stronger magnetic field." One of the mechanics had a blank look on their face. "Stronger shields," Ceres explained briefly, seeing a bright look of understanding come over the same face.

"Added point defense lasers," Ceres resumed. "I'll upgrade the Whipple shield with carbon graphene foam and aerogel in the splash-space. Mass will increase but with bigger drives and an exotic powerplant we won't notice.

"I'm going to write tight command and control apps for the datacore. I want this thing to process a jump so fast it calculates the harmonics before I think of it." He referred to operating the ryanite rings for opening wormholes, which such high-end ships had folded inboard. The men's mouths all dropped again. Ceres figured most of them did not know a freightliner rated that expensive tech.

"The elegant freedom of the Halberd Class," Ceres explained. "The twin rings of ryanite are folded in flat in the nose area, retracted for landing and docking operations." He shrugged. "I doubt a thug like Trok knew what he had ahold of here."

"You are not wrong, Jefe," Arturo confirmed with strenuous nods. "The thug did not know this." A dangerous comment with another slave master listening in, but Arturo knew he was Ceres', and he tested his new owner gently in this way. Ceres ignored it with a slight grin of knowing passing between them.

"He brought us aboard when he took this ship, it was trying to dock with the marina above Shangri-la. He found your other señorita aboard then. He sent the other ships ahead with the flagship and caught up later, just before *Marauder's* wormhole closed."

"Then I am glad I took all his toys away before he had time to break them," Ceres said. "Probably would have given this ship a bad reputation around the Periphery. Now I can shape her into a mold of my making."

"Speaking of which," he returned to his fixit wish list, "I will remove one escape pod and put in a workpod. I'd like to add a third pod port to get it back, though.

"The other ePod I will trade out for a launch that slides all the way into the core. Might rearrange the traffic flow but it will be worth it. I have to get my launch back from that arc city, by the way."

"Why a workpod instead of an escape pod, Captain?" the hologram chimed in. "Not as many survivors can fit into a work pod."

"Our Capitan is an engineer, Master Marina," Arturo guessed, naming the jelly-squid master of Cassius and Yuko. "He believes in having yet another tool to get outside and maybe fix the problem that has us considering to abandon ship."

"Right, amigo," Ceres agreed. "A launch can handle the whole crew plus passengers. A pod gives us many ways to self-repair.

"Oh, critical list: I need a hammock, too," Ceres added, surprising Trok's crew. The two larger men merely nodded. "I grew up aboard a ship. I need the background white noise of an operational starship to sleep well. Always have." He shrugged and returned Yuko and Cassius's grins.

Hmm, gotta come up with some kind of swag for them too. His gaze wandered across all the eager faces before him. Remembering prior engine room crews when he was recently part of the merchant fleet, he thought, what was missing to make us a team? "We need a crew uniform as well," Ceres said, "to let the others know you are working for me now." All of their heads bobbed up and down.

"I'm thinking royal blue cargoalls," his MeTR links controlling the clothing's settings interface, he shifted the color of his uniform top and cargo pants from the Navy's dark blue. Infusing a trace of red, lowering the intensity of indigo, it turned royal blue.

Seeing looks of approval he told the two women, "We can make one for everyone, and they can be sized right for you this time." They smiled at each other, tugging on the baggy cargoalls they wore.

"I'll have Kangee come up with a ship's logo. Maybe a patch?" They exchanged glances and small furtive smiles. Seems they sense a chance for a better life aboard *Wanderlust?* Ceres determined to make that hope come to pass for his crew.

"Now," Ceres resumed, "I looked through the supply logs and this place seems not to have some of the top gear I just listed, that I want to put aboard in those slots.

"I sent my bots out already, and you ladies are free to work your magic scrounging up more." The pair of women nodded, failing to repress their smiles. Yukozune took some initiative to step over to the crafter machines to the fore of the cargo bay, scanning for uniforms among the thousands of pre-loaded clothing designs.

When the entire crew froze in place and stared at him, Yuko eventually noticed. "What?" he challenged loudly. "Shut up!" Dismissing their curiosity, he continued digging through the files.

"Good initiative," Ceres praised. "So, for the rest, we'll have to go shopping. Who has the Carte Blanche?" Ceres patted down his pockets conspicuously. "I left mine in my other coveralls." The work crew laughed.

He thought his plan to get them on his side with a mutual love of the starship was starting to pay off. As was his intentional use of humor, finally getting to them.

"That would be your father," the holo flared to life with the Tenublian's comment, resulting in more rolling laughter. Yuko started heaving.

"Yeah, I'm sure he'll let me rack up a bill supeing up my hotrod," Yuko listed sideways holding his ribs as he breathlessly gasped for air. Ceres grinned and slapped him on the shoulder.

"Okay then. Who's good with electronics?" Only Arturo raised his hand.

"Plasma drives? Good overhaul tuner?" Arturo again.

"Anyone good at worming optical conduit through a spaceframe?" Arturo kept his hand raised.

"Well, my amigo," Ceres smiled at him. "It looks like you have job security as my crew chief. You take your three guys, and I'll take the other two and see what we can do with them." The compact mechanic nodded, rubbing his hands together.

"Oh," Ceres caught himself. "One more minor system: weapons?" Now Cassius raised both of his big hands, while even Arturo looked down at the deck.

"Until we find a combat grade fire control computer," Ceres added, "you can at least decarbonize the laser ports and polish the lenses. Oh, and," he shot gunfingers at the apparent weapon's specialist, "I need you to craft me a capacitor rod in the crafter-station. Can do?"

"Sure thing, Chief," The dark man grinned, wringing his hands. "Give me something to do besides carry the heavy stuff all the time."

"I'm not going to touch that one," Ceres deferred.

Seeming to read double-talk into their jokes that the others were oblivious to, Yuko fell over the crafter machine from laughing, his ample belly heaving, gasping so hard he couldn't breathe.

Chapter 16
Graduation Day

Hunan IV, forest
2514/10/21/1150

"Ceres, Iron: Stay at our encampment!" the venerable voice of their master called out in the boys' heads, inside the private neural comm channel reserved for this training quest. *"We have an unscheduled vessel incoming from orbit. I will return and greet them. Activate your stealth screens."*

In Ceres' mind's eye his Sensei's tone of voice evoked his oft raised finger as he pointedly said *"You two stay safely away, for now."*

Iron obeyed quickly. *"Yes, Sensei,"* he thought into the training channel.

"What's going on?" the impetuous Ceres asked aloud instead. He was so intrigued about the unknown visitor that he forgot his place for a moment. Was it his family coming for a surprise visit?

Ceres also took the opportunity to tap his Sensei on the shoulder with his bokken, showing that he had found the master's hiding spot atop a broken rock outcropping. The master turned, looked sternly directly into Ceres' holographic feathered monkey face and spoke. "Do. Not. Follow. Me!"

"Yes, Sensei," the blonde boy almost pouted as he looked downward. He struggled to comply with discipline still, wanting to do everything, see everything, and learn everything at once in his hunger for practical knowledge.

He felt stifled here, stuck on one small planet when his mother was still lost in the galaxy. He hoped his Uncle Emanuel was coming now, with news of his mother so they could go find her.

Using his grav-boots Ceres spiraled around the rocky knob, settling towards to the forest floor. On the way down he transformed his look back to appear as a normal human boy. He discovered his redhead friend at the foot of the chimney of rocks. "How did you find him up here?" Ceres asked.

"I didn't." Iron answered. "I followed silently below you, knowing you would eventually flush him down to me."

They both turned their heads back up to the nest their master had occupied, finding it now empty. They smiled at each other, in admiration that their old master had vanished in the short few seconds while they spoke.

Then they heard it, a massive "BOOOMMM" shook the rocks, leaves, branches, and their fit young bodies. The pressure wave crashing down confirmed it was the sound of supersonic entry of a spacecraft into the atmosphere. The high aerial boom echoed from nearby hills and ridges and even from the distant mountain range near the planet's horizon. The stone chimney didn't topple but the two boys backed away quickly just in case.

The artificial thunder drum-rolled across the region, accompanied by a cacophony of creature sounds, chaotic forest music erupted in response to the shockingly loud concussion. Scared pack primates hooted. Both boys, concerned for Peanut, glanced, frowning, at each other.

Lizard crows cawed angrily away, soft wing feathers whooshing as the rich, previously hidden wildlife scattered in panic. Coveys of furred quail called squirrailsburst from the underbrush around the boys and tore madly down the bloody new forest trails cleared by panicked deer-like kendor.

The stately giraffe-tall antlered herbivores thundered out of their quiet bedding piles beneath the boles and smashed headlong through the dense underbrush. In their frenzied rush they ignored the spikethorn vines woven throughout the woods, which sliced their striped hides open to gush their thin orange blood.

A very strong guttering roar of plasma drives provided background noise for the animal chorus. Clutching their smarting ears, Ceres and Iron thought to each other. *"Must have been nearby from the strength of that boom!"* Ceres sent to his friend.

"Powerful strong," confirmed Iron.

"Plasma drives are banned in atmosphere," Ceres thought back. He'd been a spacer from birth until he came to this remote planet and its secret military school. *"Galactic wide."*

"These guys are up to no good." Ceres made a logical guess as to their motives from their actions. *"Though their tactics are stupid. They should have entered the atmo over the horizon and cruised in between the ridges until the last moment."*

Ceres added, *"If it were an emergency visit by one of our parents they would have commed ahead. Nope, intimidation. Bad Guys."*

"Are you thinkin' up what I'm thin-ken' yer thinkin' up?" replied Iron inside Ceres' head.

Ceres laughed aloud and then shouted, "Oh come on! You're trying too hard now, too!"

"Yeeahhp. Made ya laugh. Means I'm a-winnin.' So, my friend, you goin' to ignore the Old's instructions by follerin' him?"

"Oh no, of course not. I have no idea which way he went. I will venture a guess—that he's going directly back to the Dojo. I am going to go around by a completely different route and just observe what's happening on the dojo grounds."

As he spoke these words, Ceres launched them into action, pushing off from the ground and "air skating." That is what the kids had finally called it when Ceres used his repulsor boots to half-run/half-float across the ground, like an ice skater but a meter or more above the ice.

"I am specifically *not* going to follow Sensei as I do that," he called back over his shoulder. He switched back to sending over their mindlink. *"Now are you going to follow me or take up solo wilderness camping in the middle of these alien woods?"* Spinning, Ceres saw Iron bounding as hard as he could over the forest floor to keep up.

"I might could," said Iron, which received more hearty laughs from his blonde friend. "Or I could say I'm going to help make sure you absolutely do not follow our Sensei. I'm chaperoning you."

"Fine then," Ceres shot back. "Just keep quiet, stay behind me, and cover my aft. I've pulled up an indirect route on the other side of this ridge. It will give us cover all the way home and an overview of the field."

"You remember that spot under the big tree branches where you caught me kissing Salei and Jessifer?" Ceres shot a glance at his friend over his cocky grin and waited for him to catch up again.

"At the same time!" snorted Iron aloud. "Who could forget that scene?" Iron rolled his eyes and blushed, but smiled. He ran up and as he passed, jumped high to slug his blonde buddy in the shoulder.

"At this pace you're gonna run out of new girls to play 'Cowboys and Angels' with before you can vote." Iron's voice changed to a mock "southern bell" voice from the Old Time 2D's, most often viewed in homeschool history courses. "Oh my, Mr. Tauri. Perish the thought. You'll have to start over!" He batted his eyelashes, displaying mock chagrin.

Ceres pushed hard like a skate sprinter, pumping his thighs and rocketing up in speed. He slugged his redheaded friend back in his shoulder. *"Oh my. Perish the thought."* Ceres teased in the same voice.

The nostalgia of the galaxy turning towards home, and with the recent Clone Wars in mind, the ancient American Civil War was popular subject matter across the WetNet once again. Equating Solman clones with ancient Earth's human slaves was the very basis for the wars. With the threat of EMP bombardment, electro-magnetic pulse, the Galactic had forced outlying systems to choose between dropping the practice of cloning or granting full equal rights to their created progeny.

Ceres grinned cockily, pleased with himself as much as basking in the fan-glory of his best friend. *"I keep telling you, Iron, buddy, I could introduce you to a couple of nice girls."*

"No, thank you, my friend. I'm saving myself for marriage. My mother would die of heartbreak. And then my big brother Grizz would pound me to death. You should wait too."

"Shush your mind, Pahdnuhr," Ceres tried to imitate his best friend's most outrageous false drawl. He coasted, lowered close to the floor of the woods, and skidded silently to a halt behind a huge red fir tree. *"Them cattle's done left the barn. We-yer he-yer, now. Come crawl snake lahk up under this here bark tree real quiet lahk and we'll see whut we kin see."*

"Oh brother," Iron transmitted. *"That accent needs work. Not thick enough. They'd kick you out of the Southern Stars."* Iron rolled his whole head, not just his eyes.

He put his hands on his knees and breathed deeply. Running through the wooded trails was second nature for these two competitive boys. They both caught their breath as quickly as would more traditionally trained athletes.

This specimen of huge evergreen tree, here called a Red Spruce, looked like a fantastic candidate for "Christmas Tree of the Century." Ceres thought that most of the forest evergreens here, well, everreds, were Spruce, but this one stood out.

The children delighted in decorating it every Sol-Earth winter as it was a perfect specimen, placed right at the end of the long red clover field where they did their outdoor training, field games and sports. The long feathery needles made for a soft overhang gently brushing the boys' backs as they slithered quietly underneath on a deep bed of fallen needles.

The lander spacecraft circled and swerved widely back and forth overhead to shed speed, its star-hot plasma space drives blasting streams of air into frothy contrails. The pilot must have cared enough about their objective not to light the forest afire, as those drives winked off while Ceres and Iron observed from their vantage point at the end of the field.

Massive grav-pulsor pads shimmered forth their lift power, the air displaced looking like heat radiating down as they pushed off from an equivalent amount of planetary mass below them. As it circled the perimeter of the main campus at tree-top height, an armored drop tube deposited dozens of troops clad in heavy black armor.

Ceres spoke into Sensei's voice-comm channel, "Look at all the different types of armors and weapons. These are mercenaries, surrounding the dojo. They're here to kidnap the kids."

"Scenario 2, formation 1!" Sensei's deeper Asianan voice burst into their heads. Everyone involved with the dojo instantly knew there was a probable kidnap-for-ransom scenario, with soldiers of some kind surrounding the building. The school's population also knew to arm and armor themselves for an orderly defensive withdrawal until they all popped through the escape telepods inside.

"Ceres, stay with Iron safely away from the compound," Sensei thought this into the general channel so everyone heard it, not just Ceres. *"Seniors, Barricade One."* The elders rushed forth to stand their ground before the main entry, where the ship was most likely to settle.

"Yeah, they're probably after you, Sport," whispered Iron, beside Ceres under the tree. "You keep out of sight like Sensei said."

"The galaxy does not revolve around me and my family, Rusty," Ceres used his newest nickname for Iron. "I'll stay away, yet help them by using this," he pulled a long flexi-band from his back pouch.

"Don't we need a third guy?" asked Iron.

"We'll circle around behind them; find a forked tree to trim for arms."

"Got it. Off to our right then." Iron shimmied back out from under the limbs. The best friends skulked along behind bushes and trees, safely out of visual line-of-sight.

Their suits' stealth mode dampened bio signatures and any electromagnetic output of their gear. Matching the forest around them, the chameleon effect of the soft fabric helped blend them into the background. The boys' passing looked like a light breeze tussled the bushes' leaves.

In front of the dojo, the large open field seemed the most obvious landing sight, and the invaders complied with conventional thinking. Settling onto her landing legs, the armed landing craft's outgassing's shrouded the ramp. Ten black armored suits pounded metal feet down to the ground from the mercenaries' assault gunboat. The largest of them solo-carried a heavy weapon normally served by a crew of soldiers.

The boys found a suitable tree behind and to the left of the merc's landing party. Iron prepared to activate his forcefield sword. *"Wait for some background noise, Rusty,"* Ceres warned him against ruining their stealth.

"Got it, thanks," Iron complied with his friend's tactical advice. Ceres readied the flexiband and laid some huge marbles at his feet.

Once the merc's heavily armored power suit units set up a defensive perimeter, a decidedly female form clad in a tight black gi sashayed confidently down the ramp. Her face remained shrouded behind a mask, her long black hair was woven into an intricate braid, adding to the giveaway.

Ceres immediately knew who that was. *"Trash doesn't always stay thrown out, huh?"* No one else broke comms discipline to laugh or respond.

Facing the mercenaries, arrayed around the small curved bridge separating the field from the building compound proper, over ten lightly armored or unarmored adults took up staggered ranks of defense. Most of them wore jujutsu gi's. Some few wore tight-fitting bodysuits and head wraps masking all but their eyes.

Heading the lines stood an elderly man of Asianan descent, clad in a traditional looking ancient Samurai armor, complete with a red flag flapping overhead. Modern armor suits extended automatically, allowing rapid entry. The nano-carbon materials were as strong as ancient light-tank armor yet weighed as little as paper.

"Hold fire, hold positions," Sensei commanded his full dojo. *"We will hear their intentions and act accordingly."*

"I came for the Tarsis boy!" the young woman shouted over the meters separating them. "Give him over and none of your precious young students need die!"

"I will parlay with you," Sensei called back. "Come forward alone."

"Of course we will not give any of you over to them. Do not worry, students," Sensei reassured his pupils, even as he and two of his best instructors marched carefully forward a few meters. *"Begin evacuating the youngest while we bid for time in negotiations."*

Sensei stopped and waited for the mercenaries' leader to arrive. "Remove your masks!" he ordered the small entourage of mercs who accompanied her. "I will know those with whom I negotiate."

"Of course, Old One," the girl laughed, tossing her hair playfully. She tore off her mask.

"Ke'inko Sakiri!" Ceres chattered into the comm channel.

"The same, young one," Sensei answered. *"Clear channel."*

"Ke'inko," Sensei Aramada addressed his dishonored pupil. "Have you no shame, no honor, returning here in force to kidnap an innocent child?"

"It is to regain my honor that brings me here again, Old One," she snarled. "If defeat is dishonor, I will claim honor with my victory today."

"Single combat then?" Sensei offered. "Same as on your last day here. If you defeat me, you get what you came for."

"Hey! No fair, you said—" Ceres whined.

"Silence!" Sensei's mind virtually shouted into the comms. *"Do not speak again! Iron, escort your friend through the forest,"* the master ordered. *"At least ten kilometers directly away from the dojo. Go now!"*

"Sorry, pal," Iron turned, "let's go," but Ceres was already missing.

"No, Old One," Ke'inko answered her former Sensei. "By 'victory' I mean, you will give me Ceres now or we will level this school and kill you all. Either way, I will have my honor back."

"Lost him, Sensei," Iron started. *"I'm sorr...."*

"Apologize later. Act now!" Sensei scolded. *"He will move toward the command group and attack from the rear. Back him up, Iron. Be safe!"*

"I cannot give you what you want, young one," Sensei waggled his finger as he disappointed Ke'inko. "He is safely away with his family, Ceres."

"It is unlike you to lie, Old One," she said. "You disappoint me. I am sure your bloody death will ease my dismay."

The cocky merc's strode forward, unimpressed with what they considered light defenses before their heavy armored suits. The Samurai at the head of the defenders drew his katana, flicking it from one ready stance to another.

A hundred arrows flew out from the grounds of the dojo', launched by hidden archers blending into and behind the stylized decorations from every world of the Asiana Sector, going back to old Earth 1.0. While the children popped away, the rest of the dojo's students and instructors had crept into their practiced positions.

The mercs stopped their forward march, hesitating while the first wave of steel-tipped arrows glanced uselessly off their thick tritanium body armor. None penetrated, so the mercs resumed their progress toward the entry bridge, undaunted and emboldened.

Sensei raised his katana to a different angle. A second volley flew forth. The mercs chuckled and laughed amongst themselves at the proven futility of these ancient weapons falling upon modern alloy plate. The second volley arced through the air. The mercs opened fire on the front lines of defenders.

One slim dojo defender went down burning in a blaze of laser fire, unable to leap aside in time. Dueling the speed of light required anticipation of the shot, a trick few could pull off.

The mercs had drawn first blood. The other defenders side-stepped behind the statuary and wielded their ranged weapons. Blowdarts, shurikens, and longbows with long arrows, they seemed ineffectual versus the heavy armor of the mercs.

A shuriken lodged in the knee of a merc's armor suit, limiting his mobility to a mechanical limp. Nanites aboard the shuriken infiltrated the system of the armored suit.

The powersuit shut down, retracting its plates into the storage position. When his armor popped the merc was exposed to the enemy. His arms were sleeved in elaborate tattoos.

One of his nearby merc's stepped over to shield the defenseless man. Arrows from the courtyard rained down, exploding in a ripple of shockwaves. The denuded merc died, his defender knocked down face first in the grass. A stone statue of a Samurai warrior came to life, the textured robot spiking its vibrating naganata down through the torso of the flattened mercenary, into the ground.

Realizing their prey were tougher than they had first thought, the mercenaries activated their defensive screens and opened fire in earnest. Shimmers of heat and color swirled around their suits, ready to push aside or absorb energy or kinetic weapons.

Flashes of explosives rippled across the field, many of them bursting on the frontal armor of the invaders. Some of them were knocked flat, a couple hit in a vital spot such as the neck region or groin. Despite their energy shields and tough armor, the merc's got bashed about hard by shockwaves from the explosive tipped arrows. In response they fired missiles and grenades over the defenders heads, lighting the dojo afire, cutting off escape routes into the compound.

Iron caught a glimpse of light shift on the boarding ramp below the merc ship's tail. *"There you are, brother! Wait for me!"*

The pilot and copilot gave each other quizzical looks, hearing a sound like a rolling marble behind them. Turning his head, the co-pilot managed to open his mouth to speak before the micro-grenade went off. Its gelatin filled the cockpit with stiff foam which solidified in place, reacting with the air. The high temp cooked the two entombed mercs until they mercifully passed out.

Climbing into the upper gun turret of the mercenaries' assault boat, Ceres found the plush tray for receiving datapins. Gunners would insert a link cable from their MeTR to assert command controls and upstream their usual settings and preferences to the device.

"Got you covered, brother," Iron hailed on their private link. *"I'll make sure no one stabs you in the back."*

"Get out!" Ceres shouted in his head. *"I don't want to drag you into my failure to follow orders."*

"If you come out, and we head to the tree line plus 10k, I'll leave with you now, pardner. Otherwise, come down and make me leave!"

"Fine. Stay," Ceres pouted. *"I perform better with an audience anyway. When I light this up they will send someone in after you. I'd come in screened up like a ghost. Be ready for that."*

"Roger that. Thanks," Iron stood in a defensive ready stance.

From the cockpit of his appropriated gunship, Ceres wound up the mass driver and tried to fire on a line of armored attackers. They were highlighted green in his HUD, and he got a target denial tone. *Friendly fire lockout, huh? We'll just see about that,* he thought.

Let's see if my training downstreams included something about security systems. What crafter built this turret? Ah, 'Target Max', my old friend Max. Upstreamed your security protocols a year ago. Ceres had a moment to comprehend the value of training he had received from this unique little military school.

Using virtual screens in his HUD, Ceres quickly assembled an override program and upstreamed it to the fighting ship. *Gonna shake your hand someday, Max. Gotchya!*

The HUD-highlighted green mercenary figures outside all reverted to red. The young gunner grinned, slowly rotating his commandeered turret. Target locking markers blinked red around the icons of merc attackers as he went. A barrage of missiles streaked out of the Assault Craft and raced up into the low clouds overhead.

"Get in there and secure that ship!" Ke'inko ordered two of her guards. They turned and marched towards the ramp. The second assault craft fell, burning, out of the clouds, twisting slowly down until the treeline obscured it from view.

Ceres grin turned to a vicious grimace as his deadly attack began scoring casualties. More of Ceres' gunboat's missiles soon returned from the couds, smashing straight down into the heads and shoulders of armored merc's powersuits. Craters of burning smoke marked their death pyres. The missiles continued to pour out of the fighting craft, looping high into the air, then raining down the curved line of attackers on one whole side of their offensive.

Ceres enjoyed his front row seat to see, one by one, merc's armed exoframes and powered suits pounded into the ground. Some of the mercenary's recognized the danger, popping off flares, returning fire with missiles or beam battery cans.

Some attackers, now coming under devastating fire from their own landing craft's heavy weapons, took to the air with their exoframe's rocket packs. A few turned and tried to fire on their own ship, finding it highlighted green in their HUDs, untouchable.

None made it far as the locked missiles caught up and fragged them, their pilots screaming as they fell to the ground, burning. Some escaped with lightly damaged suits. Ceres targeted them with the mass driver in his ball turret.

A series of powerful electro-magnets pulled their thick dart-shaped rounds through the heart of the tubular railgun. Thousands of rounds per minute travelling at two thousand meters per second shredded the merc's now unscreened armor like a shotgun blast through al-foil. All eyes turned to witness the devastation, unable to ignore the horrendous shriek of the mini-darts streaming across the battlefield.

The mood shifted across the battle line. The attackers had been confidently holding their line to contain the student/hostages within their perimeter. Then the loud, powerful, and unstoppable destruction pouring down upon them from their own assault craft intimidated the strongest and made the weakest wet their power-suits.

Iron kicked out as soon as he was grabbed by some invisible attacker, probably wearing a stealth suit as Ceres had warned him.

"Oww!" cried out whomever Iron kicked. "Get him, brother!" the invisible assailant added.

Iron threw a blind roundhouse kick. "Oooff." Iron's heel sunk into the soft middle of another attacker. Iron somersaulted further into the ship and away from the hidden attackers. Pulling his scabbarded sword from his belt, he swung it in a fluid kana, practice moves he hoped would keep them back.

First one, then the other merc de-screened. The twins, Hayaki and Sume Okiro grinned at Iron even as they nursed the bruises he had just given them. "Oh, we will have fun with you today, old friend."

"No, Sume,'" Hayaki scolded. "Ke'inko said we must have the Tarsis boy!" He turned to the redhead, Iron. "Help us capture him, and we will reward you with your life," he smiled, offering his hand. Tattoos covered his skin, turning it almost completely black."

"Are you the new rodeo clown, Hayaki?" Iron taunted, "I'd rather be dragged through the desert by a herd of snakes than shake your hand. Now, you two goats take your licks and run along outta here, while I'm still feelin' a mite generous."

Hayaki growled his displeasure, facing Iron down. His straight Wakizashi sword slid slowly out of its scabbard across his back, matched by Iron's slow draw of his curved katana from its scabbard.

"Smack," across the back of Iron's head fell Sume's armored boot toe, the kick unseen thanks to his brother's distraction. Iron came around soon, amidst being dragged into the command circle of mercs. Ke'inko wrapped her arm around his neck while the twins controlled an arm apiece.

The huge thug nearby fired a fat rocket launcher pistol at a tangent to the turret. The shell exploded, startling Ceres. The turret spun swiftly about, the white hot mass driver and missile tubes targeting the group of mercs.

"Come out, Ceres." Ke'inko shouted into her all-group channel. Her shrill voice, amplified by the speakers inside the ship pierced Ceres' ears inside the rounded turret.

"If you surrender to me I will let Iron go free. Your ransom alone is worth more than all the rest of these warugaki, these useless brats. If you save me a lot of time and effort I will spare his life, and theirs. You have my word."

"Do not trust her, Ceres!" Sensei stated into the school's comm channel. *"Her word is as useless as the air to a fish. It is why she was expelled. Remember—"* Sensei cut off his thoughts upon seeing Ceres drop from the dropship's ramp to the ground. "No." the master whispered softly.

"Deal." Ceres shouted, walking boldly towards the older girl and her hostage. "Let him go now, or I will kill you *all* now!" He glowered at her.

A thick arm wrapped around Ceres' neck. A strong hand gripped Ceres' right arm, causing the armored bracers Ceres wore to pop and creak. The huge merc in the powersuit grinned as his helmet retracted from his face.

"The Gorira!" Iron shouted in surprise. "In four years, this steer's grown up into a bull, eh Cowboy?"

"Glic—" Ceres choked as the big merc stepped on the back of his knee, forcing him down, even as his thick arm tightened around Ceres' throat.

"Ceres?" taunted Ke'inko. "I want you to think back to the day we met. That day in the forest? Does this scene look slightly familiar? Take a good look. I want you to remember this, forever!"

"Let him go!" Ceres croaked through his constricted throat.

"Okay," she directed her troops. "Now that we've got him, everybody start mopping up. No holds barred!"

"Hey!" Iron protested. "You said…arrrrhh—"

Ke'inko's Wakizashi blade sticking from his chest stopped Iron's words cold.

"Iron, no!!" Ceres surged upward, gaining enough space under Gorira's arm to breathe and speak.

Ke'inko laughed, the shrill sound cutting the still air. The planet seemed to hold its collective breath, the battle stalling as both attackers and defenders witness to it were shocked by Ke'inko's brutal murder of the teen. The apparent cease fire rippled along the battlefront. A bird called to another in the forest nearby, wings beating hard away from the stilled battlefield.

"Nooo!" Ceres' face turned red. His bowels turned to jelly, and his mouth went dry as adrenaline flushed through his body. With a flash of blue he activated the force field shield on his arm bracer. The expanding disk cut Gorira's fingers and thumb off, causing his roar of pain.

Grabbing the arm that had been strangling him, Ceres slipped under it in a reversal move, twisting it up behind the thug's back. He drew the merc's own tanto knife from his shoulder scabbard, swung it around and stabbed it through Gorira's palm into his back.

Ceres pushed downward through the ridges between armor plates, aiming deep into Gorira's body, into the hip bone where the tip stuck. The huge merc kneeled slowly, a growling scream escaping his pained lips.

From its cross-back holster Ceres drew Gorira's huge launcher pistol. Its under-stock gripped Ceres' forearm to lever the muzzle-weight against his bone structure. Tucking it under the big man's armpit he squeezed the trigger. Mini-missiles streaked out and erupted at close range, blowing away Hayaki and Sume' before they could react to the surprising turn of events. The high recoil of the fat gun slammed up under Gorira's shoulder, leaping up like a jackhammer, pounding into his armpit repeatedly.

He had loaded the weapon's helical magazine coils with what the Star Marines dubbed "Happier" rounds, HAPIR, for High Explosive, Armor Piercing, Incendiary, Rocket-propelled. These splattered their victims' remains across the command group of mercenaries. The better trained merc's shot back at Ceres or swung their weapons, but he used Gorira with his heavy armor as a body shield.

Ceres raised the launcher's barrel to clear Iron's body, but it was only due to the redhead's collapse to his knees that he missed. In his rage, Ceres sprayed the heavy pistol around like a garden hose, seemingly uncaring of the devastation he dealt out so easily.

Around the dojo the battle resumed, raged, but Ceres was oblivious to it. He focused his attack on the targets in front of him, devastating the command group near their assault ship. The high explosive blasts threw fire, debris, smoke, and carnage in the air.

When the helical magazine emptied, Ceres, teeth gritted, finally relaxed, letting the huge gun fall to the ground. Iron lay on his side, pale and motionless, Ke'inko and her sword gone from the scene.

The Gorira fell forward, face planting in the blood soaked grass when his wounded hand refused to support his weight.

"Oh, no!" Ceres shouted. "You don't get off that easily!" He leaned back and used his tractor beam bracers to pull the heavy merc upright to his knees, a feat of adrenaline-fueled strength for the lanky teen. Ceres marched around the Merc's huge body, glaring into the scared eyes of his remaining nemesis. "My uncle told me, the way to deal with bullies is to give them a heavy dose of their own medicine."

Ceres knelt, making eye contact with his fallen buddy. Iron spat out some blood but smiled, as if reassuring his friend that he was fine. His bloodstained teeth and crimson lips gave away the truth. His eyes closed, winced tight, but he spoke through his pain.

"Ceres, brother. You tell that mangy mutt I'll beat her aft in a minu—" His mouth stilled in the middle of his final word.

Ceres' eyes welled up. Face ashen but filling fast with red, he reached to retrieve something unseen from Iron's waistline and stood up face to face with Gorira.

"Your friends seem to have left you alone to bear the justice you have all earned today. Any last words?"

"It-it was Ke'inko!" Gorira stammered, his voice rising in pitch as the power dynamic had shifted heavily against him. "It was her all along. Her family is… they, they don't follow Bushido. I had to do as they said or my family would suffer worse fates. I'm innocent."

"You *chose* to do this!" Ceres shouted, his voice deepening. "This act, this *life* of evil. You will pay the price now!"

"No, Ceres!" The grave voice of Sensei sang out behind him. Ceres turned to listen to his Sensei. "He must stand trial for his crimes. Justice demands it!" The lecturing finger appeared. "Only then will he be punished as decent society demands."

"No!" Ceres shouted, defiant even to the old master to whom he swore obedience. "I told them I would kill them all, and I keep my word!" He spun swiftly, activating Iron's forcefield sword as he turned, and "O-kesa" cut all the way through Gorira, from his shoulder down through his body to the opposite hip.

With a snort, the armored merc fell in two halves onto the ground, blood bursting out of the huge, full body wound.

"Oh, Ceres," Sensei said, head hanging forward. "Your Fudoshin? I have failed to teach you a warrior's emotional balance."

Ceres fell to his knees next to the body of his best friend. The natural adrenaline downer kicking in, he puked, heaving on the grass. Twitching and crying, laying on his side where he could see Iron's still body, Ceres wondered, how could it fit God's plans that everyone he cared for had to leave him?

Chapter 17
Food Fight

A-Valhalla, Mess Hall
2525/7/14/0900

"Omelet de crab aux shallots e lay champignons, si vous play?" *Best French I could do, poorly.* Ceres smiled at the robot chef.

It seemed to blink at him, pausing, as it was in the midst of preparing several egg orders at once for the endless line of rough men and women. Ceres prayed that his order stood out.

As Ceres had shuffled up the line he had watched the chef, observed his reactions to the rude and crude beings he was forced to serve. Ceres tried to put himself in the bot's shoes for a moment. Or at least the viewpoint of those chef's whose life's works had been distilled into the programming the robot carried.

Most of the pushy customers' orders seemed pedestrian, such as eggs over easy, sunny-side-up, or scrambled with various ingredients. The frittatas he had ready looked outstanding, but those took too long for most of the impatient mob of customers here.

The bot's chest proudly displayed six bronze stars across the curved shell casing. Ceres had seen other chef's wear such stars, embroidered or pinned to their ubiquitous chef's jackets. He remembered it was an ancient system of designating the quality of the chef versus others. This one must have been programmed with at least one human chef's memories of a grand career serving excellence.

The metallic six-star worthy chefbot seemed to become irritated when he tried to persuade his customers to let him make it right for them. "Monsieur, si vous play. Allow me! All these same ingredients folded inside a proper thin omelet portioned for one? Now, that is how 'zee' finest eggs should be done!" None had the patience, until Ceres.

Shuffling forward in the line, observant Ceres had noticed this frustration bubbling up within the chef's snippy communications. He hoped his request in French would win him finer service, worthy of six stars.

"Ah, Monsieur, vous profiter des omelets, non?" He asked Ceres. The bot's thick accent confirmed it as programmed to imitate a French chef. Ceres had guessed it might appreciate being spoken to properly from that point of view. "Properly" to a French chef could only mean, in French.

But Ceres did not know the language, not really. His eyes wandered in their sockets while he tried to comprehend the robot's authentic accent. Ceres' mother had spoken it, but Ceres had downstreamed his French just to understand a college girlfriend, practicing little since she became an "ex."

Ceres' HUD flashed text into his optic nerves, suggesting translations which he tried to sort out on the fly. Finally he decided "profit" sounded good. "Oi, and if you could recommend a proper wine I'd appreciate it, Chef, ahh? Your name?"

"Monsieur, je suis le grand Chef Henry." 'On-ree' is how it came out, complete with a flourish of his multi-appendages of retractable cooking utensils. Ceres laughed, thinking the French have such a flowery way to say even such a common name as "Henry". Whatever chefs' life experiences were used to program this bot, their egos came through very strongly.

Ceres might have said so, but he was going for flattery. It is always unwise to insult those cooking your meal, especially a French chef. So many foul things can be concealed within a proper sauce.

"Chef On-Ree, it is my happy luck, to find my way into your fine dining room," Ceres covered his heart with his hand and bowed, also covering up his laugh with quick thinking and more flattery. "My French, she is not good enough, forgive me, grand chef. Mamére, my mother, did not pass enough of it on to me, I'm afraid." That Ceres had slipped into affecting a bad French accent of Galactic was amusing to the pirates around him. He was starting to think this was a bad idea after all.

"Hurry up, pretty boy!" a huge voice boomed from the line backed up behind Ceres. He did not bother to turn but continued to chat with On-Ree while the chef gleefully prepared Ceres' special folded omelet, as well as several other dishes, simultaneously.

Most of the other orders were some variation on ham and cheese, scrambled. Potatoes and onions were the only vegetables in collective favor, from what Ceres could see. These looked like hard living men and women wanting to fill up on hearty fare. With the speed and accuracy of his many arms and attachments, On-Ree kept a dozen skillets going in various stages.

"Monsieur, Bon Appetite!" the chefbot proclaimed, when handing Ceres platter to him. He even included a partial bow. With a bow, a smile, and "Merci," Ceres thanked him, Quickly he turned away from the angry line of voracious carnivores whom he had delayed from devouring their breakfasts.

"Ceres!" Kangee called out, waving his arm in a circle. "Come over." The usual "new guy at school" scene was averted when Kangee invited Ceres to sit at his table full of pirates. They scooted apart on the benches, forcing Ceres to take a space in the middle of them across from his painter friend.

"Gentlemen," he nodded, "I thank you." Ceres noted three more pirates to his right jumping up quickly, making him worry that he had offended them somehow.

Then a body the size of two men glued together slammed down on the vacant bench. Ceres beheld a mountain of a man, his arms were the size of Ceres' powerful legs, his back as wide as a workhorse and equally muscular. As a cape he wore a bone white animal fur with silver tips giving it an ashen tinge. Ceres thought it to be some kind of huge wolf's skin. *Blonde, beard, broad...Thor?*

"I am Jaeger Thorsson, Jarl of the *Star Dragon*," the mountain announced with a deep voice. "These dirt-ugly sons of whores, are my men." He turned and nodded, indicating both directions down the table. "No finer pack of wolves to be found in the galaxy!" Men pounded the table and roared with cheers and laughter at this high praise from their leader.

The loud voice behind me in the omelet line...this guy is a giant! "I am Ceres," He nodded up and down the table. "Ceres Tauri, born of the planet Ceres, and of your king, Tyrian." Men again cheered.

"You, sir," Ceres raised an eyebrow to the giant man next to him, "are well named. You are the spitting image of Thor himself."

"It inspired my Viking surname, true," the huge man answered. "Your father needed a man such as me to give image to the god. I had to earn my name in combat, of course.

"I was one of his original crew. In fact he says, his looks plus mine inspired the very concept of the Void Vikings. Our king said he secretly honored the old gods from his youth.

"When that fine new ship of yours is ready to fight, you will join my squadron, lad. Thus, we will help you earn *your* Viking name." Pirates around them grinned, and one to Ceres' left slapped his shoulder.

"We can't have you bearing the name of a Roman skirtgod of farm animals, now can we?" Jaeger pounded Ceres' shoulder blade and knocked the wind from that lung. Ceres was moved, but felt glad he was not breathless thanks to oxygen from the respirocytes implanted in his blood, a common military body upgrade. Still, peals of laughter erupted at the table.

"Once honorably earned, given your status as prince-apparent, plus your military service, your father will probably rank you as a Jarl proper, over a crew of a ship or ships. Then, you will lead raids and later plan them. If men follow your lead, and your strategies are winners, you will work your way up in stature and *earn* your rank as prince successor to your father."

The huge man leaned in close, and Ceres could smell the testosterone boiling out of his sweat. It was a silent challenge to any man: Follow me or die by me!

Ceres thought, *I bet this guy knows where my mother is! I'd better make friends with him. Where have I seen him before?*

"I have heard whispers that men and women are asking their Jarls for permission to join your crew." Thorsson's eyebrows twisted to give the strongest conspiratorial wink Ceres had ever seen. "Even some of *my* men." Jaeger the Jarl sternly looked about while his men did their best to be looking anywhere else in the universe.

"It is all right, lads. Ceres here is the newest Captain in my squadron. He will need a few able bodies to show him how we Void Vikings fly, and fight, and win!" Several pirates across the table breathed out long releases of tense breath. Jaeger turned back to Ceres.

"Too bad you have but one small gilded ship fit for a prince's tender arse, when you could fill a great warship with *warriors*," he flexed his bulging arm to make a fist, and bellowed, "to carve your legend from the hearts of stars!" Men leapt to their feet yelling guttural barks and roars like animals.

Ceres could see why Jaeger led dangerous men such as these pirates. They were vicious men and women from across the galaxy. They needed such a powerful man, graced with the body and mind to inspire their hearts to burn in their chests.

Ceres could feel it within him as this modern Jarl stirred his blood, burning in his veins. He imagined he could join these heathens, take up his uncle's old trade with a crew of these wild warriors, and rain retribution down on any who dared to steal a ship again! Of course, these very pirates were responsible for most of the "grand theft: starship" in the Periphery Sector. Slight complication.

"Every legend told among the stars, begins with one good ship," Ceres cryptically replied.

Across from Ceres, Kangee circled his dark beard in his tattooed hand and caressed it down to his belly. It was a gesture Ceres noted having seen often among the band. "Prince Ceres," he began.

Less than a week aboard this rock and they seem to want me to be their prince? Ceres thought.

"We are all excited to see how you learned from your heroic sporting days and show us your warrior's spirit in battle, to go with your Loki's cunning!" Ceres raised his eyebrows in silent question at the skinny man.

"Your holster trick in the duel. It surely was inspired by Loki the trickster, though Odin himself was known for his devious cunning as well as powerful strength at arms."

"That is why," a dark skinned man on the far side of Jaeger chimed in, "one-eyed Odin is the Jarl's god, and may be your patron old god too."

Ceres decided against crossing himself as he realized who he had surrounded himself with. He prayed in his head, *Angels preserve me. Pagan believers surround me.* If he were going to pretend to play the role his father was giving him, and these men appeared eager for Ceres to fill, he would have to fit in.

"So, our young prince," Kangee resumed, "once a sports hero, well known across the galaxy as a lover of women, tell us, men of your Wolfpack: Is it all true?" The dark beard parted in a grin of messy teeth. Ceres glanced about, surrounded by eager grins and brightly lit eyes. *Must be a table of fans?*

"No, no," Ceres teased with a dour face and bladed hands cutting down their dreams. He glanced about, seeing the expectant grins soften a bit, insulating their owners from disappointment. "That's not the half of it!" He slapped the table loudly with his palm and beamed a big smile.

The savage men roared with laughter. Between bites he told them tales confirming his college exploits in the zero gravity ball sphere and his exotic female exploits in the dorms.

Jaeger threw Ceres' delicate glass of honey colored Alsace pinot blanc against a wall, swiftly replaced by a tankard of mead and a personal bottle of dark and spicy rum, both of which these Vikings produced in the asteroid as well as stole across the sector.

Around him, the aptly named Void Vikings ate like starved animals, forking piles of bacon, sliced ham, and sausage over from heaping platters of meats hastily refilled by waitbots which seemed perpetually unable to move fast enough.

Overhead pipe works with robotic service arms refilled their hard drinks automatically. Accompanied by exaggerated belching and slobbering sounds, the pirates guzzled their rum and mead as if they were fish in the air, gasping upon the rocks, needing to refill themselves with liquids or die.

Across from Ceres, raven haired Kangee got up, soon to return with a second helping of crab omelet for Ceres, having made the chefbot create another serving for the newest member of their crew. Ceres felt fortunate to be eating while drinking to help absorb some of the alcohol. He used his storytelling to reduce his intake of drink, so he did not lose control. These vicious men were hungry for entertainment.

After the meal was cleared away some of the tables retracted into the floor and walls, creating a large common space for gaming between raids. Ceres realized the men and women remaining were fit fighters. Those with support jobs—technicians, starship mechanics, supply handlers—must report for them now, leaving the victorious combatants to their rest, sport, or training. Same as in the military.

Gamblers and rogues, they broke out cards and many other games. Seven card hold'em took over many of the tables—fitting as it had taken over the galaxy as the favorite table game of the millennium. Ceres thought it was perfect for these pirates, as it involved bluffing and throwing everything you had against your opponent to win.

A pair of the largest men in the room wrestled their cybernetic arms against each other while onlookers bet on the outcome. Dice rolled down other tables where gemstones atop velvet, and piles of precious metals stamped into coins, appeared out of personal stashes to make the games more interesting. Against one wall, other men set up a body shaped target.

"Darts or guns?" Ceres asked, licking his lips. He had thrown quite a few darts in college, one of many games of eye-hand coordination at which he excelled.

"No, lad," the big burly older man clapped his shoulder with a paw nearly as big as a dinner plate. "This is the *Viking* form of darts. We throw the space axe!" On cue, a robotic wheeled rack holding a dozen axes rolled up next to them and stopped.

A huge classic pirate weapon of the Wilmingwood Holo's, the space axe often was depicted hacking into live targets for pirate blood sport. Ceres was glad to see this was more myth than reality. The handle was usually set between one to two meters long, topped and backed by spikes, and featured a large main blade of various crescent shapes. They could vibrate at ultrasonic speeds, enhancing the sharpness of the blade's lethal edge.

These axes before him fitted half-moon blades, cut out for weight balance to match their fat and heavy back spike. It provided an awesome focus for all the force a man could generate against an armored target. The blade would hack deeply into anything softer. It looked intimidating, especially when held by dark and burly men such as these.

Ceres grabbed one off the rack and tested it for balance, finding that it hefted well at about five kilograms. Twisting hard on the handle, he accidentally extended it. Unfortunately, it poked right into the belly of Ceres' big tablemate, Jaeger.

The giant responded by releasing a very loud fart and laughing from his belly. A chorus of intentional farting and belching responded from around the room, hundreds of crude men's laughter reveled in it. Some women among them slapped men's arms and rolled their eyes. Others joined in.

Kangee cocked his head, saying, "Sounds like the bullfrogs are frisky today," and returned to watching Ceres examine the weapon in his hands. Seeing no apology was expected he offered none. His uncle had taught Ceres that, "A man who apologizes shows weakness." He needed to quickly learn this wolf pack's rules so he could fit in.

Extending the handle to one and a half meters, Ceres found the space axe was easy to spin, handle over blade. Three men from his table had taken up axes and stood in an arc around Ceres. "You go first, Blondie," teased the elder giant, Jarl Thorsson. He pulled on his golden mustache and twisted it to hold its shape.

"Perfect! I wanted to call 'first shot' and leave you in my exhaust," Ceres took his place where they pointed. Five meters back from the wall a line in the floor had been scored. It reminded Ceres of the duel he had fought in the hanger here, just days before. He took a stance familiar from his training days in Win Tao dojo, one foot forward, similar to a classic woodchopper's stance.

Ceres wound up, easing his weapon back over his shoulder, then levering it forward and releasing its handle in front of his face. The space axe flipped head over tail and squarely struck center on the body target with the base of its handle.

The room reacted with laughter so loud Ceres almost jumped at its thunder. So much for revering their star athlete. His face red, he realized now why the men had allowed him the dubious honor of going first.

"Your exhaust stinks, friend," Jaeger teased, "no matter how gilded your papers in the personal!" The men waved their hands under their noses then broke out in heaving laughs.

The artist Kangee went next. He took two full steps back from the line and assumed his stance. Ceres understood, the weapon needed more distance, more time, to rotate around its center of mass. He merely nodded with a grin on his face. *Sport is half about entertainment, after all. Be humble, watch closely, learn fast.*

The gangly trustee took a big windup. From his shoulder, he swung the axe all the way down in front, rotated at the waist, then swung up behind him before coming overhand and releasing at the target. His follow through involved a full step forward and swinging both arms in circles around his shoulders like the flapping wings of a bird. Ceres made note of this form.

Kangee's space axe had plenty of time to spin in midair, thanks to the extra range. The blade and top spike sank into what would have been the shoulder of a man if one were standing there rather than a foam body dummy. The back wall spat splinters. Ceres now noticed the walls were fairly chewed and hacked in places from their frequent sport. Applause came from all sides, and then most observers turned back to their own games of chance and profit.

"Good form, Kangee," praised Thorsson, causing the trustee to smile, "for a chicken," Jeager continued. "Next raid maybe we let you fly there on your own black wings." Laughter came at Kangee's expense, and his face fell. Ceres noted this as well.

Next up, the dark-skinned pirate who had sat next to Ceres took his turn. He stood just closer than Kangee had as Ceres marked it, but only took a half swing and a half step forward in follow through. His axe bit well into the wall, handle hanging straight down. Unfortunately, it was just right of the dummy's head, missing by centimeters.

A huge hand slapped the dark man on his shoulder. "That's a fine placement, Faruock. You cut off his earrings. You can add them to your own." The group laughed heartily, including Faruock.

The giant "Thor" stepped up and examined the target. "It appears you are the only one with points yet, Kangee. I will help you." Kangee was not thrilled to see his Jarl's devious grin.

Thorsson merely stood sideways to the targets, extending his axe's handle to over two meters. He hefted it like a spear and chucked it endwise towards Kangee's axe. His massive arms allowed him to toss the thing as if it were a toy. Ceres imagined Thorsson would carry a much heavier space axe into battle.

Thor's axe head caught on the handle of Kangee's axe, knocking it out of the wall. Both axes fell to the floor.

"Hey!" protested Kangee.

"What, no score? No winners, no losers?" asked Ceres.

Faruock held two more axes, one of which he offered to Ceres. "Two more throws apiece." He nodded towards the target. "You're up." Ceres admired the contrast of his friendly smile's bright white teeth with his skin.

Ceres took two strides back from the marked line and turned, adopting the sideways stance the others had used. Like Faruock, a man of similar body size, Ceres took a half swing, careful to avoid chopping into his own leg as the axe passed by. He followed through with a step forward, both arms swinging around like wings.

"You are trying to fly the coop with Kangee, eh blondie?" Thor seemed to enjoy joking at Kangee's expense.

But the toss was true. The handle struck, butt first, low on the target, but this rotated the head forward. The axe blade chopped into the left shoulder of the target dummy a little lower and closer to center than the mark left by Kangee's short lived hit.

Faruock threw again, planting one in the right edge of the head for the same points as Ceres.

Thor swung back two-handed over his left shoulder and then sent the blade of his axe chopping into the neck of the target. It was just inside Ceres' blade and at a slight angle, so the handle crossed several ring lines in the center of the target, what Ceres guessed must be a zone with higher scores.

Jaeger's axe handle crossed over the reddened heart of the target, too, complicating any future body hits.

Ceres' third go, he took another half step back from the line and shuffled his feet slightly turned versus before. He tried to make an identical swing as well. This time his axe hit right down the middle of the target, cleaving the lower face and neck in half.

Kangee's next shot bounced off the handles of Ceres' and Thor's axes, otherwise it would have been a good hit in the heart. "Well, I'm out. I'll tally your scores." Ceres worried the artist would wander into the target area but he wisely stayed clear for now.

"You had the best shot yet, Kangee," Ceres praised. "More practice and you'll be consistently starting off with scoring throws like that one." Kangee grinned, eyes smiling.

Faruock placed his last shot next to his second, having walked his way into the target with each throw.

Thor's last toss came from over his right shoulder, resulting in the blade chopping into the target's neck from the right side.

The three who had scored slapped each other's backs and shoulder's and traded smiles.

Kangee jumped forward and started examining the blades. He tallied up, frowned, counted again. The men walked up, ready to pull down the axes once he was done.

"It's a tie!" he announced. "Ceres and Thor each have 11 points. Ten for Faruock"

"Do we go again?" Ceres asked. "One on one?"

"One more throw apiece?" suggested Faruock. "See if there's a winner from that."

"Fair," Ceres said.

"Fine," said Thor, "though it's a bit crowded in there." Grabbing two axes off the floor, they all returned behind the throwing line.

Ceres stood still, studying the crisscross of axe handles over the body target and thinking for a moment. He twisted the handle of his space axe, extending it.

"Ah, if only it were that easy, eh boys?" a woman sitting on the lap of a nearby man teased, slapping one of the legs she sat on. Men surrounding them laughed. From his military experience Ceres knew, rough men will inject bawdy humor into almost anything. Ceres kept twisting.

"You going to reach out and stab it in there, boy?" thundered Thorsson.

"Handle it too much, it will fall out," quipped Kangee. More laughter came from the sides at the crude double talk. Finally hearing quiet settle in on the huge room, Ceres realized that more and more of the surrounding pirates were watching.

When the handle was extended to the maximum length it clicked into place on some inner detent. At 3 meters long it would be useful in a pike line for catching an enemy charge. Ceres knew the balance of the weight would now be below the head.

He hefted it by the handle, finding that point of even weight. Gripping his space-axe at the balance, he took several steps back, then a couple more, gauging his stride.

Hefting it in one hand, Ceres raised the space axe up over his shoulder. He turned aside and extended his arm full length behind him, the blade coming next to his cheek. Stepping forward with a slight running stride, he almost skipped, bringing forth laughter from dozens of men around the room.

Behind the line Ceres stopped on one leg, allowing his momentum to rotate him forward. He launched the space axe with his full strength, hurled as if it were a spear or javelin of ancient cultures. It wobbled slightly in the short distance and impaled the foam, sticking deep into the wood, its top spike embedded through the dummy's red heart.

After a second of silent comprehension, the room erupted in cheers and chanting of "Ceres! Ceres!" He enjoyed his moment, having inspired his fans with excellence in a new sport.

"Viking darts it is!" Ceres slapped Thor on the shoulder. "You're up."

"You're a clever little bastard, aren't you?" Thorsson taunted the younger man. He made direct eye-to-eye contact, testing Ceres' bearing when confronted.

Ceres recognized the classic pack positioning. *Pack of wolves' is right.*

"That word does not bother me, Thor, because I know who my father is, and I bear his name." He grinned up at the mountain of a man. "Now if you want to be friends, just don't insult my mother. We might fight over that."

"Oh, so you don't want me to call you a ... ."

Ceres stepped up, his finger thrust in the Jarl's face. "Don't!"

"What? Don't, call you a whoreson of a dirty bit—"

"CLOMKK!" The sound of the powerful blow rang out in the room. Ceres' hand already in position, his uppercut was lightning fast. He had caught Jaeger directly under the bony chin, snapping his head upwards. No matter how tough one's bones or strong his muscles, such a "Tyson blow"— a fast powerful uppercut—usually caused a knockout when the target's skull slapped into their brain.

The cheers and chants of Ceres' name silenced as Jarl Thorsson fell backwards, eyes closed, as if he were a tree felled in one titanic blow. Faruock jumped in to catch his huge Jarl, only to be buried under the avalanche of muscles.

Stunned looks on their faces, scores of men in the room stood up as Ceres marched grimly out.

* * *

A-Valhalla, Private Dome
2525/7/14/1233

"Hold still while I nurse this bruise! Y'men're such babies," Serenity enjoyed teasing Ceres. "N'matter how tough you act among men, you are delicate, tender little boys around your nursemaids."

Both of her hands wrapped around Ceres' hand, as if it were a great bullhorn she was about to blow into. Eyes closed, she imagined a glowing white warmth within her, flowing down her arms, out of her hands, into his.

Ceres wore a pleased grin, so she thought he enjoyed the feeling. *She* did. Was this man any different? Any more enjoyable?

"Terran Tor?" Ceres asked, "You're an Amazon?"

Serenity squinted open one eye. "I need to concentrate fer a few minutes 'ere, just to start the 'ealing process," she admonished him. "Try to think of something neutral. Just a color. Blue."

"Green," Ceres countered.

Serenity smiled, "Close yer eyes, love. Breathe in sync with me."

Ceres smiled back at her with a touch of smugness, she thought, playing across his lips. She did not think anything she knew of his reputation hinted he would be able to keep it clean, so she retreated from reading his mind.

The flow of warmth from her center into his hands made her happy. She had always enjoyed healing, no matter the personal cost to herself. It was a selfless act of service love, to give of your own health to another.

She felt connected to this man on a new level. It was impossible for Serenity to stop thinking that his hands, these strong hands within hers, had fought for her freedom. He had used whatever it took from his tactical training, his cunning wiles, his physical speed and talent to find a clever way to win her away from a horrible life of abuse. He had put his life on the line for her freedom.

She was grateful for his noble defense of her body, her liberty, but her gratitude went only so far. She considered whether to help him achieve his goal of finding his mother. Since she was stuck in here with him until they could escape, she might as well help him try to heal his rage as well.

The thrill within her made their touching, their share of energy somehow electric. Serenity realized his touch distracted her, She had started listening to his mind again when she heard his thoughts intrude into her solitude.

"Galaxipedia 2.0, Terran Tor," the entry played across his MeTR into his mind. A live feed pulled from the pirates' local wetnet group.

"The original colonist's battles to tame the beasts native to this wild planet, took a huge toll on the early male population, eliminating most of the colony's soldiers, hunters and explorers. The remaining women had no choice but to take on a majority of military and security enlistments. They moved into the majority of important governmental roles as well."

"I thought you said your family disapproved of joining MeTR groups?" she accused gently.

"I'm on one-way downstream," he explained, "Ghost user signature and robust firewall. These pirates are from all over the galaxy. Those who can't play by polite society's rules tend to gravitate to the lawless Rim. I'm downstreaming only. It's an intel gathering technique. Even if they detect me they can't listen to my thoughts and learn my family's secrets."

"If y'wanna' know about me planet and family of origin," Serenity said softly, "you 'kin just ask me."

Ceres' jaw dropped. "I…" he stammered, rattled.

She realized he only now figured out that she had caught him researching her background in the middle of their conversation.

"Agreed," he said in answer. "The same for you."

Good," she started. "Yes. In defense of their family, even we delicate Earth women become tigers. The Irish stock that settled Terran Tor were right hardy folk, including we women. Our ancestral Celts were among the most savage people of Europe, after all."

"Women's naturally higher eye-hand coordination probably made a difference in the field?" Ceres asked. "Enabling the use of safer, longer ranged weapons from aviation platforms. Laser rifles from that era needed steadier hands. Simple tactical use of the specialized troops at hand."

"Good analysis. You are correct," she affirmed. "Our society soon became dominated by women, within our 'Generation of Eve's, and has remained matriarchal for over 400 years since. Galactic society openly nicknamed us 'Amazons' after the legendary ancient Greek female-driven society which Terran-Tor somewhat resembles. Some of my people consider it a compliment."

"I feel," he hinted, "I should know how *you* feel about that before I say something wrong?"

"Then you are wiser as to women, than most men I have known" she said. The slight wrinkle of her lip hinted she was teasing him. He must have noticed because he broke out in a big grin.

"I'm going with 'compliment,' he guessed. "You are a strong willed person." She raised her face to look at him squarely, then cocked her head to the side. "You seem to be in too good of humor to be upset by that term."

"You are good at reading people, love," she said. "Do you still use your training to manipulate women?"

He just blinked in response. After a silent moment he asked her, "Are you relentlessly interviewing me to gauge my moral compass?"

Again, she tilted her head. She smiled more broadly, caught by his clever insight. He had already fallen very hard for her; she could tell from his words, actions, and thoughts. Her sense of his romantic, passionate feelings for her affected her own, causing her to distrust them on a subtle level.

She felt attracted to him but knew she could not give her mind, heart, body, and soul to just any rogue, especially one with such a reputation as a womanizer. She needed to know if this pirate prince was worthy of her before she crossed the lines and took possession of him as her own.

"I've learned from my mistakes of the past," he finally answered her question. "Yes, I have a colorful history. In the Academy I was... too popular. I learned the hard way, from a painful, personal lesson. I stopped 'manipulating women' for my own use.

"I am still trying to get a handle on relationships. It is hard to know if she, whomever the 'she' of the moment is, is also not using me to get to my family's money."

"Your family is rich an' powerful," she said. "Enough so to make 'appen almost what'ere they want, any time, any where. True?" She turned her statements into a question.

"Historically they have carefully resisted pushing their-" he corrected himself, "-*our*, self-interests above society's or others. It is a centuries' long dance, as my uncle once described it. He trusted people like his sister—my mother—to maintain the family's moral compass within the guidance of the Orthodox Church, so things didn't get out of hand."

Serenity heard Ceres' private thought, *Only my mother was kidnapped years ago.*

Sensing no deception in the handsome young man, she was impressed with his conviction. He knew he and his family were in the right and doing good deeds, from his point of view. She would have to ensure that his philosophy and moral compass aligned with hers, and hers was the reunified Church. She moved on to a new area to test him,

"The Commandment clearly states 'Thou shall not steal.' God wrote it into stone. That is 'ow strongly *He* feels on it. How d'ya justify stealing starships, then y've nerve to come to me 'ere today and say yer not already a pirate?"

Ceres looked down and gulped. Raising his head he licked his lips.

Feeling something internal flip a switch within her interview subject, Serenity softened her tone, deciding to let him express it in his own way.

"Okay," she offered quickly, before he could react. "I'll agree that there are often two sides to any dispute, and they can both seem right to some degree based on their own subjective viewpoints."

"That is why," she continued, "we need a solid set of universal objective moral standards, The Commandments, built into the Galactic Constitution, to base our society and laws upon."

Ceres sighed. Wisely patient, she gave him a moment to compose himself to answer her.

Finally, he responded to her question. "We were popping about the galaxy, charter hauling, delivering cargos and materials and occasionally salvaging a derelict ship here and there. But everything changed one fateful day in 2514."

"'We' is your Uncle Tarsis and you? Was your mother with you at the time?" she interjected.

"This was years after she was taken, after I had spent five years planet-side training with my master. I was back on the crew just a few months, transporting cargos by starship. My Sensei came with us after the dojo was wiped out."

"You've led a hard life. Your family name makes all of you targets?" She lifted a sculpted brow above one of her green eyes, mirroring his expression. For Serenity it was intuitive, empathic.

"Yes, exactly," he smiled at her, sighed. She thought he seemed resigned or amused enough to let her get away with this grilling.

"Owning the largest MegaCorp in the galaxy isn't just a sweet life sitting around a Roman-style villa having peeled grapes fed to you all day by scantily clad nubile women and deciding to lay off a million people just for kicks. Anyway, let me get rolling here."

She thought he threw that out there to see if she too started going greedy on him. She had mentioned their wealth and power first, after all. "Sorry, love. I'm curious, but I had to get the crew comprising 'we' in me mind. Go ahead."

She felt it was important to establish a kind of mild dominance in their relationship that women of her planet had found useful to subtly lead the stronger-willed of their men without the man knowing everything wasn't their own idea in the first place. Her people called it the "rudder" technique.

A married couple and their family might be considered "the ship" of their life. A strong man might imagine himself the captain of this ship and that would fit the biblical model well. A strong, wise, and subtle woman would have her hands on the tiller more than her husband knew, however, adjusting the rudder as well as influencing him and his work of guidance to the ship.

Few had a truly equal but different, complimentary partnership, but those happy few universally enjoyed it when they did. That was her goal. Now to find the right man, the Adam for her as Eve, together guiding their ship towards their souls' homeport: heaven.

It was a skill Serenity looked forward to mastering with this intriguing man who clearly wanted her deeply. *If he proves worthy, I might find his intensely passionate desire is my hook to get under his skin and take him as my mate.*

She smiled at him, teasing, "Go ahead, Ceres. Tell me more about how you stole starships, yet you aren't, already, a pirate?"

Chapter 18
Grand Theft: Spacecraft

MWG, Carina Sector, Racine System
Racine 4, Orbital Station 3
2514/12/07/0925

"Racine port station 3 coming up, sir," called out the navigator, a Tenublian currently colored in bright orange and reds. The vocoded voice came from the ship's sound emitters on the bridge, transmitted down one of the jelly-squid's feathery white tendrils, which pulsed with modulated flashes of light in time with the sounds of its "voice".

"The BARGE" blazoned across her bow, a large sturdy ship pushed on though the silence. To its Master, the bulky ship somewhat resembled a thick slice out of a step pyramid, with a huge aft drive section, smaller Hab/mid-section and bracket of forward thrust spars ready to push a massive load. Today such load was the container barge the tug was backing in to this remote Rimward market.

"Thank you, Med. Son, we're heading for dock 11. Sync with the station's space-control system," the deep voice of the dark haired captain shot back from his plush silver grav-chair above and behind the first bank of crew stations. From the central, raised position of his grav chair, the captain enjoyed the panoramic view of his bridge and crew.

Astern grew the shining framework of a dockyard in space. Unlike the sleek stations of the developed planets, this was a typical Rimmer, an open frame station, with docking to one side of the gridworks. Storage and housing modules seemed to have been tossed in wherever they could fit among the prior modules opposite the dock side.

On past visits, the Captain heard many local and passing spacers remark upon Racine D3's resemblance to an old ground vehicle bridge adrift in space. Beyond it glowed a small watery planet, lots of sea green peeking up through the sheets of white clouds.

"Port 3, airdock 11. Yes, sir!" called out the cracking voice of a young human male, no more than fourteen. The blonde boy was strapped into a grav-lounge to the Captain's left, forward in the bridge. The lad handled the toggles and buttons controlling the squat tug, and her fat lozenge of a barge she was braking. He had a huge grin on his face, obviously pleased to be allowed to take the ship and barge into port.

Seated behind him was a distinctly Asianan-looking elder human, his streaked greying hair pulled back into a small bun, and low grey fuzz for a beard. He slowly nodded his approval at the youthful pilot's actions. The old man did not smile, however, holding his arms crossed tightly over his chest. The Captain thought the elder might be afraid, no, uncomfortable, with moving through space?

The grain barge had its own drive thrusters, and the pair of craft pivoted smartly in space around their common center of gravity. The tug whipped around on the outside at a brisk speed. Centering on the barge's center of weight, the tug's drives lit up in massive eruptions of plasma fire, changing course to insert into the proper parking orbital path.

The captain agreed with his crew: everyone aboard *The BARGE* was grateful he had had splurged on expensive gravity chairs and lounges. They helped mitigate the crushing effects of high, thrust-simulated gravity, and the Coriolis effect of the pivoting moves, as the powerful thrusters slowed the massive grain barge at a four G pace.

The decks, laid out like stacked floors in a building, allowed for normal movement as long as the drives were accelerating or decelerating the ship at about 1 G. The normal arrangement across the galaxy, the captain thought. This allowed crew and cargo to stay put without effort during thrust maneuvers.

Settings locked into his board, the lad turned to the old man with a cocky grin. "Sensei. It's your move."

"Hai. Patience, young one. I have prepared my next several moves once again," His light brown eyes shifted over to a small holo-projector to the port side of them both. A small holographic board of glowing lights appeared.

Atop a field of square spaces numerous tiles decorated with myriad icons were arrayed in a terraced pattern. Sensei's glance moved the games holographic "hand" over to interact with one of the pieces, his virtual touch highlighting it in a grey shade. He "touched" another of the pieces, matching the tree-shaped green calligraphy pattern of the first.

The two pieces disappeared from the board, revealing more tiles below. Sensei's nimble eyes whisked the hand about swiftly, matching and discarding tiles. Finally stumped to find a match, he grunted his approval and nodded at the youth.

"Nice play, Sensei." The young man sent the hand reaching, finding a match, two tiles which were barely showing over the perspective edge of the pile.

Sensei grunted, "hrmm."

Ceres continued in a brisk fashion, matching tiles, sometimes pausing to consider taking an easy match or to await a better match to reveal more tiles below. A glowing timer on the virtual board counted down between his choices. Finally the scattered remains were all unlocked and the board flashed a green color, indicating an imminent victory for the younger contestant.

Seeing no chance for victory, the elder man fought the high gravity to wave his hand near the controls, sweeping the game away and conceding defeat. "It is a sign of wisdom when one knows to withdraw from the battlefield while still alive to learn from one's defeat. Well played." He bowed his upper body and head towards the victorious boy.

"Thank you. You played well, Sensei," The youth rotated his chair all the way around and imitated the elder man's rendition of a polite seated bow. Being merely a board game, and considering the environment' four-G's, such minimal display of the Asianan customs of respect were acceptable.

"Onscreen!" growled the captain's gravelly voice.

"Aft view onscreen, sir," replied the youngster of the crew, even as he resettled back in his chair, whipped it aright, and flipped on the huge view screen all in the same motion.

Stuck to the aft or side of huge starships as a tug often was, the crew relied upon huge display screens to the sides and overhead to provide one central view of forward progress to the entire crew at once. These yielded reliable, standard views regardless of thrust-gravity and the changing orientation of their seats.

The shared MeTR channels of information added layers to this, plus their individual station's readouts, and the central holo-display of the space environment surrounding the linked ships. Different admirals and captains were free to choose different layouts, configurations, and priorities of their command and crew displays. Not all captains—and crew—could handle the plethora of information sources fluidly.

"Looks to be the exact time for docking maneuvers, sir." The controls waggled in the young hands, the massive pair of ships shuddering in response. The main plasma drives winked off, which ended the solar fountains' eruptions.

Maneuver thrusters all about each craft spat bursts of white flames, initiating a graceful pirouette. The massive wormlike barge and its large parasite, the tug, moved fluidly like a pool diver in the Olympics.

Stopping smartly the ponderous ships aligned perfectly with the screen's virtual corridor of lights demarking their path toward final docking with number 11.

"I doubt the computer would do any better and would certainly have taken all days' time for safety measures. Just try to *appear* you are doing your job when we're approaching a metal city the size of an island, okay, son?"

"Certainly, sir. You are the Captain, Captain Tarsis, sir! Also owner, operator, employer, boss man—"

"All right, all right, smart aft!" Tarsis cut him off, "Quit talking about it, and *do* continue to show off while docking this thing already."

"No," interjected the Sensei, rising to a wide stance. "Ceres, you will carefully and correctly dock this ship in the most safe, efficient and profitable manner for your employer. Then you will apologize to your Captain for showing off while his ship and all of our lives were approaching danger."

A trace of red crossing his face, Ceres began "I'm s—"

"Apologize later. Pilot now."

"Yes, Sensei."

The older man turned and bowed towards the captain's station. "Captain Tarsis, I apologize for distracting your pilot at an important time."

Meanwhile behind them in the view screen and all the clear ports of the bridge, the framework of the huge space station slowly crept past in the total silence of space. Parts of the framework were alternately bathed in glaring white starlight or veiled in impenetrable darkness.

Some areas were lit by massive floodlights washing down a long expanse of modules and hangers, racks of thousands of containers, and the robotic pickers which shuffled them. Searchlights reached out alongside tractor emitters, focusing on the oncoming bulging barge, taking it into control of the magnetic tractor beams.

"Not a problem, Sensei Aramada. You two have only been aboard a few weeks now since the attack on your dojo. We're still trying to learn how to operate together as an efficient crew. I have been through this a hundred times with every new bridge crew I've ever flown with.

"And between you and me," he dropped his voice lower in collusion with the Sensei, "that kid could park this barge forwards or sideways, if I let him." He sat back into his grav chair. "With him driving there was plenty of time for maneuvers. Not a problem."

The Sensei bowed in closure of the matter, to which Tarsis responded with a crisp military salute.

* * *

Racine 4, Orbital Station 3
2515/12/07/2015

"Try them again, Med. We'll be heading to sleep cycle and ready for that barge to be filled up with berry corn by tomorrow. Wish they had been ready for us to do a hot swap. And it's odd that a port doesn't want to collect its fees."

"Captain, party of port agents coming up the boarding ramp now," lilted from the bridge's vocasters. For a male Tenublian, thought Ceres, Med did not know how to make his voice sound masculine to Solman ears. The wild colors didn't help either.

On the large screen appeared a cam-shot of the boarding area not far behind the bridge level. Six mercenary looking men with fat-lensed laser carbines at the ready marched down the station's access tube. Two of them stopped and took up positions just inside the demarcation line between the ship and station.

Tarsis erupted out of his grav-chair and raced off towards the access deck. "Everyone stay put!"

Of course, Ceres felt exempted from this order and ran off after his uncle. Sensei followed his young charge.

"What is going on?" demanded Tarsis of the four mercs. They were pounding boots up the main portside corridor, coming forward from the main airlock.

Not bothering to stop, the lead merc crabbed to the right but was cut off by Captain Tarsis, so the merc passed on the left and continued on towards the bridge. He stopped when blocked by both Ceres and Sensei, just outside the bridge's pressure hatch.

"Step aside, all crew! If you interfere with our orders you *will* be fired upon." His eyes shifted from the teen, to over Ceres' shoulder to Sensei behind him.

"We don't want any trouble here," called out the fuming Tarsis from right behind the merc. The captain caught the eye of the Sensei and shook his head slowly.

"Let's see those orders!" Tarsis was the kind of man who would never think himself surrounded, but rather the enemy had placed themselves all within his arm's reach. One of his key attributes was the ability to keep his head and find solutions to dire situations, which men of lesser restraint often missed. Tarsis decided, today Ceres would learn the difference between a "hasty reaction" and a "measured response" from observing his uncle.

The leader of the merc boarding party thrust forward a datapad and began reciting the basics even as Tarsis scanned at a blistering pace. The menagerie of crew and mercs shuffled towards the bridge as the captain read silently the legal details the merc was summarizing. "Your ship's been impounded for failure to report in to port authorities, failure to report your cargo, failure to pay standard and customary port fees—"

"Now just a millisecond here," Tarsis interjected. "We have been hailing the port since before we locked into the frame! We were in comms with them on the docking channel!"

"Never made contact. Never answered the Port's hails. Never sent a crewer down. It's too late now." Standing in the center of the bridge, his armed party surrounding the three human crewmembers present and standing off a bit from Med, the merc pulled himself upright. The four were obviously preparing for a fight as their weapon safeties clicked and they shouldered their carbines. "Your vessel is hereby impounded on orders of Judge Francolin, legal overseer of the Port of Racine."

Captain Tarsis looked carefully into the eyes of the young Ceres then up to Sensei. Again he shook his head very slowly, almost imperceptibly from side to side, then a miniscule smirk crept into his lips, mirth into his eyes.

The old spacefarer sighed deeply, shrugged and threw up his tanned hands. "Well I suppose there's nothing to do but go pay the fees and fines and get us untangled, boys." He turned back halfway towards the aft, towards the docking area, but caught himself.

"Hey wait a minute. There are a number of security measures aboard. I would not want to add manslaughter charges if you guys get vaporized accidentally while just doing your jobs. I had better turn some things off."

At the word "vaporized" the mercs all glanced at each other.

"Like here," went on the captain, "let me turn this containment field off so you don't get frozen on the bridge." He made a big show of slowly and carefully flipping up an anonymous switch cover on a nearby console and flipping it to its opposite setting. Nothing happened. One of the mercs breathed out, "whew."

Of course Ceres knew exactly what that switch was, the internal recorder. Adding the holocam's feed to that from the crews MeTR input into the logs and black boxes, it was perfectly harmless until these goons went to trial somewhere someday.

"Everybody stay calm and cooperate, crew," Tarsis said. "We're going to do this right and take care of our business like regular professionals here. So I'm going to switch off the security systems for these guards, secure the valuables and personals and such, and then we'll go to the port office and pay our fines, okay?"

Captain Tarsis made a point of eye contact with each of his crew during his speech. They seemed to play along with whatever line he was reeling out. Ceres noted his uncle, educated in the Academy no less, had changed to affecting conjunctions in a crustier version of his own voice.

Via the bridge communications group, via his MeTR Ceres thought, *"More salt in the ol' dog, eh, Cap'n?"*

"Hush lad. Everybody go along!"

Ceres realized, late, there was a chance the enemy monitored their comm channels. That is probably why Uncle Manny used other means to get his point across to the crew. Still so much to learn from the old man.

"Valuables?" asked the apparent leader of the mercs. "Like what?"

"Well, our personal effects and property which are none of your concern, my fine port authority friend," he smoothly retorted.

"Listen!" shouted back the merc, menace instantly in his voice. "I don't think you fully grasp the situation here." He stepped closer and loomed over the captain threateningly. Ceres imagined three different ways to attack him, and the second nearest merc.

"If you are found to resist, deadly force is authorized." The merc turned his head towards the apparent cabin boy, chuckled then swaggered cockily closer to Ceres. "You don't want your precious crew getting the vac treatment; you better give us something to make it worth our while!"

Ceres got the feeling it was not the first time this guy tried to muscle a bribe or something out of a helpless crew. *Come on, loud mouth.* Ceres thought, his teeth grimacing, looking like a cocky grin. *You wouldn't last long on this bridge. You have no idea who you're surrounded by!*

Captain Tarsis' body gave a little defeated slump. He hung his head and began to sway a bit. His hand started a nervous tremor. Looking up with moisture in his eyes he appealed, "I'm afraid I am not the man I used to be, boys," he all but whimpered. "Would you mind if an old man calmed his nerves. I've got a couple of Honey Blondes stashed in my quarters."

Again the mercs perked up upon hearing this, eyes widening and tongues licking their lips. "You have some Venusian? We haven't seen that make its way out to this end of the Carina Arm in years." They looked between each other and raised eyebrows, nodding each in turn.

"Yeah," another merc chimed in, "And it was so expensive you could only afford a single swallow. Oh how I'd love another taste of that!"

"Okay, Grandpa, we'll let you calm your nerves if you open up that stash," grinned the lead merc. He canted his head back towards the corridor to indicate it was time to go.

* * *

"Okay, behind this panel here is a corridor," croaked the nervous old Captain, shoulders filling the access way between the Captain's quarters and his private personal.

"It's around here somewhere, ah, here we go." The old man reached up and pushed a rivet near the top of the wall. At least that is what it appeared. Having lived most of his life aboard this vessel, Ceres knew that his uncle had used his MeTR to command the hatch open. The Mercs were easily fooled by the charades, one of them staring at that spot as if to memorize it for his future use.

The whole wall plate rose up quietly into a recess. Auto-lights switched on, and the passage beyond lit up. It was a bot closet, complete with housekeeping bot, folded appendages held aloft for mobility.

"Swisher, get out of there! Go clean the head for an hour," ordered Captain Tarsis. The bot whirred to life and rolled off between the assembled men. All were prying to see what was ahead of them, anticipating the sweet taste of a honey blonde.

Another hidden switch and the back panel of the bot closet slid up. Behind this lay yet another lit corridor, three meters then a turn, around which they could not see. Tarsis led the way.

Ceres almost laughed aloud, thinking of it as a tour of secret halls in a wealthy person's house. Many capital cities maintained a standard of opulence above the rest of their planet, a show of power and authority, a higher level of living to go along with governance over the people. In these places, inevitably, the ruling class of whatever system of governance is employed, goes somewhere for fine dining. Five star quality foods and beverages need an appropriate atmosphere to be properly appreciated, such a level of luxury that corresponds with the best food available anywhere.

Such places pale in comparison to Captain Tarsis' private mess, concealed behind the unassuming bot closet, behind his quarters, in the middle of his rugged looking utility tug. There is a difference between "rich" and wealthy. Hidden here was one of the wealthiest small rooms in the galaxy.

Rare wood panels with reddish hues and a warm-rubbed sheen glowed in the bright lighting, revealing a room much larger than the men imagined. Reminiscent of a paradise planet, the tropical fragrances filled their senses. Gleaming silver, a waitbot with a humanoid torso and classic greek mask for a faceplate, polished up a crystal shot glass. It poured a thin honey-yellow liquid from a clear bottle with a golden label upon it, Tarsis' usual order upon entry to his private haven from the galaxy, as Ceres knew.

Golden embellishments glittered on every rare piece of furniture and fixture in the room. Crystals and gems making up elaborate chandeliers sparkled with life from subtle lums made to move deftly among them. The floor was a sharp contrast between inlaid panels of deep yellow and dark blue tiles. Every part of every surface in the place was lit with hundreds of small, soft, embedded lights. Crisp and clean, polished and bright, the place sparkled and glowed.

Looking deeper, fossilized trilobites and ammonites raised up out of every stone of the fireplace hearth. The paintings on the wall evoked old masters of Earth brushed hundreds, maybe thousands of years prior.

La Giaconda and the Flying Machine's sketched plans by Davinci were now over 1000 years old. The Star of India, which had helped bankroll the Royal Family's founding of the colony of New Olde London, hung at the center of the chandelier illuminating the posh room, casting speculation as to the authenticity of the rest of the hundred suspended gems.

The dark expressionist flocks of ravens framing a womanly tree of life by the "American Van Gogh," Stefan Duncan, had just turned 500. Faberge' eggs seemed to be a favorite collectable of the old captain, so many rested securely behind display cases fixed to the walls.

The stone countertop of the bar, from Australia, was carved from the oldest rock discovered from early Earth at 4.4 Billion years old. On a ship that may be worth a few million dollari, this room alone had to be worth more. Far, far more.

Their jaws all agape, finally one of the mercs emitted a low whistle. Eyes sparkling with greed they gazed back and forth as Tarsis moved behind the bar and lined up shot glasses. Adding to the bottle started by the waitbot, Tarsis opened a safe-like compartment and pulled a matching full bottle from it.

The yellow honey flowed forth into the half-dozen shot glasses, which the barbot then deftly whisked across the ancient stone bar with the same stylish flare with which a professional dealer would send forth cards. The glasses slid to a stop on the counter in front of each high barstool.

Mesmerized, the mercs took their seats at the bar, licking their lips in anticipation. "Prints. Replicas, all," Tarsis casually tossed off, seeing the men fixated on the famous smiling lady. They nodded, laughed, and relaxed onto their stools.

It made no sense to common men to bring original, priceless works out into harm's way in the galaxy, Ceres thought. Of course, as heir to the greatest fortune of all time, Tarsis did not orbit within the same solar system as normal men. Ceres knew Uncle Tarsis was deceiving the enemy.

Taking up his crystal shot glass, Captain Tarsis led them in his best rendition of the most famous Scottish drinking toast, "May the best ye hae ivver seen, be the warst ye'll ivver see." Then he downed the honey liquid in a flourish with a single great gulp.

The men all answered in kind and followed suit, young Ceres excluded, of course. Some of the mercs made a great noise of gasping, losing their breath from the hard liquor, others merely inhaled crisply.

"Smooooothhh!" remarked the chief of the mercs. He wiped his armor bracer across his lips and smacked the shot glass down, in the direction of the captain, demanding another round in the traditional manner of men who have just had their breath taken away by the first round of a hard beverage. The barbot filled shots again and again.

Tarsis joined the men on the outside of the bar, lifting his glass repeatedly along with them. The celebration of this fine luxury beverage went on for some time.

At long last there was but one small dram of the tasty "Honey Blonde" at the bottom of the second empty bottle. Tarsis walked back around the bar, facing the Mercs. He made a show of carefully pouring the precious Scotch into his shot glass, lifted it and slowly tipped it into his mouth. Savoring the sweet smoothness he smiled genially at the mercs, lifting his empty glass in salute.

"Now," is all Captain Tarsis said. White tentacles snaked through and around their armor, draping across the merc's necks like feathery boas at a New Vegas floor show. Medusa had squeezed his large, flexible body through the tight passages and floated like a ghost into the room behind them.

They immediately fell under the control of the alien's mindlink ability, overwhelmed by the power of his brain, a collective of six lobes. Marched placidly aft, towards the exit hatch, the mercenaries all dropped their weapons as Med commanded along the way.

* * *

"Skritter! Stop!" shouted the young male voice from inside the starship. The guards just outside the ship turned inwards, seeing a blonde haired lanky boy running past between them. "Stop! You're out of bounds! Running off the ship is out of bounds!" the boy protested, to whom was not apparent to the men.

The mercenary port guards unslung their carbine weapons and turned towards the youth as he moved up the gangway tube. The blonde boy stopped, bent down, then stood erect with a spider-shaped bot in his hands, turning his body back towards the ship.

"Hold it right there!" shouted one of the merc guards, sighting in on the youth. "No one is allowed on or off without Port escort!" Ceres' gaze shot up at the guards, a look of shock and fear on his face. He dropped the bot, which landed nimbly on the deck. Ceres thrust his hands upwards, in imitation of a hijack victim of the old galactic frontier holovideos.

"I-I-I was just playing t-tag with m-m-my bot here," whimpered the lad, eyes wide and lip quivering with fright.

One guard snapped his carbine back to order arms, tight lipped. He must have realized their overreaction, aiming at a youth at play. Ceres' ploy intended this response.

"Get back aboard!" ordered the harsh voice of the other guard.

"Kindly rephrase that in a more polite request! He is but a young boy," the deep, distinctively Asianan voice ordered from within the access hatch. Sensei was standing within arm's reach behind the guard who had spoken roughly to Ceres. Fingers steepled together, the stern look on his face glowered at the guard who had been harsh to his star pupil.

Both guards spun on their heels, surprised looks on their faces showing that the wizened old man had succeeded in sneaking up on them. The closer guard on the left seemed irritated that he was vulnerable with a potential threat appearing so close to him. He swung his carbine along with his body to aim it at the white-haired, Asianan man at his elbow.

Sensei moved his right hand mere inches in his own defense. The first two fingers opened into a blade, which intercepted the barrel of the merc's carbine and prevented its traversing to point at the old master. "Calm yourself," he softly instructed. "One who looks to start a battle, often succeeds."

The other guard turned to bring his weapon to bear on the old man, opening his mouth to shout, but he failed to do either. Instead, his body convulsed in spasms and twitching, blue waves of electrical energy rolling up and down his body. He collapsed to the deck, a Leyden round attached to his shoulder, releasing his weapon to clatter across the tritanium deck plates. Ceres stood over him wielding a small air pistol and a big grin.

The harsh guard near Sensei coiled his muscles to react, now caught between dual threats. Sensei's left elbow and forearm shot upwards, then his hand sliced forward, the calloused fingers flattened into a steel blade, hardened by years of striking wooden boards, buckets of sand, and unfortunate enemies. He chopped the guard in the side of the neck, where the trapezius nerve bundle hid beneath the skin.

147

The guard instantly collapsed, stunned unconscious by the precise blow. Sensei lowered him gently to the deck plate, holding the lapel of the mercenary's armored vest with the hand that had just struck him.

The master's right hand that had blocked the weapon's swing now held it firmly by the barrel. The entire instant fight was silent on Sensei's side of the little docking tube.

"Next time," admonished Sensei of his young student, "grasp their weapon to minimize noise. In shinobi missions, we strive for silence, my pupil. Ideally the enemy should not know we were present until the mission is already a success, and we are safely home."

"Yes, Sensei," Ceres bowed respectfully and perfectly, then dropped to one knee to address the robot. "Okay, Skritter, go upstream my worm program into the barge. Goodbye, little friend. We can't wait for you!"

The bot swiftly crabbed its way up the hull, its small black body hiding in the shadows.

* * *

A-Valhalla, Ceres' private domes
2525/7/14/2011

"So I programmed the grain barge to open its cargo hatches," Ceres continued his story. "The ocean-seeds poured out and enveloped the platform, which provided a station emergency to cover our escape."

"Wait, what about the guards?" Serenity held her arms crossed over her chest, a skeptical wrinkle on her lips.

"We dragged them to an escape launch and piled them in. Uncle Manny cold-started the drives. Our first mate, Mr. Riverwind, had been a Special Forces operator before his leg got too wounded for ground pounding. My uncle brought him aboard not long before I left the school. Mr. R. and the others hid around the rear of the ship while we dealt with the mercs. So he shot out the docking tractor beams and we lit the dark on fire making for deep space!

"Weeks later the judge, the port master and the boss of the Longshoreman's Union were implicated in a conspiracy to overthrow the local government. Sensei and uncle had all kinds of smug looks on their faces and they would not comment on where exactly Sensei had been on his weeks' vacation. But he returned Skritter to me, so I am sure."

Chapter 19
The Seduction of Ceres

A-Valhalla, Starship Hangers
2525/7/15/0613

"Hey blonde boy. Duck!" Ceres' workout was interrupted. While he ran down the equator of the asteroid through the ring of hangers, Ka'ra yelled out her warning just a second before she would have flown into him.

Ceres dove to the ground, rolled under and back upright as the white skycycle drifted overhead, the albino girl lazily pushing pedals.

"Get one, catch up!" she taunted, soaring away, up towards the energy screens and clamshell hanger hatches overhead.

He fetched a nearby skycycle, from some pirates who were fans of his, preparing to start early, working on their ships. The young pilot who owned it had carried it in his cargo pocket, folded down into its compact form. Ceres thought the design was a simpler form than the common skycars found throughout the galaxy, often carried by commuters who needed transportation to and from their telepod stations at either end of their travels. The gangly bike folded out to full size in seconds.

He ground hard on the pedals in the highest gears, rushing to catch up with the drifting dandelion speed of Ka'ra. To brake hard and match her lazy pace Ceres banked and looped high over her.

One tip of his flyers' thin albatross wings brushed the underside of the massive hatch doors. He barrel rolled and dove back down like the slowest and lightest dogfighter of all time, dropping into formation beside her.

"Whoo, that was close! Are you always the daredevil?" Ka'ra asked. Lolling along at such slow speed, three meters over the deck and just three meters apart, it was as easy for them to speak as if they were pedaling along a ground bike trail next to each other.

"Life is cheap," Ceres said, easily matching Ka'ra's speed. "So many ways to die in this galaxy and God is not telling us how or when. So we might as well enjoy the thrills of a lifetime every day."

If I show you I am not a boy, for example? he thought.

"Seems backwards," Ka'ra retorted. "Put your faith in a God who won't tell you what's coming in your own life? What to do?"

"Oh, He does," Ceres said. "You have to know how to listen. First, you have to show up, or you will miss it. In Church. A line in a guitar hymn. A saying from today's Bible reading. A message from a sermon. An inspired answer to prayer. Even the words of wise council from fellow Godly people.

"You never know when it is going to come, so you have to go every week, read the book every day, and pray every minute. At least that is what my Mother used to say." *Lately, I am not practicing what I preach,* he thought with remorse.

Growing up in space, visiting planets, asteroids, space stations of all kinds, Ceres had long ago figured out the trick to low-grav glidebikes. They were constantly falling.

As the floor of the hanger strip constantly fell away under them, the gliders were not really flying so much as gliding downward in an endless decent through the light gravity well of the asteroid. With double, albatross-like wings on these ultralight bikes, that left a lot of lift for soaring.

In the low gravity of the asteroid, one pair of short wings easily held the bike aloft, while the other pair of wings flapped for thrust. Levers pushed down by the feet flapped the wings. Standard bicycle wheels helped when accelerating for takeoff, and landing. A crossed, fishlike tail gave stability and flexed for turning as well.

Ka'ra pulled up, dipped for speed, then seemed to try to take Ceres' wings off as she swept ahead. Ceres rolled away, swooped low and picked up a little speed, enjoying the rush as the hanger floor whipped past at close range.

The improvised race was on, to pass through the next inter-lock between hanger bays. Athletic Ceres ground away at his pedals again and easily pulled away from her. Once through, he coasted so she could catch up.

"You're in pretty good shape," Ka'ra shouted after him. "I was wondering if you kept fit after Grav-ball. Now we know."

"All it takes is about an hour of hard work each day," he answered, choosing to not mention his added martial arts work. "Without it, zero or low-G living would rob me of muscles I need just to stand up on higher grav worlds. Most spacers work hard to stay fit."

Ceres kept his lead in their linear flying formation, making it easier to slip through the frequent interlock hatches separating the endless series of hangers belting the length of the asteroid. "I want to get it done before anyone comes out here to work." He kept turning his head to call back to Ka'ra.

"Yeah, I come out early to fly, too," she said. "I'll bet these rogues wouldn't like having their heads taken off as they load missiles."

"Ha hah. Yeah," he shot her a glance. "That might slow my rise to the top Jarl's position."

"Probably," she agreed. "But you're going to have to get past me to get there. Or work out some kind of," her voice deepened perceptibly, "mutually beneficial political arrangement?" She shot a pointed glance at him.

After stowing the skycycles, they walked the hanger belt to cool down.

"You want that?" Ka'ra asked Ceres. "To run raids and take over for your father someday? Ascend from prince to king?"

"I can see forward, how to work that out over time," Ceres said. "My father might like to retire someday, settle in comfort, live an easier life, without all the planning, raiding, backstabbing to worry about."

"What if he could be, 'persuaded', sooner?" Her inflection implied the word was a euphemism. "As prince, and a very famous and popular one at that—" she stopped walking, and he turned back to face her.

Looking him up and down appraisingly, Ka'ra continued, "A case could be made for the heir apparent. You might need friends. Allies?"

I've got friends, family and allies, lady. I don't recall you bein' invited to our last barbecue. Ceres activated his auto-stim unit, injecting the medic's ACH inhibiter directly into his veins. He was not going to be caught twice by Ka'ra's chemical manipulations.

"People with influence over most of the gang, a—" her voice dropped to a low sultry purr. "—special friend to watch your back. One who knows who to watch out for, those who would need ... elimination, before they try to eliminate *you*, hypothetically."

"Yes," Ceres said softly, taking a half step forward. "I'll bet it would be good to be close to such a person. Keep them nearby?" He noted how she licked her lips when she watched him talk. He angled his head, then smiled when she angled hers opposite, as if aligned to kiss.

"Yes, you would want to keep such a friend within your sight," she stepped inside his arm's reach again, like she had the first day they met.

"Very close," he answered, nodding as if mulling her suggestion. "If only I knew who to trust." She leaned her head nearer still. Ceres drew a deep breath. They looked into each other's eyes.

After you kidnapped me? My father excused it as for my own protection, but I still hold it against you. Then this conversation about killing my father and taking over the pirates at my side? I will never trust you. You're not a Valkyrie, you're a demon with long eyelashes. Succubus!

From a couple of inches apart, Ceres said "Ka'ra, thank you very no thank you. I just got here. I am not about to push my father out the airlock. I hardly know him well enough to hate him that much." After the horrific arcology attack he had witnessed, Ceres was not sure that was true.

Ka'ra took in a deep breath, drew her shoulders up, and put her hands on her hips, biting her lip. "I'll let him know. I'm sure he'll be pleased to hear that," she smiled.

"My techniques are slipping. My parathion is not working on him," she transmitted one way to Tyrian. *"At least he is unwilling to knife you in the back, for now."*

"Now, what about the wolf pack? You have *already* started making friends, I hear?" Ka'ra giggled and grinned.

"I will think about your kind offer to guide me through the den," his head tilted in thought. "Making friends and allies, to counter the enemies. People do tend to love me or hate me." He shrugged with a sheepish grin.

"More stick," Tyrian replied in her head. *"Less carrot dipped in honey."*

"Jaeger must be sore, hmm?" Ceres laughed at his own two-sided joke. "Well, the men admitted they have a wolf pack mindset. Wolves fight for position, rank among the pack. I guess you can't just knock down the alpha wolf and slip away unscathed?"

"You need close friends, not close enemies," Ka'ra confirmed. "The pack will eat you alive and space your bones, or love you, follow you, forever."

"Give me a few days to think while I finish my ship," Ceres said. "With your help, I think I will fight my way up fast." Ceres winked conspiratorially at her along with his grin and walked away, towards the nearest lift tube.

"You are either with us or we toss you overboard, pretty Daddy's boy or not!" Ka'ra thought at his back as Ceres walked away from her.

"There is no 'slipping away unscathed' here, my little prince," Tyrian agreed with her. *"Let your 'God' tell you about that!"*

* * *

A-Valhalla, Ceres' private domes
2525/7/15/07010

Sweat dripping from his nose, Ceres barged through the hatch to his dome. "Oh, excuse me." He stopped short when he saw Serenity kneeling among the furniture, her hands clasped. *The peaceful look on her face. Wow. She really lives up to her name.*

Presently Serenity crossed herself and stood up, coming to Ceres at the entryway where he stood watching. She flowed gracefully across the room to him, handing him a towel.

He saw firsthand, the results of the tailor's efforts to cover more of her skin with fabric. He did not think this outfit would help his dilemma one bit. His mouth started watering, and he recognized the early stages of his arousal.

"Do you like?" Serenity smiled, turning a pirouette similar to the presentation of the women the day before, and then held his eyes. She wore a form-fitting cat suit, made of the sheer material that had once draped the canopy bed. Its current color setting displayed a tiger-stripe pattern, enhancing the cut.

"I—I—" he stammered, struggling. "It is very attractive, as are you, but, '*Love,*' as you say, this does not help me look at you chastely! I don't know that it will help any of the other men aboard this rock, either."

"Be careful what you wish for," Serenity quoted him, then pulled forth swaths of material attached behind her, a gauzy train of wing panels. She wrapped layers around herself and tucked the ends in, modesty restored.

"You just might get it," Ceres finished the quote for her. "Whew. That seamstress is amazing!" He smiled. "Of course, she has a fantastic model to work with." His smile beamed brighter.

Serenity smiled demurely and half-curtseyed. "Thank you, sir. Welcome home."

"Oh! I did not mean to interrupt your praying," he remembered. Please excuse me."

"You di'nt. I was covering *you* in prayer." She smiled up at him, turned and led him to the auto-kitchenette in the adjoining dome of the suite. The kitchen's arms swung to life, fixing their first meal of the day.

Meanwhile Ceres remembered what 'covering you in prayer' meant. Praying over someone who is in a dilemma, for spiritual coverage and aid. His mother had done that often when she was around. "I tried to work out early enough to be back before Dooms' guards delivered you here," he said.

"Yes, I have followed your mind along on your routine," Serenity confessed. "Every day you start with exercise; I start with prayer. Are you thankful for your life?" Her direct eye contact took him aback.

"Of course! I, of all people, have a lot to be thankful for." *She sure enjoys these sudden changes of subject.*

"Then, whom do you thank?"

Ceres blinked, thinking *She must have heard me bring this up with Ka'ra?*

"Who ultimately gave you all the gifts of your life? The gift *of* your life?"

"I see where you are going here," Ceres answered. "God, of course. I might say my family, the founders of my bloodline, my parents, my Sensei.

"Myself, even, for charting my own course and seeing it through. Ultimately though, it is my Higher Power. I owe thanks to God for my life." He smiled proudly at her, having given a Sunday school textbook answer.

"Does He know? When do you thank Him?" she smiled, then went about pulling their freshly made fastbreak shakes out of the robot's output coldbox. His consisted of vitamins, amino acids, proteins, simple carbs and fiber, the perfected blend for his post-workout needs, determined back in his Academy days and tweaked little since then. Her pre-workout fuel shake helped get her body ready for her Aerobi-dance routine to follow.

I don't think now is a wise time to tell her this reminds me of my mother? "You challenge me like no priest ever did before," Ceres answered, shaking his head at her. He dabbed more sweat off his bangs, accepted his drink from her.

"Well, maybe Father Tony," he amended. "I should introduce you two when we visit Atlantis someday. Oh the debates you'd have!" He chugged down half of his fastbreak.

"Did you just invite me on a date, to church?" Serenity asked. Her eyes gleamed and her mischievous smile erupted in laughter when Ceres snorted on his drink.

He coughed and laughed as well. *I'm dodging that one.* "So you think," he continued, "because I jump up in the morning and run off to, ah, 'run off,' that I'm not praying and thanking God for the opportunity? I do pray, you know, but I *was* just thinking this morning about how little I practice my faith. My mother would not be happy."

"I will guess that you occasionally slip it in between your other thoughts," Serenity asked. "Especially when tough situations come up. Am I right?" She raised an eyebrow at him and grinned, imitating his frequent expression.

That is twice today, two different women have given me that look, Ceres thought. *They use the body-language mirroring technique to build relatability with the other person. Ka'ra used it to draw me in to a false sense of closeness when she kidnapped me. At least I trust Serenity's motives.*

"Do you set aside a regular time early and late in the day to talk to God?" she pressed him. "Do you make it a priority, make Him a priority enough that He knows it? Do you talk to Him throughout the day?"

"I suppose *you* do," he said, "and you want me to join you on your prayer schedule?"

"If we *were* a couple, we would integrate our lifestyles more, on purpose," she answered. "I have my relationship with God, my church schedule, and you have yours. Ask your own wise counsel, ask your priests. Ask yourself!

"Examine your own conscience, Ceres. What do your thoughts dwell on all day every day? Your self-will, or God's will? You have to work this out for yourself."

She continued, "Maybe when you come out of the shower you are ready for some meaningful time with Him. Maybe you need to roll out of bed onto your knees. Maybe at night when you have exhausted the day, then your mind and soul are ready to listen. Maybe all of the above and more?"

He reviewed his morning, then thought back upon the days before. He realized he did not spend much prayer time aside from asking for God's help with his problems, and randomly and selfishly at that. He looked at the woman before him and appraised her anew. "You remind me of my mother." They both blushed. "She was the moral compass of my family. Now you're doing it."

"Is that a good thing or bad?" she asked tenderly.

"Good," Ceres answered. "I like it. You are asking me the hard questions that all add up to 'becoming the best version of myself,' which the Modern Proverbs says is the mission of every church member. You know I have failed miserably by objective moral standards, the Commandments, for example."

"Every saint is a sinner," she interjected.

"Yet you have not blinked when I answer with the hard truth about my past misdeeds. Are you still giving *me* a chance?"

"We shall see. There is more ground to cover, priorities." She dodged this line of questions as well. "How did your workout go?"

"Oh, that!" Ceres loudly clapped his hands together. She did not react. "I had a conversation with that albino gal, the one who kidnapped me."

"What side do you think Ka'ra is going to end up on?"

"I think she's going to come around. I don't trust her, but I think she likes me. I think we can save her from them." He smiled, willing it to happen.

"No, Ceres. I was listening in on your thoughts. I was able to receive hers, too, from here."

He opened his mouth in surprise. His voice dropped lower, "I have some alien friends since my youth who could do that, but not that well, that far away. You are better at that than I thought." He smiled, unsure whether he enjoyed her listening to his thoughts or not. *What did I say with Ka'ra that will get me in trouble now?*

"Telepathy can have unlimited range," she said, "once I have made some connection with the minds."

Ceres raised both eyebrows. This confirmed training his family had given him since his youth. He had considered it parental hysteria, warning that alien psionics could try to control his mind. Yet out here on the rim of the galaxy, he encountered a telepath who lived this truth.

"I'd rather not snoop in your head," Serenity offered, "but we are in a serious situation here. I am sleeping overnights in the slave pens, so I can feel out who is in their thrall, bought in on the pirate's side and would turn us in, and who we might be able to trust to help us, and who to try to save. I feel I have to eavesdrop, especially on conversations around you, since you have this blind spot.

"She was foolin' ya' the whole time, Ceres," Serenity continued. "She was playing you, seducing you. Either for them or for herself, she is lookin' for opportunities in *her* self-interest. Fear and power motivate 'er.

"She acts just loyal enough to both sides so she can end up with the winner, whichever that is. Be ya' blind to this?" Serenity raised an eyebrow again. Ceres looked sheepishly down at his feet. "You have a problem with women," she told him.

Ceres sighed. Serenity waited. He considered his past relationships with this new concept as a filter. "You may be right," he finally answered. "I'm still so upset that she so easily kidnapped me to bring me here. Considering my mother was kidnapped, by these pirates no less! Plus, I trained my whole life to be able to fight off any threat.

"She just put on a coy smile, sashayed up and took me out within seconds." They looked at each other for a moment. Serenity raised one eyebrow again. Ceres sighed in resignation. "You're right, you know! I have a weakness. A blind spot."

"All men do," Serenity turned away, towards the triangular crysteel panels of the dome. She shut her eyes as if to ward off a bad answer to her question. "Can ya' be sure, it in't a blonde spot?"

"Oh, good one. Look who's doing it now, trying to draw me in?" He walked closer and put his hands on her shoulders. He liked her soft strength under his hands, powerful yet gentle. He noticed her shudder, her rising goosebumps, her reactions to his touch.

"I just had a thought," Serenity said. Stiffening in alarm she turned and moved half a step back from him. "When I get so into listening to someone, maybe their thought patterns are getting into my head? Ka'ra's jealousy, her playing all sides against each other. What if I'm still not quite right because I was just attuning myself to her while I was listening in to her thoughts and yours?"

"Then I need to teach you those blocking techniques my family uses to protect from alien minds," he said. *Are you off your namesake "serene" game, due to sensing my passions for you?*

"Per'aps," she agreed, making him wonder if she replied to his words or his thoughts. She blew out a breath and forced herself to relax. "This will take some thought and experimentation with my abilities. Maybe later, when we're safely away from 'ere."

"I have been with too many women of all kinds, true," he admitted, back to her main point. "I do not think you will be able to let that go; you will hold it against me in the end, my past. But I care so much for you, I—"

"I think you are infatuated with me," Serenity said. "I think you are reacting to pheromones, which is normal for men and women of our age. An' in your 'ead, you're drawn to the unreachable."

"Because I don'na throw m'self at you like most women do,"she said, "it causes you to follow me like a puppy. Like any carnivore, you're drawn to chase what runs from you. I don'na think you love me. Not love me *true*. This is a grand physical attraction." Her arms raised wide to illustrate the words.

Uncomfortable, Ceres opened his mouth but said nothing, his head spinning. For the first time in his life he had no idea what to do or say to make progress with a woman. It was obvious to him that the dynamics of their relationship had changed inside this conversation. She was going to be in the lead from now on.

Serenity continued, "I think you *could* fall in love wi' me, for real, and I could you, the next step after the initial attractions are owned up to. We will need to go through the process, experience things together, talk about compatibilities and differences of interest, all while enjoying a proper romance. Let me tell ya' mister: without a proper romance first, there will be *no* proper marital passion t' follow, 'ear me now."

Serenity's hand gently turned his jaw so he faced her and Ceres gazed into her eyes. She forced herself to listen in to his private thoughts, despite her newfound hesitation.

He could not look into those sea green eyes without seeing his home planet of Ceres and smiling. She listened to his mind as he thought *It's amazing, this color. I've never seen it on a woman before. I wonder why her eyes change between darker and lighter shades of green?* He felt drawn into her eyes, warm and enveloping, familiar, like he had seen them in his dreams of home forever.

Serenity blinked up at him. *Those weren't all his thoughts.* It was a hard truth for her to accept, but she realized she was swept up in his emotions. She now knew not to trust her own feelings if they were influenced by his feelings, by those of the women who flirted with him like Ka'ra had earlier.

This was huge! It implied her whole escape strategy here had a major flaw. What if, in reading these pirates, she got caught up in their ways, lost herself to their behavior? She could end up as Ceres' concubine in truth if she did not preserve herself from his mind and heart as well as his body.

She would have to put a stop to this budding romance, until she could figure out how to share his thoughts without internalizing his feelings at the same time. "I know this sounds cold to you—" she said.

"You're the bluntest person I've met," Ceres cut in, "outside of the military—my uncle the admiral, for example. You seem to have turned relationship counselor on me, too," he said.

Her eyes softened, and she tilted her head to match the angle he hung his. "I can tell by the way your eyes just glazed over. I'm sorry. Right now, I need you to be my warrior, not a lover. This is not the time 'er place for a romance. We have yet to escape from over 3000 pirates 'ere.

"And we just may die trying, he interjected. "Or worse."

"I am grateful to you, Ceres. You nobly jumped in t'save me from Trok and did what you had'da do," she said in an even voice. "Thank you. Now, I need y'to put the idea of 'us' on hold for a wee bit, and focus on yer mission, soldier. Ya' still have a great, grand bit o' rescuing to do!"

"Kiss me for luck?" he grinned incorrigibly and raised his eyebrows.

"Yer gonna have to be patient, Mister." Serenity waggled her finger at him, grinning. She realized she had to learn a new skill, to separate other's thoughts from their emotions. For now, when she shared his thoughts she shared his feelings too. No way around it yet. She decided to go along with it until further notice. Maybe she could learn to control it, use it against him?

"Good fruits take time t'grow." Not against him, maybe, but to understand him, to help her redirect him to the greater goal?

With an encouraging smile, Serenity took a small sip from her fastbreak and carefully stepped away out of Ceres' arms reach, which seemed to break the tension between them. The energy she felt when close to him lingered as goosebumps on her skin. "It's hero time, love! Show me."

My head is spinning and I feel like negative G's in my guts. Why do I think I like it? Ceres' grin slipped into a determined frown as he reviewed their strategy and the tactics he planned to use to dig them out of the deep gravity well they were caught in. He marched for the hatch, loudly clapping his hands together.

Serenity giggled at his thoughts, flattered. Her head snapped up in surprise when he repeated her exclamation. "Hero time!"

* * *

A-Valhalla, Hanger Decks
2525/7/15/0825

Arms full of spare parts, Ceres strode into the lift sphere, an extra bounce in his step. He had collected items from three different hangers where he had scanned for spare parts during his morning workout. The lazy flight with Ka'ra had helped speed the search.

Crews gladly donated spare power pistons, so their famous and friendly prince could add some variable geometry control surfaces to his new ship. The craft's flex skin was old tech, but inside her, new actuators would give her new flight capabilities. Ceres' load of pistons stacked up in his arms like cordwood. Low gravity made him seem as strong as a superman.

The spherical lift was separated into two hemispheres. Flooring was all gravity plates, to help stabilize crew and cargo using the lift. They could stand upright on either side of the sphere, top or bottom, as needs and capacities required. The sphere even rolled to allow use of both halves at once, but he wouldn't need that feature today, just a low grav setting.

Various intersections in the tubes branched off to different parts of the asteroid, similar to the system used aboard space stations and the largest starships. The lift tubes saw much more traffic than the central walk-shaft piercing through the heart of the asteroid. Ceres interacted with it via voice commands, as his MeTR link had no command access yet. "Lift: 50% Grav," he commanded, easing the weight of his burden.

Women! Ceres thought, grinning. *One minute I'm being seduced by a she-devil, the next I'm in catechism then being shot down by the one I want. They've got my head spinning. I have to re-focus on the game plan here!*

Stopping at the next level, five pirates boarded the lift. Ceres noticed their eclectic collages of combat armor. Judged it to be gathered in pieces, probably looted off the bodies of fallen enemies? Side arms strapped to their hips and legs looked like a collection various energy weapons. He knew these would prevent shooting through the hulls of space vessels during aggressive boarding actions.

Ceres thought they only let their officers carry weapons aboard the asteroid. *Something's up?*

The first of them to shuffle in was Slim, as Ceres had dubbed Trok's tall and skinny lieutenant, followed by Farouk of the Viking darts game. Then in lumbered three other large men. Ceres recognized them from Thorsson's crew at the breakfast table the morning before. Nice crew of muscle, armed for a game of murder.

Today they all had cold eyes for Ceres, in contrast to the jovial breakfast and games of yesterday. Used to being greeted warmly across the galaxy by people he had never met before, let alone those he had, Ceres knew something was wrong.

His gloves creaked, fingers flexing. He looked forward to finally getting a good fight! The bloodlust he had felt, watching these pirates descend upon the helpless city, came flooding back, enflaming his veins, filling his lungs with every deep breath.

I'm going to have to raise my level of aggression and violence over theirs, otherwise hundreds will continue to bully me. Ceres' shifted his armload to balance on one arm, easy in the lowered gravity.

"Okay boys, before we play, who's the leader?" Ceres raised one hand and beamed a ridiculous jovial smile at the gang. He hoped this would work. They seemed taken aback that he would start a conversation with them.

"Who speaks for the group, who gets credit with the boss, eh?" The excessively tall, skinny one raised his hand. This was the first time he had been so close to him, but Ceres remembered the stretched, low-grav man had bullied Serenity the other day at the death-duel. *Long hair. Horn tats. Goat beard. Trying too hard?*

"Okay, Slim. What do you want?" Ceres stepped even closer until almost touching the skinny man. Ceres had to look upwards to confront him with eye contact. *I am sure I can snap this scrawny guy in half if I want to. And yes, I want to!*

"We're friends of Trok. The, the thick guy you melted the other day."

Goat breath too, whew. Ceres thought, "Yeah, about that—"

"He was a leader in our pack, Jarl Thorsson's squadron." Slim cut Ceres off. "We're here to settle up his old debts. He took a lot off the top from each of us. You took it all. We, we're taking our shares back."

"Sure, sure," Ceres agreed amiably. "We can get a bot to take an inventory, fill out a list and we'll sort it all out, no problems."

"I don't think you understand, little prince," Farouk cut in, his deep voice squeezing out between his gritted teeth. He stepped up, pressing his chest against Ceres' shoulder, his mouth centimeters from Ceres' ear.

"We've been here for years, fighting our share, bleeding our share, enjoying our share of the spoils." His head waggled to the side to punctuate the inflections of his voice. "Working our way up to enjoy more of the fruits of our blood and labors. That's how we're supposed to do it.

"Then, what? You just show up on your first day, start shooting and punching our leaders and take everything? No, sport, *we're* not cutting *you* in." His hand inched closer to his holster.

"Ah, so you all want his starship?" Ceres took one step back, away from Farouk. He opened his hand and made a gesture like an offering towards the other men. They looked back and forth between each other, confused looks on their faces.

This was not going according to plan? Good. Ceres was trying to throw them off their game plan and onto his.

"You want your own domes? Your own girl?" he noticed some eyes light up around him. "The girls huh? Oh yeeaahh. The giirrllss," Ceres drug out the word, then grinned and nodded his head, seeing a couple of them nod along with him.

"Okay guys, raise your hands if you're hoping for your share of alone time with that hot redhead? Huh? Huh?" His devilish grin flashed from face to face as his hand raised and waved at them. *Over my dead body would any of you get a shot, but that* is *why we're here, right?*

The pirates' sheepish grins faded as they seemed to realize they were being set up. None of them raised their hands. Slim was eying Ceres' fat disruptor pistol, stuck in his right hip holster.

Ceres turned back and forth, teasing them. "Oh come on, so you guys aren't normal men? Maybe we can work out a deal here. Come on, raise your hands if you want her?"

Two of them raised their hands, filled with their laser pistols. They grinned, aping Ceres' cocky grin.

"Ah, right. Play time!" Ceres' grin broadened. "Lift: Negative 2 G's." He activated the tractor beams in his boots and knelt quickly to the deck. Over Ceres' head, Farouk's rabbit punch whiffed by, then his fingers clawed for Ceres as the pirates all fell upwards. *Here we go. This should be fun.*

The two with their guns drawn both shot, but they were falling awkwardly up towards the ceiling, the unfamiliar reversed gravity pulling their aim high. One's shot hit a fellow pirate across from him, then they all crashed into the ceiling, pressed there by the two Earth gravity equivalents of thrust upwards from the lift's gravity plates.

Usually this feature helped secure or move heavy objects in and out of the lift system. Ceres exploited it to throw off the attack of these pirates. As they crashed upwards, Ceres' armload of power pistons was pushed upwards by the reversed gravity. He released them so the metal pistons fell on the men's heads and shoulders just as they started to gather their feet under them.

"Lift: one G and lock," Ceres commanded again. He rolled acrobatically to the edge of the circular lift, out of the way of the mass of men who once again fell hard on their heads, this time amid the power pistons. Much groaning accompanied the fallen pirates as Ceres drew his service issue plasma caster with his left hand.

He headshot the three burly pirates quickly as they staggered to their knees or thrashed dizzily on the deck. They should've worn helmets, but that would have been too obvious, right?

Farouk rolled to his feet, coiled up his legs and jumped at Ceres in a flying tackle. With years of practice and excellent reflexes, Ceres grabbed one of Farouk's wrists, spinning his body about quickly. Farouk, launched by the aikido move, flew past Ceres to smash headfirst into the wall.

He might have been knocked out, but Ceres guessed the guy's neck was broken from the way his body crumpled to the floor. Probably the best way to go. Ceres shot him anyway, down into the neck gap above his large plate of chest armor. The plasma fireball expanded to burn into Farouk's chest, finishing him off.

Three seconds to take out five guys? Not bad.

Slim rolled about, finally sitting up at the edge of the circular deck. Shaking his head did not help clear the cobwebs.

"Stop shaking your head!" Ceres ordered. He knew this was only adding to the random spinning of inner ear fluids and causing still more dizziness. "Nod your head straight up and down, no turning to the side!" Slim did as ordered. Ceres stood over him and waited for him to come out of his daze.

Slim tried to get his pistol out of his holster, still snapped down under its retention strap. He stopped when the hot barrel of Ceres' plasma caster singed the side of his face.

"Amateur," Ceres smirked and shook his head. He planned a test question to see if he should bother interrogating the weasily guy. "One chance. You *liked* bullying that redhead before my duel with your Captain, right?" Ceres accused.

"No, he made me—" Ceres shot him in the side of the head.

"Never lie to me again," Ceres ordered the grotesquely long corpse as it stilled.

The series of solar flares from the plasma pistol had brilliantly illuminated the sphere's panels, lighting up the darkness in the lift tubes. Four reports, a fifth had echoed through them, then the sphere slowed to stop at another deck. Ceres lifted a power piston off the floor. He stood there holding it, vacant look on his face, and surveyed the battlefield.

After-action report jargon crossed his mind, filling automatically into MeTR forms, vestigial from his recent duty billet. His military training and programming took over as the combat's adrenaline rush turned to downer effects working to chill Ceres' racing metabolism. Trembling, he tried to calm his aggressiveness while the cold fingers of remorse started to grasp at his heart.

How do I reconcile this with my faith? Ceres prayed silently in his head. *'Thou shall not murder' is how the ancient Talmud records God's Commandment. To kill for justice—is that, not, murder?*

Father David? How did you go from musician for the king to kill the giant at God's command, to great general of God's people, to become a wise, poetic king?

The hatch "Shiikked" open, curved triangular leaves of the sphere sliding apart on tracks like a pocket door. Ceres thought *Speaking of giants....*

Jarl Jaeger Thorsson wore surprise on his face, finding Ceres standing amid a pile of bodies, pools of blood, fluids, and fallen power pistons.

"You must have expected the opposite?" Ceres grinned cockily.

"Good," Jaeger growled. "This game, I get you all to myself." He grinned through his broken teeth and slapped the blade of his huge space axe.

It looked more than twice as large and heavy as the throwing axes from the day before. A heavy hammer provided back-weight, replacing the usual thick spike. The custom axe blade elongated downward in a large crescent.

Ceres taunted him with a broad smile. "Another playmate! I'll even the odds up a little for you." He dropped the piston on the deck between them, making a show of holstering his slender plasma caster, snapping its retention strap. "Best I can do. You got anybody good left to help you?"

His advantages are size, strength, and weight, Ceres thought. *Gee, is that all? He probably never fought anyone fast and nimble.*

"Let me shut that smart mouth of yours!" Jaeger yelled. He lurched forward, rowing the huge axe down past his leg then up over his shoulder. It came down towards Ceres' neck and shoulder, looking to chop its way down into his ribcage.

Ceres leaned back out of the axe's range and pushed off with the repulsors in his boots. He back-flipped to the edge of the lift, into a handstand, then pivoted on one hand, so he was facing inward.

Jaeger kept his axe swinging in the fluid motions of a brutish axe-kata as he stepped forward over the obstacles on the floor. He swung in sideways and low, towards Ceres' head.

Stretching his uniform sleeves, Ceres' bracers expanded to glowing rings around his wrists. Lifting his arms up to his sides, Ceres shot up to the ceiling of the lift. The tractor-pressor bracers and boots drew him up effortlessly to stand upside down on the center of the curved dome of the spherical lift.

Jaeger was surprised by this flying move, distracted enough that he rolled his foot on the power pistons strewn across the deck. Startled, he straightened up quickly, worried look on his face while losing track of his opponent mid-fight. He turned around just in time to get Ceres' boot right in his face.

Staggering back, nose bleeding, Thor slipped again on the power pistons and tripped over a fallen pirate's body. He fell flat on his huge back onto another corpse, crushing it.

Eyes wide, Jaeger sat up and quickly staggered to his feet, watching Ceres gently settle from ceiling to floor of the lift like a flying super hero in the holovids. Jaeger showed his experience by jumping up and landing hard, nodding his head down with his momentum. This helped stop the spinning in his head by stilling his inner ear fluids.

Ceres licked his drying lips then smiled, relishing the challenge of a worthy opponent. His adrenals were flowing again. Danger did that for him and he liked it.

"Let's clear the playroom, shall we?" The giant Jarl grinned. His space axe hummed and sparked with energy. He twisted the shaft, swung up and around into a powerful hammer blow on the deck. The shockwave bounced everything into the air—bodies, pistons, Ceres—sweeping it to the walls.

Ceres' head hit the curved wall of the lift sphere and his back slammed into it. It pitched him forward towards the deck. Eyes watering, dizzy, the last thing he saw before hitting the floor was the grimacing Jaeger, swinging his hammer back behind him, winding up for another crushing blow.

Ceres curled forward, landing shoulder first to roll across the deck and to the side. The energized hammer smashed down again next to him, the shockwave sending energy ripples across Ceres' jumpsuit. Futech fabric absorbed the energy surge to recharge its own threadlike power cells, protecting Ceres from electrical damage. Navy uniforms were designed as proof against several energy weapons commonly used in the galaxy

The force of the hammer blow sent Ceres into the edge of the lift, spinning on the stack of retracted armor plating layered like a turtle shell on his back. It would extend to cover Ceres' flexible space-grade suit on command. Drawing up his knees and arms, Ceres easily slid and spun across the deck on the graphene plates.

Jaeger grinned viciously, likely seeing the tables suddenly turned, his quarry downed and cornered. He hefted the axe, preparing a side slice down into the confined space where Ceres lay. It would be a hard blow to avoid.

Ceres' feet against the wall, he reached out with both arms, seeming to plead for a moment of respite. Jaeger laughed, swinging back for a mighty killing blow.

That looks familiar, Ceres thought. *His square jaw, towering over me. Was he personally there when mom was taken?*

Drawn across the floor by Ceres' tractor beams, the long body of Slim ran into Jarl Thorsson's legs and swept under him, taking him off his feet. He crashed on his back again, the weight of his fall knocking the breath out of his lungs. He recovered, but found Ceres standing across from him holding one of the power pistons upright like a spear.

Several blows to the head following a concussion? Ceres assessed. *Tactics limited to brute force via frontal assault. I bet I can goad him into charging again.*

"Nice dance moves, Jaeger," Ceres taunted the larger man. "But you're a bad partner. You're not very nimble on your feet."

Thor stood up, bruised but angered. He popped his back, stretched to full height, and hefted his axe.

"Yield?" Ceres asked, smirk on his face. "You're right, though. I *will* enjoy *Star Dragon* as my first flagship. I could use a good Lieutenant like you in, *my* wolfpack."

Jaeger's eyes lit up, and his nostrils flared.

Ceres dug deeper, pointing a finger and waggling it derisively. "You will have to behave, though, like a good doggy."

That set the Viking Jarl off. Thorsson yelled and swung the axe up overhead and down on Ceres with all his fury.

Moving one leg, Ceres' body pivoted aside from the axe's swing by a mere decimeter. Ceres swung the piston like a staff and slapped it across the side of the Jarl's head.

It rung with a metallic sound. A cut in Jaeger's skin showed dull and gleaming metal inside the bloody gash of the open wound.

"A cyborg! Excellent!" the observant Ceres said. He activated the force field shield in the right forearm of his uniform. Standard equipment for members of the Galactic military, Ceres only used it when needed. The uncoordinated sometimes maimed themselves with poorly wielded force fields. Ceres had never been accused of being clumsy.

Thorson grinned, swinging around again.

Ceres caught the long axe blade at an angle with the flat of the round force field, wincing as his elbow and shoulder tendons pulled under the heavy blow. He slid the axe, sparking energy versus energy across his shielded forearm before elbowing it aside. The axe tipped the shield close to cutting into Ceres' abs. Despite his elbow injury he thrust the end of the power piston at Jaeger's face.

Thorsson nodded his head forward to head-butt the end of the piston. "Clonngg," it rang dully, but both men were forced to step back, separated for a moment by the force of the blow. Jaeger seemed dazed.

The auto-stim pack embedded in Ceres' suit filled his veins with neurotonin, erasing his pain so he could move freely. Ceres waited to set up the opening he desired. The thrill of combat brought a grin to his face. *God knows I love to feel this alive.*

"You were lucky yesterday with that uppercut, boy!" Thorsson shouted. "That is the only soft spot in a tritanium skull implant, the brain within. Time for upgraded cushioning. I'll need new teeth too. But with your fortune as my claim, I will be able to afford them."

"I might as well knock some more teeth out of your face for fun then!" Ceres spat back. "You think you're tough enough to claim my Trillions? Molon, Labe!" he quoted the ancient Spartan's taunt meaning "come and take it." Ceres turned to a sideways stance, twirling his piston end over end.

Thor powered up the energy in his hammer until it vibrated and buzzed in the hemispherical space. He wound up for another crushing blow and marched forward, determined to test the power hammer against Ceres' tweaked arm supporting that shield.

Ceres triggered the power piston, firing it open directly into the Jarl's chest. With the back of the piston pushing off the lift's wall, the front shaft punched into Thorsson's upgraded metal ribs and knocked him off his feet.

It stuck between Jaeger's ribs like a spear, retracted into its compact length, and waggled over him as he wheezed. Ceres reached and pressed the control button again, extending the piston's shaft up to the ceiling, pinning Jarl Thorsson in place like a big blonde bug. He groaned and gasped for air as the piston bore down into him. That lung collapsed and filled with blood.

Ceres stepped over, calmly lifted Jaeger's custom heavy axe-hammer and knelt above the Jarl's head. Severely wounded, Jaeger started to come around from the stunning blow.

The lift slowed perceptibly, causing a light feeling of lightness which the gravity plates in the floor quickly adjusted for. The lift must be approaching a junction, or the end of the run, Ceres thought.

"I want to know, Jarl Jaeger Thorsson," Ceres asked calmly, "where is my mother?" Thorsson's eyes flitted up to Ceres's.

"I remember you," Ceres whispered, lifting a lock of Jaeger's long blond hair up where Thor could see it. "You came into that layover box, threw me and my mother around."

Thorsson turned his head away in the start of a denial, distracting from his arm's reach for Ceres' leg. Ceres dragged his shield edge across the deck, scoring a line in it. The electron-thin force field sliced Thorsson's arm off at the elbow, spouting a gush of blood.

Ceres' fist hammered down on Jaeger's forehead, bouncing his head off the deck and silencing his painful howl. The multiple concussions nearly caused Thorsson to black out. The lift shifting to the side as it transferred into a connecting branch tunnel didn't help Jaeger stay lucid.

"Yes," Ceres resumed his questioning. "Don't lie to me. I kicked you. You remember *that*, don't you? I do." Ceres grinned.

Jaeger nodded very slightly and closed his eyes, grimacing.

"Good man. Thank you for remembering," Ceres said. "You took my mother from me." Ceres' anger melted his smile into a grimace. "15 years! Is she here aboard Valhalla?" He struggled with his emotions, on the verge of answering the burning question that consumed most of his life.

Jaeger turned his head to the side.

"No, that would be too easy, right? Do you know where she is?"

Again Jaeger turned his head aside.

"Does my father know where she is?"

Jarl Thorsson's eyes popped open, making contact with Ceres's. He nodded his head slightly, wincing. A blood bubble escaped his lips.

"Thank you. Now, I am going to repay you for the kidnapping of my mother. Under Galactic law the penalty for kidnapping is death. You and your crew were convicted *in abstentia* 15 years ago. As the closest thing to a representative of the Galactic within hundreds of light years, I am going to carry out the sentence.

"In addition, I am going to show you how I feel, all these years, growing up without a mother, not knowing where she is, if she's alive or dead, or worse. But because you answered me with honor, I will make it quick."

Ceres plucked the cluster of data pins out of Thorsson's implant tray behind his ear and stabbed them all into Ceres' own tray. He launched a MeTR program, sifting through the datapins, searching for information about Ceres' mother, her kidnapping, and location.

Another prog scanned for intel on the Void Vikings and their base. Ceres had many unanswered questions and he just captured an intelligence motherlode. Meanwhile he turned back to the matter at hand, standing above Jaeger's head.

"Let's see if you were right earlier," Ceres grimly teased. "Let's just see if I can get through that thick skull of yours?" The vengeful part of him, originated in his bitterness over his mother's kidnapping and hidden well by years of training, flared up in moments like this. It caused his adrenaline to pump even harder, fueled by old, unvented anger.

Ceres stood, releasing a low animalistic growl. He swung the heavy axe around once slowly, hitting nothing, growling louder in his chest. Around again overhead, faster and then, Ceres, roaring with bloodlust, smashed the blade down powerfully into the Void Viking Jarl's brave, unblinking face.

The space axe's blade, buzzing with ultrasound vibrations and powered up with a full electrical charge, cleaved deep down into the face of Jaeger Thorsson. It cut through the cleft in his jaw, smashed down into the openings for the nose, and bit into the top of Thor's skull. The electrical discharge arched his huge body upwards, trembling, then it relaxed.

The sculpted metal ridge across Jaeger's tritanium brow was very strong though, and the axe did not deliver a killing blow into the brain. Jaeger howled in pain and sputtered blood out of his ruined face, flesh divided by his own heavy axe, burnt by electricity.

Ceres stepped around so he stood over the bleeding man. "Impressive. You were right. You looked death right in the eyes, too. I respect that. Jaeger Thorsson, do you wish to die with honor?"

Thor, stunned and bleeding, was only able to groan in pain. Ceres stepped back and kicked the axe handle upwards, cruelly but effectively wedging it out of Jaeger's metal face. He grasped the handle and laid it into the outstretched left hand of the pinned and bleeding Jarl. Ceres was careful to keep one boot pinning the axe handle to the floor, and thus Jaeger's hand.

"There. Under your belief's you can die and go to Valhalla, the other Valhalla, if you die in combat, weapon in hand, true?"

Jaeger did not respond, continuing to groan.

"These several 'One Father' faiths can't all be right. Let me help you settle that question, once and for all eternity!"

Ceres stood over Jarl Thorsson and drew his plasma sidearm. The lift's speed slowed and it settled like a cloud, stopping at the final floor, the hanger deck opposite the start of this journey.

Raising his pistol, first Ceres saluted the man with it, then made a sign of the cross. "May God forgive you, all of you," he generalized it, glancing around at the other bodies around the lift. "Go ask God the truth!"

The triangular leafs of the spherical lift slid open at the hatch, the hanger crew gasping in shock. Many of Jaeger's crew had assembled near the lift doors as ordered, seeming to await their Jarl's exit.

I imagine, Ceres thought, *the sight of a layer of their friend's bodies bleeding across the deck, with me standing over their downed and blooded Jarl, is hard to believe?*

Ceres looked Thorsson in the eye through the iron sights of his feather light plasma caster and shot him once. The body twitched in response to the star-hot electrons and protons erupting into the nerves and brain.

Ceres turned to the open hanger, his face dark with menace, a vicious grin of bared teeth, and stared down the witnesses. His blood boiled up for combat, he felt more than ready to take them all on. The crowd murmured amongst themselves, but stepped back as Ceres, defiant, with violence in his eyes, stepped forward in their faces. *Time to change the game!*

Ceres reached out with his hand, using the tractor-pressor in his gauntlet, and drew the huge space axe out of Jaeger's relaxed hand and into Ceres' own. Gasp's came from many in the crowd of superstitious pirates, few seeing the tractor-ring glowing blue around Ceres' wrist. He extended the handle on the heavy axe, found a balanced length, and began twirling it. Hand over hand the heavy axe-hammer flipped before the dazzled pirates.

Ceres spun it overhead, twirled it around his body, even around his neck, executing a pole arms kata, an old practice routine from his years in the dojo. He pressed the stud to power up the energy charge in the blade, then whirled the axe out at arm's length in a giant spin, almost touching the grave faces before him.

Ceres twirled it back behind him, up over his shoulder, he let his hands slide out to the end of the handle. The huge heavy space axe of the late Jarl Jaeger Thorsson circled up overhead and finally hammered powerfully down on the hanger deck.

The force of the blow, the energy wave rippling across the deck, pushed back a couple of the closest and lightest of the Void Vikings. Many of the onlookers were shocked, tingled by the energy release.

Dozens of bedazzled eyes accompanied him as Ceres stepped backwards, closer to the lift controls, most of his attention focused warily on the crowd of superstitious pirates observing him. Ceres' MeTR had quickly tested Jaeger's datapins. One of the three gave him command access across Asteroid Valhalla.

The lift sphere doors slid shut, and it traveled even higher, twenty meters more to the surface of the rock. The petal-like triangles opened up like a flower, releasing the atmosphere and contents to the void. Blood and air crystallized into a cloud around the bodies, which froze in random poses, drifting out towards the screen of glowing nebula haze surrounding the asteroid hidden within. Stunned silent, the crowd of pirates watched through the energy shield of the open hanger overhead.

"Anyone else?" Ceres roared in challenge. No one said a word. "Then get back to work!"

Dozens of pirates and slaves, hardened by the common execution of spacing unwanted hostages and the losers of duels, merely turned back to outfitting ships and preparing for the next raid. As they milled away into the hangers, a low grumbling arose among them.

Kangee, Thorsson's artist, now on Ceres' repair crew, made a gesture of peacemaking to Ceres, left hand palmed over his heart, right hand opened, palm towards Ceres.

Chapter 20
A New Business Plan

R'an, Himinglaeva, StarSys Trade Platform
Pub, Private Room #3
2516/5/4/0900

"What's Plan A, sir?" Med wanted to get down to business. He seemed to hate meetings almost more than his captain did. From his studies, and his observation of his colorful friend, Ceres knew the brash Tenublians were known for craving as much action and adventure as they could survive. It helped them mate with higher ranked females back home.

"Go there and retrieve the ship. What else?" Tarsis joked, knowing such lack of detail would only frustrate the multiplex mind of his navigator.

"Kinda sparse on the per-ticulars, sir. You gonna fill us in?" Ceres slipped into a slight drawl reminiscent of his old buddy Iron.

He loved crew meetings. He loved the planning, the intimate details. Mostly because the crew welcomed Ceres to this table as a full partner, like an adult. He loved brainstorming sessions like this one, learning firsthand from the experience of the crew. He especially enjoyed it when his ideas earned him their praise.

"Watch your mouth, son." Captain Tarsis chastised.

That is, Ceres loved it all except for the risk of again being called a "smart-aft" by his uncle, a frequent occurrence when the young man's brains were showing and his tact was not.

"Do we have a *detailed* Plan A, sir?" Medusa asked again, more precisely. Ceres appreciated his friend coming in to back up his question.

"Oh, detail? Correction:" Tarsis rarely stammered, "that is our *objective*, you have me there. Table is open to suggestions. Anyone?"

"Why are we even doing this… this risky business, Captain?" asked the brown skinned woman with the red dot above her brow. "It is not our ship?" The Medical Officer often provided the voice of caution and reason to the crew. She had an almost maternal concern for all of them, not just Ceres.

Ceres appreciated the female presence on the crew but it was bittersweet. She inadvertently made Ceres miss his mother.

"Good question, Doc," Tarsis continued. "Word of our save over Racine must have gotten out, or the handful of starship recovery ops we've done for StarSys over the last year. We've been bragging over drinks, eh girls?" He noticed several of the crew avoiding his direct gaze.

"Loose lips vac ships," Tarsis scolded his men. "I brought half of you aboard after your distinguished military careers ended for various reasons." Ceres watched his uncle's piercing eye contact wither first the huge man obviously from the Asianan sector, then the Rokkled, then the strong bald-headed black man from the New Orleans colony world. "I'd rather not have to start interviewing. Or worse, work up some obituaries!"

"You men should know better!" First Officer Riverwind cut in with an angry tone they recognized as a former drill sergeants' standard voice.

Ceres remembered different circumstances where every one of the former military badasses aboard burst into that tone. *Must be a military thing?* he imagined.

"This work is as serious as our Special Forces careers," Riverwind continued chastising them generally. "If the criminals we're up against get wind of this, they could be over-prepared for us one day. We could all die doing this job. You are putting your mates at risk, your friends next to you, even our families back home."

"Sir, we could," Jerome suggested, "make ourselves available to other Captain's and companies besides StarSys, to go retrieve *their* lost ships. I think it is only charitable to consult for the owners, see if their stolen ships are recoverable or a loss."

"Yes," Tarsis cut in, "now that the word is out, let's let it filter through the shipping community and see if StarSys gets inquiries to pass on to us. Let's agree, men and women, we will not discuss it any further outside of this crew, outside this ship! Agreed?" He asked the question with such commanding strength it came through as an order more than a question.

"The request of the commander is as good as an order. Yes, sir!" Riverwind replied. Most of the crew matched the statement of compliance.

"This is not a military ship and crew," Tarsis sat and bowed his head forward, his body language softened to release the tension among his crew, "even though we are embarking on a paramilitary adventure here."

173

Ceres realized his uncle the admiral was using a different tone than his commanding military presence when in uniform. Ceres was often subject to that persona when being disciplined by this beloved father figure. Maybe there was more depth to the "Old Man" than he had thought.

"We will have to toe that line, people," Taris said. "If we trip up we could see one or all of us suffer for it. None of us want to be that guy who gets our shipmates killed. Agreed?" this time softer than the first.

"Agreed," all of the crew said in unison.

"We will let it go at that, then. Discipline yourselves, so I do not have to discipline you. You wouldn't like that." The captain finished the subject.

"Besides that," he transitioned with a more optimistic tone, "with the owners or underwriters covering our fees, I sense a unique business to be had here. A potentially lucrative one for all of us." His nodding head drew a couple of the crewmembers into nodding with him.

"Now, back to the mission at hand." Tarsis drew a deep breath and resumed the briefing. "We will all infiltrate the port under cover identities and gather intel, then form a plan there in situ. We don't know enough about the current lay of the space to form one from here in the dark."

"Sir," Jerome raised his hand, "are we gonna kill some folks, juss ta steal back property?" He laid his huge palm atop his bald pate. From their side conversations during down time, Ceres knew him to be a man of deep faith. He guessed the sensitive man was concerned about the crew losing their moral compass in this shift of their mission. A relevant question.

"Subjugating the enemy without the use of force is the true pinnacle of military excellence," Tarsis quoted in reply. "Does anyone know who said that?" Ceres' hand shot up instantly. Tarsis raised his eyebrow in his direction and nodded.

"Sun Tzu, sir," Ceres answered correctly, "in *The Art of War*." Jerome gave Ceres a wink and a nod. Others smiled on him with admiration and approval. Ceres ate up the positive affirmations. It was one reason he continued to downstream mass amounts of information from all fields of interest. As part of this crew Ceres had a special interest in learning all about the ancient and modern art of warfare so he could fit in better.

Ceres' uncle smiled approvingly. "You are going to downstream the entire Library of The Galactic pretty soon, son." He ruffled his nephew's hair. "Now, take us out of port."

Chapter 21
That Father & Son Talk

A-Valhalla, Tyrian's Personal Domes
2525/7/16/0945

"Come, sit with me, son," beckoned the tall pirate king, his blonde hair beginning to turn white with age. The father and son walked away from Ceres' hanger, down to the central spiraling corridor of the asteroid named Valhalla. Tyrian's brace of pistols swung from a wide ribbon that hung around his neck, slapping his hips in rhythm with his long stride.

He must not trust anyone, Ceres thought, *even here in his sanctuary, with his returned, prodigal son.*

Ceres moved with a slight swagger, highlighting the heavy double-barreled disruptor holstered on his hip. It felt poorly balanced by the ultralight plasma caster on Ceres' left hip. Knowing his father wanted him to take Thorsson's place as a captain in the Void Vikings, Ceres tried to look the part while he searched for a way out of his moral dilemma.

Riding the lift down the tubes with his newfound father, to Tyrian's private domes, Ceres eventually stepped off into a foyer of sorts. The lift unfolded under a dome buried in the rock of the asteroid. Three branch tunnels fanned away from it. The flooring here changed to a black and white pattern that dazzled Ceres' eyes, making him glad he had downstreamed Thorsson's maps.

Tyrian charged out of the lift at a brisk pace, forcing Ceres to lengthen his stride to keep pace. His father said nothing, branching and cutting back as the tunnels zigged and zagged. Guarded by four well-armed pirates, a sturdy hatch opened as Tyrian approached. He turned hard and the pair continued, now climbing slowly up a long ramped tunnel.

They emerged into a bright hemispherical room with hundreds of opaque triangular panels arching overhead. A scattering of large stones lay in a random arrangement, embedded in a sea of white sand. The map showed them to be on the surface of the asteroid. Thorsson had marked the map with a special symbol reminiscent of a pile of marbles or stones with an arch overhead.

"A Zen garden?" Ceres asked. Tyrian nodded. "Surprising," commented Ceres, "I recognize it from my years in a dojo."

"Yes, authentic late Earth 1.0 period reproduction," affirmed Tyrian. "It is supposed to help me calm down between raids and keep focused."

"One of your wives' suggestions?" Ceres guessed, seeing his father's eyebrow twitch as he asked. *He gets annoyed at many things I mention. I bet I can get him off balance, and he will blurt out what I want to know.*

Tyrian nodded with a frown.

"Hmm, well, I hate to tell you, these 'Zen' gardens are not authentic, not classic oriental gardens dating back into thousands of years of Japanese culture. No, this type came into favor around the start of this millennium, just 500 years ago aboard early space-age Earth. It grew in public popularity though, as it gave practitioners a visual aesthetic and a light physical hobby they could meditate with."

Tyrian looked annoyed. He closed his eyes and took in a deep breath. Ceres felt pleased and inwardly amused that he could so easily manipulate his father's turbulent emotions. "Do you find peace here? Does it help calm your mind?"

Tyrian did not answer. His channeled brow and deep frown said, "no" to Ceres.

Doesn't like being challenged or contradicted, not even by his 'princely' son. Noted, Ceres thought. *Game on!*

Tyrian rose and roughly snatched up a wide-toothed wooden rake leaning against the inside edge of the entry hatch. He marched out to the center stone in the dome, stood there and drew several deep breaths. After a moment, he started smoothing the parallel lines scored in the white sand, erasing them with the flat back of the rake. Ceres watched from the bench

"I have heard some details from your time on Hunan IV," began Tyrian. "Interesting childhood. Did you have any friends there?"

Ceres thought his father must think that pointing out Ceres' isolation from his family, and lost friends, would help cement his recruitment. Ceres' smug smile vanished. "Yes. My best friend was a kid named Iron."

Tyrian turned his head, flashing a grin at his son.

Oh, that's where I get that from, Ceres thought. His father continued to rake grooves around the garden's center stone for a minute, going through the motions, but seemed unable to get into the act, the zen of it. Ceres' comments about the questionable authenticity of this type of garden seemed to have ruined it for him?

"Iron?" finally, he spoke. "Sounds tough. Might be a good pirate name. What's he like?"

"I miss the tough little son-of-a-gun." Ceres gripped his chin, remembering Iron connecting a hard punch once upon a time in training. "Definitely worthy of the name. He died the day I left that planet."

"You've had a number of major losses for someone so young," Tyrian pointed out. "Seems like you need more friends? New friends. A new family." He kept circling, redrawing the same pattern in the sand that he had just erased.

"Well, I think I've earned my way up your ranks here pretty quickly."

"Look, son," Tyrian stopped abruptly, turning to face Ceres with anger coloring his face. "Stop killing my best men!" He flipped the end of the rake in Ceres' direction, stared down at it, and then decided it was a good time to give up on the frustrating effort. He strode to the bench but stood there.

Ceres looked at his father with a hurt expression. "When your 'rising star' challenged me, I killed him in a duel and took his place."

"All fair under our rules," Tyrian confirmed. "I was standing right there, too. Your point?"

"You said 'the spoils go to the vikrant." Ceres' faced turned quizzical, confused.

Tyrian nodded, confused himself.

Ceres quickly moved to the center, took up the rake's handle, then back-stepped in a growing spiral to erase the entire dome floor of lines.

Tyrian seemed puzzled. He stroked his beard, sat, and continued with the grooming gesture. He shrugged and relaxed back on the bench as if waiting for his son to explain.

Done flattening the pattern, Ceres returned to the bench and sat, contemplating the design he wanted to trace. He decided he had given enough time to let his father's anger simmer down. He wanted to escalate the tension, but under his control. *Let's play.*

"When Thorsson sent his men and then fought me himself, I killed them all. Law of the wolf pack, as Jaeger called his squadron. If you want to crown me as your prince, I *have* fought my way to the top, haven't I?"

"No!" Tyrian stood up and shouted, echoing in the dome. "I told my people to talk with you first, to bring you into the squadron in Trok's place and show you how we do things," he lectured, pacing, shaking his finger down at his son.

"If you throw me to the wolves," Ceres quoted "don't be surprised if I come back leading the pack." He grinned, his eyes lighting up. He enjoyed this verbal taunting, dueling his father. He could see from the slight grin, his father could appreciate his logic, respect the bravado of his phrase. *He might be buying this.* Ceres sat there quietly, looking about the garden for a few moments for inspiration.

"Cute, but no," Tyrian said. "It seemed to have started well, until you had to take offense at a common joke of questioning someone's parentage." Tyrian smirked and changed to a nasty tone. "You shouldn't be so sensitive about that—" he stopped himself, glancing at Ceres.

Ceres shot upright and raised a warning finger. His other hand was on his hip above his disruptor's hilt, the rake falling off his shoulder into the sand.

Tyrian's hands gripped the ribbon dangling his pistols close to his hips, but his smile was anything but hostile. The two Tauri men stared each other down for a moment. Then, Ceres caught his father's smile and laughed, shaking his head.

Enough defense! Ceres thought. Time to change the game. The best defense is a good offense.

Ceres grabbed up the rake and carried it with him, out to a stone positioned off to one side of the arrangement. He squatted to heft the big rock, then lofted it into the air like a champion Highland Games stone thrower. It fell heavily in the sand, in an open space. The lowered grav setting of Tyrian's dome had made it easier to handle the weight.

"This reminds me of a quote," Ceres dragged the wooden rake through the sand in a new pattern, different from what Tyrian had just casually re-drawn. "'When we direct our thoughts properly, we can control our emotions.' The ancient thinker W. Clement Stone said that. Fitting for this place?"

Tyrian merely nodded, his brow furrowed as he looked at the rock his son had thrown.

Ceres circled the newly placed stone, in his hands the rake drawing rings of measured lines spaced perfectly, like a ripple on a pond, frozen in ice. He stepped farther from the stone and traced the ring of ripples larger.

"This garden must bring you peace?" he started again, having intentionally disrupted his father's peace here.

"Sometimes," Tyrian sounded annoyed by Ceres' subtle criticism. "Not right now."

Hmmm? Ceres thought. *Is he annoyed further by the destruction of the pattern he had carefully redrawn. If that's a sore spot, let's poke it!*

"Let me guess: you recreate the same pattern?" Ceres asked. "For consistency, trying to bring order to your troubled mind?" *Good luck, with me flipping through a list of subjects on you.*

"The stones," Tyrian answered. "They each represent one of the planets I control."

"Ah," Ceres said. "So this restructuring must be annoying?" Turned away from his father as he spiraled in the sands, Ceres snuck in a grin. "It is a visual metaphor for me and you. *I* am the stone tossed in, to disrupt the prior pattern. Now we have the opportunity to create a new dynamic."

Tyrian smirked. *Maybe he is aware,* Ceres thought, *that it is me creating the new pattern? At least he gets it now.*

"I'm glad you did not make the same mistake as your dear late Jarl," Ceres said, mirroring his father's expression. "I don't let anyone insult my mother." Ceres shrugged, seeing his father's look turn cool. "You told Jaeger it was okay with you to bust me up in front of his men? To regain some of his honor?"

Tyrian nodded with a predator's grin that made Ceres shudder. It was as if they discussed the leash training of a dog, not encouraging the multiple assault of a long-lost son missed, pined for, for over 20 years.

"You forget, they told me about their wolf pack mentality, and you told me about your spoils honor system. I decided, to survive here, I had to outmatch their level of violence. I had to make it clear: to fight me is death. They came to fight me, they are dead."

"You had to show respect for our ways," Tyrian countered. "Take your place and earn your way up the ranks. Prove to them and to me that you are with us—one of us!"

"You never have to chase people down to command their respect or loyalty," Ceres said. "They are either with you, or they're not."

"No, "Tyrian started, "I just wanted them to beat you into your place."

"Strong people don't tear others down. They build them up," Ceres countered.

"Exactly!" Tyrian grinned broadly. "You see, son. You and I are so much alike," he gloated.

Ceres raised his eyebrows at his father, confused.

"You got angry and killed men who intended only to hurt you. From the cams it seemed that you enjoyed killing them too," Tyrian continued. "How does that figure into you and your *holy* mother's faith?" he sneered it, every time.

"Doesn't your Bible say 'Thou shall not kill?" Tyrian seemed gleeful while taunting his supposedly pious son with his own hypocrisy.

Son of a ditch! He's good, Ceres thought. *He turned it around on me while I'm doing it to him? Impressive.*

He finally circled in to the center stone. *This is why Sensei taught us to end fights immediately! Go long enough, and the enemy will find gaps in your defenses and exploit them.* He shook his head, smirked.

Ceres started scoring reflection rings off this boulder, like ripples in a pond bouncing back off a rock or tree in the water. The trick lay in overlaying the new subtle ripples without erasing the first pattern.

"The oldest scrolls of the Bible," Ceres explained, "written in the ancient dialects of Hebrew, use the specific word for 'murder' which God prohibits in that Commandment. God wrote the flawless principle, 'Thou shall not murder,' into stone. Man, prone to sin and error, edited in the word 'kill' leading to generations of confusion and accusations of hypocrisy due to *man's* fallibility.

"Our Father sent David out to kill Goliath," Ceres continued, "and later sent his worthy men of Israel to kill many challengers and occupiers of the land God gave to Israel. God gave His blessing, even His command, to kill unbelievers and enemies on behalf of His will for His chosen people. God does not contradict Himself. If we had historically kept the translation correct we'd see that more clearly.

"Early in the new Millennium," Ceres was lecturing now and his father seemed to resent it, frowning below his scowling eyes, "the Second Revelation of Saint John was finally revealed, inspiring mankind into the Modern Exodus out among the stars. God's commands then caused us to kill as we left Earth to take new worlds for God's people by His new command."

"He is close to exploding, Ceres," Serenity warned, telesending to him. *"Better ease off the Sunday school lesson and give him something he can relate to without anger."*

"God gave us the natural emotion of anger." Ceres shifted tactics after a slight pause, continuing to drag lines around the stones in the sandy dome. "The natural adrenaline rush in combat is not the same thing. I enjoy that rush, the speed and strength, the feeling of slowed time."

He looked up, caught eye contact with his father, and noticed Tyrian smiling and nodding with him. *Too rapid emotional changes. Something's wrong with him, but I am not a psychologist. I imagine I'm here as an operative, and he's the mission.*

"I did not enjoy killing them," Ceres pointed out. "But I did not choose it. They did." *Considering their part in killing thousands last week, I think it is at least partial justice, too.*

"It is true," Ceres continued, "anger flares up within me in fights like yesterday, but I'm already fighting when that happens. They provoked my vigorous defense. If they hadn't brought lethal weapons and put their hands on them, I would have just knocked them around, like you say they planned for me.

"Someone higher up in the pack gave them access to their weapons from the armory. I take blame, or credit, for killing them in self-defense. But, are their deaths partly your responsibility, since you armed them and sent them to fight me?"

Tyrian's brows furrowed.

Okay, smart guy, back on offense. Ceres thought. "That is hardly equal to executing a major strike on civilian targets. I learned a lot about you, Pop, when you killed over 20,000 people in minutes just to impress me." He watched Tyrian's face, seeing him frown.

Oh, he didn't like 'Pop?' Perfect. "You crave power, Pop. Money, fame, yes, but power. Control over others."

"No, son," Tyrian started justifying himself. "This family I have created and lead brought purpose to the chaos of the sector—"

"It's why you take slaves," Ceres cut his father off, ignoring his argument, "why you demand tribute, why you started this whole scheme of basing the Void Vikings on the ancient Viking cult of pagan gods and men of battle, trying to earn the false reward after death of mead and maids in Valhalla. It's just a cult to enslave them into fighting and dying for *your* goals, serving *your* thirst for power, isn't it?"

"Don't contradict me, son," Tyrian warned. "I don't like that."

Found it. Jugular time! "My mother contradicted you, didn't she? Her disagreement, your wife, your *chattel*," Ceres emphasized the word with a sneer in his tone. "She stood up to you. She refused to disavow her faith. She disagreed with your plans for your future?

"She had the nerve to want an honest man to be proud of starting a family with?" Ceres pressed on. "She didn't take her demure place in your scheme of life. That made you angry. Is that why you hurt her?"

"Like you, I get out of control when I get angry," Tyrian said. "I'm fighting myself right now since you seem to be trying to make me angry with your clever words. But don't push me any harder, son. My anger gives me strength in a fight."

"Another wise man I know once taught me," Ceres continued, "the true strength of a man lies in his strength of control of his anger."

"Most of my men are smart enough to respect my anger and not provoke me."

"Well, let me take another wild guess, then. You think fear is the same as respect?"

Struggle showing on his face, his moving lips, Tyrian chose not to answer. Instead, he took out a ribbon studded with tiny green pearls, peeled one off and put it under his tongue.

Ceres was betting that Tyrian did not want to kill his son when Ceres could be so useful to him. The hope for a successor, to bring such a famous son back into Tyrian's bloodline and to finally win out over Ceres' mother, was probably too great an urge to give up just yet.

"Your dear *saintly*," Tyrian sneered out the word with distain, "mother did not respect me as her husband, so I tried to make her fear to disrespect me, fear to leave me."

"Backfired," Ceres interjected. "She feared you enough that she left anyway, out of justifiable self-defense."

"Right!" Tyrian picked it up again. "She had you, and then had one of those annulments you churchers use in place of divorce. That erased our marriage. She made you illegitimate, didn't she?" his Cheshire grin implied he thought he had won the verbal fencing match with this killing blow.

"No. You misunderstand. I am here, am I not?" Ceres spread his hands and shrugged. "I was born while you were still married, and, she ensured I am known to be your son so I am legitimate. I kept your name. Annulment does not defacto de-legitimize children, anyway."

Tyrian frowned. *I must have stalled him with that argument?* Ceres thought.

"Why did you attack Shangri-La?" Ceres picked up where he had left off. "I have a theory but I want to hear what you say first."

"They angered me again, just last week. That fifth tower finished its skybridges. They didn't include me in their ribbon cutting ceremony, opening the completed city. They should have invited me!"

"Exactly!" Ceres jumped in, "They do not respect you; you are their King, after all. You want to be in control of them, their city, their society. You want that power over their lives. So it made you angry?" *Not to mention you are crazy, petty, and bloodthirsty.*

"Obviously!" Tyrian shot back. "They have been paying me tributes for years. Money, gifts, food, resources. Releasing their criminals to join us. Honorary mention in social events, befitting the king of planets!"

"They completed their city center and celebrated *their* achievement," Tyrian went on, "without inviting me, honoring me? So I reminded them who's in charge, who can destroy them! I can blow out those arc's support buttresses and kill them all in an hour, if I want."

"You would kill a million people because they didn't invite you to their party?" Ceres accused. He sat back in shock, on the striated boulder next to Tyrian's bench.

"You have to rule sheep with a strong fist," Tyrian said. "Sometimes they need a reminder of who is their master."

"Yes, but you are not a benevolent shepherd; you are a wolf," Ceres countered. "Sheep need the sheep-dog, and the Shepherd's staff, to keep the wolves from eating them one by passive one.

"Look at the names they chose for their place in the galaxy!" Ceres continued. "The ancient mythical utopias of 'Shambhala' System, Planet 'Nirvana', and the mythical City of 'Shangri-La'? These people came out from various planets outside the Galactic to try to create their own idyllic world of a peaceful commune.

"Their mistake was leaving themselves defenseless. Words and signs of 'Peace' do not stop hungry wolves like you. They show you who is easy to attack."

Tyrian's grin became savage. "They were languishing. Sitting around all day like the early arc colonies, but these people brought no robots to do the field work to support them. They wanted to eat but nobody was motivated to work enough to feed their own families. It was the first non-Galactic colonies all over again! They were going to starve of laziness." He started to raise his voice.

"They needed me! A strong leader to motivate their lazy butts to work. I took over, and they finally started to move, to build, to grow, to contribute to supporting their own worthless lives. Before I made them work hard to pay tributes, they wouldn't even work hard enough to feed *themselves*! I brought in food from elsewhere and made them work to earn it.

"At gunpoint, I made them work hard to plant crops, mine resources, craft, and build. The way I see it, *I* saved them from starvation. I made their fantasy of a city function and flourish. The final arcs immigrated because of my success."

He raised his voice into an emphatic growl. "It's not their city anymore! It's *my* city! It was *my* celebration!"

"He that is slow to anger is better than the mighty, and he that rules his spirit than he that takes a city," Ceres' calm quotation was a stark contrast to Tyrian's vocal rage. "Proverbs has been guiding righteous men to wisdom for eons."

"It's *my* planet—*myyy* Sector, and you are my prince!" Tyrian taunted, the venom dripping from his lips like bitter wine. "Tomorrow I go back and remind them the price they will pay to live in peace. First, I will get a nice fat tribute, ransom for returning all the people we just took. Then we'll see who rules the city, and the sector!"

Tyrian's anger continued to grow, the more Ceres teased him about controlling his anger. The Bible quotes especially seemed to annoy the anti-religious senior Tauri. Ceres was trying to get him above simmer but not over boiling.

"I'm worried about you, Pop," Ceres was relentless. "'He who reigns within himself, and rules passions, desires and fears, is more than a king.' Milton." Ceres switched to a secular thinker's quote.

"I *am*, more than a king, don't you see, son? A mere king rules a planet. I will install my top men as kings across this sector because *I* rule this entire sector! What do they call the one above a king?"

"God," Ceres calmly replied.

Tyrian swung a swift backhand at Ceres' face, scrambling up to stand over him. It appeared he was not going to take any more smart remarks from his son —especially not a religious rebuke.

Ceres raised one hand, his palm easily countering Tyrian's swing. Ceres sat there, still, eyebrows raised. He remembered downstreaming the move at age nine, his first lessons in karate the month he had joined Sensei's dojo.

Of course, Ceres' years of practice and excellent reflexes made it easy. What was hard for him was restraining his combat instincts, his Jeet Kun Do and Krav Maga training, pushing him to retaliate, to attack as his defense.

Tyrian's rage played over his face, clenched fists at his sides. He turned to face Ceres while his son remained seated on the rock. It implied the impotence of Tyrian's ability to threaten him.

"I don't think it would be wise for us to fight, Pop," Ceres said. He considered standing up to face his father, but thought it would be taken as more of an aggressive challenge than Ceres intended. His plans for Serenity and the slaves' escape did not allow for a real fight right here and now. He awaited the pirate's next raid away from the base.

Then, Ceres glanced over at the center stone of the garden, noticing something new. *I wonder what those scratches are about?*

Tyrian took another cannahol tab under his tongue, taking the edge off his rage. The top note of the designer drug had an immediate impact; the full effects took time to catch up.

He must use a lot of that stuff, to need two to feel it, Ceres thought, then asked his father, "Do you want me at your side? You want me to join you and become your second man? Your prince?"

"We shall see!" the senior Tauri spat back. "For now, I want you to join us on the run tomorrow, to see how I take tribute from the civic leaders and make them honor me where they forgot me before. I'm going to make them grovel and bow, kneel- all but crown me."

"Tomorrow." Ceres answered casually, almost bored. "I will begin running space trials on my new ship tomorrow. I need your raiders to clear the space around Valhalla. To join your fleet, we would need at least one

185

more part to repair the radio inside one of the plasma drives. Maybe you can bring it back for me?"

Tyrian did not seem surprised by Ceres' bland response.

"If it hadn't fried, we would be flight-worthy," Ceres shrugged apologetically, as if there was nothing he could do. "As it is, there is a long list of repairs and upgrades I need to make *Wanderlust* worthy of my princely stature, you understand?" He grinned his boyish, impish grin, making it hard for Tyrian not to join him.

Finally, Tyrian broke out in a mild smile and nodded, his anger mellowing.

Ceres stood, slowly, eyes on Tyrian. *He bought the lie.* Ceres extended his arm formally, offering to trade grips.

"I will decide anew, where to fit you into my fleet, after tomorrow's raid then," Tyrian said instead. "Killing two of my best men? You have spent the goodwill of your star-appeal, son. I can't just let you off without paying a price. You will give me that redhead," he snapped his fingers, "all of your slaves, in fact."

"I won them in a duel to the death," Ceres disliked the lustful look on his father's face. "Your own code of honor is at risk in front of your men."

"*I* rule this sector and this asteroid in particular!" Tyrian thundered. "I made the rules we live by, and I remake them at will. *My* will."

"I will decide your ultimate fate after our next raid," Tyrian raised an arm, pointing at the exit hatch. Four armed and armored guards stepped in, emphasizing Tyrian's orders that this conversation was now over.

Ceres nodded towards the exit and then looked back to his father. *Now or never,* he thought. "It is unfortunate that we are quarreling. I came here to learn if everything my family told me was true. I have to know if you were behind my mother's disappearance, and if you know where she is now."

Tyrian grinned in a way that made Ceres' stomach knot up. He took one step towards his father and stood tall.

"Last chance, Pop. If you tell me where she is now, I could forgive all the rest, all the years—" Ceres doubled down.

Tyrian laughed. "Well, you are my boy after all. I have to respect your nerve, to bottom line me. I am telling you nothing about your dear *holy* mother that you don't already know, my boy." More sarcasm emphasized Tyrian's words, but he could not hold Ceres' gaze for long.

"He is visualizing a church," Serenity thought to Ceres. From Ceres' domes, he realized, she had been reading Tyrian's mind too, while he spoke with his son.

"She's not here, then," Ceres thought back. *"There is nothing church-like here." Caught you!* Ceres thought of his father. *"Thank you, Red!"*

"Now," Tyrian popped yet another green tab under his tongue, and Ceres saw the whites of his eyes finally turn that distinctive shade of green. "It's time to introduce you to another of our customs and laws." His visage darkened, the stern father, the hungry predator look Ceres had seen first when his father tried to recruit him during the hanger tour.

Ceres nodded towards the exit, grinned at his father again. He moved his hand in the sign of the cross in front of his chest. Ceres, looking down at the lines in the sand, the disruptive ripples he had scored, grinned more broadly.

Obviously something has disturbed his Zen. Ceres kept grinning at the puzzled guards, saying, "Carry on, men," and saluting crisply as he marched towards them.

The hatch opened allowing Ceres a view down the garden dome's entry corridor. Pirates lined both sides as far as he could see. They were armored, helmeted, and seemed ready for a fight. Their hands were filled with blunt weapons of various non-lethal designs which several hefted and slapped into their palms.

Chapter 22
Paid Thieves

Alford's Star, Vanuatu, Loganville Freight Platform
2516/6/1/0730

"Listen up, boys, 'cause this ain't no dirt!" Captain Tarsis began with the standard opening for all military tall tales. In the field fighting alongside his men, his demeanor changed slightly, affecting a seasoned combat veteran the same as them. His audience, the long term crew of his space tug, *The BARGE*, rewarded him with the usual chuckles and grins.

All but Medusa. That giant floating jellysquid showed his mirth in ways the humans had never deciphered, all but observant Ceres that is. The youth let his xenomorphic friend's secrets remain so, turning his attention to the master storyteller who was also the ship's master.

"Our intelligence operatives are just as good as the Galactic's," Tarsis went on. "Better, in that ours are still covert. They gave us this initial report, and it is sounding like this M.O. is growing in popularity out here on the Rim.

"Judge Breyer thought he was very clever," said Tarsis. "He thought of a loophole in the Galactic Law of Space that even the Rim sectors honored. Of course they had to if they wanted any Galactic shipping interests to respect their ports and bring precious cargo to and from the outlying sectors.

"Breyer must be getting greedy, though. He decided he could impound a ship under even the most minor infraction of local laws. 'Local' means Vanuatu for those of you taking notes.

"As you all know, if the owner's—that's us, well, StarSys—did not come forward within the specified time, the ship could be impounded to pay for its mounting port fees and fines. Then it could be resold at auction. Once sold, under the Law of Space, the past ownership history would be wiped clean."

"What?" exclaimed Ceres.

"Old laws," Tarsis said, "going back hundreds of years to seaborn ships of Old Earth, lad," Tarsis explained. "Naval traditions translated off Earth into our spaceborn Navy and trade ships. Downstream some lessons from the Merchant Marine Academy, which trains the professional officer corps running all the Capitol type ships in the galaxy, and you'll see what I mean."

"Then it makes no sense for the Galactic to honor their laws out here on the lawless Rim," Riverwind said, indignant, "where they don't honor our Constitution, or the basic principle of property ownership. Why can't we just float in with a gunboat and reclaim it?"

"I could make a call," Tarsis replied directly, "but I leave gunboat diplomacy to others. I am still an Admiral in the Reserves, but that duty is only a couple of months per year. Let's do this our way. Without risk of life and limb." He shot a hard look at Ceres to indicate this line of debate was over.

"Our 'Honorable' Judge," the captain resumed his monologue, "intended to ensure that all of these so-called 'legal' transactions passed through his hands, the writs of ownership bearing his name in the end. Seeking retirement, he was hoping to branch out into multiple incomes and prepare for continuing the wealthy lifestyle he had come to enjoy here on the gold-rush Rim.

"His connections in the legislature passed some laws that might be harder for some Captain's to comply with, especially if they didn't know them or interpret them properly in order *to* comply. Such interpretations were our Judge's specialty.

"*Breadwinner* was a perfectly good medium sized freighter built on the open frame design plan. She has a heavy spine fore to aft with plenty of attachment points for standard cargo containers. A starship, she was never expected to dive far down into the heavy gravity well of a planet or moon. She had been tramping around the non-Galactic Rim sectors taking cargos where she could connect the dots and keep her crew fed.

"So, when she backed in to the vicinity of Loganville station, Captain Mulzac had no idea of the recently changed local laws of space prohibiting use of shipboard plasma drives within 10 kilometers of the station. Considering the Galactic standard practice of parking orbits at three to seven km distant, the captain was rather proud when his cargo-filled vessel came to rest at four kilometers on the wellward side—the planet's gravity-well side—of the station.

"Prouder still, he was, that she had efficiently parked in the sweet spot. Just two km in orbit below her lay the small fleet of transfer ships waiting to remove her standard shipping containers; like a pack of ravenous alien Insectoids feeding on an African elephant back in the 2050's." Ceres chuckled, imagining the horror of that spectacle.

Tarsis pressed on, "When the first ship to dock spit out a contingent of Vanuatu soldiers, Mulzac's pride in the efficiency of his crew turned to bittersweet objections falling on deaf ears. For 'operational port safety violations,' *Breadwinner* was impounded, her cargo seized, and later auctioned cheap.

"The Judge ordered the ship immediately sold, unfortunately the announcement of the auction coming too quickly for the captain to cross to the *other* space station servicing the tropical island-based agricultural Rim planet, Vanuatu. Mulzac thought it odd that there was no spaceborn transportation or popper travel times allowing him to get from the trial to the auction in time.

"Breadwinner was auctioned for exactly $1000 Dollari, ironically the exact amount owed in fines, sold to a dummy company secretly owned by local shipping bosses in partnership with Judge Breyer himself."

"Wait," incredulous, Doctor Kauri, interjected. "They claimed a multi-million dollari starship for just 1000 Di?" She used the short name for dollari.

"Yes," Tarsis affirmed. "It is an obvious rip off when you look at it plainly like this. Especially when you consider the auction occurred within a minute after the Judge gaveled his conviction, on the orbital altitude charges he had invented."

"The captain was probably still stuck inside the courtroom." Dr. Kauri said. *"No* chance to pop over in time." Several heads nodded agreement.

"StarSys received the call over a month after the auction, seeking us," Tarsis resumed his tale. "It took that long for our stranded Captain Mulzac to bum a ride far enough away from danger of reprisals, to contact the owners, who contacted their insurers, who contacted us today. He is a good man, though. He put his crew up safely first." Tarsis's crew nodded their approval.

"Over a month has gone by and now our crew of specialized 'merchant commandos' has arrived." The crew chuckled amongst themselves at that colorful job description. 'Spacer bums' was just as apt in their minds, Ceres thought.

"A month ago *Breadwinner* was renamed *TradeWinds*. Pretty good name considering Vanuatu was terraformed into a tropical Ag planet that developed coconut oil for export, mostly for premium cooking.

"*TradeWinds* exports the local variation of coconut oil, favored by chef's, bringing back high tech goods to and from ManHolme. That's the manufacturing planet nearby in the Carina Ends rim sector. They hoped it would become a standard route. We won't let it come to that."

"Suggestions?" Tarsis leaned back in his chair. By opening his arms he opened the table for input from the crew.

Finally! Ceres thought, licking his lips in anticipation as he called up schematics in his implanted datapad. His MeTR's HUD created the illusion of screens of data and scenes of images, before his eyes only. Brainstorming was one of Ceres' favorite intellectual activities, and at this table he felt he was treated as an adult.

He actually was not, his unique perspective as a youth allowed him to see the world from different angles, which the "Olds," as he called them, just couldn't see. So while initially unwelcome to chime in, and Uncle Tarsis frequently called Ceres a smart-aft, Ceres' comments were often ground breaking. He sent the crew off on tracks towards solutions they wouldn't have seen without his perspective looking in from outside the established norms and routines of generations of space business.

* * *

A-Valhalla, Ceres' Personal Dome
2525/7/15/2120

"So, Jerome got a job as a bartender in the ship guard's favorite nearby pub," Ceres continued his storytelling to Serenity. "He got Akebono on as a bouncer for the place. When the ship was back in port, Jer waited for them to come in off duty and slipped them a mickey."

"What's that?" Serenity asked. She had downstreamed a good education, but this spacer's knowledge reached far beyond hers. She was intrigued by it, willing to learn what he knew so she could understand him.

Merely willing, or eager? She considered her feelings, trying to separate them from his and once again feeling challenged by him in new ways. *Perhaps.*

"Ancient name for a drug put into a drink," Ceres answered her. "This one made them suddenly seem overly drunk. Doc was sitting there as a patron and helped the guards wobble to the head, where the crew pulled them out the back hatch."

"Riverwind, that's our First Officer, and the Doc had the best skin-tone matches for people from this sunny planet so they had their faces scanned. We fed it into a crafter station to spray-print a facemask. They fit the wearer's scanned face perfectly on the inside but looked exactly like the other guy's scanned face on the outside."

"Number One and Doc had observed the guards for two weeks, practicing imitating their manners of walking, gestures, so they took their places on the next shift and let me and Sensei inside. I infiltrated the ship's datacore—my size was just right—and plugged myself in.

"Only problem was, before the rest of my crew came aboard, the ship's crew found me. I must have pulled some cable loose, and someone came to check on it in there. In prying me out of the core one of them made the mistake of calling me an 'S.O.B.' Do you know what that means?" Ceres asked Serenity.

She nodded and bit her lip as she let him tell his tale. She could see from the way his fight response flared up in his body from merely recalling the incident, that he relished some fights more than perhaps he should.

"Well, I don't allow anyone to insult my mother! So, I knocked him out," Ceres snapped his fingers. "Just like that."

This reminded Serenity of the injury to his hand from knocking Jaeger out. She reached over, took his hand, pulled off his glove, and began her healing ritual again.

"One of the guards turned his rifle on me," Ceres continued, "so, I took him out too. Then the rest. By the time my crew got in there everyone was out cold or dead." Ceres looked at Serenity expectantly but went on when she just held his eyes without comment.

"We got the ship out of there quick. That's about it," Ceres shrugged.

"Vengeance is mine, I will repay, says the Lord," Serenity quoted from the New Galactic version.

"Yeah, well," Ceres justified, "how do I know He didn't send me to do the dirty work for Him? Psalm 144: 10: 'You give victory to Kings—'"

"You delivered David your servant," Serenity picked the quote up immediately, now curious to know how he learned his scripture. It was an important indicator to her that he might be more qualified to be her God-given mate than she had first imagined.

"From the menacing sword deliver me," Ceres added.

"Rescue me from the hands of foreign foes," she said, "This particular Bible verse I prayed to our Lord, as *Wanderlust* landed in Valhalla, just b'fore I saw you standin' in the hanger, Ceres," Serenity smiled.

She had prayed for God to send an angel to protect her among these hungry wolves, with hands and swords to deliver them into His justice for their atrocities. Had Ceres been the answer to that prayer?

"Their mouths speak untruths," he continued with a slight squint of his eyes at her. *Now I am certain, I had felt her watching me as her ship landed.* She heard his thoughts.

"Their right hands are raised in lying oaths." When Serenity finished the prayer they sat silently a moment, then she asked, "So tell me. Do y'feel the ship thieves brought God's justice down upon th'mselves, by coveting another's goods, by stealin', and by lyin' oaths to steal the starship?"

"Yes."

"And y'feel God used *you*, as 'is hands no less, to rain God's justice and wrath down upon th'm?" She studied his face and his mind and knew he answered as he truly felt.

"Yes."

Chapter 23
Run the Gauntlet

A-Valhalla, Tyrian's Personal Domes
2525/7/16/1035

Ceres looked back at his father in question, his exit from the king's domes blocked by over a hundred angry pirates. He thought this could turn bad fast if he had to fight all of these warriors at once. Not great odds. And he didn't want to kill his father. Not without more info about Mom.

"See, son," Tyrian said, "Thorsson helped me found the Void Vikings. He was beloved by all of his crew." Tyrian nodded to the hallway.

Ceres recognized all of the faces as having sat together around Thorsson's table for breakfast. *His* crew. Great! Got it.

"All but worshipped as the physical embodiment of the great god of lightning. He was 'Thor' himself among us. You have gained a lot of enemies today." Tyrian went on.

"When a member of the pack over reaches, commits an offense against the whole of the Void Vikings," Tyrian pointed his finger at Ceres, "they usually die at all of our hands, in a public reckoning. Right the wrong." Ceres fingers flexed and he started breathing heavy, oxy- loading like before a big game, in preparation for the battle of his life.

"But if they are someone we have hopes will get in line," Tyrian resumed his chastisement, "someone with potential, if they can learn, if only we give them another chance,' his grin turned vicious, his eyes alight with pleasure at the thought, "we have a special way of dealing with it." Tyrian ran his hands down the ribbon around his neck, finding the energy beamers held there at arm's reach.

"You said I could fight my way up in position," Ceres said. "How is that over reach?" This looked dangerous. Out of control. Overwhelming odds. Ceres guts cramped up as adrenaline took away his blood and fluids needed elsewhere.

"I assigned you to Thorsson's crew to learn from him over time, not kill him in the first week," Tyrian said. "You were supposed to fit in and gain some experience. Prove to the wolfpack why they should eagerly follow you. You haven't even proven yourself on your first raid yet!

"How can I promote you when we don't know if you aren't still an outsider? You haven't shown your commitment to be one of us. You haven't earned your Viking name by doing Viking deeds!"

Ceres nodded at the logic of that. He hadn't figured to stay around long enough to need to beg off raiding, secretly on moral grounds. He had no good excuse besides preparing his new ship first, to go raiding with them at the helm of his own command from the start. Time was up for that. Time to play their game.

"Okay," Ceres' forehead wrinkled, one foot shifted forward as he leaned towards his father, a determined look on his face. "Let's get this game over with. I have work to do."

He breathed deeply, filling his lungs. Tyrian raised the beam pistols in the general direction of his son, squinting at Ceres. The nearby guards too, shifted their aim towards the younger Tauri.

Ceres pushed back, off his forward foot, spinning towards the exit. He flashed past the hatch at a sprint and passed the first several pirates in the access tunnel before they could even react. Ceres' armor extended as he ran, rippling out of its backpack-like pile across his shoulders.

A fist crossed Ceres' jaw from the left. He reeled and staggered into the body of a huge woman on his right. She held a large metal plate shield that she used to throw Ceres off her and against the opposite wall of the corridor.

Ceres rebounded to the floor on his hands and knees, feeling the blows of several fists, feet, and blunt weapons rain down on his shoulders and back. The armor held, it would take a titanic and focused blow to crush through the graphene plates, but inside the suit Ceres' body was jostled, bruised, and battered from the blows.

He thrust off with his boot repulsors at a high-g acceleration. His chest smashed against the wall, he spiraled, scraping, up to the ceiling of the downward sloping corridor, accelerating past half of the assembled crew.

One of them reached up with both big hands and caught Ceres by the shoulders. He held on as Ceres' momentum lifted the pirate off his feet and smashed him through his crewmates. But the added weight changed their trajectory downwards into the hall. The sea of pirates reaching out brought Ceres down.

At least his fall was softened by the big man he fell upon. He heard the corridor behind him fill with the chaos of tangled bodies and shouting, cursing pirates as he tried to rebound back into the air.

Someone huge raised their foot and caught Ceres' shoulder, stomping him down flat to the deck. He felt several heavy impacts as several pirates jumped aboard to stop his flight. He ground to a halt to one side of the hall under a dogpile of the pack wolves.

Pirates wrestled with his boots, succeeding in pulling one off. Others undid Ceres' suit arm's ripfast, pulling the bracer off his right arm. Ceres considered flipping on his force shield to save it but decided that would just earn him a painful death if he used lethal weapons in this crowd. The conversation with his father taught him that, minutes ago.

These guys just meant to give him a beat down. He turned off the auto-stim features of his suit as well, reserving the limited onboard supplies for a later, dire need. *This is gonna hurt.* He pushed up to his hands and knees.

A pirate kneed Ceres in the left side of his face. His helmet came askew, halfway off and obscuring his vision. His eyes watered, the taste of blood in his mouth and its scent coming from inside his nose.

He thrust up to his feet, staggering, and limped forward, feeling kicks to his legs and knees, trying to cripple him. His armor's power braces prevented a serious injury. Still, he felt them trying. Probably want to leave a more lasting impression. To ward off the blows to his head he raised his left arm protectively.

One man crouched, then leaped from the left in a classic groundball tackle, smashing Ceres up against the wall again. The helmet popped off his head and skittered away, retracting into its compact state.

Twisted inside the armor by the pirate's tackle and then his body's impact with the wall, Ceres' ribs exploded in pain, the wind knocked from his lungs. The respirocytes in his blood put out oxygen to make up for the pause in breathing from the spasms in his diaphragm. His mind racing due to the adrenaline of combat, Ceres felt fortunate that these artificial blood cell nanites were standard issue in the Galactic military. He had to await the end of his amateur sports career to get the upgrades.

Falling to the floor Ceres rolled onto his side in a fetal position. He covered his face protectively with his right arm, his left covering his ribs as blows rained down from wooden training sticks, padded space axe handles, and booted feet.

Yes, if they left marks, they would have a right to brag that they did that, they dealt that blow. Bragging rights. Pack positioning. Perfectly understandable. Perfectly painful.

The chaos, noise, and aches seemed to slow in time and cease as the lums shone through the shadows of bodies standing over him. Bright light washed down upon him. The shadowy figures seemed to part, their angry shouting quieting down.

Ceres pushed up to his hands and knees once again, blood dripping from his face. *Who the hell is this?* Straining his sprained neck, he turned his head to see who the crowd had parted for, only to be flattened by a stunning punch to the jaw. He nearly lost consciousness. Certainly a concussion.

"I will help you finish." A hand reached down and took Ceres' hand, grasping above the wrist as if in greetings. With a twist and pull, Ceres was slowly flipped face down, only to be dragged, sliding, down the griptread surface of the corridor.

"Go on!" It sounded like Ceres' father but the blood pounding in his ears made it hard to be sure.

Bruise upon painful bruise thundered up and down Ceres' back and legs as he melted mercifully into the darkness of the floor.

Chapter 24
Brainstorming

Epsilon Eridani, P2, StarSys
2018/4/14/1300

"Listen up: here is the intel we've collected so far," Tarsis said. "Captain Barrwick himself arranged to have the ship impounded and a fast auction, so he could claim the ship for himself." The crew spent a moment uttering words of disgust at that captain's betrayal of his sacred duties to owner, ship, and crew.

"The original owners called StarSys and asked for us to help reclaim it. So, we have *The Palomar*, mid-sized freighter touring the Loose Ends on a charter hauling circuit. The captain conspires with the crew and a lawyer in 3Parthneid system to trump up a local impoundment and auction. The lawyer buys the ship at auction on behalf of the partnership between the lawyers, the captain, and crew.

"Barrwick takes over the route of the charter and goes right on with business as usual. They've stolen the starship from the rightful owners, cut them out of the deal, pay themselves the same wages as before plus split the owner's profit margin within the partnership.

"Now," Tarsis went on, "this is not the first time we've heard of a business or starship's buyout into a worker cooperative or employee owned company. StarSys itself makes such deals through our S.E.E.D.S. program, for a crew corporation to buy out their ship and jobs and go into business for themselves.

"We have been encouraging private entrepreneurship for hundreds of years because economic freedom is the ultimate personal freedom and drives the economy like nothing else."

"You don't need to convince all of us to go into business for ourselves, Uncle," Ceres joked. "You are setting a fine example."

"Ahem," Tarsis cleared his throat. "Let me finish my briefing and we will get to the brainstorming, then." Ceres beamed at him, convinced his uncle was more annoyed by his nephew's interruption than that he had been caught pontificating on a favorite subject.

"What is illegal here is the captain and crew's piracy based on the invented charges that cheats the proper owner of their ship. That's why we're here." Tarsis finished up. "Questions?"

"Are they on the same scheduled route as before?" Med's voice fluttered from the vocasters. "As navigator I wish to begin plotting intercept locations." Ceres knew his secret; that Medusa's networked brain lobes allowed multi-tasking in ways the Solman crewmembers could not imagine. Only the huge Rokkled could match it, and Carver was better suited than Med as an AB, 'Able Bodied Spacer', moving cargo in space. Ceres imagined Medusa blowing up like a gas-giant blimp in the vacuum of space, forcing him to repress his laugh.

"Yes, Med," Tarsis answered. "Go ahead. They went right back into their route without interruption. I doubt some of the stops even know there has been a change of ownership. As soon as they do, there might be a change, but we got the owners to hold off legal notifications while we investigate. This should allow us to get ahead of them and prepare."

"Stupid," Ceres commented. Young people his age were often indignant when others failed to follow the rules of society.

"No one ever said criminals were that smart, did they?" First Officer Riverwind chimed in.

"Crime doesn't pay," Ceres uttered the cliché.

"Au contraire, my young friend," said Jerome, setting loose his slow Cajun drawl. "Crahm *does* pay. Oth'uh'wise crim'nals wou'nt bother."

"If it did not pay enough or often enough," Riverwind said, "and resulted in hard consequences more often, then it would not pay. The smarter criminals would find more profitable, honorable ways to make a living. Tends to be more crime like this out in these rim sectors where the Galactic fleets do not patrol."

"But," Tarsis interjected, "in this one case among the many, our job is to make sure it does not pay for long. Correct?"

"Agreed," Jerome replied, affirmed by the crew's nodding heads.

Medusa said, "Let us have a look at that route."

Ceres 2525

* * *

Cordova, Valdez, Dock 2
2518/4/22/1645

"A fine mess o' ribs, son," Jerome grinned at Ceres.

"You're the bess cook here, 'Ol fren," Ceres did his best with his friend's Cajun accent. "Figger n'take your stake an' open a rib joint?" Ceres and Jerome had enjoyed cooking up a mess of ribs reminiscent of Jerome's southern style honey-slathered barbeque. Ceres usually took the opportunity to cook alongside each of the crew as they rotated through kitchen duty. It gave him a chance to get to know each of them on a personal level, and make friends. He bussed away the bone plates and towels.

"We see when dee time come, my young fren'," Jerome answered.

Ceres slipped into his more frequent rendition of a Southern boy he once knew. "Yup, pardner. We got a lot uh trail t' ride before we sell off the herd."

"Ha!" Jerome's laugh was as big and booming as the rest of him.

"Well if ya do farh up yer own barbeque pit," Ceres encouraged his older friend. "I'd be proud to work a grill for you or with you."

"We all need to have somethin' t'fall back on," Jerome added. "People always need tuh eat, lil' brother. Someday, when I'm too tired or too busted up to work starships, I'll take my savings and open a grill of my own. I'd be honored to have you come eat as my guest then, same as now."

He nodded and that was the end of it. The pair finished cleaning up and took their places among the assembled crew.

"She's leaving tomorrow and will be back here in two weeks," Tarsis's deep voice overcame the din of chatter and clanking of drinks, referring to the *Palomar*. "We have that long to take our places among the locals and iron out the details. What kind of ruse can we pull this time?"

"Can we hire prostitutes to distract the crew, a repeat of Atlantic City?"

"No, Mr. Riverwind. While we don't judge them, we should not support their lifestyle. Besides, those women were killed after the local boss investigated what happened. We learned from that situation and wise council with Father Mick about it afterwards. Now we know better."

The first mate nodded his head in agreement.

"We can pose as a repair crew and get ourselves hired on to refit her, then separate and disable the crew?" suggested the moving statue known as Carver. "This plan worked efficiently at Hatteras Bay."

200

The ship's vocaster speakers translated his thoughts into Galactic for the rest of the crew's ears. Silicon-based Rokkled's grew up in space and had a digital nerve network equivalent to Solman's implanted MeTR's, for communicating with others of their kind. They had some handicaps when trying to speak audibly as did the other sentient species.

"Yes. Possibly repeatable," agreed Tarsis.

"How about I slip aboard by myself and take it out of the harbor," Ceres offered nonchalantly. "Meet you all at the bottom of the hole?" Ceres suggested, meaning the far end of a wormhole jump out of the star system. "I can do that easily, the way I infiltrated the ship's datacore on Loganville."

"No!" bellowed Tarsis, popping his hand on the table, causing some of the crew to flinch. "You know that turned out badly when they found you in there. I won't risk you again that way. We will find another means."

"More suggestions?" The crew returned to murmuring and chattering while Ceres sat in a comfortable chair and tuned them out. He breathed deeply, eyes closed but roaming under their lids, his placid face turned up to the ceiling. Even if his input was now unwelcome to his uncle, Ceres still worked the problem in his head.

The crew dispersed to sleep on their ideas, recheck sensor data the next day and return for another session of brainstorming with fresh Intel. Ceres and Sensei lingered with Tarsis.

"Captain," Ceres called out. "I have a plan to submit."

"What? While we were all arguing the last two hours?"

"Meanwhile," Ceres nodded, "I have polished a plan. It will risk only one crew member."

"I assume you want to repeat your performance from *The Breadwinner?*"

"No, sir. This is a major improvement on that *successful* plan. This involves the same infiltration to the core of *Palomar* as I performed last night while you all slept." Tarsis' jaw dropped in shock. "How do you think I acquired the intel on the crew station's, berths, and the ship's layout?"

"Absolutely not!" ordered the captain. "I will not lose you too, son. You are going to have to find a way to help us without putting yourself at so much risk. Get some sleep. Dismissed."

Ceres stood to attention and saluted smartly. He pivoted on his heel and marched off, foot strikes echoing down the passageways. Marine drill instructors would be proud of his execution of parade drill standards.

His uncle recognized, it was not out of respect but a physical statement of sarcasm. Ceres was not in the military. His sharp salute and drill amounted to a statement akin to "Drill you, *sir*!"

"Sir," Sensei said, "A word please?" The elder man used words of proper respect due any captain aboard his own ship, no matter the relationship.

It was not, however, a request, and Tarsis saw that plainly. From Sensei's tone of voice, he took it not as a challenge to his authority but as a serious matter to which his old Sensei gave great importance.

"I gave my sister my word!" Tarsis went first. "I have protected this boy since before he was born. Surely you of all people understand family honor, the importance of honoring your word? I know he's not the angry little boy I presented to you for training, but he is still the one I call 'son.' I love him as if he is my own."

"You have a crew full of special operators," Sensei said, "likely the most overqualified freighter crew in the galaxy. And yet, Ceres has been doing work which none of the others can do," the master pointed out. "And he can do far more on his own."

"Another reason I can't afford to lose him!" Tarsis argued.

Sensei warned, "Sir, if you don't let him go, you *will* lose him. You have been holding him back because you can't see him.

"He is no longer your sister's little boy bouncing around your ship. He is on the verge of manhood, eighteen years old in a matter of months. In many ways he is a man already, just needing the additional knowledge and experience of," he paused, "his *own* experience."

Tarsis persisted in shaking his head.

"He is capable of far more than you allow," Sensei continued. "Observe, he can succeed alone where we have failed to find an effective way for all of us to act as a team. We have been grooming him all these years, for what?" While his old master paused, Tarsis was wise enough to await Sensei's summary.

"If the Eagle does not push the eaglet out of the nest, it will never learn how to fly. If it cannot fly, it is not an Eagle."

"Ah, yes, you just had to go there didn't you?" Tarsis sighed deeply, eyes closed. "Very well. We will promote him soon, begin his next level of challenges so he can develop more complex skills. He said something recently about the Academy."

The two men held each other's eyes for a moment. Tarsis was known for making his mind up quickly and never changing it. Now that his wise counsel had led him to a decision, it was set. He crossed himself and prayed.

"Lord grant me wisdom. What is Your will for me, for this boy whom You have entrusted to my guidance?" He thought back to his own Academy lessons. He thought *Presley O'Bannon just got it done.* A story of warrior leadership he had shared with his nephew.

"Son, do it!" Captain Tarsis transmitted via MeTR.

Ceres, caught amidst donning his infiltration gear, shot upright in surprise. He had been preparing to leave. If *Palomar* was gone the next morning, they would eventually figure it out and follow him. Unable to respond momentarily, finally his tongue loosened with excitement.

"Yes, sir!"

Chapter 25
Release My Heart

A-Valhalla, Slave Prison
2525/16/1230

"Help me get his shirt off!"

Babushka looked stern, disapproval on her face at Serenity's suggestion.

"With skin contact I can heal 'im faster. This is medical, Anastasia, not improper. Y'r gonna just haf'ta trust me."

'Two' lifted one of Ceres' arms and Babushka the other. Serenity peeled his white "2nd-Skin" t-shirt off, wet with his sweat, revealing a minefield of black and blue. Ceres' major armor plates were outlined on his skin in red, a few spots were tinged greenish, covering Ceres' entire body.

"Worse than I thought," Serenity frowned. "This will take all of my energy. You must assist me. Do you know about aikido kai energy transfer?" she asked the medic, 'Two.'

"No, but I know someone nearby who does."

"Go get 'em," Serenity ordered. "I'll get started. He needs me and I need him. We don'na have…" she cut off, in case the slave guards were listening. In fact, she was sure they were. Still, one must do what must be done.

She decided against peeling off her own top. The skimpy bustier style bra-top the pirates had given her left plenty of skin contact. Good for the connection she needed to form between them. She lay down on Ceres' prison bed, curling herself behind and around him like a pair of spoons in a drawer. Her legs tucked up behind his, her arms pulled his back tight to her chest.

Serenity closed her eyes and began synching her breathing with Ceres'. Then she matched his heartbeat with hers. Her mind reached out and she entered his dreams.

"I am here, Ceres," she thought. *"Are you well?"* She looked in on his dream as an observer.

* * *

"Mom!" Ceres shouted down the tunnel. "I'm coming!"

Through the hazy murk of the thin atmosphere, Ceres turned corner after corner. The asteroid's tunnels connected and turned like an endless maze. He raced from one corner to the next, always pausing before the turn, bracing himself for a fight or a surprise.

He could hear the heavy boot steps of someone following him. Ahead he heard a woman's soft sobbing cry. Always he got to the next bend and... found no one.

The cries echoed in the tubes and tunnels. It sounded like it was coming from overhead comm speakers. It sounded like it's behind him. Ahead, right next to him, all around him.

Down the hall a hatch like a jail cell door appeared. The woman's crying was louder. Ceres raced down the hall, which seemed to stretch farther the faster he ran. Finally, he leapt from the floor and flew like a superhuman hero from the holofilms. With a great strain of speed he caught the hatch and held on, settling beside it.

"Mom!" Ceres shouted. "I found you. I'm here." He found a solid durasteel hatch. The sobbing seemed to come out through the ventilation slats in the door. He pulled, finding it stuck. It was rusty. Flaky patches of rust seemed to grow before his eyes, encrusting the hinges. Sobbing echoed all around.

Ceres braced his foot next to the door and summoned Herculean strength, wrenching it free, shoving the rusted door open, aside, where it stuck out into the hall like a metal flag.

"I am here, Ceres," his mother's voice said. "Are you well?"

"I knew you were here somewhere!" Ceres shouted, "It was just a matter of finding you. Now we can get out of here."

"My handsome young man!" mom cooed softly. "I knew you would come. I always knew. Look at you! The same as I have always remembered."

Ceres seemed a small boy of ten, maybe younger. He waddled sleepily into the cell and up to his mother. A thick chain draped from a ring overhead in the ceiling, curving down to a thick manacle around her wrist. She sat on the edge of her thin, fold out bed, itself suspended by chains from the ceiling. When she reached open arms to him, he put his head on her shoulder and cried.

"You look exactly the same as I remember, too," Ceres countered. "Listen, momma! I came here to get you. Let's get going, you can tell me all about it when we're safely away."

"Okay, my happy boy. Now will you break my chains?"

"Oh, no problem," He fished around in his little pants pocket, pulling out a pocketknife. He flipped it on, a small force field blade erupting from the end of the handle.

No matter that her chains were as thick as her wrist, when the little blade touched them they shattered like a comet's ice crystals. He smiled at her.

"Oh! You've freed me!" she gushed, grabbing him for a tight hug.

Ceres beamed at his mom, pleased with her praise.

"Now, how will we get out of here?"

"Oh, no problem. We'll pop out." He reached in another pocket, producing a small ball of nested rings, like a bangle bracelet. He rolled it on the floor into the far corner of the cell.

"Hurry Ceres!" Mom shouted. "I hear people running this way!"

The rings expanded and grew to a ball of three meters, filling the space to the ceiling.

"Okay, Mom, get in," Ceres waved his arm and pulled her by the hand. They climbed into the interior of the rings.

"Hang on while this thing powers up!"

The rings started spinning and gyrating, building up speed. The hinges squealed as a huge muscular Viking pirate flattened the door open to the wall. Wicked space axe in hand, he filled the frame.

"Hold there, slave! There is no escape!" He reached over and grabbed Ceres' mother by the wrist,

"Help Ceres, save me!" Mom shouted.

In a blur of speed draw, Ceres pulled out a double-barreled pistol so big it was a carbine in his tiny arms. He fired, hitting the man square in the chest. The pirate flew back from the blast but started melting away as well. Dissolving in mid-air, there was nothing left to hit the far wall of the tunnel.

"Oh, you saved me again! When can we go?" Mom pulled her arm back through the spinning bars, seemingly unscathed.

"We're ready now. Let's go!"

"POPP!"

They appeared in a telepod on the hanger decks, next to an open airlock hatch.

"Okay let's go Mom!" Ceres shouted, excited.

"You've thought of everything! My smart boy!" Mom praised him, ruffling his short blonde hair.

Through the airlock they could see *The Barge* slowly maneuvering in to dock with the asteroid.

"Oh, I have you both now!" Tyrian's voice thundered from behind them.

"NO!" Ceres and his mother both yelled in terror.

"Don't let him take me again, Ceres!"

"Run, Mom, into the lock!" Ceres commanded. He turned on his father, fingers hooked like claws on a great cat. "AHRRRAAH!" he roared, leaping at his father.

The tall blonde pirate turned his purple cape and swept up Ceres in mid leap, bundling him like a constrictor snake. The pirate king tossed off his cape and Ceres with it, throwing them to the deck. The cape tightened while Ceres wrestled to escape. Over and over he tumbled, merely bruising himself, no closer to freedom from the tight bonds.

"Well, my dear 'sainted' wife," Tyrian sneered. "If you wish to leave, I will let you go."

Ceres gasped and looked up in surprise.

"Not without my beautiful boy, old husband," She answered. "I have served your purposes all these years. Let me have this one wish. Let *him* have this one wish."

"Oh, no," Tyrian said. "If you want to go this badly, there is a price to be paid. What was it your old favorite saint used to say? Let me see, 'Go in peace.'" Tyrian popped the hatch controls, blowing off the outer airlock.

The roomful of air blew out immediately into space, sweeping everything in the room with it. Ceres' mother screamed in terror, reaching out to grab the frame of the airlock hatch. "Ceres help me!" she reached for him with her off hand, body twisting in the hurricane wind of outgassing air.

"Mom, No!" Ceres screamed, horrified but helpless as he watched his mother begin to freeze in space. The escaping air took its heat with it. *Can't get free. Can't find her. Can't reach her. Can't save her.*

"I like another phrase better, dear wife," he sneered the words as if he loathed her rather than loved her, "'Until in death we do part.' So under the rules and laws of your 'Holy' faith, I consider this marriage over!"

Eyes glazed with frost, Mom's grip on the hatch slipped free and she drifted away slowly. Her body tumbled off the hull of the hovering *Barge*.

"Now, my boy," Tyrian turned and addressed Ceres, bound so tight within the constricting cape that he felt some of his bones and joints popping. "You are free of that old baggage. You are now *my* son. *Only* mine. Are you ready to take your place as my prince?"

Can't save her. I waited. She's lost. Too slow. She's gone. Too late. She's dead. My fault. She's dead.

* * *

A-Valhalla, Slave Prison
2525/17/0330

"Shhh shhh shhhh," Serenity consoled Ceres, whispering soothingly into his ear. She held him tightly around the chest as he heaved, sobbing, on the bed. "It was but a dream, love. A dream. A nightmare. You're safe. I have you. Your mum is safe."

Covered in sweat and tears, Ceres awoke with panic on his face, eyes darting around. Serenity reared her head away from his. He shook his head, breathing deeply. With a quick tactical scan, he glanced about the room, noting the medic, Two, and the grandmotherly babushka.

Settling back into the warmth of Serenity behind him, Ceres relaxed, her arms holding him close against her body. His neck exploded in fire from his sudden movement, his body afloat in a sea of pain. "Mmm, oooooooohhhhh."

Serenity gasped and winced, biting her lip. Linked to him as she was, his burst of pain crossed over to her too. His thoughts came laden with emotions, and now pain too? Tricky business, this gift. Much to learn. She tucked away the reminder to find someone capable of training her beyond her mother's ability.

"You're safe," Serenity cooed in his ear. "It was just a nightmare."

"Tell me you didn't-" Ceres cut himself off. Fresh emotional pain, his failure to free his mother, topped with sharing his weakness, his deepest secret fears, with the woman he wanted to impress with his strength? Not how he wanted to woo her.

"Yes, of course, I did what hadda be done," Serenity said. "I do understand you better now. Don'na try an' impress me, love. Just be true."

Ceres rolled his eyes and moaned again. This new nightmare hurt more than the rest, the old ones. The fact Serenity had shared it with him was somehow both troubling and comforting at once. His body was like a minefield of painful bruises interrupted by bomb craters full of flames.

"We will talk about that in the future," she said. "Right now I need your trust. Remember what I did for y'r hand, after you rightly punched Jaeger in his steely jaw?"

"Mmm hmmm," was the best reply he could offer. He mumbled, "Ooh, I can't feel any part of me without pain. Can you heal all of that?"

"I've been doing so while you slept, love," she answered. "Now that you're awake, I need 'ya to go into a state where you are detached from your body. Focus on visualizing something else in your mind. Can'ya 'elp me heal you by doin' that?"

Ceres drew a deep ragged breath, winced and lifted his bruised arm so his palm could protect his rib. She covered his hand with her own. He faded out of consciousness.

* * *

"Sore there?" Serenity asked.

Ceres blinked, nodded, and winced as the pain returned.

She drew a deep breath, closing her eyes. Linked with his mind a visage of pain crossed her face as she focused again, her kai flowing into the spot, ablaze, in his body. Babushka Aneka reached out and patted her shoulder to comfort her.

"You've a few cracked ribs there," Serenity confirmed. "So far that is the only major injury I find. They were trying to bruise you all over but not kill you, not cripple you. Not yet anyway."

"Did... good job," Ceres gasped out. Rolling to his side he balled up. He started breathing to a measured, counted pace, exercises learned in Sensei's dojo. He shifted his mind away from the pain, as taught in his military training. Distracting himself with tactical thoughts helped. Assessing his injuries mentally, he scrolled through one part of his body after another.

She understood the problem. Even if he acted stoic now and didn't speak it, she read his thoughts. Out of combat, his adrenaline was a memory, leaving all his ragged pain nerves to overload his senses. Without fresh combat to awaken his fight responses, he would remain awash in pain.

"Okay, breathe with me now, long and slow," she coached, hypnotically. "Breathe in. And now out. Slo-oh-ow. Good."

Complying with his nurse, he closed his eyes, breathing with her.

Serenity closed her eyes, to better visualize her own healing life force as a white aura within her. Her psionically enhanced vision allowed her to see the fields of energy around her, within her. The center of it, the source of kai in her abdomen, her soul, glowed brightly like a lum underwater in a sun lit pool.

Shifting "the sight" outward, her hands over Ceres' body, she saw inside him, seeking out his kai energy. Ceres' injuries glowed as spots and areas of angry red flame within his luminous body.

"Yes, you still're bruised all over, Ceres. I'bin 'ealing the worst of it while you slept, so it is much better now than it was before, but I hadda rest. This drains me. Though now I am ready to begin again, if you are."

Ceres thought about that a moment. "I didn't need you to look within me to tell me that. I can feel it. I can't move any part of my body without pain. They took my suit, didn't they?"

"Yes, stripped you and threw you in 'ere," she confirmed. "Dooms and Felsten took turns kicking you too, not wanting to miss out on the fun, it seemed. We girls came in and covered over you to stop th'm."

"They let you in, from your cells?" he coughed then winced, his ribs aflame.

"They called us in t'nurse you back to health. Afraid of your dear loving father's mercy, if his prince died, it likely was. They wouldn't do it, of course, heal you. So your slaves, they put us all in here with ya'. Plus the medic, remember her?"

Ceres lifted his right eyelid, the only part of his body not red or black with bruising. "Two" was busy programming an auto-injector to measure enough med out of a pack of stims. She smiled back at him.

"Can we trust her, to speak openly in front of her?" he thought.

She felt comforted that he counted on her to be listening for his thoughts. Despite her concerns they were growing more used to each other, more in synch, and more dependent upon each other to escape the looming terror the Vikings posed to both of them.

Her initial plan was for Ceres to fly her away from the pirates' asteroid base. Since then she had grown fonder of him. She didn't trust if it came of this new bleeding of emotions along with her mental connections? Or was she growing feelings for him? How to know the difference?

"So far, yes," she thought to him. *"And that includes the first time we healed you together after your duel. I can tell Petalia 'ere is afraid for her life, as are most of the captives. I haven't heard her thinking about anything but 'er life as a slave, and concern for you. If anything, she's too fond of you."*

Ceres felt a new pain in his thigh, then a warmth spread through him. All the little pains everywhere disappeared as heat flowed like slow lava down his legs, his arms, across his chest. *"Oh. Must be parathion, or ketamine?"*

"Yes, how can you tell?" the medic asked.

"Had it before, last wu—" That was all he got out before his jaw tightened up as well. *"Son of a ditch! I can't believe you are all doing this to me again! I thought she made us doses of antidote to this poison! Now you use it against me?"*

"Sorry, love, we-"

"I am tired of the people surrounding me, forcing me to lie here immobile while they make me do what they want. If we're going to get out of here alive, I have to take action. Now!"

Two dripped a drop of some bitter liquid under his tongue. Once again, the disjointed feeling alarmed him. His entire body was paralyzed, but he could now move his lips, his mouth.

"Calm yourself, Ceres," Serenity said aloud, "We're doing this to you again, yes. For your own good this time, not to take advantage of your helplessness." She laid down behind him again, wrapping her arms around him, her body mirroring his fetal position in her spoon position. "You will hold very still now, am I right?" she smiled sweetly. Two reflected that smile, bright eyes blinking.

Futilely Ceres attempted to roll his eyes and glare at Serenity.

She closed her eyes and once again visualized his reddened injuries, her body full of warm white kai energy. It flowed down her arms into his body, from her chest and stomach directly into his back, his internal organs. The white flowed over him, through him, into him, permeated him. Red zones of injury turned pink, eventually white.

She shifted her hands, healing energy needed elsewhere. Her body distracted her, reacting naturally to his body pressed against hers. *At least his pain and frustration at being injured and restrained, is keeping him from responding to this otherwise arousing situation.*

He grumbled low, sounding angry, "Mmm I seem to have no choice."

"To pass the time and distract us all, tell me more about your exploits with your famous Uncle Manny," Serenity suggested. "You were telling me about the one key mission at the end that helped you get into the academy? How did that work?"

Chapter 26
Solo Op

Cordova, Valdez, Dock 2
2518/4/22/1645

With vision enhanced by his HUD, Ceres detected the emission beams of multi-wavelength scanners watching the framework of the *Palomar*. He crouched on the exterior of the station module and activated his suit and shields. The reflectin weave of his chameleon suit shimmered, mirror-like then blended perfectly into the background.

His absorptive energy shields captured radiations of wavelengths below visible, effectively completing the stealth suit, while converting them to power stored in his capacitors. *One downside* thought Ceres with regret, as his vision went dark. He pushed off blind.

Forcing himself to keep breathing regularly and deeply helped to calm his nerves. Internally Ceres was ecstatic. He finally was off the leash and allowed to do his thing his way. *My mission. Mine!*

A tiny adjustment formed a small opening in the absorptive screen, allowing his suit's visor to receive in ultraviolet. He dared not turn towards the system's star or he would be blinded. The starship's reflective hull contrasted with the absorptive clouds and water of the planet below, allowing Ceres to "see" it on this angle.

Gently grasping a tubular strut of the cargo ship's lattice frame, he spun his body around. This minimized the vibrations to the ship so no crew or sensors aboard felt his impact.

Standard resupply operations were under way. One of the hatches allowed robo-tenders to push in and out with their magnetized pallets of goods. Right behind one of the robotic workpods, Ceres swung down and slid through the corner of the energy screen like a fish through a hole in the ice.

* * *

The load operator noted the energy spike and looked up. She saw the robot pushing the pallet of food stores towards the pantry corner of the hold. The hatch leading to the mess deck was askew. *I knew I should have loaded in vacuum. No noses nosing around,* she thought.

The operator moved some screens and menus aside in her HUD and initiated hatch closure. She sent a MeTR message to the cook through the crew group's link. *"Make sure all inner hatches are closed during open-bay operations. You don't want to get sucked out with me if something goes wrong."*

"Whatever, Parkins," the cook transmitted his voice. "You monitor ammo loading because that's your main concern. Food is my baby. Let me do my job, and I'll let you eat." The cook dismissed the load operator's concern, floating sacks of tubers into the mess so the bots could start peeling.

* * *

Ceres slid along the top corner of the wall like a snake. Zero Gravity ops were always his favorite. He could have bounced from surface to surface quickly through the ship if he didn't care about being heard or felt. Instead, he flowed like water through the ship, undetected.

That evening, the load operator reverted to her duty job of weapons officer. She reloaded all magazines for the projectile weapons, replaced two fried Ion Cannon capacitors and recharged the rest. Done for the night and ravenous, she finally enjoyed a delicious meal, spoiled by late suspicions of the secret ingredient of cook's spittle, and retired to her quarters for sleep period.

In the morning, *Palomar* would float out to the cargo zone and take on her load for the next leg. Captain Barrwick was sure to have arranged yet another tidy profit for them.

As Parkins slept she did not notice as her lungs filled with wisps of dramimune, above the MediCorps recommended dosage. She would not be waking up for days. Ceres extended a short length of nano-cable and linked his MeTR with the sleeping officer. Her body nestled snugly in her ZG bag, secured against her wall.

Officer Parkins seemed to log onto her terminal in her dreams. She used her own command bypass to access the central controls. She overrode all the alarms: hatchways, systems, environmental, and initiated a slow change to the air mix. None of this was visible on the bridge due to "Parkin's" fresh security lockout programs isolating the bridge duty watchman's screens to loop every 30 minutes.

Ceres retrieved the filament and stowed it, pushing off to complete his mission. Along the way to the bridge, he injected a large auto-syringe of dramimune into the air handler's humidifier. He disabled the auto-kitchen with his ion stunner, then carefully tucked the free-floating cook into the stasis freezer.

Entering the unattended bridge was as easy as floating down the corridor, through the hatch. No opposition at hand. Easy peasy.

Mrs. Molling had been slightly distracted from her duties as shift watchman anyway, faithfully observing her marital vows in the captain's quarters. Captain Barrwick wore no wedding ring as he fell asleep on Molling's shoulder.

Ceres slid carefully into the command seat of *Palomar* and took up the control chip from the pilot's array. Sliding it into his socket in his temple, Ceres booted up his cascade program and ran a search through recent password usage.

Her husband's name? Hmm, that was only my fourth guess. Ceres did not need to link to the captain to pull his passwords. Plan B remained on standby.

The hatches to the bridge slid shut and cogs spun into place to secure them. Now sealed in, Ceres grinned as he took full command of the ship.

With the oxygen level at 1/3 normal and a powerful sleep aid to overcome, most of the crew were sleeping far too heavily to wake up when the mooring beams cast off and the cargo ship's plasma maneuver thrusters burst to life. The massive ship jerked sideways out of the docking clamps and slid free into space. Fountains of blue-white sun erupted aft and *Palomar* burned for higher orbit, as the space platform went crazed trying to hail her.

From Dock 2, Tarsis and his crew popped over into *Palomar*'s telepod, armed to the teeth. They arrived just in time. Station security shut down exit systems a minute too late. From aboard the *Hasting's Haven*, a ship in drydock for repairs and refueling, Ceres popped over to *Palomar* last.

"Well, son," Tarsis began, beaming from ear to ear and grabbing Ceres by both shoulders, "you were right. Good mission. Well planned and well executed. No one truly at risk. Now, do your redundant crew the honor of flying us all back home, Captain."

Ceres accepted salutes and slaps on the shoulder from all of *The Barge*'s crew. He passed the gauntlet of their honor line in the hallway, taking command. The crew of special forces operators were geared up to pop over for their takeover of the system's civilian wormhole station.

Ceres petted Skritter when he moved him aside, pulling a datapin from the little robot's receptacle, ending the transmission link he had used to infiltrate *Palomar* by tele-robotics.

"Goodbye, Valdez Harbor!" Ceres waved. Entering the coordinates for their exit station into the auto-pilot, he snapped it shut.

* * *

A-Valhalla, Ceres' Cell
2525/7/17/1109

Serenity's energy faded fast. She needed backup. Focusing on healing Ceres' body, she was not aware of all the minds—all the people around her. The green armored guard Felsten surprised her at the grate-like cell door.

"Delivery!" he was always making jokes. She already thought of him as one of the sickest beings aboard the base, partly due to his morbid sense of humor. She'd be glad when he oozed back down the corridor and left them to the dire work of healing Ceres.

Yukozune, the immense human slave held deeper in the prison complex, filled the door, then entered the cell. "You called for my help?"

"Yes, Yuko," Serenity answered. "I need an orderly. Strong arms to help me move Ceres as we do physical therapy to heal him."

"Thank you, Master Felsten," she played her role. "We will begin more active therapies on the prince so he doesn't get bound up from all of these bruises and cramps. You don't want him to seem crippled when the king comes to see him, correct?"

"Well," Felsten seemed oblivious, "just get him mobile. Two days tops, when the fleet returns—" he stopped himself. "Never you mind that. Just get him well enough to stand before the master!" He turned and stomped off.

Serenity made eye contact with Yuko and clamped her lips tightly shut, to indicate silence for the moment. Once the guard was well beyond earshot she nodded. If they had listening devices then they would have to live with the outcome when it came.

"I hear you know how to transfer kai energy for healing purposes?" Serenity asked Yukozune.

"What?" he shot a blistering glare at the medic, who turned away, unable to face his anger.

"Yes," Serenity confirmed, raising her arm and waving off his anger, "she revealed your secret to me. I needed to know. We have urgent need of your ability. I have been healing him all night."

He took in a deep breath through his nose, blew it out of his mouth as a warm wind across the cell, then nodded. "My bloodline has done so for generations," He looked at Ceres, then back to Serenity, eyes squinting. "You want me to heal *him*? Even though he is a Master?"

"Yes. He is a good man. I am drained by this. Tired and weak and empty. I need your 'elp, love. Take a turn, please?" To cover up for how weak, how drained of energy she truly was, Serenity sat up and lowered Ceres' head and shoulders across her legs. She reclined against the cold cell wall, closing her eyes. She knew it would take time to recharge her batteries, so to speak.

Yuko grinned. "I'd rather give *you* my energy," he grinned, his hands rubbing together, both big as dinner plates, "You look more—"

"That would be unwise, my sumo friend." She smiled with confidence. Summoning her remaining strength, she commanded him, using psionics to aid her persuasion. "Do not anger an Amazon. Do as you're asked."

Yuko froze when she claimed her title, then wisely bowed in compliance.

She thought it might be worth some time having Yuko re-energize *her*, if Ceres was not more desperate for the healing. She was going to need him to do his part in breaking out of the asteroid complex. Large parts of their plan counted on his expertise, and he had to be mobile for action.

Everyone had a role to play. If Ceres couldn't deal with the base defenses and the fleet, she was stuck right back where she started when stepping off Trok's captured ship a week ago. Worse. Worse for all of them.

Yuko knelt before them on the cold duracrete floor. Closing his eyes, he made silent gestures which they all took to be silent prayers. Then he put his hands together and rubbed them warm.

He slowly ran his left hand down Ceres' body, pausing here and there, finally returning to the injured ribs. His right hand drifted down Ceres' leg, resting on his severely sprained knee, Yuko's hand wrapping around it.

With a bow of his head he began his hands-on healing ritual, breath shifting into a slow meditative pattern.

"Go on with your story, Ceres," Serenity bade him.

"Right. Just wrapping up the aftermath of that mission."

"The crew remained unconscious in their quarters," Ceres explained. "Only one little problem: worried about pursuit, I got caught up in the rush of our escape—taking her out of harbor, our commandos raiding the jump station, hole transit, system traverse on the other side—" he paused. "I forgot to re-oxygenate the air."

Serenity's eyes opened, bulging in mock alarm.

"We were all suited and helmeted. One of the ship's crew never woke up, brain damaged." Ceres stopped, winced. A tear formed in the corner of one of his eyes.

Serenity gasped, her hand over her mouth, feeling his dread, she worried he had killed an innocent. She was not yet sure how she would deal with dark parts of his past like that if he had. Would she be able to invest herself fully in helping him get a handle on his need for vengeance?

"I was released without charges, mostly due to my age. The magistrate could not believe I intended to harm them and said it was a natural consequence of their crimes. Uncle put the family's resources behind it—"

"To get you off easy?" she accused.

"No, to save *her*. Our best doctors, best hospital, all of that. Unlimited."

Serenity nodded, relieved. This sounded like a family with its priorities right, then. That felt better. She breathed out the tension she had just felt amp up.

"But, she's never woken up. Not yet," He lifted his eyes to meet Serenity's moist green eyes. She felt his strong emotions affecting hers.

"Thing is; I did not have remorse. Don't. The lovely young Mrs. Parkins was an enemy caught by the consequences of her grand-theft: spacecraft. In the moment, I had thought of venting the entire atmo but changed my mind. The rest of the thieving crew stood trial, were convicted of multiple felonies, and were transported to a prison colony planet. My uncle took me aside and told me two important things."

"What were those?" Serenity played along, knowing from her newfound empathy that his true feelings were remorseful, despite his callous words. She could feel it within him even though he denied the truth, even to himself. *He talks a good game, the tough guy act, but he's like a candy bar: crisp, crunchy, and covered up on the outside, with all the tender good stuff you like inside.*

"He said," Ceres adopted a deeper voice. Serenity assumed he was impersonating his uncle. "One: you did what you had to do. Two: I am proud of you.' I have never looked back. Until telling you about it today."

"I entered Navy boot camp and then the Academy shortly after that Op. Uncle Manny continues to be proud of me. I work alone so I don't endanger anyone but myself. I don't want the responsibility again after losing…"

"Iron," she finished his sentence for him, plucking the name right out of his mind. Her people confronted their fears and failures in a direct way, differently than did he and his, apparently.

"Yes," he finally said. "But I do whatever it takes for my mission."

Serenity breathed deeply while she contemplated this. *Can I trust you? She thought to herself. In the end are you good, or a bad man? Will you be an ally, or will you hurt me? Do you want my love, or just a lover? Same question for myself.*

She asked him again to explain himself. "Do the ends justify the means? Or are we held to a higher standard?" They shared eye contact silently. "How are these ship recoveries not just, piracy on the pirates?"

"With our business license, judicial backing, and letters of Marque from the original owners of the ship, we were technically privateers," he answered her. "We received more and more such jobs as the stories spread across the shipping industry.

"That same crew is still around right now doing ops exactly like that, recovering stolen starships and sometimes rescuing kidnapped people." He looked at Yuko with dead eyes, who swallowed, returning the blank look.

"To date no one has been seriously injured let alone no deaths, though the judges have indicated it would be justifiable.

"My uncle went back on active duty in the Navy when I entered the Academy. Three years of college, four years' compulsory service in the merchant fleet, done. I am on indefinite leave while I decide what I want to do next with my life. I came to meet my father, looking for my mother, and here we are."

Breathing deeply, Serenity had to decide what to do with this dangerous young man she was falling for, use him just to escape the asteroid, or more? Far more? She clasped her hands, set them on Ceres' hands, which he held together on his chest, and smiled sweetly back at him. "Here we are."

Chapter 27
Who Rescues Whom?

A-Valhalla, Hanger Deck
2525/7/18/1030

Before putting their daring plan into action, the vivacious fledgling Psion with flaming hair, did a mental inventory, ensuring that a high percentage of the pirate band had headed off on a major run.

The trustee Kangee was the sole exception to the current lockdown order. As daily, he trudged with his bags of paints and gear through the vault-like hatch from the slave prison leading to the strip of hangers belting the asteroid. Just through the hatch he dropped a handful of rolled canvases.

"Oh, hold up, Felsten," he called out to the controller. Taking a moment to re-roll one of his sketch canvases, Kangee secured them under his arm. Standing, he saluted the holo-cameras atop the hatch then continued up the tunnel towards the hangers and his latest commissioned work of art.

"Always daydreaming, his head lost in his work," muttered Felsten. He thumbed the manual controls for the hatch on his desk-wide control console.

"Yeah, distracted," agreed Dooms. "If not for the galaxy class work he does for the boss, I'd love to help him get right." Dooms tapped his shockrod on the deck to emphasize his meaning.

"Well," Dooms stretched and yawned. "The fleet's away. We're in change now." He grinned at his henchman Felsten.

"You know what they say?" Felsten replied with a knowing look.

"When the wolves' are away, the sheep will play," Dooms stoked his beard and grinned as he walked deeper into the slave prison, oblivious to the old adages he had mangled.

* * *

Kangee sat atop the freshly "painted" sky-blue surface coating the last spacecraft in the hanger, deep in meditation. Surrounded by his canvass concept sketches, he prepared to program the ship's skin to depict the grand design he had conceived for Ceres. He sensed Serenity's contact with his mind as a faraway feeling, her use of his vision as a slight haziness like when he woke up early.

Distracted, he looked up and gazed across the quiet emptiness of the vast hanger. The open hatch at one end stood silent vigil over yet another barren hanger, the deck curving over and down, away from him. Kangee inhaled deeply, closed his eyes, returning to his reverie of his latest epic mural.

* * *

"Ladies," Serenity spoke to her cellmates. "There comes a time when you have to be your own hero. I must go now. Be careful." She transferred Ceres' sleeping form from her lap to the grandmotherly Babushka's knees. Serenity turned the tiger stripes of her vari-fab outfit black, creating a solid color scheme, then tucked her hair up and in.

The two older women both nodded, but neither got excited with hope. "Be safe, dear," Babushka said, then bowed down her head. She silently prayed *Father please preserve us innocents from reprisal due to this brash traveler's actions.*

I forgive you, Babushka Anastasia, Serenity prayed in return, having heard the mental prayers of her cellmate. She thought it would be more helpful if the grandmother had prayed for heaven to intervene. She and Ceres could use divine aid to ensure success in freeing Babushka and all of the slaves from these evil pirates.

"Well!" Dooms presented himself at the cell door, drawing himself up imperiously. "It seems your owner finally has a good use of you, Ginger," his nod indicating Serenity. "Let's go." The slaver tossed a set of power cuffs through the bars, gripping his electro-staff with both hands.

Serenity startled when the cuffs clattered on the floor. She rose slowly, rubbing her eyes and yawning. Stretching like a sleepy cat she moved, listlessly, to pick up the cuffs. In slow motion, she put on one, then a second bracelet, sighing. They retracted automatically, tight enough to dig into the skin above her wrist.

"Oh!" she gasped when the power snapped on, the electromagnetic bindings pulling her hands together. "It tingles!"

"Heh, heh, yeah," Dooms oily voice purred. "You have more surprises coming today. Okay, you two grandmothers, stay put there!" he ordered.

"Yes, sir," they replied in tandem. The older slaves were years beyond hope of resistance gaining them anything but pain or even death. They did not raise their heads.

Dooms slid the metal grate door open and waved his hand, beckoning. Serenity rose and shuffled forward into the hallway, jumping at the loud clank of the door slamming closed. Dooms chuckled again, his hand drifting to Serenity's back, he guided her down the corridor. She did not respond.

"You are in for a treat today, my dear," Dooms said. "A special lesson in how the underground economy works among us Void Vikings. You see, we barter, gamble, trade, sell among ourselves, that which we own or control." They were almost to the junction with the main control station and access hatch into the rest of the base.

"During raids, our king demands that the slave cells be locked down, so those of us remaining don't take advantage of your proper owner's absences. But you begged me to let you and the medic heal him. You asked for that big man to help you as an orderly to move your master's body as needed. You asked for the favor of staying at Ceres' side overnight."

"In his own quarters—though I say he cheated to steal them from his predecessor—there, that would be his natural right. But in here, considering the lockdown, considering our king may well throw him out the airlock tomorrow... no. It is not permitted for prisoners to have visitors."

"I bent these rules for you because I am the master of these cells and all within them. You and your young prince now owe me a favor. I am sure he enjoyed the pleasure of your company. Having watched you sleeping here this last week, I can understand why."

"Save some for me!" Felsten, Dooms' henchman, said from behind the command console as Serenity shuffled docilely by under Dooms' close lead. Felsten pushed the old prison's stolen keyboard to open the main hatch, allowing Dooms and Serenity to leave the slave pens. The thick hatch slowly swung outward like a bank vault.

"All favors have a price, and I am collecting on those favors now," Dooms went on, seeming pleased with himself. "He will enjoy your company again later,"

Dooms turned Serenity to face him, cornered her against the hatch frame, and lifted her chin so he could see her expression. She thought it would be part of his sick fun to see the horror on her face when she realized what he meant. She determined to deny him that moment.

"I will enjoy the pleasure of your company now," He smiled.

Serenity grimaced as he lifted her long hair locks and smelled them. *If I don't vomit on you, you, loathsome thing,* she thought.

He tilted his head towards the exit corridor, pointing with his shockrod.

Serenity took a careful long-legged step over the large sill. On the next step, she tripped over something on the floor. It was a roll of canvas. She fell to the floor.

Dooms, puzzled, picked up the canvas, rolled it open and took a step toward Felsten, where the lighting was better than in the outer corridor.

"Kangee missed one. What's on it?" asked Felsten.

"A weird, horse-bird hybrid?" replied Dooms. "Like those squids are always creating? Kangee, lost in his daydreams." He shook his head. "I will definitely give him something to get his head straight." Energizing his shockrod, Dooms turned back toward the hatch.

"Pask!" he swore, using one of the Vikings oldest Scandinavian slurs, "where is she?" he shouted as the two observed the empty corridor beyond the half-retracted armored hatch.

"You idiot! You let her escape!" The fit Felsten vaulted over the command desk and ran out the hatchway.

Passing Dooms and then the half-opened hatch, he pitched forward, launched by a blow from behind. He sprawled unconscious onto the deck, his body racked with spasms as waves of energy rippled through him.

"Yes, Ceres," Serenity thought, *"these guys are as dumb as you said they would be."*

Dooms stepped back as his eyes widened. Serenity stepped around from behind the open hatch, scowl on her face. Dooms, bewildered, just shouted, "You filthy slave, what did you do to him? Get back to your cell, wench!"

Serenity marched through the hatchway, stalking confidently towards her captor. Dooms backpedaled slowly as she approached with long, slow steps. The capacitor rod in her hands chinked as she extended it to three meters long, its short spikes bristling.

Dooms recognized the threat. "A capacitor? Drain the energy out of me, like an electrical vampire, huh girl?"

She realized his chainmail suit, electrically grounded, protected him from other electrical weapons, but not this one. Ceres had told her he had noted Doom's armor days earlier. Cassius crafted this device to counter it.

"No, this is but a tool," Serenity answered. "The real threat is the one who welds it. Have ya' never wondered why they call my people 'Amazons'?"

Dooms eyes widened in horror. His mouth opened, chewed the air, silent.

"Because we women, conquered the beasts, which killed most of our men, in the colony landing party," She twirled her staff. "Beasts to give you Vikings, nightmares." Her eyes widened to punctuate the word.

Her voice dropped to a low, menacing growl, as if she were telling horror stories around a campfire. "Dragons and dinosaurs and demons, they called them. We women proved more ferocious than they are. You will see why."

Dooms ran around the security console, making a dive for a big red button on the commo board. His hand missed the panic button, though, slapping down beside it as if his hand had been pushed aside. He looked up in shock, seeing that Serenity had closed to within a long step away.

With a dark look of determination on her face, the young redhead swung hard, across the board and up towards his head. She grimaced at the "CRACK!" of the tritanium cap against the sadistic slaver's jaw. Doom's helmet went flying across the command center. Continuing her fluid move to spin on her heels, Serenity followed the first blow with another, this one landing high on the side of his head.

The force of the strike to his temple, plus the energy surge—body electro-chemical energy pulled through his spine up into the rod—the fat human fell over the commo board. In the throes of a seizure, his body bounced back, nose bleeding, and fell into one of the operator chairs behind the desk.

He slumped, twitching, as the chair wheeled back against the wall behind the security station. Serenity growled, taunting him, "Enjoy yer' lunch."

Plucking the datapins from Doom's head, her MeTR analyzed them. Soon she rolled him over to the security station, placed his palm on a reader pad, and pushed buttons nearby.

"Clack, sshhk, cklank!" The sounds of multiple doors unlocking, sliding, and slamming open echoed down the first corridor.

* * *

"Ceres," Serenity yelled from beyond the cell bars. "On your feet, soldier! Alert condition one!"

Ceres shot up out of bed in a stance ready to fight. Finding no enemy at hand to fight, he realized how much pain he was in. Nostrils flaring, he breathed in deeply to awake his mind more quickly, with more blood oxygen flowing to his brain, adrenaline fueling his fight instincts.

"OOoohhh," he moaned. "Crewman." He over-extended an arm, popping his elbow joint.

"What?" she asked, puzzled. She came around the open cell door, holding forth his uniform jumpsuit as if it was a birthday cake. His boots represented the cake beneath the frosting of black fabric with its design of sprinkled star points.

"The Navy has crewmen," Ceres groaned. "Soldiers are Army ground pounders." He stretched to work kinks out and find the real wounds among the minefields of mere bruises remaining across his body. "They come along after, to occupy planets the Navy and Marines take in combat."

Glancing up he noticed her eyes roll and head shake. Over her shoulder hung his belts of weaponry and gear pouches.

"I've seen this scene before," he tried, weakly, to joke, pulling the legs of his suit on, covering his boxer briefs.

"You w'r actin' so cocky n' foolish, like the prince apparent," she teased.

"Yes, I get the irony of this," he rolled his eyes, laying the ripfast seams over each other to seal up his suit. "Here you are breaking me out of captivity. My hero. Our roles reversed quickly didn't they?" He palmed a lump in his suit over his liver.

"Your father is fickle. A sign of his mental instability and drug abuse. Now, get your gear on, soldier, and go be the hero I need y'to be."

"Plan A?" Ceres asked. Pausing, he closed his eyes, taking in a deep breath of relief. Pain meds, stims, and anti-inflammatories flooded his veins from the auto-stim unit embedded in his suit. He pulled on his boots, long gloves and gear belts while Serenity went on.

"Kangee don'na see any ships or pirates around your ship. We need to scout the hangers, to make sure we're safe to fly away."

"We can tap into the internal holo-net and the flybots. First step is to secure the prison," Ceres said. "Did you close the hatch?"

Serenity's wide eyes told him what he needed to know. Belts unfastened, Ceres raced down the corridor with Serenity right on his heels.

Sliding into the command center, Ceres turned right into the exit hatch corridor just in time to leap up, power-assisted by his boots, kneeing the staggering Felsten under the chin.

"You woke up at nap time!" Ceres teased him. With a crunch of his armored knee versus the guard's armored helmet, Felsten rebounded from the wall and slumped to the floor. "Back to sleep, bad boy!"

Ceres dragged Felsten inside the security anteroom, plucked out the guard's datapins and thrust them into his own socket for analyzing.

"Here," Serenity said. "These were yours, Thorsson's, and Dooms'." She handed him a small nest of pins. "Dooms was analyzing them all."

"Great," Ceres thanked her. "I am confident in my security." She looked at him expectantly. "Even if they figured out what we planned, we have to go forward now. The ball is in bounds, play clock's counting down. Time for our team to take the sphere!"

Serenity smiled, shaking her head. "You boys and your sports."

"Hey, I am..." He cocked his head to the side, spread his arms and grinned, but let the thought die on his lips.

"Okay, next step: we lock these guys in a cell." He pulled Felsten by his ankles; sliding across the deck made easier by the guard's graphene plated outer armor.

"Yes, sir!" Serenity gave him a half mock-salute, half upwards wave. She wheeled the unconscious Dooms down the corridor to the nearby cell, where Ceres dropped Felsten. Probably the only safe place for them once the slaves were free.

The cells she had opened earlier were devoid of slaves. "Dooms must have liked it quiet," Ceres speculated aloud, "so he moved them away from his 'office' at the front?"

"Poetic justice, but not mob vengeance?" she ignored his question as rhetorical, asking her own.

"Yes, exactly," Ceres slammed the sliding cell door then melted the lock with a short blast from his disruptor pistol. Seconds later the metal disintegrated and ran like warm putty. It fused together when it cooled.

"Handy little thing," Serenity joked.

"Little?" Ceres shot her a sideways look, peering down at the huge double-barreled disruptor pistol in his hand.

"Boys and their toys," Serenity teased him, wrinkled lip repressing a big smile while she gently shook her head.

He grinned as they returned to the control console. Ceres looked over the analog panels of buttons and lights. "It must be a security protocol to have a manual control board? That, or, this is what they could steal and bring out here. It's not like they could hire a contractor to install modern systems."

Ceres stabbed Felsten's—now Ceres'—datapin into the socket. In his HUD, he saw a pop-up screen of the cam views now linked to his neural network, bridged by the datapin with the asteroid's security network. He scrolled through several cameras installed around the slave prison complex, returning to monitor the anteroom and approach corridor. These he slid to the side of his vision so he could focus.

"Looks clear," He ran down the corridor towards Serenity's former cell. *"They must not get many escape attempts-"* he turned to mental communication with her, easier when running. *"-being trapped on an asteroid. Futile."*

"Nowhere to go," she responded. *"That explains the desperation, resignation of the slaves to their lives. Why some go over to their side."*

"Sort out the beings in here," he advised. *"Whoever you trust, get them ready to run for the hanger deck. Remember, if you don't trust them, if they have crossed over to the pirate's side, just stun them and move on. They are responsible for their choices."*

Yes, love," "Serenity answered. *"As when we founded Terran Tor, we will not lose the all, for failure to sacrifice the few, as needed."*

Ceres arrived back at her old cell, at his three cells for his three groups of slaves. He stood outside them, to speak to the household and boudoir women, and the starship mechanics.

"Listen, all of you," Ceres called out. "We are leaving this asteroid today, while the pirate fleet is away. We can free you, or you can stay here. Who wants freedom?" Ceres raised his hand.

The men all stood up, one coming to the cell's door. Arturo raised his hand, grinning at Ceres. He glanced about, seeing the others' heads hanging.

"What is wrong with you?" Arturo chastised his cellmates. "This is our chance to escape! This man has treated us very nice, very good."

"I'm no fighter," one said.

"I'm afraid to die young," said another, returning to sit on the bunk bed.

"Si, we are no caballeros," Arturo agreed, "but I know you, amigos. We four have been stuck here together for over a year. More of us have come and gone, lost to the whims of these bad men, these banditos. We all wish to live free or die trying. Let's get out of here, no? Yes!"

"I am here to free you, all the slaves here," Ceres asserted. "If you want to survive the day, help each other get to the crew hanger, to my ship. Anyone left behind will not survive."

Serenity found the cell numbers on the old prison manual control board and punched them. The three doors slid open.

"You are free to choose," Ceres said. "Sit down and wait for death, sooner or later, dead is dead. Or, come with me and *liiiivve!*" He emphasized the word with a lot of zest in his voice. With that he turned and strode down the cell-way towards the next junction.

Arturo followed him around a corner and down a few doors. "273," Ceres called out to Serenity, although she already knew this from reading his mind.

"Men!" Ceres smacked his fist into his gloved palm, getting the attention of the two huge men inside the cell. "I'm breaking everyone out of here, right now. Cassius, Yuko, are you crew or jetsam?"

The two cargo specialists usually labored under the thrall of the Tenublian jelly-squid pirate. They had been working for Ceres on the ship repairs, but today they were locked inside the slave prison during the pirates' run. "Crew!" they both shouted, shooting upright and coming to the bars of the door.

"If you cross me, I will kill you immediately," Ceres warned them, turning to include Arturo in his threat. "I need you to keep the crowd of slaves safe while I gather ships to fly you all out of here. Will you do that in trade for your freedom?"

"Been waitin' for my chance to rip some tentacles offa that slimy squid!" Cassius growled. "If I kin do that, Ah'm in." Ceres nodded sharply and looked to the other man.

"Same here," Yukozune grunted. "Deal? But you must free us first."

Ceres grinned, made gunfingers, pointed, fired. The cell door slid aside thanks to Serenity following the conversation in Ceres' head. He blew across the tips of his fingers as if blowing away the smoke from a chemical-launched slug thrower. Ceres smirked, offering his hand to one of the towering men. They shook on it firmly, moving to the door. "Deal," Ceres answered. "Glad to have you on board."

"Jefe, we need armos," Arturo said, walking alongside Ceres. He made gunfingers with one hand and swung a blade shape with the other. "We'll be blasted like parked asteroids." The group passed the cells where Arturo had joined Ceres. He waved his hand at the remaining men and women, bidding them to join in the escape.

"I'll have Serenity open the locker room, the guard's armory inside this prison," Ceres said. The other three mechanics poured out of the cell, hustling to catch up. The women's heads popped out of their cells. They glanced among themselves, then started down the corridor after Ceres' entourage.

"I'm on it," Serenity replied in his head.

"She's looking," Ceres told his men. "You help her free the rest of the slaves. Secure the prison until you can guide them to freedom. Taking care of the rest of the base is my mission."

"By yourself?" Arturo sounded horrified.

"I work better alone," Ceres frowned at him. "It will be safer for you all when I draw them away from here." The group of escapees arrived at the command center where Serenity held court as the warden's usurper.

"He'll be ahright," Cassius smacked his big palm hard on Arturo's shoulder. Arturo nodded, pursing his lips.

"Si, Jefe, you run off on your loco, Don Quixote adventure, yes?" Arturo said. "I will have our ship ready in case we see you again," he poked a thumb at his chest. "Oh! You must find that fire computer for my Señorita'! We can't fight our way out with no guns, Señor'!"

"We will have all the guns we need. Don't worry, amigo," Ceres answered. "You men, help her," he pointed to Serenity. "Secure the prison and handle the rest of the slaves." They each nodded assent to him.

"Okay, next phase," Ceres said, punctuating by clapping his hands. "I will go by the gun range, grab a bite of lunch," he teased, "think I'll go shopping after that. Let me know when you've got the ship loaded." He faked a nonchalant face.

"You run along and go play, little dear," Serenity tried to play along like a motherly character in a children's holo-film. "I'll just pack th'ship, an' take care of everything." They both laughed at each other's sarcasm. The men traded knowing glances between each other.

"Be safe," she said with that uniquely feminine ability to combine the sounds of genuine warmth with worry. She frowned at his enthusiastic answer.

"Be right back!"

* * *

A-Valhalla, Armory
2525/18/1057

Tyrian walked briskly down the corridor towards the armory. "Okay, crew, check in. I popped back from the fleet early, to check up on you." He flashed his hawkish scowl at the holocam above the vault-style hatch. "My upstart whelp of a son hasn't come around here trying to get his hands on anything, has he?"

"No, sir," Olavir Gunnelson answered his king through the vocaster. "We're all clear. You're the first customer we've had since the lockdown."

Tyrian, a smug look on his face, nodded approvingly.

"Sadly," Hleidi added quickly, "no sign of that handsome young prince of yours. We haven't had the pleasure, since he first arrived." She batted her heavily painted eyes dramatically and waved a plump, bejeweled but carbon-covered hand as if she were suddenly hot.

She knew it would make Olavir, her husband, irate with jealousy. Olavir and Hleidi had been working the armory together for many years. Eventually they married, making it much easier to flirt and fight.

"Then that whelp better stay clear of my airspace!" Olavir suddenly outburst, his fat belly wiggling under his black leather apron. "I'll show *him* how to melt down a pirate!" He stalked over and, with a flourish, yanked the covering tarp off a huge multi-barreled laser called a rotary cannon, Olavir's personal weapon of choice for defending the armory.

"Hold, old friend," Tyrian chuckled as he warned. "He is my son. Let me in to check on the supply room, personally."

Hleidi winked in exaggerated fashion towards the door, apparently thinking to open the hatch. With a "Clonk" the massive vault door opened and rolled slowly aside like the seal stone of an ancient tomb. A low humming sound to one side tipped Tyrian off that it was magnetically controlled.

Tyrian marched in with long strides, continuing, "Thanks. Ceres said he needed a new fire control computer to get his fancy new civilian ship ready for raids. Didn't we scrounge one up a few months back?" Olavir nodded, lips squashed into a pursed frown. "Show me that it's still secure," Tyrian ordered his armorer.

* * *

The fat man waddled down the halls, leading Tyrian through the locker rooms, babbling about the mess this ship's crew left lying about, dirty weapon problems due to that negligent pirate, and rival crews pulling sabotage-like pranks on each other's guns, which he and his wife had to repair.

The ship's crews each had their own sports style locker rooms to secure their personal weapons between raids. Colorful nicknames and graffiti decorated many of them, too rude for any but pirates to proudly display.

"Here we are," Olavir gestured at an airlock hatch. Through the view port Tyrian could see the clear outer port shining with red light from the nebula beyond.

Tyrian raised an eyebrow at him in question, "Isn't this an outside escape hatch?"

Olavir moved a large fanbeam lase, hanging beside his leg, out from under his work apron. Its multiple barrels spread apart as he gripped it. "You should know the layout and contents of this place just fine, sir, *if,* you were in the MeTR group with the rest of the crew left behind, as I am now."

His amiable smile turned to a grim scowl. "Hands up! Don't move."

"How can I put my hands up but not move?" Tyrian quizzed his man with humor.

"You got 'im, honey?" sing-songed Hleidi's voice from beyond the locker rooms' hatch. She sounded close. The blonde man's forehead wrinkled.

"Yes, dear," Olavir answered her. "That reward is our ticket to a rock of our own! Whoo hoo! Stay there, honey. Cover my back."

Tyrian tilted his head to the side and grinned as if his weapons master was crazed. "Are you feeling all right, old friend?" He slowly raised his hands in the usual show of surrender and caution.

"Dump the pask, young prince!" the armorer barked, his meekness emboldened by the laser shotgun he wielded. "We've been on to you since you couldn't open the hatch by yourself.

"Pretty good impersonation of your father, I'll give you that, but no ribbon of pistols, either. Your father, our king, warned us to be smart. Now, into the airlock!" He gestured with the fanbeam towards the airlock besides them.

"How much?" Ceres-as-Tyrian asked.

"Huh?" Olavir did not understand.

"What size of bounty? What's the young prince worth?"

"Oh, that. Uh, 10,000 Dollari dead, 50,000 Di alive." He used the currency's abbreviation, pronouncing it "dee-eye."

"Insulting!" Tyrian's face showed Ceres' frown. "I am far more valuable than that! I guess, if actions speak louder than words, you gotta prove it sometimes."

"Tyrian's" hands partly up, he braced his foot behind him and made a push gesture at Olavir. Thrust by pressor beams, the shotgun smashed across the fat man's stomach, knocking the wind from him. The shotgun fired a spread of laser beams that punched a line of pockmarks, fist-sized duracrete chunks exploding from the walls of the armory. Their ears filled with pulsing laser bursts, millisecond buzzes like robotic bees on overload.

"Tyrian" reached out with his right hand, grabbing one of the outer barrels in the duck's-foot brace of them, flashing his plasma pistol out with his left hand. He moved his foot beside Olavir's leg, turned his body using the slung shotgun, and pushed.

Olavir shouted as he fell back, spinning as he went, landing heavily on his side. "Tyrian" went down with him, landing behind him on the deck. There was no other cover in the middle of the room than behind the fat armorer and he expected the man's wife would retaliate.

A volley of laser blasts burned through the air over them, the room echoing with a loud series of buzzing shots. Hleidi wielded the massive rotary cannon, floating easily on its repulsor mount, held in place by tractor beams and protected by its own force field shield, glowing blue around the protruding barrels. "Get him, sweetie!" she yelled through the echo of the blasts.

"Uuhp, ahh!" were Olavir's last words, before a plasma blast shot the back of his head. A military-style plasma caster thrust out under him. Low across the floor flashed packets of star-hot plasma into Hleidi's foot and calf, followed by the distinctive "pahk-pahk" report of the pistol.

She fell to that blasted knee, screaming in pain as she continued down to the ground. Still holding the firing handles of the heavy weapon, Hleidi slewed it around, firing blasts at the hatch, wall and ceiling. Her large body rolled out from behind the protective shield, quickly dispatched by two shots in the ribs.

The Galactic Military favored plasma weapons for their ability to melt through most un-shielded materials like a blast-torch through warm butter. Effective modern security defenses required the right combination of physical and energy protections against the attacker's weaponry. Each of Ceres' favored weapons required different kinds of energy screens to ward off.

"Tyrian" quickly pulled his arm out from under Olavir's remains. He stood and shucked off the mess from his left arm, hand, and plasma caster. He decided not to reholster it until he cleaned it. First he reached down and removed the datapins from the late head armorer of the Void Viking clan.

"Hmm, this disguise was short-lived," he said to himself, removing the blonde wig his female slaves had loaned him. "Tyrian's" holographic disguise shimmered and cut off, and Ceres stood tall over Olavir's body.

Sticking the datapins into the socket in the back of his head, Ceres' MeTR started analyzing them. He tore off the flowing shirt his father had loaned him for the duel versus Trok days before. Repaired by his Babushka, it was again stained in this latest battle.

With the clean parts of the shirt Ceres' mopped up his tight sharkskin-like glove and the sleeve of his Navy blue uniform. He frowned, but knew the futech fabrics would not stain. His armor plates being blood red, he preferred the under-suit remain a sharp Navy blue.

"Step two complete," Ceres thought to Serenity. *"They know we are moving against them. Stay locked in the slave pens. The armorers said they were MeTR grouped with the remaining pirates. Most of them should come here to collect some kind of bounty on me, my father's way of expressing my low value due to my inevitable betrayal."*

Ceres grabbed Hleidi's datapins, too, then pushed the hovering multi-laser back towards the entrance to the armory. Using Olavir's datapin Ceres quickly reset the security controls, denying access to any but a group of at least twenty pirates, such as a ship's crew coming to gear up for a raid. He went to their nearby repair room, dunking his plasma caster in a parts cleanser tank before holstering it.

"We opened the guard's wardroom," Serenity replied. *"Plenty of non-lethal weapons left here. These two big slaves you freed have taken the best. They seem to know how to use them. We are preparing the slaves to defend themselves. We're safe behind solid walls and hatches here. You be careful out there."*

Ceres locked the rotary laser in place with its tractor beam braces, setting the onboard reactor to slowly overcharge each barrel's capacitor. With a cable and mini-plasma torch from the repair supplies, he hot-fused a port connector to it, plugging it into the hatch controls.

Ceres bonded the cable to the hatch face with a life support emergency sealing strip, the latest version of the essential engineering supply known for hundreds of years as "duct tape." He then reeled out the cable to plug the other end into the firing controls of the rotary cannon. Inserting one of his datapins, he quickly reprogramed the controls. Last, he fine-tuned the aim of the device, shifting it to cover the huge roll-out hatch leading into the armory.

"Good, then. Stay sharp, Red. They may have a way to override the hatch controls. Remember what you learned from my REM training datapin. I'll work my way back to you."

Ceres left the huge cannon and scouted for supplies. He expected a final battle, to break out of the base. Better carry a select few extra items with the standard kit. He draped himself with a fat bandolier, filled it with a variety of grenades. Checking the charge on a pair of rapid-cycle lasers, he clipped the fat-lensed pistols onto his wrap-around gear harness.

His MeTR found no fire control computers in the inventory on Olavir's datapin. Ceres jogged to the starship-grade weapons locker and rifled through the bins and shelves, double-checking. Nothing.

In the next locker, he tracked down his helmet, chiming away on his beacon channel. The folded part looked like half of an Asianan fan. He clipped it into place on his back, HUD screen showing all green when it reintegrated itself into his armor's defensive and communications systems.

Not concerned, Ceres returned to the exit airlock at the back of the armory locker rooms. Cycling the airlock, he pulled the hood of his Navy uniform over his head, preparing his suit to automatically deploy its integral armor and helmet upon the slightest sudden drop in atmo pressure.

The retracted plates of graphene-tritanium alloy, layered and folded and tucked together on his back, slid out, crimson red, looking like dried blood in the dim light of the airlock. Small segments filled in, his angular helmet and gold visor of diatanium locked into place.

Large plates with extra layers, capable of withstanding hits from large caliber weapons, covered Ceres' major organs. These leaf-shaped overlapping bands, and gaps between, allowed him the flexibility his training required. Three seconds later, Ceres stood in his full combat armor, ready for war.

Stepping to the open hatch of the airlock, Ceres jumped out of the asteroid, into open space.

* * *

The tractor-pressor beams in Ceres' arm bracers and boots worked in concert to push away from the surface of the asteroid and pull him to the side. His MeTR displayed a HUD image of a map of A-Valhalla, taken from Thorsson's datapins and fed directly into Ceres' optic nerve "HUD". His NavWay program provided a virtual beacon trail across the barren surface.

Domes and crags of rock stood like mute sentinels, watching Ceres pass in the ghostly silence of space. Only the sounds of his breathing and heartbeat accompanied him. Relaxed, Ceres grinned. Space was his home.

Taking long slow breaths he enjoyed the sensations of microgravity as he drifted along on his tractor-pressor beams. In a stance similar to a groundball lineman, Ceres stood just a meter away yet anchored close to the surface. He grinned as he virtually flew over the face of the asteroid.

"Phase 3 underway," Ceres thought. *"Ready to receive guests. How goes it with you?"* He flitted through views of the slave quarters on side screens of his HUD, seeing open doors and slaves remaining in their cells, unsure what to do now that they were freed. After the fight in the armory drew pirates in that direction, Ceres' ship crew had made it down the access tube. They worked on pre-flight preps even now.

"I am a little busy right now," Serenity called back in his head. *"We are doing fine. A few slaves so far were unsure which side to take. They are sleeping in cells near our hanger access."*

"Copy," Now mid-op, Ceres used military terminology out of habit and training. *"Everyone is responsible for their own choices in life, and lives or dies by them. Out."*

Between the rocky outcroppings of asteroid, Ceres' trail of virtual breadcrumbs led him to a series of large domes. Lit from within, they poured light out into the nebula.

"Must be the place," he spoke aloud in his helmet. Completely isolated from the rest of the universe, Ceres took comfort from a human voice, even if it was his own.

Landing gently on the edge of one dome, Ceres saw row upon row of hydroponic plant racks inside. Each rack was split into meter-square buckets. Each bucket held one or more tall green plants rising several meters

234

in height. Some were almost touching the inner curve of the dome, their giant hand-like leaves seeming to reach for escape.

Ceres reached for the side of his thigh. The armor split down a middle seam and parted, much as the hanger bay doors of the base would. The inner Navy suit being space-tight by itself, Ceres was unaffected. From his lower cargo pocket Ceres retrieved half of a hollow ball.

Leaping up to the top of the dome in an effortless bound, he placed the palm sized grey cup on the surface of a triangular dome facet and tapped it twice. The dull metallic surface rippled and waved like the surface of a creamy coffee, when the last drop of cream falls from the bottle. It grew larger like an inflating balloon. Ceres looked about, scanning for signs he had been detected. The ball grew until it touched the three edges of the triangular struts of the frame, then stopped.

The external view of the long corridor leading into the armory popped up in his HUD. A pair of pirates in full eclectic armor warily stalked towards the hatch, laser carbines at the ready. Ceres grinned.

"Come on in, little mutts," Ceres' voice taunted outside the Armory hatch. He transmitted from his MeTR to the datapin he had placed in the hatch controls. His voice came over the vocaster system Olavir had used to speak to him when Ceres posed as Tyrian earlier.

"The cat wants to play with you. Heh heh," Ceres chuckled. More pirates approached the closed hatch from down the corridor.

Ceres focused again on his task at hand. He tapped on the grey sphere three times, seeing the hemisphere spin in a circle upon the crysteel pane of the dome, cutting through the surface. Four taps and the sphere grew round on the inside of the pane, completing the sphere. Two taps and the outside hemisphere retracted, leaving a hollow cup in the dome's face, like a giant golf ball dimple.

Ceres used the tractor beam bracer on his forearm to pluck the crysteel circle out. A small outgassing of atmosphere puffed off into space, flipping the clear circle away from the dome, turning over and over like a tossed coin. He tractored it in, juggling it with small bursts of his tractor/pressor settings in his bracers. Eventually it settled down, and he set it gently on the next triangle of dome, where electrostatic attraction held it in place.

He climbed carefully into the cup of grey metal and hunkered down on his knees. With four taps the sphere grew whole again, fully enclosing its human occupant. Two taps and a pop of his palm and Ceres slipped out of the cup's bottom, inside the dome, a slow motion descent owing to the unassisted low gravity of the agricultural domes.

Reaching up, Ceres hung by one arm from one of the dome struts while he observed the surroundings. His other arm held the grip of his plasma caster, still tucked in its holster. Ceres used his boot tractors to pull his legs flush with the dome, laying inverted against the top of the curve. Brief mechanical whirs and clips came from below, and the low vibration of repulsor pods moving air ultrasonically.

His MeTR reported an unbreathable atmosphere inside the dome, unsafe levels of carbon-dioxide. He kept his helmet sealed. High oxygen content was detected, likely thanks to the plants' "exhalations," but lowered nitrogen levels, which would not bother him.

Like most colonies, the pirates appeared to design their base's life support to pipe in "used" air from the domes inhabited by human and alien pirates. The inhabitants consumed some of the oxygen and breathed out carbon dioxide gases- CO_2. In a local area the CO_2 might be allowed to build up to as much as 0.5% concentration, or one part per two hundred.

The waste air was returned first to the agrifarms aboard the base so the plants could benefit from the higher CO_2 which they breathed in. The plants converted this gas—poisonous to humans—into oxygen, as part of their natural growth process.

Then the air cycled on to the life support system for processing into breathable mixes for the inhabited parts of the asteroid. That meant, this dome would be sparse on people and heavy on robotic tenders. Good for Ceres. Bad for the pirates.

Ceres repulsored down among the sun lamps, tucked behind each connection of the domes' crossed struts, then between the leafy plants, which reached up towards their life-giving lamps. He encountered a handful of agribots carefully picking their way through the lush plants. Some were culling dead leaves. Some harvested ripe serrated leaves, others sprayed fertilizers or misted water on selected plants.

He chose one of these bots and tapped its shoulder, reaching in among the ten appendage's attachment "shoulders." These agribots, modular in design, looked like metal jellyfish. Their central repulsor movement held arms of all kinds, hanging underneath and attached around the hull. For different tasks and jobs, different arms and attachments mounted as needed.

"Yes, sir? I am Agribot-Pruning/Harvesting One Dee Seven, or 'Aphid7.' How many I serve you?" it asked in Galactic. The current 1D series agribot was ubiquitous across the galaxy thanks to StarSys' great marketing and price point of a flexible and functional design. Ceres, like most galactic citizens, knew it by its marketing friendly series name.

"Aphid, I am Prince Ceres Tauri, son of our pirate king, Tyrian Tauri," Ceres claimed the truth. "Do you have apparatus for removing infested plants?"

"Yes, my Lord," Although without programming to recognize who was whom, the bot did know the Galactic language, and the rank structure of the Void Vikings, for interface purposes. It proved this to Ceres when it responded appropriately. "We all have antifungal, fertilizer, and flame sprayers, as well as quarantine destruction protocols to contain a parasite or fungus—"

"Good, Aphid," Ceres cut it off. "Take this programming." He opened an armored hatch on the back of his helmet, so he could remove a datapin. He stuck it into the socket in the center of the robot's body.

"The entire crop!" Aphid7 exclaimed. "I will initiate the protocol you have programmed, my Prince!" Instead of taking immediate action, Aphid7 whisked over to the nearest agribot. The two interfaced for a nano-second, then rushed apart and on to new partners for data transfer. Soon the nearby robotic crew were reprogrammed. They all flew off throughout the series of interconnected agricultural domes, spreading the word throughout their brethren, about the crop emergency.

Ceres chuckled as he flew back up to the dimple in the dome, tucked in and reversed the series of taps, exiting onto the surface. He retrieved the cut circle of crysteel from the next dome triangle he had set it on. Replacing it in the sphere cup, Ceres tapped to get his giant grey cup topside. Now he slid a finger over its surface and waited, standing in space atop the dome.

Ceres' HUD popped open the virtual screen showing the access tube to the armory. At least ten pirates had moved up, right to the hatch. Two were squabbling between themselves over how to hack their way in.

"All you brought is ten pups?" Ceres teased them, transmitting via MeTR to the datapin he had inserted in the hatch controls. The pirates froze while he spoke over the comm vocaster.

"I am insulted! In the lift I took out five at once and didn't break a sweat. I cut Jarl Thorsson's head in half!" Ceres dropped his voice to a growl, low and menacing, "You might want to bring more pups...."

They argued among themselves, waving in more pirates to advance down the corridor and tinkering with the controls with fresh agitation. Ceres minimized the screen in his head.

Outside on the dome, Ceres' grey cup's aerosolid material exuded a clear gel into the cut line between the circle of crysteel and remaining triangle rim attached to the frame. When the sphere shrank back to a palm sized half-ball, Ceres plucked it up and returned it to his cargo pouch. The gel repaired the triangle panel, turning almost as clear as the rest of the pane.

"Phase 3 done, on to the next," he thought. Hovering just over the dome's surface like an ice skater, Ceres balanced his tractor-pressor settings. He pushed off behind him with one leg, sliding down the curved face. His legs pumped hard, gaining speed and shooting him across the surface of the asteroid. The next dome cluster rose before him.

He leaped high, halfway up a dome, crouched as he skated upwards, released his tractor beams and pushed off hard. Grinning as always, Ceres flew high over the surface of Valhalla.

The popup screen in his HUD showed the status of the bots. *They move fast in an emergency,* Ceres thought. Via MeTR he transmitted thoughts to the datapin he had placed in his lead agribot, A-PH1D7, *"All Agribots, execute protocol, tool 3."*

Ceres drifted in a high trajectory, a temporary satellite of Asteroid Valhalla. Opening his arms, he flew like a bird of space. He admired the view of the nebula, the folds of gas, the stars buried here and there, birthed from gathering the remnants of the nova which long ago had thrown off these sheets of gas.

Gravity from the baby stars and their father, the white dwarf remnant of the nova, kept the asteroid from escaping the veils of the nebula. When he turned towards the nearby stars, Ceres' gold visor automatically filtered the bright pinpoints of blinding light.

The gravity of A. Valhalla being low, Ceres could have leaped away and out of orbit with his strong legs. He used his tractor beams to pull himself in a large swinging arc, to the other side of the giant potato-shaped asteroid.

Fires erupted across the many cannahol hydroculture domes, bots everywhere burning the blight Ceres had reprogrammed them to see and destroy. They had shut down the fire control systems so they could do their jobs efficiently. Flamethrowers quickly consumed billions of Di of crops, filling the hydroponic agridomes with billowing smoke.

The life-support systems went into overdrive to filter out the smoke. Prepared for a single dome emergency, they were immediately overloaded. Filtration lost its effectiveness. Cannahol blew throughout the ventilation system across Asteroid Valhalla. Designed to enter the bloodstream through moist tissue such as the eyes or under the tongue, it found its way in through the lungs even more easily.

That should keep the rest busy, heh heh, he thought. To Serenity he intentionally thought, *"You are going to get downed. Use the blue jumpsuit and mask in the tool bag I dropped off. Outer pockets. Anti-narcotic stim in the inner pocket."*

"I remembered," she thought back to him. *"I am wearing them already. Thank you. It is already working here. Nice way to settle these agitated slaves down for me. Everybody has pretty green eyes, like me. Thanks."*

"Oh no," he disagreed, *"Nobody has pretty green eyes like yours. They are unique."*

Repulsor beams firing strongly, Ceres landed near a cluster of domes highlighted in his HUD thanks to his NavWay program. The triangular panels were set opaque for privacy. Repeating the entry routine with the grey cup, Ceres soon dropped inside.

* * *

He hung from the ceiling for a moment, checking out the area below. Tyrian's Zen garden looked much the same as he remembered. "Heh heh. You *had* to erase my changes, huh Pop?" Ceres commented to himself, absently teasing his father, who was away on the ransom mission.

"Must be an isolated air-system just for the king? I expected smoke," he continued to speak to himself. Ceres moved to the entry hatch and let some of his hijacked robots inside.

Since taking over his first pirate bot, his dome's floor cleaner, Ceres had his robots virally spread his own command and control worm programs throughout most of the asteroid's complement of robots. His MeTR linked to the one he had designated his foreman, which grouped itself with many of its metallic brethren. Now he called some of them in.

The 20 or so of them had slowly made their way here from throughout the hangers around the base, answering his earlier marching orders for the foreman, a huge autonomous loaderbot, to gather his cadre of workers. "Okay, boys," Ceres spoke to the bots, "let's get to work."

The pair of loaders with their heavy cargo graspers, large power pistons, and six thick extendable beams for legs, a handful of medium labor units on treads, and several small carriers that looked more like flatbed go-carts with multiple wheels, the robotic platoon paraded across Tyrian's lushly carpeted foyer, trampling it to ruins. Ceres led them up into the sand garden dome.

"Move the stones aside, to there," he pointed for the loaders to a clear space under the edge of the dome. "Start digging those spots once the loaders have moved the big rocks away," he told the laborbots.

In his HUD, he saw a red flash of warning and switched his attention to view the armory holo-cam. The pirates stacked up outside the armory had reached critical mass, and the hatch unlocked as programmed for the full crew of twenty or more. The pirates in the access tube grabbed their weapons, clicking off safeties and powering up energy screens.

The big lock pistons retracted and the thick metal hatch started to roll. Ceres grinned. From inside the armory his voice growled to them, "Come on in to my lion's den, you mangy pack of dogs. I'm ready for you."

The rolling hatch pulled the thin cable taped to it free from the control pad next to the massive door. The loss of signal automatically initiated the rotary cannon set in place directly behind it. The lasers fired off in rapid series. Ceres watched, grimly determined.

The ten large barrels stayed fixed in place while the sequencer triggered off one then the next, in a rotating series around the group of barrels. Needing mere milliseconds to complete one cycle, each barrel had time to cool and recharge its capacitor before the sequence came around again.

An endless buzz, buzz, buzz roared and echoed back into the cavernous locker rooms of the armory, as the pirates took the brunt of the heavy weapon in their faces at close range. Each laser's cycle of several millisecond pulses burned layers of material out of their target, the pulses making that distinctive buzzing sound.

"Close the hatch!" men shouted. "Shut it! Shut it!"

"Get out of the way!" Some tried to run back up the corridor, others tried to dive to one side or the other.

His datapin giving Ceres control, he remotely shifted the huge weapon from side to side by adjusting the tractor beams bracing it. The blazes of focused light swept the long approach corridor from side to side with heavy laser blasts, mercilessly mowing down the twenty$^+$ pirates within seconds. Tens more down the corridor were caught as well, and soon the weapon merely burned more holes into dead men and the acrid, smoke filled air.

They must have thought I was in there for some reason, heh heh. The murderous scene had distracted Ceres. He blinked and looked up, questioning his eyes.

One of the stones laying nearby moved. Stony arms and legs unfolded from beneath it and stood up into a plump, vaguely humanoid shape. Towering over Ceres at three meters tall, the alien, a Rokkled, reached out and fought hand to hand with the loadbot that had tried to pick it up.

"MY STONNNES!" it bellowed slowly with a grave voice, the lid of a sarcophagus sliding to the side. It twisted the foreman's arm at a high angle.

"LEAAVVE DOMMME!" It snapped the robot's arm off. The alien Rokkledds had great difficulty speaking the over 200,000 different words of Galactic based on combining 70$^+$ different sounds. They usually plugged directly into robots or computers that translated and vocalized what they meant into the more complete sentences of other sentients' languages.

"STO-O-OPP!" The xenomorph pushed the loader back steadily, bashing its lift arms and legs with fists like small boulders. In their native voices, Rokkledds used simple Galactic words in short sentences, about all their crude sound boxes could handle.

The living statue broke one of the loadbot's thick legs off too, and started beating it with its own leg. Smashing the loader's control module, the moving statue continued beating its shell casing in for an extra moment. Then it jumped onto a nearby laborbot, toppling it off its tracks and riding it down to the sand, crushing its torso like an empty trashcan.

The Rokkled warrior showed his strength, rebounding from the sand to leap at another bot, swinging the robot leg like a massive club. Its surface looked like large granite quarry stones, with seams of gleaming silver and black metal between them. Flashes of light travelled down these metal ribbons as it moved.

Ceres drew out his plasma pistol and started ripping off shots. The huge moving target was an easy hit, but red circles of lava formed on its stony surface and slowly dissipated.

"AAHH!" It roared in apparent pain and turned towards Ceres. "FLESHY NOT MELT!" It swatted aside a laborbot and stalked towards

Ceres. Its massive legs, each the size of human statues, cratered down into the sand, every blunt footfall slamming down like a pile driver.

"Pask!" Ceres tried the Vikings exclamation he had recently learned and ran behind a low boulder for a moment's cover. Holstering his plasma caster he drew the huge disruptor from his hip. Double barrels made it unwieldy and slow. *Wish I had Thorsson's axe-hammer right now!*

Ceres' eyes widened as the Rokkled leapt into the air, arms spread, easily cleared the boulder, soaring toward his prey. The disruptor's beams blazed up into the three-meter tall statue as it fell like a massive gargoyle at him.

"RRRRUUUUHHH!" the Rokkled roared, whether from pain, anger, or warcry, Ceres did not know nor care. It scared him all the same, goose bumps covering his skin inside his suit. Ceres held the firing stud down on his disruptor, pouring out the deadly beams.

How do you headshot something without a head? Traversing from the alien's chest area up toward its rocky lump that he knew had some functions of a head, he inadvertently hit one of the many metallic seams spider-webbing across the raised mound of silicate sensor organs.

The nerve network of Rokkledds consisted of bio-refined veins of platinum, other conductive minerals, and streams of nanites. When Ceres hit this network, his disruptor's ionizing electron beam travelled throughout the nerve seams, throughout the body and its several brain clusters. The disruption beam of alpha particles blasted apart molecules, even some of the atoms themselves. Ceres' extended blast crushed gravelly bits out of the silicon-based xeno's head, chunks that flew like popcorn into the air.

The huge statue froze up and fell over Ceres, pinning him to the sand. Its raised fist punched down on one side of Ceres' head, the base of its robot-leg weapon narrowly missing his arm on the other side.

"Yep, handy little thing! I gotta keep this handy little thing," he praised the disruptor pistol that was now pinned against his chest, crushing down on his armor's graphene plates that could bear a rhino's weight. The heavy weapon's housing popped and groaned.

The mass of the Rokkled settled heavily on Ceres, crushing his armor like a steel turtle under a tank's tracks, squeezing the wind from his lungs. His respirocytes, artificial red cells, started pumping out their oxygen into his bloodstream. Despite the inability to breathe, Ceres had many minutes' worth of oxygen in his blood, enough to save his life in many desperate circumstances.

These respirocytes, implanted nanomachines, were a mandatory upgrade in the Galactic military. Being a top college-level athlete, Ceres had to wait until his last amateur sport season was over before receiving the military standard implants.

He only now realized his error. He had stuck only one of the bots around him with a control datapin. This xeno's smashing of the loader foreman cut off Ceres' control link to the bots. He had summoned them through their own network link back through his lead bot carrying the datapin. Having thought of it as a less detectable system, he now saw the downsides.

He could not easily command them to free his body. Ceres snapped his fingers, pounded his free hand down on the sand, and slapped the stony corpse pinning him. Nothing seemed to summon the robots' help. They continued moving large stones and broken robot corpses aside, following their last orders. *Eventually they will see the danger I'm in, follow their base programming, and lift this guy off me. Hopefully soon.*

Minutes passed while Ceres debated calling out to Serenity to help him. Disciplined, he avoided intentionally thinking messages towards her, not wanting to draw her out of the slave prison she was safely locked within during the progress of their breakout mission. He popped up a screen viewing the slaves' pens. They milled about, now zombie-like in their shuffling, drugged state, but he could not find a view of his beloved redhead.

The stone shifted, pressing his shoulder further into the sand. The massive weight lifted off him and he reeled, starting to see stars in his extreme need of fresh air. His lungs were both aflame within. Ceres disciplined his mind to prevent panic. He could not tell if they were punctured by broken ribs. They burned throughout his chest and throat.

He had survived so far, only due to the emergency oxygen supply pouring out of the respirocytes in his blood. Now even that was about to expire. The edge of his vision darkened.

One of the first signs of oxygen debt. Gotta upgrade these nanos to a higher count or capacity if—no WHEN I get out of here! he thought. The opaque whiteness of the dome overhead cut out, and he closed his eyes. *Lord, forgive me my sins. I ....*

Ceres imagined Serenity kissing him, the kiss he had never enjoyed, the first kiss of love.

"HuuhhAAHHHH!" he gasped a ragged breath. Flexible woven cords in his suit squeezed his chest, then relaxed. He drew another painful, wet breath. "How—?" Ceres sputtered weakly, blood on his lips.

"I'm here," Serenity answered. She looked ravishing, wearing the form-fitting blue coverall he had concealed under the bottom of the toolbag along with the capacitor rod.

"The big bot was lifting the statue when I arrived. Then I breathed for you, until I remembered your Army suits have rescue settings. It did this whole cycle of breathing and shocking you, injections—"

"Navy," he said weakly.

"What?" She seemed bewildered, gently tossing her waves of hair.

"Navy, not Army."

She blinked at him, kneeling in the sand and sitting on her heels.

"While the Army drags its aft in the dirt, Baby, I can *fly!*" he repeated one of the unofficial recruiting slogans, then coughed.

Just as she opened her mouth, he drew her down for another kiss. For this one he was conscious. After a moment, they both drew back, awash with the rush of inner feelings. She shook her head, unable to respond between her feelings of exasperation and desire welling up inside her.

"Thank you for saving my life," Ceres said. "No one has ever done that before, not since—" he winced. *Iron.*

"You're most welcome, Love. We c'n talk about Iron later. Now, on your feet soldier! Back to work. Hero time, remember!" She stood up and helped pull him up to his feet, leaning back to balance his weight.

He admired her strength and fitness. *Good match.* The robots had continued moving the large stones away, including the body of the Rokkled. Ceres patted his body down, moved each limb carefully. Aside from a bruised shoulder and lungs, he was ambulatory.

His suit's first aid module injected him with stimulants and pain neutralizers. He noted the cracked housing of his disruptor pistol when he holstered it. *Better not fire this thing until I get it repaired.*

Serenity helped Ceres limp over to the Rokkled's corpse, a frozen statue, now dragged to the side of the dome. Turning to the remaining undamaged bots, he saw they continued busily digging away the sand. Piles of stones and sand appeared in some places while funnel pits opened up in others.

"Okay, boys," he said to the bots, "focus on one place, then work your way around the room. Everybody over here," he pointed. "Come dig out this spot in the middle." With a Solman to organize their work cooperatively by voice command, the gaggle of robot's efficiency skyrocketed.

Serenity following, Ceres walked gingerly over to the bench nearby, where he had sat with his father the day before. He gestured, offering for her to sit first, and then he sat. She smiled at his regard for her as a person worthy of respect.

"That Rokkled must have been a special bodyguard. Yesterday it was a rock right here," he pointed to the divot in the sand where it had stood up. "I sat on it." Ceres took one of Serenity's hands and smiled at her. She smiled back, but he saw a twinge of concern for him in her eyes.

"Can I show you one of the beautiful secrets of the universe?"

"Sure," her eyes twinkled. "Surprise me."

He felt her presence in his mind retreat. *She might be surprised for once?* Ceres called over the remaining big loadbot and inserted a datapin, so he could control the group.

"Here, smash that stone," he pointed to the Rokkled corpse. "Crush it," he ordered the three-meter-tall robot, showing it his gesture as if squeezing a ball in his fist.

"But, no. Isn't that—?" Serenity gasped in horror.

"At the heart of these xenos is the seed of their essence," he watched the loader get a grip and start compressing. "The one part of them that makes them alive and unique as individuals." The robot's power pistons whined in a higher pitch with the strain. Serenity's eyes widened, her face ashen.

"It is a rare and beautiful thing," Ceres smiled at Serenity, seeing her face pale. Cracking sounds emitted from the boulder body of the vanquished stone warrior.

"In their society, this is considered a prize, a gift of honor from the fallen to the victor." Hollow "pop, pop, pop" sounds echoed in the dome. Serenity's head canted to one side, she squinted, and her eyebrows wrinkled.

"SNAPPcrrushcchh!!" The former torso of the statue alien cracked on long seams, several major chunks coming free like old shattered concrete.

"Stop!" Ceres ordered the robot before it could continue on with its task, crushing the smaller pieces. He knelt forward and gingerly crawled to the pile of broken rocks, clearing some away, and sweeping gravel with his hands.

"Ah," he smiled warmly, tucking something into his cargo pocket away from Serenity's sight. Carefully, he stood, using the bot's leg to steady himself, then walked back to the bench. He sat, tenderly, next to the puzzled but quiet redhead.

"Now, Rokkleds like our late friend here are an ancient sentient race of silicon lifeforms from the Greater Magellanic Cloud, a companion galaxy to our Solman's Milky Way. That silvery platinum you saw is part of their nerve network, where they host trillions of nanites of all kinds. See those black veins?"

She nodded.

"Those are the glue, the cement that binds together and powers the other parts of their body. The nanites are so small they flow almost like water, or maybe graphite dust is a better description, understand?"

"Are you going to tell me this great mystery of the galaxy? What's in your pocket?" She cut to the bottom line. "I know you're hurt and regaining strength, but we need to complete this escape, soon."

"Always to business with you," Ceres chided. "This is our 'stop to smell the diamonds' moment here. The pirates are all vaped out, and we gotta wait for the bots to find something anyway." He grinned, reaching towards his pocket.

"Here, 'Miss Patience.' I present you with... a soul gem." From his cargo pocket, Ceres drew out a clear crystal longer than his illuminator, glowing red from within.

Serenity's jaw dropped and her eyes moistened when Ceres handed it to her. "Is it still alive?" she stammered. "These swirls of inner movement... and I can almost sense something in here."

"The progenitor nanites *could* start the process of assembling another body," Ceres replied. "The memories are all in there, like a master computer's memory core. You can decide later what to do with it." He stood up again and formed up some of the robots into a line, leaving her reeling, blinking, her gaze wavering between the gift and the giver.

After a minute, Serenity stood next to him. She reached through his suit's neckline, placed her hand over Ceres' shoulder, and meditated. He felt the same warm flowing sensation as before. Something interesting was happening and it was not the meds. Okay, many interesting things were happening.

"You're extremely good at this healing," Ceres complimented her. "I never encountered a master so skilled at transferring kai energy as you." He did not care what the cause, he enjoyed her hands on him. Their warmth. Their feminine softness. He never wanted her to stop.

"I'm not a martial arts master," she retorted. "Well, not in your traditional sense. We Amazons do have our own combat arts, don't we?" She smiled and Ceres nodded.

"Herbal healing is as ancient as mankind. The first African healing woman to bind straw to a hunter's wound founded this ancient art. I have studied it my whole life at the side of my mother."

"Plus, what we have called 'the gift' since the days the Celts wandered Europe, handed down, grown through 'proper breeding,' as my grandmare would say." Serenity rolled her closed eyes, which Ceres took to mean she was frustrated with her bloodline, as were many young people with their own ideas of how to run their own lives.

He squinted, thinking, *Or maybe disagreement with her form of society? I wonder if they get to choose their mates, or if the matriarchs arrange marriages for the good of the bloodline?*

She shook her head slowly. He thought she had heard him but chose to ignore his thoughts on purpose. "I combine these arts into seeing inside," she went on, "feeling what is damaged inside your shoulder in my mind's eye, and redirecting the tissues into their proper places, sealing up ruptured vessels, opening lymph ducts to flush away excess fluids, reversing the inflammation. I calm down the pain nerves and activate the pressure nerves to overwhelm the pain."

Wide eyed, Ceres stammered, "I, hmm. I thought you were using the same kai energy-transfer techniques as learned in Aikido. You describe finely detailed internal effects, as a micro-surgeon would see them. What exactly do you call this power, this, whatever you do?"

"That is the foundation of it, the same bio-energy system, understood in the same way as kai, maybe with different words in ancient times but now the same. I do not know what to call my adding the gift on top of it, inside of it. A 'healing insight' is the best phrase I can find so far."

Ceres nodded, opened his mouth—

"Clunk!" sounded out from the pit.

"Okay, sweep it clear," Ceres ordered the bots, hopping to his feet. Excited, he overdid it, leaping into a high arc, landing near the pit. Serenity walked closer to see what was happening. The rounded corner of a smooth metal case appeared. Ceres grinned at Serenity. "Payday!"

She raised her eyebrows at him in question. He grinned back at her, sliding down the sand to the bottom. Ceres winced, digging out sand with his hands, uncovering the first metal case. He pointed, and a general labor robot gripped the handles, tugging. It popped free and the genbot fell back.

"Thanks," Delicately he handled the case, hopping up to the flat sand near the exit. Ceres laid it carefully on the bench. He and Serenity examined the locks and straps, both frowning.

"Any ideas on how to crack that open?" Serenity asked.

"No inputs showing? Looks like a MeTR activated lock. Bet you five Di my father set it to unlock when he thought of the password."

Serenity pouted. "What's in it? Treasure?"

"Sure, the best of the best, most compact, high dollari treasure he wants to stash away from his own rogues and thugs." He looked at her. "My guess is gemstones. Big ones. The only other thing worth hiding like this might be ryanite ingots, and they would float up to the ceiling."

"What?" Serenity questioned.

"Exotic matter. Negatron mass, immeasurable at least. If you irradiate it, with, say, a laser beam, it re-radiates energy as the gravity or anti-gravity effects we depend on." He pointed at his wrist, the armor bracer with its blue ring around his wrist that emitted tractor/pressor effects. "Refined to this purity, far beyond military grade, this is worth millions."

She opened her mouth in shock, closed it slowly.

Ceres drew his double-barreled disruptor, aimed carefully and released a small dual burst at the lock mechanism.

Serenity's hands shot up in surprise. "Why?"

The lock bump on the case melted away and dripped to the floor, a hole spreading open on the edge of the case. Ceres popped it on the top and pulled the handle, flipping up the lid. "Because it worked," he said.

The case sparkled, filled with large gemstones of several colors, some cut and polished. Most were raw shapes looking like melted composites. Protective webbing held them all in place. Ceres grinned. Serenity frowned.

A GP robot delivered another case to them then returned to the pit. Ceres melted open this one, too, causing far less damage to the case. He smiled triumphantly then froze when he flipped the case open.

Light from below filled their faces. Twenty crystals, each glowing from within, ranked in a staggered three by four pattern, swirled with internal colors. A network of lights flashed among them at high speeds. Tiny threads linked each crystal in the pattern. These too flashed with inner light. The crystals strobed from the high-speed pattern of flashes.

Mouth agape, Serenity pulled the crystal Ceres had given her out of her utility suit's pocket. "More of these? Rokkled soul stones?"

Ceres kept a tight lip and nodded. "What does heaven look like? Is this it for them?"

Gulping, she drew her mouth tight, sucking in her cheeks. She placed her crystal at the corner of the last row of three, where there should be a fourth crystal on the corner to carry the pattern through. It dropped into the open spot.

Immediately, new metal threads snaked out from the neighboring crystals, snapped straight under tension, and solidified. The strobe pattern changed to one of flow, of waves of light to and from the newcomer.

"Welcoming him into their own little cloud of heaven?" Ceres posed.

"This is the most beautiful thing I have ever seen," Serenity said breathlessly. Her eyes watered and overflowed down her cheeks. "Why?" she glanced back at the pit.

Ceres reached around her shoulders and hugged her. "Probably just another ransom for my father," Ceres said.

Serenity shot him a look of confusion.

"What would you pay the devil, to return your family's souls?"

She put her hand over her mouth and closed her eyes. Finally, she swallowed, but nodded in agreement.

"Buried here for safety, so his pirates don't try to sell them on the black market for their own profit. If you knew what these are worth!" He pursed his lips in a silent whistle.

"We must rescue them, too," she said. Hearing more metallic scraping sounds behind her, Serenity turned around slowly, foreboding and wonder fighting for control of her face. The robots continued to clear away the widening funnel pit. Five more such cases now peeked out of the sand, as well as trunks, metal boxes, and chests. She gulped.

"Let's get out of here," Ceres said to her. "My MeTR estimates the pirate fleet is probably finishing their business and due to start their return."

"Can the bots finish up and catch up with us at the ship?" Serenity asked, then, urgently said, "We have more rescuing to do than just the treasure!"

"Put all the boxes on the flatbeds and haul them to my ship in the hanger," Ceres ordered the mechanized work crew. "I'll take one of you with me. When you finish here, link to him." He picked out the last of the cargobot haulers waiting in a line, patted the flatbed and smiled at Serenity, her red hair... "Let's ride, Strawberry!"

Serenity's jaw dropped. "My father called me that. How—? You—?"

"Just came to me mid-sentence," he shrugged. "Do you like it?" He thought that could go either way. She may not like it if he hijacked her father's nickname for her. Or she might find it the sweetest thing yet that he figured it out on his own.

"We'll see," she tilted her head in a wistful way.

Ceres thought she had done that before in a good context. *Sweet,* he decided. He waved his hand over the cart in a welcoming manner.

Serenity snapped out of her daydream. "Oh, sorry," she blushed red among her freckles. She sat on the robohauler, and then he joined her.

"Are you always the gentleman?" she asked, biting her lip.

"Always," he answered her. He thought she was trying hard not to seem too pleased with his romantic efforts. Or, too angry with his misogyny?

"Except when you are the bad boy," she chided him. "I can tell."

"True," Ceres said. "I'm not sure which part you like better." He grinned. "I think it's because *you* aren't yet sure which you prefer. Maybe both."

Serenity did not answer, crossing herself for silent prayer instead.

I bet she's praying for help deciding to love me or hate me, Ceres thought.

Popping his hand on the front of the flatbed he commanded the hauler. "Pod please." A small egg extended up from the front of the robot. Ceres pulled yet another datapin from the back of his head and inserted it. He was sure he was going to run out of these pins if they did not get out of there soon.

* * *

Spinning on its wheels, the robot shot out of Tyrian's surface domes, into the access corridor trailing down to the tube piercing the center of the asteroid. Ceres laid back on the flat cargo bed and breathed steadily. To help its passengers stay aboard, the bot raised its cargo handler arms as side rails.

The hauler rushed down the tunnel, electric motors in each wheel accelerating it quickly with high torque. Interfaced with its sensors, Ceres drove with the HUD feed in his vision, rapidly turning corners and racing the bot to its top speed rating.

Skidding out into the central shaft cored through the asteroid, the robot slid around the last turn, chattering wheels. The passengers, thrown over to their sides, clung on desperately with all hands and legs as the bot held them with its cargo manipulators. "Ha hahahh!" Ceres laughed, enjoying the thrill ride he was taking Serenity on.

"Who taught you to drive?" Serenity shot him an accusing look, fingers turning white from gripping so tightly to the hauler's load arm.

"You're right," Ceres shouted over the rushing air. "Delicate cargo aboard. I thought you Terran Tor women were tough."

Projectiles and beams ripped through the air over the robocart. "Duck!" Ceres shouted. He did the opposite of his order, rolling off the back of the robot and leaping up towards the center of the shaft. Serenity laid back the way he had.

For a moment she gazed up in shock as Ceres floated overhead, his momentum keeping him in pace with the hauler. Grimacing, he ripped the pair of rapid repeat pistols free from his gear harness and flew down the shaft.

"Drive!" he shouted to the redhead on the careening cart, the robot struggling to regain control as Ceres' focus shifted to combat. The leaves and segments of his armor helmet wrapped around his face. *"Hard to drive and fight at the same time, if I'm not on that thing!"*

Serenity reached behind her head and pulled out her own datapin. Ceres' lack of drive control left the robo-cart to go around the loop of the central tube in robotic self-preservation. The centripetal force at least glued her to the top of the flatbed, so Serenity could lay low on it as shots pocked the central shaft around and behind her.

"Pod please!" she spun around facing forward and slapped the load bed, stabbing her own pin in while the egg rose up. She maneuvered the cart around in a wide turn up the sidewall at high speed, heading back where they came from.

Ceres was busy fighting and flying. He was an easy target, fully exposed up in the center of the shaft, so he flew like a crazed eagle caught in a tornado. The spiraling cart paths lined with gravity plates looked like roller coaster tracks twisted into a barrel roll, spiraling down into the heart of the asteroid from end to end. This allowed the entire asteroid surface of domes and hangers to have direct paths to the center that came out aligned with the walkway.

Ceres exploited this tube's design to fly down its center, a move he was uniquely equipped to pull off with his tractor-pressor boots and gauntlets. He worked his legs at crossed angles to keep him aligned, pushing his two pistols out to arm's length where his tractor beams pulled him forward, twisting along with the cart paths. Passing yet another exit onto the corridor, Ceres used his peripheral vision and fired a laser burst down that tunnel. He grinned, satisfied to hear a pirate yell behind him, the clatters of body and weapon on the floor of the side shaft echoing in the tubes.

Pushing the robo-cart to its maximum speed, Serenity caught up behind the crazed flying man, seeing him shoot their enemies with hardly a glance, flying along in a classic hero pose from the holofilms.

"Amazing! Or insane!" she thought to him.

"Not now, busy!" he responded in his mind. The adrenaline rushed in his veins and he inhaled deeply, relishing the feelings of combat flowing through him. Beams of light flashed the length of the shaft as the pirates tried to track the spiraling Ceres at long range. *They want a fight? I'll fly one right down in their faces!*

Ceres spiraled down the length of the asteroid like a living bullet down a rifled barrel. He looked ahead, pointing one arm forward to shoot at heads that popped up in the tunnels he approached. His other arm swung at passing corridors. Blindly firing bursts down them, he was rewarded often with the wounded screams of unseen would-be ambushers.

The pirates down the tunnel ahead changed tactics, shooting at Serenity and the robotic cargo carrier she rode. As she spiraled down towards the hidden shooters, the laser beams lit up the traces of dust in the air, tracking closer to her. Some of them splashed off the front of the robo-cart.

"Roll your body right!" Ceres shouted over the cacophony of gunfire echoing down the tube. He landed on his side next to Serenity, atop the cart as it rolled up under him.

His ribs and lungs screamed in pain from the impact, especially after his crushing experience under the Rokkled corpse had aggravated the bones broken thanks to the Viking's gauntlet. The numbness up his left arm caused Ceres to drop the repeater pistol under the front of their robot-hauler. It clattered along behind them for a while then slid to a stop.

On landing, Ceres had noticed the metal case gripped between Serenity's legs. He pulled himself forward, snapping his left arm's shield on. Red rippling pools on the clear bluish force field showed the laser's hits grew closer to their mark. "Went back for that?"

"Yes, it fell off when you bailed out," she said. "I rescued them from your rescue." They traded glances. "Who just jumps off a high speed roller coaster?" She shook her head with a rueful expression.

"Me," he shrugged one shoulder. "I thought to draw their fire away from you. We're closing on the inside hanger access near my ship. They are waiting for us down at the end of the line. Probably want to pin us in the middle of the central tube."

His repeater pistols lost in his crash landing/boarding move, Ceres' angled his plasma caster over his shield, lancing flat blue plasma bursts ahead at open tunnels and the pirates waiting there for ambush potshots. Serenity lay flat on the cart so Ceres tried to cover her with his armor.

"Excuse me," he said, laying half atop her body. Pirate laser beams reflected off his shield and to the left, effectively pinning down any pirate ambushers on that side, so he concentrated his own shots to the right.

"Look out!" she shouted, ignoring his concern about too intimate a pose, warning him of the looming obstacles ahead.

Piles of ship parts, cargo crates, trash, robot bodies, and miscellaneous junk filled the tunnel ahead. At least twenty pirates' helmets peeked through the barricade, heads showing over their weapon barrels. The barrage of energy beams and projectile fire turned Ceres' shield opaque, now that they were close enough for greater accuracy.

"Time to change the game, this isn't going to hold!" Ceres yelled. Between shots he popped the deck of the cargobot with the butt of his pistol. "Pod!" He pulled his grenadier's belt off, over his arm and head. "Retract side arms!"

His fractured ribs, still knitting, caused him to grimace in pain as their frayed ends shifted, firing pain through every nerve they touched. Gritting his teeth, he did it anyway. Sweat broke out on his forehead. He concentrated on completing his tasks, submerging the pain beneath his willpower, the force of his anger.

Hooking the belt around the protruding egg, Ceres retrieved his datapin and stabbed it into his H-harness for safekeeping. Quickly thumbing one of the grenade's safeties off, he shouted to Serenity.

"Hold on to me!" He rolled to his side. She faced him, pulled the case up behind his back, and hugged Ceres. Both of her hands held tightly to her case of precious cargo behind him. "Keep the bot driving forward, despite its protests!" He squeezed the spoon trigger closed on the red grenade and started counting down from five on a HUD screen with his MeTR.

Ceres rolled backwards off the side of the cart like a diver into the ocean, but this ocean was like rogue wave surfing in a spiraling vortex of spraycrete at 100kph. As soon as he collapsed his shield the robocart took hits and slowed. Ceres whisked them up off the flatbed, the two escapees careening towards an opening in the wall.

Cranking his tractor beams up as high as he could stand, Ceres managed to skim the deck, then turn, bumping down the connecting tunnel. A pirate waiting in ambush with a laser carbine took Ceres' armored knee in the face and flew back, limp and lifeless. Ceres' leg exploded in pain, adding to his major injuries collected this day. *Time to limp! Good thing I'm flying,* he thought.

Serenity flattened against Ceres' chest and face, barely hanging on to the handles of the metal case as it scraped the deck. He barrel rolled and flew along in a groundball stance, Serenity hanging on underneath.

A great "Whoosh" sounded down the tunnel and around the corner. The grenade's foam flushed out, expanding into the main tunnel, covering the pirates' barricades. With a "FWOOMP!!" the thermal foam ignited, then lit off the rest of the grenades in the belt in a series of supersonic concussions.

Shockwaves vibrated the tunnels, causing bits of asteroid rock and spraycrete to fall or lift into the air briefly. Debris rushed past the end of their side tunnel, dust and smoke filling the air and creeping down after them. Slowing at the bends in the tunnel, their flight soon approached the hanger deck.

"Whew!" Serenity gasped, eyes wide. "Is your life always this exciting?" Her face lit up and flushed.

"Hmm, lemmee see here: kidnapped, Vikings, duels, inherited slaves, pirates, space-axe darts, damsel rescue, gang-on one fights, and sabotage," he mused. "Mmmm, kind of a light week for me, why?"

Serenity grinned, cocked her head and raised both eyebrows.

"Okay, yes," he confessed. "I have noticed a little extra excitement since I met you."

Serenity pulled herself up on his armor and kissed him, long and passionately, leaving them both breathless. Ceres slowed their flying pace to walking speed and tried not to crash, angling his body up to settle them to the deck.

"Okay, a lot of excitement!" he amended.

He winced when he put weight on his knee. Winced when Serenity clung to his shield arm. Winced with every breath. His suit was out of healing agents. Time to tough it out.

"Are you ready to fight our way out of here, soldier?" Serenity challenged him.

"No worries," he assured her. "Adrenaline is my combat buddy. It's like runner's high. I'm in for whatever it takes."

Walking down the tunnel together, Ceres limped while Serenity wobbled. She gathered her feet under her after the dizzying changes in gravity and orientation.

"Same here," she breathed, beaming her brilliant smile at him. "You din'na tell me you can fly."

"I can fly," he shrugged with a sheepish grin. "Been doing it for years. You really never heard of my sports days, much less watched a holo?" He clucked his tongue.

"No. Should I have?"

"Your loss," he frowned. They stumbled and limped towards the end of the tunnel.

"Usually, you are the one," he pointed doubled gun fingers at her, "reminding me," he pointed at himself, "...the game clock is ticking." He waved his hand forward, pointing to the hatch ahead. He half shuffled, half limped towards it quickly.

"Aye, right," she blushed and wobbled after him, increasing her pace.

"No sentries," reported Ceres. "Coming up this tube surprised them."

"How do you know?" she asked him, already seeing the answer in his mind. She focused again, closing her eyes, letting Ceres lead her with his arm. She did what her brother once complained as "broke in on his mental channel." The same as she had done to Kangee hours earlier. She saw in Ceres' mind that he watched a HUD screen, transmitted in his optic nerve, a view of the inside of the hanger.

The holo-cams were perched at least three meters above the deck, providing a panoramic view of the length of the hanger and the port side, or left side, of the curvy blue starship he had modified over the last week. From their hiding place, within the airlock door into the hanger, the pair of escapees saw several pirates.

"They may be well protected if we had come in from the lift tube end of the hanger, where I threw Thorsson overboard," Ceres analyzed the impending battlefield. "But from here they are side on and easy to spot." He pointed and Serenity nodded.

"How do we get past them?" Serenity asked.

"We don't. We blow them away," he grinned. She looked puzzled. Ceres pulled out Thorsson's datapin and inserted it into the hanger's hatch controls.

One part of his MeTR's processing power he had tasked with finding links to the master hanger controls and asserting command using Thorsson's authority, his datapin's stored knowledge of the Void Vikings systems, access codes, and security passwords.

"Don't watch," Ceres warned Serenity. "You're strong, but still sweet and innocent of the horrors of war. Some things you don't want to see."

He flipped through HUD screens to select the right datapin among the many he had placed of late, finding the right system controls. This one he promoted to the top of his priority list.

In the hanger, several parts of the blue and white painted starship emitted "FluuUUSSSHHH" sounds. The pirates below his craft looked at each other with worried expressions. One stood up and tried to open the crew hatch. Three tractor-pressor pods bulged out beneath the ship's underhull, each shaped like half an egg.

Serenity stopped herself, mouth open. "Oh. OHH!" Horrified, she squeezed her eyes shut.

"Thermal batteries," Ceres answered her unspoken question. "Liquid sodium, heated by the ship's thorium reactors that charge all the capacitors and power the ship. It flows into the plasma drives for a quick, hot start."

His face took on a menacing look, turned back to the enemies surrounding his ship and preventing their escape.

Serenity shook her head and hummed.

Ceres realized what was happening. She wanted to block out the visions of coming carnage he imagined as he set things up in the hanger. To help her, he flexed his mental muscles of concentration, of willpower, to block her telepathy.

He imagined a heavy duranium safe around his mind and closed the door firmly, hearing the "Clank!" sound. He visualized turning the manual lock dial, shutting her out of his thoughts. To him it seemed similar to the willpower technique for blocking out pain. He saw Serenity's eyes open, her mouth open in surprise.

Shaking her head, squinting at him, she wrapped her hands around his injured knee, huffing out a breath.

Ceres shrugged with a wry smile and turned back to his sensor feed and ship's controls. *My family was right. This mental blockage works against those grey-skinned Xardyon's too, they say.*

Drive coils of super-electromagnets created intense magnetic fields. These both shielded the ship from energy damage, and contained the radio waves and plasma inside the engines. The powerful radios inside the plasma drives quickly superheated their hydrogen fuel to sun-like temperatures, separating the atomic elements. With a "BRROAARRR" each of the plasma drives spewed a small solar prominence down upon the hapless pirates hiding beneath the spacecraft.

The tractor beams kept the ship anchored above the deck, despite the thrust of the engines through their magnetically vectored exhaust ports. The pirates' screams quickly silenced. If Ceres' little military pistol could melt their armor, they had no chance against a starship's engines. Controlling the ship remotely, he spun it around slowly to angle the plasma engines into each corner of the hanger and over pirates waiting to ambush him there.

Star-hot plasma output swept the deck free of ash and coal-like graphene flux nuggets, the remains of the pirates' armor. Overhead, the hanger's clamshell doors opened and the ashes blew out in a grey rushing cloud, along with all of the air. The ship settled on its landing struts once again, plasma drives already cooling down in the vacuum of space.

Ceres flipped through numerous holocam views throughout the asteroid, scanning for more intel while waiting for the space hatches to close and the hanger air pressure and temp to return to livable levels. The armory looked secure, the massive rotary laser guarding it ultimately triumphant over many tens of pirates in the access corridor. The diversion had served its purposes.

Burning debris filled the end of the central access tube from the incendiary grenades and their large pile of fuel. Using the cam's ultraviolet spectrum to see through smoke and ash, Ceres scanned for movement. The hanger side cleared by Ceres' use of *Pegasus'* thrusters, the ambushers were burned away from both sides of their blockade.

Spread by the ventilation system, cannahol vapors anesthetized those pirates without protective suits and breath masks. Serenity was still protected from its effects thanks to the counter-agent Two had crafted for them.

A few ambushing pirates in the hanger access tubes now wandered aimlessly, like narco-zombies, as did hundreds of freed slaves. Those slaves who, through years of brainwashing, had gone over to the pirates' side, were effectively neutralized as inside threats to the escapees. Cannahol users were highly suggestible, but without some guidance to follow, they were more dangerous to themselves than anyone else.

"I think the vapors downed them," Ceres told Serenity. Still working to deal with what she had initially seen via Ceres' mind, she kept her eyes closed. Ceres scanned the asteroid, viewing cam after cam seeking movement, seeking stray slaves to rescue or pirates to fight off.

Air volume and temperature restored in the hanger, Ceres opened the hatch and swept in, little plasma pistol drawn. He imagined opening the safe in his mind's eye too, letting Serenity back in touch with his mind. Another hatch "ShhCLUNK"ed open down the hanger, causing Ceres to wave Serenity back as he took cover against the wall.

The parade of wheeled cargobots rolled in and processed towards Ceres' starship, treasure cases and crates atop them. From the other end, APH1D-7 floated towards the ship as called.

Meanwhile, the hatches of the ship popped open. The handful of Ceres' armed crew dropped down into crouching stances, waving stun carbines and pistols around, seeking pirate targets, and securing the craft for those coming aboard. Ceres thought they looked as untrained as any random militia he had ever seen.

Kangee, seeing no enemy, stood, walked to the edge of the hanger and looked up. Smiling, he gazed up lovingly at his handiwork.

"They're gorgeous!" Serenity marveled at the beautiful white wings painted with feathers to fill the entire topside of the atmo-wings. The muscular body, head, and flowing mane, filled the central raised portion of hull, a mighty mural of the ancient heroic horse. The downward curve of the wings allowed them to see it from the sides.

"Thanks," Kangee smiled broadly but humbly, almost seeming uncomfortable with the praise.

"Why didn't you tell me?" Serenity asked them both.

"It's his work," Ceres shrugged.

"It was his concept, his commission," Kangee said. "He wanted to surprise you," he waited a beat. "Surprise!" His arms opened and he smiled wide. Ceres mimicked his gesture, the two looking like singers presenting their big finale in a concert.

"I like surprising you with beautiful things?" Ceres glowed at her, pleased that she liked his idea for making the luxury spaceship even more beautiful. Serenity caressed his cheek with her soft warm hand, which made him wonder if she had misgivings about their earlier passionate kisses.

"Jefe!'" Arturo shouted and waved, encased in a silvered hard-shell space suit. "Ah, bella doma," Arturo grinned warmly at Serenity, "we are all about to taste freedom, si?"

"Si, Señor' Tapas," she called him by his last name.

Ceres ignored his mildly flirtatious manner, for now. He did not consider Arturo as a serious threat to his relationship, so he thought no more of it. Let alone he knew she was in complete command of her own life and body. She said she would one day give it only to her husband.

"Let us make haste, gentlemen," Serenity raised her eyebrows expectantly.

"We're all clear and ready to launch!" Arturo agreed. Turning to Ceres he added, "Did you find what my Señorita needs?" His big smile made Ceres smile in return.

"No, my amigo," Ceres said. "We will have to leave unarm—wait! What about this?" He turned and took the silver case of soul crystals from Serenity, presenting it to his mechanic with a grin.

Arturo opened it and whistled, the lights playing warmly on his brown face. "Señor," he said. "We have no doubt. You are muy loco, no?"

"Install it in the fire control system and isolate it from the rest of the systems," Ceres replied. "I think the Rokkled souls will want to escape from those who killed them just as much as we want to get out of here."

He shot a look at Serenity, silencing her probable comment about the one Ceres had killed. "We can form an alliance to escape our mutual enemies. Talk to them. Ask them."

"I'll 'elp if you need it," Serenity offered. "Call on me when you're ready to plug 'em in."

Arturo looked to Ceres for confirmation. "Whatever works," Ceres said with a shrug. His mother's motto came in handy many times.

Running up the boarding ramp into his ship, Ceres was pleased to see his bots from the dome loading crates aboard, the best of the bounty from their king's private stash. Serenity ran to the access corridor leading to the slave pens, the same entrance nearby which Kangee had strode up earlier in the day. She waved her arm in a large circle, then led a small group of the oldest and youngest slaves to the ship first.

As he settled back into the pilot's grav chair in the cockpit, Ceres noted sullen or fearful looks still gripping some, but a dim sunrise of brightening hope now gracing others' faces. Ceres shared a knowing look and smile with Serenity through the crysteel cockpit panels. The pilot's manual panel swung in front of him. Round half-spheres raised up under his palms, at the end of his grav-chair's arms.

Behind them all Cassius and Yukozune—their armored suits and helmets could not conceal their immense physiques—held up laser rifles also liberated from the guard's armory, saluting Ceres with crisp port arms gun salutes. Ceres snapped a sharp military salute in return.

Yuko turned back down the corridor to protect the remaining docile slaves until their turn to go. The Tenublian's two clone slaves stayed close to Yuko, helping him with crowd control. Seeing the four large men together, Ceres had the odd thought that they looked related somehow—a question he would file away on his MeTR for later.

Cassius crept down the hanger's edge with quick but lumbering runs from cover to cover, deactivating the nearby telepods the pirates used for moving loot and slaves to and from the fleet ships left out in space. They didn't want to leave any open access for the pirates, now that they were this close to escape. The dark giant looked like a war robot in his stolen grey armor.

"Cassius to Ceres," the escaped slave voice commed from his helmet. "Where is this big luxury cruise ship you promised us, boss, to get all of these people off world?"

"Patience, patience," Ceres teased. "It will be here in a moment, friend. Be careful what you wish for. It could turn out to be full of new slaves. No room for you."

"Ha-ha," Cassius said. "As long as it's not full of pirates, and arrives before them. And if you leave us hanging here, I will kill you immediately. Shoot it back at you, boss. Cassius out."

"It's a deal," Ceres answered. "I'll be right back." Ceres, eyes closed, was deep into the full preflight checks when Serenity sashayed in and perched on the navigator's seat next to him. He could tell she arrived just from the vanilla and jasmine scents filling the cockpit. "Ready to load the nav coordinates?" he asked his favorite redhead.

"Yes, Captain," she smiled, sliding a datapin into the control board's receptacle. "We should backtrack the route they flew me in on. Good thing they let me watch from the view-lounge." She nodded to him. "The last container should be coming up now. I'll go double check." Serenity turned away down the tube shaped corridor out of the cockpit.

Various ship's systems powering up filled the hanger with sounds while Ceres finished the preflight checks on cockpit screens and controls. His control datapin in the console before him, used earlier for remote control of the whole ship, directed into his HUD more system reports then he could track without using his MeTR. He had programmed a preflight checklist, which rapidly cascaded from all red bullet points through yellow to green.

Shortly the redhead sat in the cockpit again, this time on the co-pilot's seat. The curvy spearhead-shaped ship lifted off on blinding blue pillars of plasma, up beyond the clamshell hanger doors and out into space. Viewing the ventral holocams on the belly of the ship as they rose, something didn't look as expected down in the hanger, but Ceres couldn't place what it was just yet.

The squid-like Tenublian pirate filled the corridor, drifting silently up into the back of *Pegasus'* cockpit. While Ceres and Serenity busied themselves at the controls, the alien's tiny white tendrils lifted up and reached out.

Ceres, cocky as ever, gripped the manual control balls, dialing up the speed. He called out to Serenity, "One rescue, coming up!"

Chapter 28
Push the Eaglet

Milky Way Galaxy, Central Gyre
Galactic Capital Station Atlantis, Joint Academy Headquarters
2518/6/5/0900

"I am submitting an application, Ma'am," Admiral Emanuel Tarsis looked sharp in his full regalia, his dress white uniform tailored, pressed, and spit shined. One arm cradled his flat-topped uniform hat, rimmed with gold leaves. He thrust a datapin forward.

"Are you attaching your reference, Admiral?" asked the intake clerk, a Lieutenant. "Giving your recommendation?" She took the pin and inserted it into a datapad for viewing.

"No, Light," Tarsis used the current nickname, common among officers for their most junior grade. "I am using my annual Admiral's appointment to directly insert this applicant into the next class."

The lieutenant's eyebrows raised in surprise as she noted the chosen academy. "But, sir, this is just for the Merchant Marine, not one of the military acad—" eyes lifted, she took in Tarsis' commanding gaze.

"I—" she stammered. "I'm sorry, Admiral, it not my pla—"

"Do not lose your bearing, Lieutenant, hmm, James!" he leaned forward, squinting, to make clear he was reading the nameplate over her collarbone. "It is unbecoming an officer to apologize. Take responsibility and resolve the issue. Execute your orders."

"Y-yes, sir!" she saluted. "I will run this to the Admiralty's attention immediately. Yes, sir!" she saluted again.

"Confirmation of receipt," he growled even lower. "I'll wait."

Admiral Tarsis' eyebrow lifted, noting her haste as Lt. James vanished like a ghost, into the back-office access hallway, the admiral's datapin stabbing into the palm of her shaking hand. His face carved in stone for a moment, he grinned. *I still have it.*

Chapter 29
Way Ahead of You

Wisp Nebula, Veils Region, Exit Mouth
2525/7/18/2100

"We're surrounded," Ceres said as calmly as he could. He did not want to panic Serenity or the others aboard. When the spaceship pulled out from the nebula's haze of gasses, Ceres could see the starships. The entire Void Viking fleet lay before them, dispersed into intercept positions, a blockade formation.

"I see nothing but space," Serenity said. "Aren't they all black?"

"Look," Ceres pointed. "See the twinkling stars?" Numerous stars seemed to wink off and back on as Pegasus moved before the midnight black armada. If he chose to run for it, any number of escape vectors could be cut off by intercepting pirate ships within weapons range.

Ceres looked darkly at Serenity, who had returned to the cockpit to assist with the takeoff. He opened his mouth to speak.

"It's okay," her fingers hushed his lips. "I know you'll do your best to protect us, all of us, no matter what happens." The comm crackled to life.

"Son, what in the dark heavens are you doing?" the menacing voice of the pirate king asked.

"Hey, Pop," Ceres answered cheerfully. "Glad to see you made it back already. I'm just taking her out for a trial run here, you know?"

"Don't try to con me boy, or I'll blow you out of space right now. I'm very disappointed. I'll be taking command of my new ship. Take her back to the rock, and we'll make this short and painless."

"I have a better idea," said Ceres, holding up a datapad so the comm recorder's lens would see it. He smiled, touched the little screen once, and sent *Pegasus* flying towards the net of pirate ships. "Bye Pop, nice meeting you."

"You mean you actually thought you could just send a couple of bots around to install a kill switch into each of my ships?" Tyrian roared. "You really think we would miss that?" His voice rose in anger.

"Why do you think the base was so lightly defended, my boy? I left the weakest ten percent of my people behind for you to cull for me. I *let* you get to this step, to see if you would take it. I'm so disappointed in you, my son."

"Marina, take control!" Tyrian yelled into the comm.

The Tenublian floating above and behind them grabbed the backs of the grav-chairs in the cockpit, securing Ceres and Serenity, who both looked up at him as if helpless.

Tyrian's flagship, named *Marauder* leapt forward, taking *Pegasus* roughly in tow via magnetic tractor beam. The larger ship extended its weapons pods on struts. At least ten laser turrets jutting from the underside of the larger warship covered *Pegasus*.

The rest of the fleet of over 300 smaller craft quickly accelerated. They poured like flocks of birds with their tail-feathers afire, down into the clear lanes between sheets of nebula gas and dust, to return to their rocky roost hidden within.

Ceres held up the datapad again. "You mean you think that was all I'd do to prepare to get out of here? You don't think I'm that smart then, do you?" Holding the datapad up for the lens, Ceres slid his thumb across it. Like fanning cards in a poker hand, out from behind the first slid a second datapad, which had been hidden from view.

"Really Pop. I'm so disappointed in you," Ceres keyed the second pad. Tyrian's command and control screens, holotank and fleet MeTR feed all died instantly. Only the transmission to and from *Pegasus* remained.

"Did you really think that obvious bot program was all I'd do to escape from here?" Ceres voice sounded amused, playful. "While you focused on that, did you ever wonder what else I might have slipped into your fleet systems. Hmm, hmm hmmm?"

"Marina, get them!" the elder Tauri screamed. His bridge crew pounded on control pads and furrowed their brows as if trying to force mental MeTR commands through dead comm channels.

The Rokkled airboss seemed particularly furious, shaking his pillared fists in rage. He easily re-asserted command of his nanites, those he had reluctantly donated to Ceres earlier in the week upon his King's orders.

Ceres gritted his teeth when he noted the loss of signal from the nanites he had reprogrammed and distributed. *"Pask!"* Ceres sent via MeTR to his command group of the escapees.

"That didn't last long. There goes my control of their systems. Rokkled technology is alien to me, after all."

The Tenublian behind Ceres and Serenity stood up on its thick tentacles to full height and folded its thin white tendrils into a hammock, the xeno's approximation of a Solman's crossed arms. Ceres decided to project confidence while his mind raced, thinking of new solutions now that they were committed to escape.

"Problem is, Pop, in your line of work, you never know who to trust," Ceres teased, maintaining an air of control of the situation, even as he subdued his panic at losing his main means of escape, the nanites distributed throughout the Void Viking fleet.

"See, this is my old friend Medusa, formerly of my Uncle Tarsis' crew," Ceres flipped a hand over his shoulder, towards the jelly-squid, receiving a tentacle pad complete with dozens of suckers wrapped around his forearm in return. Tyrian's stunned face turned red with fury.

"Jefe," Arturo called out loudly from the cockpit access corridor. "Things okay up here?" All three turned to see Arturo pointing the fat rounded lens of his laser carbine at Medusa.

"Yes, Arturo," Ceres answered. "This squid is my old amigo. He was just showing my father the ruin of his plans for us. We go back over ten years. I trust him with my life."

"Medusa, Arturo," Ceres introduced them. "He's my new Maintenance Chief on my new ship." Medusa lifted a tentacle in imitation of a human's handshake gesture, which Arturo reluctantly accepted, his eyebrows raised high as he traded arm grips with the squid.

"Fair breezes," cockpit vocoders emitted Medusa's lilting voice in Galactic, even as the sound of air escaping bladders cut through the air. Medusa's skin flashed when he quickly turned from his aggressive red hue to blue then green.

"Well," Arturo said finally, breaking out a huge warm smile for the Xeno filling the back of the cockpit. "Any friend of my savior here, is a friend of mine. If my Jefe trusts you that much, who am I to disagree with him, no?"

"Engineers report?" Ceres asked, taking the conversation into the command group over MeTR's. He did not want his father to listen in. Arturo finally let go of Medusa's tentacle.

"Si, Jefe," Arturo answered him. *"I can plug that suitcase of soul stones in."* He sounded hesitant, even in the voice created in his mind.

"Are you sure you want to do this, just to have a gun computer? Seems mighty risky to me, giving control of your weapons to a box of dead aliens? They might have their own agendas."

"We may need them shortly, my amigo," Ceres thought. *"I hope they wish to get away from their captors as much as the rest of us caballeros. They may be willing to help. I am willing to risk going from a civilian model, to no target assist system to see if I am right. I can shoot manually better than any civvie computer anyway. Do it."*

"Fwheew," Arturo whistled aloud. "All right, Señor, as you wish. She is your ship as much as mine." He shrugged, throwing up his hands as he walked down the hall. Ceres and Serenity smiled at each other.

"Very touching, son," Tyrian growled. "I'm still going to vac you all. As soon as we clear the nebula and my fleet can witness firsthand, what I do to traitors, even fam—"

"That's nice, Pop," Ceres cut him off. "Thanks for the tow. Helping us conserve fuel, very thoughtful."

Ceres pulled out a data pin from the socket behind his ear. He inserted it into his datapad and pressed the screen with his thumb. He transmitted a thought command, relayed from his MeTR through the datapad, through his ship's comm system. Stepping up to stronger transmitters in each link gave him greater signal strength and range.

Despite this, Ceres' nanites embedded in the fleet's systems did not respond. "Problem detected," Ceres rued, "I can't regain control from that airboss." With a thought, he cut off the external comm transmissions so he could speak without his father hearing it.

"I'm using the nanite security programming I downstreamed from an old Rokkled friend, but those nanites out there *belonged* to that guy to begin with. He has an affinity with them that I just can't match from outside."

"What else can you do?" Serenity asked him, "You must have backup plans?'

"Plan B is," Ceres answered, "I will have to shoot out that tractor emitter manually and race to clear space to form a wormhole, ahead of the fleet."

He gave Serenity a wry grin and shrug. "Doing so would require leaving the slaves aboard A-Valhalla."

"No, we're taking them with us!" Her determination was clear, final. "Let me see. I have an idea. 'Plan A, 2.0, let's call it?" Serenity rose, slipped under and between Med's tentacles as if she was dancing with him, and swept down the access tube into the ship. Ceres followed her through the ship's internal sensors and cams, relayed to his HUD.

* * *

"Arturo?" she called out. *"Ceres, I can't find his mind now. I sensed him earlier."* She found him in the center of the ship between the power access and data core.

Arturo' head dripped sweat on the floor, frozen in a prayer-like position over the case of Rokkled soul crystals. She pulled the datapin out of the tangle of threads in the case and eased the slumping mechanic to the floor.

"Ceres!" she shouted. "Come quick!"

"Already here," Ceres' boots slid on the deck as he rushed into the space outside the ship's data core. "Amigo, what happened?" Ceres patted Arturo's face.

"Let me," Serenity said. She stared at him and reached out to access his mind her way, mentally.

"Arturo?" she thought to him. She had been able to converse with her brother and Ceres, even in dreamlike states. *"Amigo, where are you? Are you all right?"*

"No answer," she reported aloud. "It's like he's in a deep coma. His mind is swirling, like fast forwarding through a Holo. They overwhelmed him? Over 20 minds intruded upon by one mind, xenomorphic to them. He was the alien shouting inside their heaven?"

"So, they scrambled his brain?" Ceres speculated, "Why?"

"Maybe just to punish him for waking them from their final sleep?" she speculated too, "We really don't know what's going on in there. Maybe they don't like intruders. Many species, and many individuals across our galaxy, are like that."

"I have to believe they wouldn't like being held hostage even more than being woken up from a nap!" Ceres said, "I will speak with them, then."

"No!" Serenity shouted.

"I will keep an image in mind of what we want to do with their help," Ceres persisted, "to escape the pirates who killed and kidnapped their soul stones. Maybe that will get through to them first?"

"No," Serenity said. "I'll handle that. I was a fellow prisoner of these pirates. They'll accept me as friendly."

"I can't let you—" Ceres cut off, noticing Arturo's body moving on the floor between them. "Hey, Amigo. Are you alright? We're worried about you. Wake up. Speak to me." Ceres looked to Serenity for help.

"No!" he saw her head slumped forward over the case of crystals, just as Arturo's had been when Ceres raced into the room. "No! What are you doing? Come out!"

Ceres reached for her datapin, and then realized he might hurt her if he disturbed her while she was mindlinked. He looked over to Arturo, worried that he might have brain damage either from the link or from their breaking it abruptly.

"Damn! I guess she couldn't mindlink her usual way, to this kind of digital mind?" he shook his head. "I'll jump in there with her and try to get us out of this."

"Med, come to the core!" Ceres shouted unnecessarily over the comm system. Instead of the floating jelly, the raven-haired artist walked in.

"I thought you may need a hand," Kangee said, "with all the shouting going on in here. How can I help?"

"Help revive Arturo," Ceres suggested. "Get some clues to help us come back out of… in there, whatever it is."

"I've got your back." Kangee offered his support. "Remember, when you dream quest, you are in the hands of the Great Spirit. Be mindful of who you are and who He is."

"I'm not sure that's what we'll find in there," Ceres said. "Thanks for watching over us."

Ceres took out another of his datapins, his last one, the one he had taken from the Rokkled guard in his father's treasure dome. "I'm sure this is the dumbest thing I'll have done all week." He stabbed it into a junction of nano-threads connecting the stones in the silver case.

* * *

"Hello? Where is everyone in here?" Ceres saw nothing but a powerful, blinding white light coming from everywhere at once. No floor, no walls, or ceiling. He put out his hands. *"No hands? Okay."*

"Hello Ceres. Come towards my voice," Serenity beckoned, her voice seeming to echo from everywhere around him.

"Where are you? I see nothing but white glare?" he replied.

"Think of me, think of being beside me," she answered.

He thought her voice came from a particular direction. He turned, imagined her, and with that thought, Ceres noticed Serenity beside him, radiant in white robes. "You are an angel!" he said. "Your eyes are emerald green, almost glowing. Your red hair stands out against the white... everything."

"This is their representation of heaven, based on our assumptions of where they are in their link, Ceres," she explained. "That's why you see an idealized version of me from my mind, and you appear here as the ideal version of yourself *you* see in your mind."

Ceres looked down at himself, stunned to see a super powerful body, as if he were remade into a hero by the holo-film industry. "Every man is a super man in his dreams," he quoted. "Is this all in my mind?"

"No," she explained. "It is all in their mind, with added input from ours. Their collective unconscious is like a supercomputer network, to our understanding. It is a higher mind than we can understand with our one brain, single mind, and personal unconscious."

"Okay, so," Ceres, results oriented and driven to action, raised his head and voice to address the blank white sky overhead. "We have a mutual enemy. The pirates who killed you and captured your soul crystals are trying to recapture us all. I am trying to get us away from here, as well as hundreds of others like us. Perhaps thousands more like you."

"They know, Ceres," she said. "We've been talking for hours."

"Oohh, Sweetheart?" he said, "You were only mindlinked with them for seconds before I joined you."

"Yes, the speed of dreaming thought is far accelerated beyond the speed of our waking lives," she explained. "Maybe I should say, it seems like I've been in here speaking with them for hours."

"Understood. Introduce me to your old friends, please," he asked her. "I feel like we're standing beneath the throne of heaven being judged by God, who we can't see because we're still in purgatory, not yet accepted into His presence in heaven."

"They are not gods," she corrected him. "This is not heaven, even for them. It is a group mind, a shared dreamland even. Displayed for us like an immersion holotank but with so much bio-feedback it seems real in every way. A moment, love."

"Diamion," Serenity said, while bowing from her waist and opening her arms like wings, "I bring before you Ceres of Ceres. He represents your old friends, the Tarsis of Ceres."

The apparent sky and ground they seemed to stand on shook as if a ground quake rumbled throughout the simulated heaven. Vibrations fell as sound into Ceres' ears.

"FRIEND," echoed in an avalanche of sound, as if great stone monoliths dragged roughly across their massive foundations.

Ceres grabbed his ears, even though he knew they were not real and it did nothing to dampen the immense sounds echoing inside his skull. *Dreamland, she says?* Ceres thought. *That sounds familiar.*

"Ceres of planet Ceres, the asteroid that grew up," The Rokkled voice lowered in volume, becoming more bearable. "I am Diamion. It is well to meet you.

"I knew your grandfather as a friend," the voice filling the sky continued. "He stayed the hand of his mining fleet from our adopted home in your galaxy. I showed him veins of thorium that fueled his fleet for twenty of your Sol-Earth years."

In an instant, the image changed. The blinding white light dissolved and Ceres and Serenity felt like they were suddenly hanging in the middle of open space. It was dark but billions of brilliant points of light surrounded them.

"Oh!" Serenity cried out. Feeling as if she should be falling, that is what happened to her virtual body. "It seems we create our reality here based on our perceptions of it?"

Ceres grabbed the collar of her blue jumpsuit as she dropped next to him, his idealized virtual body moving at the speed of his mind. Thanks to his tractor/pressor devices, Ceres could fly. Thus, inside the digital dream world created by the Rokkled mind network, he flew like a holovideo superhero. He pulled Serenity back up to him and they grabbed ahold of each other for stability, mostly hers.

"Easy," Ceres reassured her. "I've got you. You're safe." The surrounding image rushing through space as if beyond the speed of light made her nauseous.

"I *know*," she said, exasperated, "Intellectually I know my body is kneeling in the middle of the ship. It's just so *real* in here—beyond the holovideos, even beyond an immersion holotank!"

"This virtual mental landscape—" she grasped for words to describe it. "The sleeping Rokkled soul stones—their dreamscape uses cues from my mind and gives sensory feedback that I actually feel. It makes me feel like I really am in space and falling. I hate falling!" she said.

"I have you. Trust me," Ceres said. "I will teach you how to enjoy flying."

Rushing past stars, the surrounding scene slowed, tracking down into one particular star system. A brown dwarf star emitted very little light as Ceres and Serenity flew by, on a flight path towards a vast asteroid belt around a bright white star. The binary stars shepherded the vast rings of smaller bodies between them.

"Ahh, I see now," Ceres said to Serenity, "Hang on to me while you get used to this." He turned his attention back to his conversation with the Rokkled group mind.

"I am surprised to learn that, Diamion. That you are an old friend of my family, thus a friend of mine. If you know my Papa you know loyalty is an important principle to my family." Ceres stopped squinting his eyes as the pressure in his head lessened. "Is this a depiction of the mining region you showed my grandfather? Or of your homeworld?"

"From our races' homeworld in a nearby galaxy, *this* is where we settled in your Milky Way Galaxy, as you call it," the powerful voice replied. "We call it a "Greater Belt."

The dreamscape raced back as if a distant camera had zoomed in to millions of magnifying powers, now reversed. Star systems raced by and their surroundings resolved to show the entire galaxy from afar. The bright gyre around the central black hole. Ceres realized this perspective might be from one of the Magellanic Clouds, small galaxies near the Milky Way.

Ceres smiled, both in the dreamscape and with his physical face outside as well. "I am here to ask you to collaborate with my family once again, with me. In return for aiding me today, I will deliver you and your fellow souls to that location. Agreed?"

"It is not that simple, young friend of soft flesh. A new soul among us is as displeased with you and your family as I am happy and proud."

"Convey my remorse, please," Ceres said. "I did not wish to kill him but I had to defend myself, as is the natural right of every creature. He could have asked a question before attacking me, perhaps? I am sure if we had spoken before fighting, he would have joined me in liberating you from your sleeping prison on the pirate's asteroid. Do you agree?"

As Ceres imagined the Whisp Nebula and A-Valhalla within, so the dreamscape flew at immeasurable speeds to the location. Serenity gripped Ceres tighter as they raced down as if to wreck upon the asteroid. They stopped smoothly, hovering over the domes of Tyrian's apartments.

They seemed to slip effortlessly through the dome's crysteel panels as if Ceres and Serenity had ghostly bodies. Ceres could feel the sand on his bare feet when they came to rest on the edge of the pit, where Ceres' crew of robots had dug out the cases full of Rokkled soul stones. The dome was empty of robots. It looked as it had when Tyrian verbally dueled Ceres here.

The sand beneath the large central rock rippled, dark streaks between the sculpted white lines left by raking. To the low hissing, crystalline sound of a dune flow, these streaks coalesced into a river, flowing across the sand towards the entry. They passed right around and under Serenity's feet as if they weren't there.

"It tickles!" Serenity laughed. Ceres lifted off the floor to avoid contact with the strange phenomenon.

The river of dark sand climbed up the low stone to the side of the entry triangles. Enveloping it, the stone vibrated, the sand parting beneath it. It appeared as if the thin dark sand dragged the rock beneath the white sand filling the floor.

With an uplift, the stone reappeared, white sand pouring off it as it vibrated free from its burial. The stone seemed to stand up, sections breaking free, attached by the black sand and threads of silver lacing through it. A stone statue arose before Ceres and Serenity.

"This is the same thing that happened earlier today!" Ceres shouted, aghast. "I was here with my team of bots to dig out whatever treasure my father had buried here. This guy stood up and started fighting my loader bot. It was trying to lift the stone and the Rokkled started fighting it, then turned on me!"

"Yes," Diamion said, "our son was protecting us. It is why we conceived him. We now show you the scene of his birth."

"I didn't know!" Ceres said, "Oh, what have I done? Diamion, I didn't know! I…" he might have apologized, but remembering his uncle's advice against it cut him off. His Sensei obviously set a different example. Ceres had to make up his mind which principles to live by and how.

"Diamion, forgive me. I intended to salvage my father's treasure, which I concluded must be in his domes from Thorsson's data on the entire base. Then I noticed my father's odd behavior when he brought me here, the scratches on the rocks hinted at bot handling. I didn't know…." he trailed off, head bowed to his chest.

The Rokkled folded its legs under and rolled over towards Ceres' virtual body. It brushed past Serenity as if ignoring her.

Ceres settled onto the sand then dropped to his knees. "Forgive me. How can I make it up to you?"

The Rokkled unfolded its limbs, towering over the kneeling human. It reached out with a powerful arm, gripped Ceres head in its huge hand, fingers wrapped around all sides.

"Yes, you, young one," Ceres realized this live addition to the historical scene must have come from the young guard. "I can understand your desire for personal revenge. But this is a virtual scene, isn't it? Your soulstone is in the case aboard my ship along with your elders, your parents."

"We must find another way for me to make it up to you besides allowing you the hollow vengeance of seeming to kill me in this world created from our collective minds."

The rounded statue sagged, relaxing its body along with its grip on Ceres. It rolled back to the entry, to the depression in the sand next to the bench viewing the sand garden. Finally, it folded itself back up, tucking its rocky limbs underneath, resuming its disguise of a boulder, so perfect that Ceres had sat upon it.

"How are we 'here,' Ceres?" Serenity asked by telepathic thought. *"Mental travel, out of body, back in time? It feels we are truly here in the dome at this moment, even though I know we are still kneeling inside the starship."*

With that new thought the pair flew out away from the dome, beyond the asteroid, soaring past the folds of nebula, past flocks of black star fighters, their glowing plasma drives thrusting them home. Ceres thought, though they were silent, the Rokkleds were interacting with them by moving the point of view of the dreamscape to match the pair of Solman's side conversation.

Coming abreast of the mothership, the *Marauder*, the dreamscape showed *Pegasus* in tow beneath the larger ship. The view zoomed in and squeezed through the hull to hover over the scene in the ship's core— Medusa floating over Arturo and Kangee while those two gently held Ceres' and Serenity's kneeling forms.

"We are in a form of group mindlink with them, right?" Ceres asked with his "voice, no longer bothering trying to converse privately with Serenity via thoughts. "You called it a dreamland at first. In our dreams, anything is possible and it feels real inside its own reality."

"This 'dreamscape' as you named it must be their version of a holo-tank?" Ceres guessed. "Full 3D immersion with inputs from any mind viewing, or, which has previously viewed, the displayed area. They probably use guesswork, imagination, to fill in the unknown details. That side thought of revenge by the young one was able to alter the historical scene, add to the data they showed me of how he was progenated."

"They must have—no *be*—a vast yet compact database of their many mind's lifetimes of experiences. The ultimate mainframe of crystal data storage. It is extremely impressive."

"An interesting perspective on our new member," Diamion finally answered. "You speak well, Ceres of Ceres." He seemed to ignore directly answering Serenity's thoughts. "He is young, having not yet grown a head. No achievements to mark upon his body and give him his name."

"I see," Ceres suddenly understood the xeno's lifecycles better. He visualized the various forms of Rokkled bodies he had seen in his lifetime. "The young rollers don't have a head to interfere with their locomotion. They have no accomplishments yet tattooed on them. As you grow you sprout a head?"

"Later you grow taller still? I've heard of five meter tall Rokkleds. Is that your elder class?" The scene around them changed back to floating freely in space where they started, but did not show the Rokkled bodies Ceres imagined it would. *"I think he is modestly withholding what they know,"* Ceres suggested privately to Serenity. *"Not answering my concept of their life cycles."*

"We will discuss that at another time, if at all.' Diamion dismissed. "Our two new fleshy friends carried images of your efforts to free others of your kind from our captors, Ceres of Ceres. You have fought better than we against these, harvesters of our soul gems."

A momentary image flashed—the dreamscape transforming instantly—of Ceres flying Serenity down the central shaft of the asteroid. It seemed to be from Serenity's perspective, clinging to him in flight, just as she was now in the dreamscape. The shockwave from the many grenades' explosion seemed to whip by despite the solid walls of the asteroid.

"Ceres," Diamion asked, "will you be our champion, in the physical realm? Protect us from those who would exploit us and our brethren in our connection in this mental realm?"

"I will," Ceres agreed without hesitation. Being called on like this suited his self-image as a defender of others perfectly, playing to his ego. "To make amends for my ignorant destruction of your child, I will protect all of you just as fiercely as I have those of my own race aboard this ship, Diamion. You have my word."

"I will carry your prayers to my brethren." Diamion said, "They are disturbed from their bliss. You have requested our aid. We will decide your fate."

"It is the fate of us all, old friend," Ceres renewed his diplomatic appeal. "I offer to make it up to you. What do *you* want? Your freedom to slumber in your final bliss?

"Where could you do that, a place better than here, trapped by these pirates? Perhaps in your adopted home, among the stars and stones of your full brethren?

"If you help me I promise you, on the honor of my family, your old friends and allies, to return you and all the others we have liberated, to your home stars."

"Wait while we discuss." With that the sonic trembling of the dreamscape ceased. Ceres and Serenity seemed to drift on in space.

"That's it?" Ceres turned, asking Serenity.

"They are rather blunt and to the point," she commented.

"Like you. I can see why you are already old friends." He grinned and she smiled back at him.

"They don'na like a lot of talk and diplomacy.... Politics! If you kept talking you could have blown this deal, Aye." She shot him a rueful smile.

"They are used to deciding things by instant consensus across their networked mind." She taught him some of what she had gleaned from what seemed like the last few hours. "No debate. Well, so fast we wouldn' notice it, likely. We must be incredibly slow minded to 'em. Probably annoy—"

"YES!" boomed Diamion's voice. "Plug us into your void craft's main systems, and we will help."

"I just need you to assist the little civilian-grade defense laser's targeting," Ceres replied to the white sky. "Help us shoot out their tractor beams. We must hit several emitters and laser turrets while I fly like crazy!"

"I can do that all myself," Ceres admitted, "but our odds go up with your digital targeting and my intuitive flying." *Flying like a duck scared of a brace of booming shotguns will probably do the trick.*

Serenity snorted, choking on her laugh. Ceres was reminded that she was always in his head, even here in the dreamscape where they were both in these Rokkled's collective heads. Ceres thought Diamion's final comment was positive.

"We will do what you need us to do."

* * *

Eyes squinting open, Ceres felt strong hands roll him from his knees to his back. Seeing the large colorful canopy of his old friend Medusa floating overhead comforted him, while Arturo and Kangee kneeled over Serenity.

"What did you learn?" Kangee asked them.

"I'm okay!" Ceres moaned, muffled through a stiff jaw and numb lips. "Bad headache." He tried to move but felt frozen as when Ka'ra had poisoned him with her paralytic pheromones.

"It will wear off soon, Jefe," Arturo said. "Kangee has an herbal remedy that helps, if you can stomach it."

Moving in jumps and starts, Ceres reached up to massage his throbbing temples. "Check on her."

"I am well," Serenity reported, seeming less effected even though she had been under for a longer time than him. "They use our bodies' natural sleep paralysis, so we don't hurt ourselves while dreaming."

Kangee handed her a container of tea that she sipped from, grimacing, her small nose wrinkled. "Powerful medicine is often hard to swallow," he advised. "Pinch your nose and slug it back. Just a mouthful."

"What is it?" Ceres looked on with concern.

"It will knock your headache out in seconds." Kangee said.

"Trust me, amigo," agreed Arturo. "It works!"

Serenity passed the cylinder over and nodded her approval.

Ceres gulped the remaining beverage down, hoping for relief from his headache. His body was coming around quickly. Merging with so many minds and communicating mentally for what seemed hours in mere minutes was a mental feat that challenged him.

"I feel like my quantum chips got hot and overloaded." The throbbing and pain subsided immediately as promised, a wave of warmth spreading down from his lips to his fingers and toes. Ceres gasped, looking with surprise from the cup, to his artist friend.

"My people have preserved much of our ancient wisdom from old Earth," Kangee said. "I will tell you more another day."

"Fair enough, my friend," Ceres said. "My mother's motto is 'whatever works' and this works! Let's get out of here already."

The pair got to their feet with assistance. "How long were we down?" asked Ceres, already wobbling his way towards the cockpit. He knew they had little time before the fleet approached the asteroid.

"About five minutes, six?" Arturo answered. "I only just got back up myself."

"Funny, I thought we were in there for hours!" Ceres called back, concerned. "I wonder what else happened. My MeTR reports under six minutes too, but I'd swear it was far longer!"

He rotated the pilot's chair into its reclining combat position, climbing on like a repulsor-bike rider, also the way most star-fighters were flown. Kangee lifted Ceres sluggish feet into the footwells aside the pilot'schair.

The front half of the grav-chair folded back over Ceres' chest, holding him securely, pinched between cushions and gravity emitters. The armrests shifted to find his hands over their rounded half-ball controls, fingers finding the touchpads for manual control of various thrusters. Redundancy with the linked controls allowed choice of the pilot's preference.

"It was a matter of several hours for me, Ceres," Serenity said. Arturo helped her to her chair at Ceres' right. "I seem to have less of a headache than you but more lingering physical effects."

"Maybe because I was trained for immediate action when I awake," Ceres suggested, "while you are used to being in multiple minds at once?"

"Or maybe I'm just smarter than you and you're an athlete?" she teased.

"Hey, did you just call me a 'big, dumb jock'?" he went along with her humor. "You're probably right," he answered diplomatically, with a grin. "I don't need to be the smartest one in the room. Just the last one standing."

"*Then* you will be the smartest one in the room," came over the vocasters, informing them that Medusa had followed them to the cockpit and followed their conversation as well. Serenity and Kangee laughed. Ceres grinned sheepishly, then shrugged when Arturo slugged him in the shoulder.

The *Marauder* still held *Pegasus* in its tractor beams, towing it along. They approached the inside end of the folds and channels of the nebula's dust cloud leading to the vast inner pocket cleared by the gravity of Asteroid Valhalla circling the distant white dwarf. The fleet of smaller ships was far ahead of their flagship, half way to landing on their base.

"Time to change the game!" Ceres claimed. He closed his eyes, focusing on working his way through the command functions of the bridge of his father's ship. Over the last week, Ceres' robots had passed on a rather obvious infiltration program, which Ceres had almost intended for the pirates to find. If they were just smart enough to look at all, that is.

Meanwhile, many nanites had jumped from bot to bot to computer to pirate ship as well. Each stop of a robot spread more molecule sized Rokkled nanites, eventually into all the pirate's systems. With Ceres' reprogramming and his worm aboard they would give him internal control over any system they swarmed into. The Rokkled airboss had reasserted control of his nanites, though, cutting Ceres' control.

"*Ceres to Diamion*," Ceres' MeTR called out to his new friend via the datapin he had left in their network of connective fibers.

"WE SHALL HELP," the grave voice boomed over the vocasters.

"We?" Ceres had not expected the whole group of Rokkled minds to break out of their dreaming network to assist him. "I'm not sure what they are doing?" he said to the cockpit crew of Medusa and Serenity.

"I explained things to them more fully than you," Serenity explained. "Maybe they are taking their own initiative to do what they think best for us? They do combine many lifetimes of experience."

Explosive shudders rocked the pirate's flagship, weapons and shield capacitors erupting in overload. The tractor beam switched off and *Marauder* drifted on through the last cloud layers of interstellar gas making up the bright nebula, now helpless to resist the inevitable gravity of the asteroid base or its star.

"That is what I had intended to do," Ceres said. "My plan which I just thought about, in there with the Rokkled sleepers. I had not counted on the big guy taking back his nanites once he donated them to me. I'll have to plan to counteract that next time." He shared rueful looks with Serenity.

Tyrian yelled into his ship's command comm, "Get back over there and secure our slaves!" His slave guards were all aboard *Marauder* below him. Ceres' HUD displayed the internal holo-feeds and system status. One by one Tyrian's bridge status display lights winked out. System by system the flagship's command bridge lost power. The Rokkled crewman rushed the open lift hatch in the center of the bridge's floor.

"Wait your turn!" Tyrian yelled, "Captain first!" The statue-like airboss used a thick arm to block and shove Tyrian back from the hatch. He squeezed himself through, his huge body scraping roughly over the metal and plasteel surfaces of the hatch. He slid down the shaft inside the spar raising the bridge above the hull of the starship.

Explosive bolts ripped the bridge free of the tower, emergency hatch sealing them in. Bursting out of the damaged tower, the Rokkled spun in space but soon righted himself with twists and spins of his arms. Vented atmo blew him up against the bottom of the bridge, drifting away from its former starship.

Landing then leaping off from the bridge structure, the rocky alien drifted down, grabbing the now sealed tower that had held the bridge above the hull. He climbed down to *Marauder's* hull, standing there defiantly, immune to the vacuum of space.

Hatch closed, the bridge became an escape pod for the remaining command crew. The capsule twisting end over end in the void inside the nebula, Tyrian's rant was lost to silent space.

"Grantite has joined us," Diamion reported, naming the Rokkled airboss. "We will use his natural control of his nanocytes for your flight plan."

"Well, that simplifies things," Ceres replied. With the greater signal strength of a network of minds and nodes, Ceres' relayed mental commands opened the waiting links to the telepods back on the asteroid, targeting the pods the flagship used to disgorge pirates and looted cargo, and to load and unload slaves. Earlier in the day Tyrian had used them to transfer the ransomed hostages back to Shangri-La.

Aboard the flagship hull, Tyrian's pirate guards noted their poppers powering up, destination A-Valhalla, and climbed inside. They were eager to get off the hulk and wanted to recapture their slaves, per their King's last orders.

* * *

The teams of slavers and prison guards popped out into the asteroid's hanger deck, weapons shouldered and ready. They found the decks vacated.

"We're on the far side from the slave pens!" one of them called out, "Run!" starting a stampede down through the empty landing bays.

The slaves gathered on the far side of the asteroid, near their former prison. They hurried to escape before the guards arrived. Tens of robots assisted hundreds of them into the telepods.

Leading the wave were the two burly slaves Ceres and Serenity had armed—Cassius and Yukozune'.

* * *

Popping out into the troop cargo holds of *Marauder*, they ran down the interior of the derelict pirate flagship, engaging the remaining crew of pirates still manually operating various ship systems. These two men were ruthless and efficient in their revenge against their former captors.

Watching their progress on the capitol ship's internal holocams, Ceres could tell these men had been hiding their skills. They must have had some high level military training in their younger days. They were still proficient in shipboard combat after all these years. Working in tandem with cover and cross fire, soon they cleared the pirate resistance. The derelict hull of *Marauder* was theirs.

Podfulls of slaves popped over to the flagship, flooding eagerly out of its cargo and boarding pods. Within minutes, the asteroid was emptied and the *Marauder's* hull filled with refugee slaves.

Ceres used his MeTR link to Grantite's nanocytes to take over controls for the flagship's dislocated bridge, powering up its system's and comm screens so he could safely speak with his father. "I wish I could say it was nice to finally meet you, Pop, but I could *never* be your pirate prince."

"Not an issue, son," Tyrian spat back. "I have others. Better, more obedient sons and daughters. I declare an end of your branch of my bloodline. I will cut it off. Cut *you* off. I will have my fleet follow you to the ends of the galaxy! We will destroy everything you ever loved!

"To warm up, we'll start with burning alive that city you seemed so concerned about. Then we'll go to Old Earth and pay my in-laws a visit. Should be exciting!" His face lit up with manic glee.

"I am sorry to hear that," Ceres replied, troubled look wrinkling his brow. "I was just going to disable your fleet temporarily so we could get away.

Now...?" he trailed off. "You've really left me no option but the last contingency I had planned. Pity. So many nice ships."

"My nanocytes have left a few minute's power in your comm system, so we could watch this together." Ceres keyed the pad again, switching his command pathways from his father's flagship to his pirate fleet. There was no hesitation as the networked mind of 21 Rokkleds used Grantite's commands to reawaken Ceres' worm programs in the fleet's datacores.

The top academy pilot closed his eyes, leaned back comfortably in the grav-chair and settled in to his dreadful work. His face grim, Ceres determined to do what he had to do to end this threat to his family and the galaxy.

First linking his MeTR HUD to the sensor feed from his ship, his NavWay program overlaid a holographic icon highlighting each of the dark ships hidden against the blackness of space. Ceres sent the view feed to the cockpit display screen in both his ship and his father's derelict bridge capsule.

"This is your Captain speaking," Ceres said in a classic flight controller voice. "Please direct your attention to the nearest screen, or out the viewports if you purchased a window seat. We will begin showing our inflight movie in just a few moments." He joked with the flight crews of both his ship and Tyrian's bridge, trying to ease his own building tension with dark humor. Then he gulped and his mouth went dry. This really wasn't funny business.

Ceres closed his eyes and merged back into the Rokkled's dreamscape. He slid into a clear global exterior scene as if he had dropped out of the ship's lower airlock, now outside watching from space. The fleet of highlighted black pirate ships popped out against the background nebula. At first Ceres saw *Pegasus* hovering overhead, beneath the derelict hull of *Marauder* and her drifting bridge.

Ceres gasped as he felt himself merge into the hull of his sleek new ship. His body now floated free in space, observing his surroundings, his starship missing from the scene. His arms swept back, he had the distinct feeling of vibrating with restrained power.

"Are you doing something, Diamion?" Ceres thought, though in the dreamscape he spoke aloud. A strange sensation, being the body of a spaceship with a mouth? Stranger still, speaking in open space.

"We are doing what you need," came the cryptic reply from the Rokkled voice. "Your link remains. We are helping you see beyond your sight."

"Ah, yes. I left my datapin in your nodes," Ceres remembered. "You are using the dreamscape to show me everything? I feel like I am flying in space. Is the *Pegasus* being represented by my body in my mind's eye?"

"Yes, your understanding is sufficient for you to comprehend. Proceed with your mission. We will do what you need."

Ceres felt integrated into the ship. As if he had become it and it had become him. His fingers felt like the tips of the flight surfaces, extending like feathers as he flexed them apart. His abs tingled due to the power core's hum.

Chilly, his skin felt touched by the cold of space yet his toes were notably warm—the engines? Ceres' eyes seemed wide open, unblinking, and multi-pane like an insect's, the sensors of the entire ship feeding into his brain. *This must be what it would feel like to be a living starship. Exhilarating!*

Ceres thought of sending a command through the network to freeze all the pirate ships in place. In response to his mere thought, the idea, controls locked up in the hundreds of pirate ships on approach vectors to their landing zones, inside or on the surface of the stony asteroid.

On his HUD passed a list of commands Ceres had prepared for each flight of ships, each separate squadron. The pirate ships changed direction, some reversed and backed away from their base, while others altered course to pass the asteroid. *That's odd. I meant to transmit the command, but they reacted to my mere thought?*

As each squadron approached its glowing holo-graphic nav-mark the ships rotated and fired their plasma drives, the classic turn and burn to halt their forward momentum. Some ships stopped in space while others drifted into formation alongside them. They pivoted to face Asteroid Valhalla.

Across the powerful pirate armada of hundreds of attack craft of every kind, fission power plants switched into overload. Thorium catalyst withdrawn, the nuclear reactions raced out of control. The slowly drifting command ship pushed through to the large center space of the nebula, clear space carved out by the asteroid called Valhalla and its dwarf star.

Ceres and Tyrian had an encompassing view of the whole scene. The command holotank filled the dead bridge with light, depicting the three-dimensional scene of the asteroid and fleet surrounding it.

"What the stars are you doing, son? I can see perfectly well out the ports here. Turn off the damn power!" Tyrian understood the inevitable result of draining the finite amount of power left in the bridge pod batteries. It would be getting as cold as space soon without full life support.

"Oh, no, Pop. You didn't have an integrated fleet control system linking all of those space-black ships, did you? Oops." With a look of mirth, Ceres dramatically tapped his datapad again, then gulped in chagrin at what he was about to do. Still not funny. Dead serious, in fact.

Closing his eyes, he concentrated. Tyrian strained to look, watching his son on the command screen and his fleet on the big holo filling the bridge.

Ceres' eyelids looked like he was dreaming, eyes moving rapidly as he glanced from one HUD view to another even while inside the dreamscape. The Rokkled minds helped, taking control of whole sections and squadrons as Ceres laid out his plan in their collective mind. Across the pirate fleet, pilots and captains called out in alarm as their ships became unresponsive to their control inputs.

Ceres thought about Tyrian's voice, opened his mouth and spoke. Tyrian's voice said, "I'm uploading new controls to the whole fleet. Don't panic. This will soon be over." Ceres grinned. One of the many HUD screens he monitored showed the ongoing violent ranting of his father, trapped in the bridge capsule.

"You don't seem to appreciate the chance to sit back and watch for once, Pop," Ceres teased in a mocking tone, using Tyrian's voice. He switched to his own voice, "You must have some desperate craving to be always in control. Relax. This will be an interesting father-son moment for us!

"You get to watch from the bench. I've taken control of the game. It's the end of the fourth quarter. I have the ball. I will take the final shot!"

Tyrian's face turned white as the blood drained from it. Ceres figured, surely he remembered as well as half the galaxy did, Ceres' winning gravity ball tactics?

Fanned out in space, the pirate fleet maneuvered into a ring around the asteroid. Whole phalanxes of Ravens, Needlers, Bombers, Dragons, and more, arrayed in squadrons on line, facing directly at their rocky home. A pattern arose.

The pirate fleet blockaded their own asteroid base. Ships with high acceleration rates formed an outer ring, while slower thrusting ships tucked in closer. A line of Needle fighters aimed at each end of the rock, where the central shaft pierced through the length of the asteroid.

Ceres beamed a huge grin, squirming in his seat, anticipation high. *With these guys helping share control I've finished what would have been hours of squadron maneuvers by myself, achieved in mere minutes!* Ceres cut sound transmission from the ejected bridge, silencing Tyrian's impotent screams of rage.

Arrays of ships fired all of their weapons at once. Hundreds of missiles and thousands of laser, proton and plasma weapons all pouring forth their destructive energies into their asteroid home. Dozens of habitat domes shattered and flash fires burned off the oxygen of the base. Maneuver thrusters cut off on the ships, no longer holding them in place against the slight gravity pull of their asteroid base.

"A reading from Jeremiah seems appropriate now," Tyrian's voice spoke to his fleet as Ceres recalled reciting the ancient scripture. "Behold, he comes up like clouds; his chariots like the whirlwind, his horses are swifter than eagles—woe to us, for we are ruined!" he finished low and deep with a voice of dread.

Plasma engines erupted their little solar flares out the aft of every ship. They surged forward, trying to catch up with the barrage of missiles racing forth. A bright halo appeared in the heavens, surrounding the asteroid—two rings of blue-white fiery prominences of the ship's plasma drives, erupting at full blast.

"It's so beautiful," Serenity said. "Ironic, their power."

Just as the fleet reached the surface of the asteroid, every weapon fired again at point blank range. Then came, the impacts.

The pirate fleet of hundreds of ships all crashed into the hangers and surface rock with a synchronicity usually seen only in a flock of birds or school of fish. The lines of needle ships smashed through the docking hangers at each end of the asteroid, lodging inside the central tunnel. In a second, the armada decimated itself, slamming at full throttle into the huge rock.

Fire and light erupted out of every hanger ringing the asteroid, every dome and hatch gouted enormous flares. Debris and bodies were thrown spinning into the vacuum of space. Some live pirates twisted and jerked, legs trying to run futilely in space until their lungs erupted from violent decompression, spewing fountains of blood out of their mouths to freeze in space.

Over 300 ship's power plants exploding at once caused a massive shockwave, engulfing the hanger waistline of Asteroid Valhalla. The tunnel bored straight through the core, with all its connecting tunnels to each hanger and surface dome, proved to be a structural weakness. Ceres exploited it with this massive, shaped-charge attack, the internal explosions of the needle ships' power cores fracturing the massive rock.

Asteroid Valhalla cleaved nearly in half and one of those huge hemispheres shattered into millions of pieces large and small. Serenity breathed slowly, as if reacting to the death toll.

Ceres retreated from the dreamscape view, blinking as he adjusted to the cockpit light. "A mere mortal again," he sighed. "Pity."

Tyrian, hot with impotent rage, slid his hands down the ribbons around his neck. Short-barreled pistols appeared in each hand. Flashes lit up the bridge pod as Tyrian executed his screaming crewmembers one by one with the energy beamers.

He continued shooting bodies strapped into their seats until his weapons overheated and deactivated themselves to cool. The dethroned king went on defiling the corpses with unrestrained kicks and slamming his defunct pistols down repeatedly. Eventually Tyrian exhausted himself, standing, panting in the center of the blood and smoke filled bridge pod.

"Oh, dear," Ceres said. "Was your greatest strength your irresistible armada of ships?" Ceres' mocking tone irritated his enraged father. Ceres switched to a more menacing voice.

"I just used your strength against you," Ceres said. "And your arrogance. But that was not the last of my special surprises prepared for you today."

Ceres made a show of putting his finger back over the datapad. He could blow the bridge with a thought but that would be hard to show his father the threat. "Now, *dear father*," Ceres' contempt was evident. "Let's have this little talk again. Where is my mother?" His furrowed brow, red skin, and heavy breathing revealed that his combat adrenaline had kicked in.

"I don't know," Tyrian sat stiffly on his command chair, presiding over his crew of corpses.

"If you tell me who you sold her to, I'll let you live," Ceres guessed. "She was not aboard Valhalla. Where did you sell her into slavery?"

"I wouldn't tell you if I did know," Tyrian's breath began to show in frosty vapors as the bridge capsule cooled in the deep chill of space.

"I'm sure you sent the men who took her," Ceres confirmed. "Thorsson was there. I remembered him. That is why I took special care with his execution.

"I didn't find the other kidnappers' faces here. So, let me guess, Pop. You meant to kidnap me as well, didn't you?" It was more statement than question.

"In fact, my guess is that you meant to get me away from her, so you could torment her with dramatic threats to me. Just keeping us apart would be torture to her, right? But your men settled for Plan B when I managed to escape them.

"Instead of stealing me from her, to cause her pain, you stole her from me, to cause her pain. Therefore, she has been held captive somewhere else, forced to be subservient in ways she *never* was to you, while she is prevented from contacting me all these years!

"What you forget, *dear father,*" Ceres' voice turned snide, "is that you have also caused *me* pain all these years!" Ceres boiled with rage and had to force himself to calm down. It felt good to finally confront his father and vent his full emotions. Now, wound up, he feared pushing the button and killing him out of spite before learning anything new.

When Serenity put her hand on his arm Ceres inhaled sharply, calmed, nodded to her. There was always something comforting about her soft touch. Her healing method must apply to emotions too? Maybe that was the secret to her name.

Ceres took a couple more deep breaths and continued. "I love my mother. I want my mother back. Tell me what you know!"

"She was a thorn in my side the entire time she was with me," Tyrian yelled. "Always pestering me to do things the way she wanted, nagging me not to do what I wanted. Then she left me, just as I began to start building all of this!

"I was going to put her on a throne over a planet, one day an entire sector. She was to be my queen, one day my empress. Instead, she left me?" He had an incredulous tone, then turned angrier, "Taking away my prince, my blood!" Tyrian rose to his feet as his anger grew. "She stole my bloodline. Away from _me_!"

"So, you took her away from me in return, and put her in a church somewhere?" Ceres guessed, then prompted, "Where is she? Did you kill her? Are you envisioning her church funeral, a graveyard? Is my mother still alive?"

"You're a smart boy," the elder Tauri smirked and gloated in an animalistic growl. "Not smart enough though. In a way, I'm proud of you, even as I am disappointed."

"Ahrrrr!" Ceres shot to his feet and pounded the arm of his pilot's chair, furious to know the truth that was right there in his father's head. Serenity merely sat quietly in the co-pilot's position, concentrating as she listened. Ceres held the datapad, his finger still poised over it.

After a short time of visibly wrestling with himself, Ceres sighed and straddled back onto his grav-chair. "No. As you have done to me, I will let you think about it for the rest of your life. Best wishes, Pop. Try and make it 15 years!" He tossed the pad down.

"*If* you find her *holiness* alive," Tyrian spat the words, "send her my regards... from hell!" The last image Ceres saw in his holo screen was Tyrian pointing both of his energy pistols at the bridge holo-cams.

"Great!" Ceres barked, frustrated. "Now I will never know. Two more clues than I came here with. Almost worthless!"

Serenity patted his shoulder, holding her eyes shut tightly. Ceres lay back in his chair and closed his eyes too. The only sound for a moment was from the chair, moving to wrap over his body again.

Pegasus, expertly driven by Ceres' newfound mental control system, maneuvered smartly down to land gently atop *Marauder*. He was getting used to popping into the Rokkled's dreamscape and enjoyed the unique new feeling of *being* the ship.

Kangee's natural remedy was still suppressing any headaches but Ceres felt more accustomed to the expanded viewpoint of the dreamscape and the many minds sharing it. It was an upgrade far beyond the detail of any holographic navigation system.

Tractor-pressor nodes and landing struts held the sleek Halberd Class liner fast to the larger warship's hull. In Ceres' dreamscape-view he stood atop the warship as if he too were a Rokkled, indifferent to the vacuum and radiations of space.

The Rokkled airboss, Grantite, climbed around the flagship's hull and entered a hatch through an airlock, surprising the slaves. Yuko warmed up with his sumo posturing, slamming one foot down then the other in preparation for hand to hand combat against the big statue towering a meter over the giant Solman.

Cassius started squeezing the firing stud on his laser carbine when Ceres commed over by MeTR.

"Wait one, crew! The Rokkled airboss switched sides," Ceres spoke to the escapee command group. "His name is Grantite. He just helped us crash the pirate's fleet. Let him stay aboard, but watch him."

"Good thing you said so, boss," Cassius replied, "I was about to melt him down."

"Prince friend," Grantite growled out loud. Cassius and Yuko nodded, but persisted in covering him loosely with their weapons.

With a thought, Ceres set the nav vectors back out through the dusty lanes through the nebula. The flagship full of refugees moved out under Ceres' direct control of its drive components, seeking clear space to open a wormhole to their destination. With the bridge controls physically removed, the Rokkleds, linked through the nanocytes Ceres had spread, extended their role as *Pegasus'* computer brain to control all systems aboard *Marauder.*

"You have ended the threat of our captivity and won our revenge, Ceres of Ceres," Diamion still spoke loudly enough in the dreamscape to tremble it with his voice. "You have honored your agreement to free us. You have proven your family worthy of the loyalty you require. We will continue to aid you in your quest to return all the slaves to their homes."

"Thank you, Diamion," Ceres said, still feeling like a floating starship in the dreamscape. "There is much yet to do." Finally, reluctantly, Ceres left the virtual world of the dreamscape and opened his eyes.

Serenity moved next to his command pilot chair. Looking deeply into Ceres' eyes she couldn't miss the mixture of strain and relief on his face. She leaned gently over him, comforting him with a hug. Awash in eerie light, the bright red glow of the nebula bathed the cockpit as the conjoined ships blazed steadily through it.

In a long open channel between sheets of dust, Ceres let the ship carry them on. The forward view played on a screen in his HUD. Contingency alarms would notify him if any status changed, in or outside the ships.

Serenity took Ceres' arm, and he led her aft. Trusting the former slaves and bots aboard *Marauder* to fend for themselves while the Rokkled sleepers ran the ship, the pair made the rounds aboard *Pegasus*. They saw to the comfort of refugees, assigning various household bots to tend to them individually.

Two, the former slave medic, tended to bumps and bruises, but found no major wounds among them. The long-term psychological damage of the months and years of slavery they had all endured was beyond her combat-medic expertise. Besides that, she was one of them, in that sad regard.

Other rob-units made ready the staterooms that made this F/L ship a Liner in addition to a Freighter. Ceres claimed the master suite for Serenity, for her privacy. His pilot's gravlounge would suffice him for this short run.

The French chefbot, On-Ree, with his strong personality, set to banging about in the galley, swearing beautifully in French. Seeing Ceres walk by the robot vocalized his displeasure that he was now head chef of an auto-kitchen. "Flash-cooking allows moi no creativity!"

After several minutes of stepping over freed slaves and robots Ceres called out to the redhead, "Hey! Where did all these bots come from? I thought I brought only my few aboard, but there are at least twenty in here?"

The beautiful redhead at his side explained, "Thirtyyy—plus? I kept 'em all aboard when they loaded ever'thin' earlier."

Snapping his fingers, "That's it! That's what seemed odd in the hanger. No bots hanging around! Maybe you *are* smarter than me. Nice thinking," he smiled.

She chuckled at his mixed compliment. "After we do some research with the Sector Marshalls, to restore the traceables to their rightful owners, we c'n let these poor people split the remainin' treasure and get on with their lives. I figured you might know where to sell a small shipment of bots to get your stake."

Ceres' lips pursed, eyes narrowed, "I'm figuring it the other way around."

Serenity's red-painted mouth tightened, and she marched right up to him, insisting, "They have lost ever'thin', their entire former lives and families!" She shook a fist and stomped a foot to emphasize her points. "Splittin' the spoils will be just enough to get 'em all home, t'begin to put their lives back in order!

"You have this ship," she went on. "A few thousand dollari times tens of bots is enough to get you started on y'er own, without your family's money and 'elp!

Her voice dropped lower, "Overcoming your sinful human nature and living virtuously would impress me, Ceres. You *do* want to live up to your family tradition, that you can start out and make it as your own man, true? Show me."

Quickly sizing up a situation and deciding on the best course of action was one of Ceres' trademarks. He hated to let millions in booty go, but reminding him that the treasure really belonged to others jarred him loose from the wave of greed he had felt.

If I keep the pirates' treasure, profiting from their pillaging, I will be just as much a pirate as them. It's not like I will ever need money, anyway. He wrinkled his mouth, but sighed and nodded to himself in resignation. Then Ceres noticed that Serenity had an amused look on her face, her freckled nose underlined by a smirk.

"What?" he asked, puzzled.

"I was just enjoying watching you work all that out," she replied. "Now that you remembered that you're a good-guy, let's see where all these folks call home an' plot a hole."

Floating on a cloud of love, the puppy Ceres followed Serenity's fantastic blue and red form, sashaying down the hall. Focused on her words "enjoying watching you," he momentarily forgot that she could easily read his mind. He felt amazed that she could read his face that well.

I will remember that when we play poker, he clapped his hands together, echoing down the ship's corridors. *"Game on!"*

Chapter 30
Aftermath

Wisp Nebula's outer reaches
2525/7/17/2330

"Ceres, love," Serenity called out. "You grew up in space—you called it your home. Explain t'me now, how wormhole travel works."

He thought about it for a moment. "Come with me!" Ceres beckoned Serenity. Excited, he ran like a kid down the access tube, turned a corner, tiptoed over various rescued slaves and the bots tending to them. Serenity caught up as he entered the forward lounge.

The Halberd Class design featured a large atrium-roofed view lounge, forward in the hull. Several rescued slaves were recovering there, enjoying the first comfortable room they had experienced in years. The two newcomers were warmly received, a space cleared for them on the couch among the grateful former slaves.

Ceres called up a music file, saved among his MeTR's petabytes of data. The room filled with sweeping orchestral music, then the building tune of a four-part harmony choir. The rich acoustics of the largest cathedral in the galaxy, filled with the gospel choir of Saint John's, reverberated in the lounge. Ceres added his baritone voice to the soundtrack, causing Serenity to turn in surprise.

"Oh Lord my God, when I in awesome won-der,"
"Consider all, the worlds Thy hands have maaade,"

His closed eyes and warbling voice showed his feeling for the music. His head turned and tilted, adding emphasis to match the flowing highs and lows of the classic tune.

"I see the stars, I hear the rolling thunn-derrr,"
"Thy power throughouuut, the universe displaaayed..."

He asked her, "You have heard the adage that 'music moves the soul?"

"Yes," she answered softly. "How does that matter? In space, no one can hear you sing."

He chuckled, "Space hears our starships sing."

"I'm listening." She settled back to enjoy the view of millions of stars visible in deep space.

"A brilliant man, Nikolas Tesla," Ceres started, "once talked about harmonic vibrations as a secret to constructing the universe. He reportedly built a huge machine that produced macro scale vibrations—like small earthquakes but modulated, pulses. By tuning the harmonic frequencies just right he could tremble different buildings around his city."

"Not possible," her frown displayed her skepticism.

"Quite possible. In fact, proven! Tesla claimed each building had its own harmonic frequency unique to its design. Records show building collapses around the area in the same timeframes when he ran these experiments.

"In addition, we have long held String Theories and Brane Theories, trying to unify the large scale universe operating under the known laws of physics with quantum theories about sub-atomic particles.

"Quantum theory is all about tiny particles and packets of energy in the quantum foam, which whisk in and out of existence in nanoseconds, each vibrating with a unique harmonic pattern. Cosmic strings link the massive structures of galaxies spanning the observable universe.

"Considering every atom of your body was once matter in the heart of a star, is it any wonder we follow the same rules as every other bit of matter in the universe?

"Scientists who are also Christians believe, these ideas from different fields are all onto the same truth. They meld together the large-scale universe, small-scale atomic structures, Tesla's observation about harmonic vibrations, and the fact that the right music, the right 'vibes' can make your pulse pound in your chest and bring tears to your eyes."

His voice joined the choir in the rising volumes of the stanza. He reached out and held her hand for a moment so they could share the feeling.

"Then sings my souuulll, my savior God to theeeee,"

"How great Thou arrrrt, how greaaat Thou arrrt."

He could tell from her responses to his touch, that he had a moving effect on her. The slight sway to her body, her increased rate of breathing, showed that the music too had the exact effect he expected, backing up his words. Her pulse raced. She looked into his eyes, hers moistening.

"Music is a secret to life, the universe, and everything. I believe it is part of God's 'magic,' if you will, used to run the universe."

She gasped, placing her palm over her heart.

"Everywhere throughout the universe, in the middle of space, right here between my fingers," he held his fingers apart for effect, as if grasping an invisible egg, "tiny particles, wormholes, even black holes, appear and vanish every nanosecond."

She nodded, "Still basic home upper school science."

Ceres nodded with emphasis, "Yes! So out there," he looked away from her, nudging his head forward. She turned her head and whole body to follow his gaze, seeing two large rings opening up ahead of the ship, thrust forward by four spidery arm struts. Between them a small flash of light added to the background of the brilliant stars around them in deep space.

"The two rings house a circle of ryanite discs, like a set of drum skins. They can absorb electromagnetic radiation and convert it to radiate gravity output. Reversing the magnetic polarity flips it to anti-gravity output. So we use lasers as our drumsticks to beat them in the exact harmonic patterns to match the target location where we wish to appear."

Throughout the ship, everything, everyone felt a humming, throbbing sensation. Despite the dampers, the vibrations translated down the struts holding the rings forward of the hull. Serenity's hair stood up on her arms. The flash of light outside had grown into a bright sparkling spot. A girl nearby gasped.

"A wormhole flashes into existence and the harmonics give it energy," Ceres continued. "The gravity pulses grab it, hold it, and pull it open. Once it grows it has a little more gravity of its own, so it sucks in those other wormholes, particles, and micro-black holes appearing nearby. It feeds itself, a ravenous worm, devouring, inhaling, the very stuff of space."

The bright spot swirled and expanded like a ball, a sphere of light.

"The end of the 'hole we have captured grows here. The far end is at our destination. The cosmic string connecting them becomes heavy with all the quantum stuff and interstellar hydrogen molecules falling in."

The wormhole grew before their eyes, a giant fisheye lens with an alien world on the other side, seen in short flashes as the swirling pattern of the event horizon allowed.

"All we need is enough power to pull it open on our side so we can fly through. The hole does the rest naturally. The gravity of the wormhole itself pulls us forward—that's why we need the struts to hold the ship away until we're ready to transit. We add a bit of thrust with our plasma drives so we can escape out the other side, and 'Poof' we're there."

With dramatic speed, the Ryanite rings folded up like an umbrella, retracting down flush and into the hull of *Marauder* ahead of *Pegasus* acting as its bridge. The swirling wormhole event horizon flashed before them, then they felt the kick from behind, of the ship's drives firing.

Ceres helped Serenity fall to the couch by hooking his heels under it. He held her with one arm around her shoulders. She looked at him sternly for a moment then back at the spectacle before her. They were stuck fast in the gravlounge cushioning, held in by the antigravity field surrounding them, anchoring them against the movements of the ship.

"Coming out here on my journey," she said, "I've done this a few times now. Of course, everything you said is covered by basic science, downstreamed in homeschool." She turned to him, "But I've never heard it explained so beautifully. You have a gift for this, don't you?"

Realizing modesty was something she wanted to see him try, Ceres withheld comment for a moment. "If you say so," he nodded, but turned away, looking behind her head, to hide the huge smile he could not suppress.

"Well done. Fake humility for a while and you just might achieve it," she said. They both laughed. "Good enough for a start," she added.

"Why, thank you, Miss," Ceres smiled.

The nose of the ship disappeared, stabbing into the spherical event horizon, concealed behind the swirling fisheye lens effect.

Marauder slipped through the hole. Ceres enjoyed the feeling of being expanded in all directions at the same time as being crushed from all sides. He had come to regard it as a feeling of being one with the fabric of the universe. Considering the mass of the quantum string connecting the hole mouths was compressed into a one particle chain the length of their journey, it was not a far leap to imagine this true.

Serenity, and the majority of the freed slaves aboard the pirate's former flagship, were sickened by the unfamiliar experience. It was a common human response in modern travel about the galaxy since the Exodus, the start of the Galactic Era of Man. But each individual had to gain enough experience travelling to get used to it, if possible.

The redhead breathed deeply and steadily to calm her nerves and stomach. It felt like 30 seconds or more of transit to most, but the true elapsed time was instantaneous from entry event horizon to exit horizon of the wormhole.

* * *

Shambala System, Planet Nirvana, L2
2525/7/17/2335

"It is like stepping out through the doorway of your house," Ceres explained, "but in completing that step your foot lands inside the doorway of your destination, say, your office across town."

As soon as they passed through the spherical event horizon, the galaxy seemed to have changed. No longer was the ship back-dropped by the beautiful Wisp Nebula, but now the closer stars near the heart of the rim arm known as the Periphery Sector filled the forward views.

"Would you care to see where I've taken you?" he nodded his head towards the forward view again.

The particularly bright star nearby was Shambhala, in its blazing glory and splendor. The ship turned to port and the Super-Earth planet, Nirvana, filled the left side of the view, causing an eruption of cheers from the passengers.

"This looks familiar," she said. "I was right here for the transit into Nirvana space over a week ago. This is where Trok had his men hold me while they took us through the wormhole and flew in to Valhalla."

"Ah, so this is where you first laid eyes on me, is that it? Mixed feelings?" he looked over, drawn into following her red hair as it cascaded down over the back of the lounger.

"Yes, then and now."

"Well, if you want to get off this is the first stop, Strawberry."

"We'll see. We're not done with this mission yet."

"You keep reminding me," Ceres sent the conjoined ships flying down on a landing pattern approach he found recently used, in the navigation logs of *Pegasus*.

"Hey, Sweet Strawberry?" Ceres asked her, "How about this time, you get to *land* in this ship? No more hijackings?'"

"Sounds interesting," she teased him back. "It *is* kind of unusual for us. Let's try it for variety's sake, and see what happens?" She smiled back at him. Ceres was pleased with her use of his style of humor.

They began their fiery descent through Nirvana's dense atmosphere, huge energy screens ballooned like an umbrella, engulfed with the flames of air particles super-heating as the ship blasted down like a long meteor, plowing into the dense atmosphere of Nirvana.

Judging from the eruption of WetNet feed, Ceres thought Planet Nirvana was collectively stunned when a wormhole opened in the nearby Lagrange-point, and out came the *Marauder* for the second time today. It took the usual hour landing the craft, shedding speed above the atmosphere, burning off more speed inside the thick layers of gasses of Nirvana's heavy air.

Ceres landed the pirate flagship at sunrise, in the city square amid Shangri-la's five arcologies. Most of the debris had been cleared from the pirates' bombardment a week past. *Pegasus* floated off the back of her carrier and landed next to it.

Boarding ramp down, Ceres and Serenity welcomed their passengers to the ground. Out poured the hundreds of freed slaves from across the Periphery Sector, delirious to be home, incredulous that they were finally free. Long accustomed to the lower gravity of Asteroid Valhalla, most of the slaves were incapacitated by the high gravity of Nirvana, needing needed robotic assistance to disembark the spacecraft.

Thousands more robots filed out from the arcology tower's bases, preceding their owners. The remaining families of kidnapped slaves came after their bots, to find out if their family members had survived the horrors of pirate slavery.

Once she sat on the huge parkland lawn at the heart of the enormous city, Anastasia froze in place, now realizing what was happening. Tears in her eyes and words choked up in her throat, she mouthed, "God bless you!" towards Ceres and Serenity.

Cassius and Yukozune dropped their weapons inside and saluted Ceres.

"Well done, Jerome," he called Cassius, "Akebono," he said to Yukozune. "You guys earned two years pay plus a double bonus. Now, go get that old squid Medusa out of there before he molts, and enjoy your leave time." Ceres saluted them and turned, grinning and shrugging, to Serenity's surprised face.

"You hired your uncle's old crew?" Serenity asked breathlessly. She caught on quick, recognizing their names from the stories of his upbringing that Ceres had been telling her lately.

"Thank you, men," she said to the huge crewers. "It is amazing to find such loyal men these days."

"The Tarsis family attracts fanatical loyalty, because they treat their people so well, Ma'am," Jerome deferred her praise. "We were like Ceres' adopted big brothers growing up. It tweren't nuthin' fer us but anothuh family picnic."

"You've got your own stake now," Ceres said. "You can sell your share of the recovery business, or keep it and ease out of the Ops? Take advantage of the Tarsis SEEDS program to get you going?"

"What about 'seeds,' Ceres?" asked Serenity.

"Second Enterprise, Entrepreneurial Development, & Stimulus." Akebono answered on Ceres' behalf. "The Tarsis family helps any employee with a decent idea start their own side business and help it grow. They provide training in entrepreneurial skills, and have spun off more employees into their own businesses than any other way of retirement from employment."

"Does it work?" she asked, again directed to Ceres.

"It works," answered Jerome, "for those who work hard. ...work smart. 'Sessful people like StarSys know how to teach people to do the same for themselves. They are the biggest business seed starter—all time. It works."

"So, go open your own restaurant already, old friend," Ceres traded arm grips with the massive man. "I will buy out my own table, reserved in the best spot, if it means I can always get in for the best Cajun food in the galaxy."

"What are you going to do with your bonus, Achey?" he teased the sumo-sized man.

"Party loud and large, my young friend," Akebono said. "The three 'F's' of the single man's life: Fun, food, and females! I intend to spend it all, so I need to go on another adventure."

"You could be the doorman for his restaurant?" Ceres looked at Akebono but hooked a thumb at Jerome. "Keep working together like the brothers you are? Akebono's eyebrows raised and he mashed his mouth to the side.

"Thank you, my brothers," Ceres said to both men. "I value loyalty, and you guys have proven yourselves to be family. Come visit home any time. You are always welcome!"

"What about you, little brother?" Jerome asked, leaning his head forward, he looked through the early grey flecks in his eyebrows.

"Unfinished business," Ceres answered cryptically.

"We'll be there!" Akebono said. "Do not leave without us."

"You don't even know what he's talking about," Jerome obviated.

"Does it matter?" asked the big Asianan.

"Nope, I 'spect not," Jerome said with a chuckle.

"This is something I should probably handle alone," Ceres said. "I don't want to risk your lives again."

"Di'n't you just learn?" Jerome whacked Ceres' shoulder blade with a heavy handed swat. "With a team, you increase your odds of success, you multiply your capabilities by those of your crew."

"Iron is long gone, but not forgotten," Serenity added. "Even when he fell, it was his choice to follow you, was it not?"

"You sound like my old Sensei," Ceres replied, hanging his head in deep thought for a moment. "Yes, I see that the group of us achieved more together than I would have solo. I agree, I—we, *we* would never have rescued all those slaves if not for the team, including you, Strawberry."

Jerome smiled broadly. Looking from Ceres to Serenity, he nodded his head with a satisfied look on his face.

"In fact, wasn't breaking them all out of there, your idea?" Ceres only now realized she had led him into expanding his mission beyond the search for his mother, to save and free Serenity, and then to free all the slaves. He decided *how,* that to save them all, to protect his family, and to end his father's predations on the Periphery Sector, Ceres destroyed all of the Void Vikings.

"Thank you for your capable help," Serenity planted a soft kiss on Ceres' cheek. "I couldn't have done it without you, too, without all of you!" she amended. She gave both huge operators a kiss on the cheek, causing them to grin and blush.

Ceres offered a handshake towards the men, then leaned in as if to hug his old friend and brother, Jerome, but gave him a kiss on the cheek too.

"Hey!" Jerome pushed him off, his booming laughter giving the bass beat to that of the rest of the group. Akebono held his ribs as his chest heaved.

"Rest, relax, and regroup for the next Op, then." Ceres bowed towards Akebono and shook Jerome's hand again, then the two men headed back into the ship.

"Seeing you for the first time from inside *Wanderlust*, before we ever spoke I had that odd feeling you were a man with plans," Serenity teased Ceres. "What else are you scheming to do?"

"I am still on the same mission of my whole life," Ceres answered her. "I will find my mother. The next adventure starts where they all do: home."

The city leaders' delegation had walked out from the civic building, Tower One. They finally approached as triumphant Ceres swaggered out among the freed crowds, the hundreds of impromptu family reunions.

Serenity traded looks of shock with Ceres, when the Gendün Lama asked, "How much more do you want in tribute for these units, my Prince?"

* * *

Wisp Nebula's outer reaches
2525/7/17/2337

Ka'ra lined up her targeting reticle on the drifting bridge, blown free of the fleeing *Marauder*. "This is it!" she squealed, thrill of the kill creeping into her voice. "I can finally be free of that—" she paused, squinted through the holographic sights at her helpless prey, "—that maniac!"

"Hmmm," she reconsidered her options. "That maniac still has contacts and connections, other sons lacking such a haughty moral code. You should think. You may still take advantage of him." She slumped in her pilot's chair, lip wrinkled, reflective of her conflict.

Sitting upright, she sprayed on some of her special pheromones. – Sprayed some more. "I don't know if you're stupid enough to do this or stupid enough not too, vac girl!" The fact that she often talked to herself made Ka'ra worry about her own sanity.

"I know. Let's get on with it!" It was more that she answered herself as if a different person, that most concerned her.

Docking her craft with the *Marauder*'s bridge pod, tractors compressed the torn strut-tower against her ship's armor. One of her long white gloves set to stun, Ka'ra opened the hatch, greeting her king with a demure smile.

"Follow them!" Tyrian screamed, flying headfirst through the hatch even before its leaves had fully retracted out of his way. "Get within combat range so I can shoot them down myself!"

"Master," Ka'ra soothed, her voice calm, "remember, 'revenge is a dish best served space-cold.'" She immediately resented using the term identifying herself as property, but subservience felt like the way to survive his infamous rage this time.

It barely stayed his tirade as they raced after the bulk of his flagship, escaping towards open space. Poisoning his rage with her persuasive pheromones, plus a handful of proffered cannahol tabs, likely made the difference between her life and death. *The more you take, the more you need to take.*

Tyrian squinted at Ka'ra, mouth drawn tight in a grimace, but he reserved his answer. After a few tense breaths in the cockpit of her white starship, he calmed down a bit. "What do you have in mind?"

"I suggest, let's let them *think* they have escaped. Let your son follow his little clues he thinks he found here, and when he finally finds his mother, she will not be there."

"I'm listening!" The sneer in his voice confirmed, her magic was working. She was persuading him to at least listen instead of rush forward into a futile duel with the larger combat ship which Ceres had somehow wrested away the control of.

That her king had forgotten about that concerned her deeply, so blind was his raging anger against his traitorous son. Ka'ra manipulated him in her every way, appealing to his cunning to delay their attack, and it barely saved their lives to fight again another day.

Two minutes after *Marauder* left the fringe of the nebula, just as the wormhole started to collapse, a small, ivory colored ship slipped through into Shambhala system, otherwise unseen.

"So, where is she?" Ka'ra asked.

"Set wormhole coordinates for the Patriarch Stars. Tip of Saint Michael's sword." Tyrian smacked his palm into his fist, growling, "I'm gonna make her pay for this!"

Ceres 2526 (Book 2)
Chapter 1: Freefall

Sol System, Earth 1.0, Polar orbit
Starship *Pegasus*, airlock
04/15/2526/0700

Ceres dove out into space.

Passing the lintel of the airlock's hatch, his forcefield shield grew to extend around him as a sphere. Pushing through the hatch's energy field, he brought the air enveloped by the shield with him. The enclosed bubble drifted away below his starship *Pegasus*.

Ceres' freed his forearm bracer from the limpet-shaped shield emitter, the magnetic fastener released. Swinging his arms overhead as a diver over water would to execute his championship moves, he spun around in space, to face back whence he had come. Ceres fanned his arms again, in the reverse directions, halting his spin.

Drifting, seeming to stand erect in space over the planet below him, Ceres saluted. His grin morphed into a warm smile for the stunning redhead woman watching him from above.

Lips pursed, arms crossed, she stepped closer to the hatch in her royal blue, tailored unisuit.

Ceres noted her piercing eyes, her tight smile, losing sight of her as his drop bubble slid away below the spearhead shape of his spacecraft.

"I'll be right back, Strawberry," he reassured Serenity via their crew comms link, using the nickname he recently coined for her.

The orange glow of friction from *Pegasus'* aerobraking maneuvers had all but faded from the belly of the craft, the spaceship now inserted into a polar orbit. Her skin displayed glorious details at his close range. Ceres' newest friend, the artist Kangee, had completed his epic mural depicting the mythical horse with wings, the namesake of the sleek vessel. Drifting beneath the belly of the orbiting luxury freightliner, Ceres enjoyed the perfect vista for admiring the intricate squiggled quills sprouting from muscular wings programmed into her photoreactive skin.

Ceres' private moment of appreciation for this art ended as two small spherical drones popped out of the belly hatch of the craft, sentinel companions for his journey. They reminded him of the alien Rokkled's "Foo Fighter" drones, which had mystified ancient Man before the day of Second Revelations.

"Talk," Serenity replied, curt. "Now you will show me how well can I trust what y'say." She set the hook he had put in his own mouth.

"Oh!" Ceres groaned into his comm channels. "What the right woman can inspire us to do to prove our love!"

"Roger that," growled a deep male voice.

"Copy, Barnes," Ceres replied, prompted by the military jargon to focus on the mission. "That passes for our external comms check. Ceres Out." He grinned, glad to hear from his old friend's voice, graveled from frequent shouting. He knew Barnes and his storied team of commandos awaited him far below on the surface ice. The ship's proximity allowed a through-connection for now. He looked forward to the quiet isolation of his entry burn's comm blackout.

Drifting through space, Ceres rolled back, feet towards his ship above, spinning facedown. Grasping the shield emitter with one hand, his other reached to his lower back, detaching a brick-shaped battery pack from his gear harness. Snapping the power-pack into the shield unit, he gripped it in front of him. Boot pressors thrusting off *Pegasus'* mass, one arm's tractor beam pulling at the Earth below, at a shallow angle Ceres flew towards the glowing bow of sunrise warming the edge of Man's frozen homeworld.

Show her! Ceres thought of Serenity again. Was she testing his worthiness as her lifemate? He knew she did not want to hear him explain. She wanted to see for herself how faithfully he kept his word. Despite his success in freeing Serenity and thousands of slaves from pirates, still she challenged him. Ceres knew his real work lay ahead: to prove his sins and character flaws remained in his past, and no longer part of him.

At the Tarsis family banquet celebrating his successful return from visiting his father's pirate band, Ceres, arrogant, prideful, and vain, had boasted among his cousins. He bragged he could visit Solman's ancient home unharmed, retrieving Earth's greatest lost treasure.

"Show me!" the Irish redhead had called out his bragging. Leaving Asteroid Valhalla, Serenity had been the most excited to discover that he could fly. So here he was, a meteor falling from space to Earth's surface.

Ceres thought she couldn't help but be thrilled along with him, right? Was it a good sign, for her to get a thrill when thinking of him? Certain he felt thrilled when thinking of her, he thought, let's even things up?

Pushed at four-G's of acceleration by the powered rings in the soles of his boots, Ceres rocketed towards the edge of the black planet. He raced forward to meet sunrise, the dawn terminator, as it crept around the globe to greet him. Aurora borealis shimmered below him in sparkling green ribbons, as ions from the sun rained down along Earth's magnetic field lines. Ceres realized firsthand, that Earth's "shield" had inspired those engineered by man to protect their starships.

Why is my nose lit up on one side? he wondered. His gaze panned over to take in a shining moon, to his right. "Where mankind first stepped out into the night," he recited the ancient line of space poetry.

Beyond Luna's bright glare he found his home, among the background stars piercing the velveteen blackness surrounding him. As much as he loved this spacediving, it was the "Twilight Star," always climbing into Earth's early morning sky, that spread Ceres' lips in a warm smile. His home, his planet, his namesake: planet Ceres.

The former asteroid Ceres, moved to the fourth Lagrange point, had preceded Earth in its march around Sol for nearly 500 years. From there the Tarsis family watched over Earth 1.0, while managing their galaxy leading multi-corp, StarSys. Ceres' Papa Joe described himself as the most patient gardener in the galaxy, carefully tilling, fertilizing, and sowing, for the eventual rebirth, the bloom of man's ancient home.

"Snowball Earth" his History homeschooling and Planetary Astronomy professors called it. Earth 1.0, now over 400 years since it froze to death. The result of a global nuclear winter, thanks to Man's ancient war with the Insectoid Infestation. Short version: To kill the human-sized bugs eating Mankind, we killed our own planet. It had cost us our ancestral home, he thought, but at least the survival of humanity was secure now, spread out across the galaxy.

Those few we could save. '*We,*' thought Ceres, *those few the Tarsis family could save.* Terraforming their nearby planet Ceres, the Xardyons helped them raid the asteroid belt and Kuiper belt to build the fleet of Arcology space cities that had saved mankind. The survivors, launched across the galaxy to colonize hundreds of worlds, became Man from Sol, or Solman. The tailings piled upon Ceres until the asteroid grew into a planet.

When Earth froze and, tragically, no further rescue arcologies could be filled, the Tarsis family then assumed the role of caretakers of the ancestral home of Solman.

The silvery teardrop protecting him hit the first molecules of the planet's uppermost atmosphere, what spacers such as Ceres called "atmo." Red-orange flares erupted across the drop capsule, throwing splashes of flame across his flattop. Performing a handstand against the slight push of air resistance, Ceres steadied the backside of the shield emitter. Expecting a cold reception below, he did not want the shield to singe the scruff of hair off his face.

Scanning the planet ahead and below, Ceres tried to visualize his intended landing zone, still hiding in pre-dawn darkness. Spring for the Northern continents had not yet reached up into the Arctic Circle.

Flares of atmo molecules increased to more steady gouts of flame. The intense energy striking the force field turned the drop pod opaque. Rolling down to his shoulder, Ceres turned and lay against the effective floor, placing the pile of graphene-armored plates stacked on his back, upon the glowing white cocoon. Wrapping his arm around the shield emitter he tucked it against his side, using his weight as ballast to steady his energy bubble in the intensely burning winds of reentry.

The battering intensified as the atmosphere he fell through increased in density. Air molecules striking at his orbital velocity of thousands of kilometers per hour, burned against the outer shell. The robotic probes tricording while falling with him, saw Ceres' white teardrop as a tough marshmallow in a blast furnace.

The goo- Galactic spacer's other slang term for a planet's atmo- could not get out of the way fast enough. An air cushion built up, pushing a shock wave and heat layer forward and away from the spherical forcefield. With most of the hot gases removed from contact with the shield, the heat remained in the shocked gas layer. It squeezed around Ceres' energy capsule to ooze back into the goo.

He had several minutes of isolation to review his strategy, how to achieve the long mission which dominated his whole life: Where's Mom?

His mother was one root reason for being here today, falling into the planet at hypersonic velocities, coming to steal one of Earth's most precious assets. Ceres' goal: nothing less than improving the lives of every Solman, including the lives of his family. Troubling thought: does this equate him with a cast away angel of the Old Testament? Or Prometheus of ancient Greek tragedy?

Where is Mom? Finding her, kidnapped and hidden among the galaxy's over 500 inhabited worlds, had bested the Galactic Marshalls, Military Intelligence, even the Tarsis family's vast resources. Promising leads had dried up over a decade ago. It frustrated Ceres, his mother's vanishing. There were just too many blind planets off the radar to hide in and on.

Recently, hope had re-ignited. Grown and trained, Ceres had crossed the galaxy to find his father, hoping to find his mother too. The elder Tauri's personality, small clues in things he said, and revealing thoughts of his ex-wife, each yielded new vectors to search for her. Serenity had read new clues from Tyrian's thoughts while aboard Asteroid Valhalla. The family—especially Ceres—was anxious to begin rescue operations, once they finally located Ceres' mother.

Preparing for that eventual stage, Ceres had hired a team of combat experienced heavy mercenaries, known and revered as the "Blood Tide." His next step was to rendezvous with them and see how well they worked with and for Ceres, on a live field Op. Now that he crossed over his original horizon, the Arctic Circle, they should await him only 150 kilometers below. At drop speed, he would reach the top of the world in minutes.

Thickening air burning away outside had slowed Ceres' drop-capsule. Falling now at mere hundreds of kilometers per hour, air molecules compressed but flowed around the sphere of energy. Unlit, the streaks of flaming atmo vanished, taking their death pyres with them. The shield reverted to its transparent bluish tint. Clarity restored, Ceres' mental and atmospheric buffeting subsided. *Game on!* he thought.

His drone's feed into his implanted Heads Up Display, or HUD, morphed to show him beyond the visible light range. The two spheres rushed deeper into the atmo ahead of him, racing to see beneath the clouds. Pulling his suit's hood up from his back neckline, Ceres covered his hair, then pulled the hood all the way under his jawline. Out of the fabric a visor of golden diatanium hardened as it covered his face, memory-form fitting to its wrap around shape. It darkened to protect him from the sunlight striking him at this altitude.

Another visual check of the Landing Zone, or LZ, below yielded nothing observable, it was still dark until the morning line of sunrise crossed the island. There, his bots showed him the peak of the ice mountain above the

LZ shone pink with the first thin light over the horizon. Beyond that, nothing but the endless dark, uninhabited North of this renowned planet of ice.

Had it been full daylight below, at best he would have seen endless white sheets of snows and ice fields that encompassed the entire world. Drone radar scans, translated into a wireframe display in his HUD, revealing an island hidden deep below the perpetual snowpack. Its protective mountaintop caused the slow flowing glacier to raise broken crags, the protruding spine of a massive monster from B-holo films.

The Viking-styled pirates Ceres had defeated had regaled each other, reviving old stories of the world-spanning Midgard serpent. According to legend, the titanic beast lay slumbering until Ragnarok, an epic battle to destroy the gods and the world. He pondered, was he flying over ancient Viking territory, after all. Was this the mythical Wyrm's shoulder, carelessly lifting the kilometer's deep glacier with a shrug?

A lifelong Christian, Ceres did not believe pagan myths. He smirked at those ideas. His father had used the cult of Viking legends and lifestyle merely to control his pirates. He motivated them with hollow promises of rewards in Valhalla, the heaven of Viking afterlife, for great deeds and death in battle. Ceres knew his father was neither a god nor *the* God. Patricidal Ceres had killed Tyrian himself. It weighed him down, threatening to sink his soul, so he shoved the thought aside and focused on his mission.

Rolling to the side, Ceres popped the battery out of the shield emitter, returning it to the rear of his gear harness. He latched his bracer back in behind the shield, centering the falling ball under his weight. His armor extended, graphene scales flowing across his inner suit, his visor growing to encompass his face. Blue plates wrapped around him, sliding under his battle harness of gear, encasing him in cannon-proof protection. The teardrop of shielding melting away above him, violent sounds from his supersonic travel blasted and buffeted his body.

Ceres enjoyed his freefall from a hundred thousand meters above the surface, racing down at a dizzying rate. Protected by his golden faceplate, his grin betrayed his love for this rush. How alive he felt! Calling "Nick," one of the drones, closer, to capture him on its holofeed, he felt certain that she, his Strawberry, would love to see this.

Rolling, he stabilized, using his body as an aerodynamic wedge, a wing, to glide toward a beacon marker on the horizon, a green pillar of light in his HUD. NavWay, a navigation app embedded in his HUD, led him on a path of crisscross maneuvers to shed airspeed and loiter over his objective. His Galactic Navy suit lightened its color as he flew down, matching the sky's changing color, masking him from would-be ground observers.

Adjusting his arms and legs, Ceres changed direction as he plummeted through the cloud layers, seeing glimpses of the snow peaked island below. Ceres' foo fighters revealed crustal sea ice rushing by far beneath him. Switching back to view their radar he saw the bulk of an island ahead, buried beneath two kilometers of glacier, surrounded by an icy ocean full of blocks of thick sea pack.

Nearby major islands in the Svalbard archipelago remained buried under their glaciers and record sea ice, excluding the re-activated volcanic island of Nordaustlandet. Ceres called it "Nord," for short, his mission briefing noting that it had recently erupted, the icy caldera refreezing as a bullseye of muddy slush. This gave urgency to today's mission. Thrusting hard aft with his gravity gear, Ceres shot across the arctic as a living meteor, until directly above his destination waypoint.

Noting the extreme altitude, Ceres made use of his hang time. There was more than one way to get from A to B. He thought he might as well make it more interesting.

As both an adrenaline junky and uniquely equipped for expertise at this freefall sport of planet diving, Ceres remembered another reason he so enjoyed it. Twisting his arms about, he initiated a variety of spins and cartwheels. Randomly pushing out one hand or foot to drag the sky, Ceres careened like a starship wreck, wild turns and chaotic spins buffeting him into random gyrations, out of control.

He delighted in seeing how much or little effort he needed to right himself, only to set off on yet another wild tumble. Mixing in slight pulls or thrusts with his tractor boots or pressor gave him a unique range of motions and moves for sky dancing.

A buzzer went off in his MeTR alarms, just as Ceres again sent himself gyrating. He fell through the standard warning height of the "pull altitude" for Earth's gravity. Marines inserted from orbit for planetary ops would pop parachutes or fire landing rockets at this height. Gathering himself in, head down, Ceres rushed even faster at the ground. Then the emergency "pull" alarm blared in his head, red notices flashing before his eyes in his HUD.

Breaking through the cloud layer he now saw firsthand, sunrise highlighting the peaks of jagged ice of the arctic glacial field, a permanent cap atop the world. Buried mountains of the island archipelago thrust up the glacier as if through clouds that had frozen in place. The jagged edges of flowing arctic ice pack made a ski jump for titans as they towered into the sky, ice mountains themselves.

Gritting his teeth at the extreme speed, Ceres tucked his knees and arms up into a flying stance. He imagined himself a super hero flying off to save the planet. Humming with feedback, pressor beams in his bracers and boots thrust down and aft, pushing back toward the mass of planet Earth below him.

Transitioning his downward speed into transit speed across the snowpack, the strain of four-G's neared the limits of his strength. Gravity being the weakest force, though longest ranged, only now near the planet's surface did his personal-scale gear have the strength, the mass resistance feedback, to support his weight. Ceres struggled to change his lethal fall into thrilling flight.

With life or death stakes, he tested how much power he could endure and still overcome gravity and his momentum before his body plastered into red mist across the ice field. Adrenaline flowing, he reveled in it as always. Ceres never felt more alive than when facing death, and right now he felt very alive!

He flew! Bending legs and arms, feeling powerful, fast, and strong, his trajectory curved flat. Ceres rocketed low across the ice, jinking between jagged flows and huge blocks squeezed up from the global icepack, ridges and peaks of an ice-cream mountain.

Pulling up, Ceres spiraled, regaining hundreds of meters of altitude, teasing his holotographer Nick, and the other silvery dropbot, "Sput," as if he would catch them. As with their great-grandfather robots, Ceres' drones were strong enough to smash through a light aircraft and survive.

"Thank you, Lord," Ceres prayed aloud, "for leading me here." His arms moved over his chest in the ancient sign of Jesus' cross. "Everything in my life: every lesson, every person, every prayer, every motivation... has led me to be here and now so I can fully appreciate the gravity of this moment."

"For thousands of years, man has dreamed of soaring bodily through the air, just like the birds. Today, in this moment, I am the first in history to fly over the Earth, as my ancient forefathers dreamed."

a

Galaxipedia 25.25

Aft: The rear of a ship. Slang: The rear of a person.

Arcology: A hyper-building, 12 kilometers tall with a 1.5 km wide base. Arc is the short form. These are often built in space enabling an entire colony to move from source to settler world.

Army: Galactic troops tasked with ground ops on the surfaces of planets.

Asiana: That sector of the galaxy settled by former Asian Earther's.

Atmo: Atmosphere.

Bird House: A space station housing a squadron of fighter craft.

Bloodline: Family lineage, tribe, clan.

Cargoalls: Coveralls with several baggy pockets, loops, and straps for holding numerous parts and tools.

Carina Ends: The end of the Carina Arm of the Milky Way Galaxy is a wild, uncivilized sector with few colonies.

Ceres: 1) Terraformed into the smallest planet in Sol system, Ceres was once a dwarf planet, the largest of the Sol system asteroids.
2) The most eligible bachelor in the galaxy, Ceres Tauri was the MVP of the Zero Gravity Ball League, leading the Navy Stars team to the championship title in "The Game," in two of his three seasons of play.

Crafter: The crafting station is a robotic machine that builds items out of stored base materials. It essentially prints parts to build almost anything.

Di: "Dye" on some planets, "Dee-eye" on others. Short for Dollari.

Diatanium: Alloy of tritanium with diamond latticed graphene. This clear metal is harder than diamond and stronger than tritanium.

Ditch: A "dirty" swear word.

Dollari: Currency used in the Galactic Confederacy of Worlds.

Duranium: Depleted uranium, an extremely dense, heavy, and strong metal used for the most extreme armor or projectiles, as it is still radioactive.

Earth 1.0: Old Earth, the birthplace of mankind. In the 21st century, the Insectoid Infestation led to a global nuclear winter. As the ice sheets advanced, now "Solman," evacuated Earth onto new worlds.

Exoframes: These lightest of 'Mechs, three meters tall, are heavy powered armor the user wears more than climbs into. They are capable of carrying crew-served and vehicle scale weapons, heavy armor, portable power plants, and racks of missiles. Many are flight and space capable.

Farmstead: See: Homestead. The price of passage on early Earth colony ships, colonists had to agree to settle their own plot of land for a minimum of 10 Earth years. The cramped space and no comforts forced most colonists out onto their new worlds. The land grant of 10 square kilometers per family over 300 original colony words collapsed Earth housing and land prices, precipitating the global economic collapse.

Force Field: An active, powered energy field for defensive use. Sometimes shaped into thin, perfectly sharp weapons.

Gi: The martial artist's uniform. Each major art form has its own special style of clothing, but they are all referred to as "gi's."

Groundball: Old Earth 1.0 would call it Rugby.

Head: Naval term for a zero-gravity bathroom.

Homestead: See: Farmstead.

HUD: Heads Up Display via optical nerve implant. A multitude of virtual screens, displays, and overlays can appear in the user's vision.

Jetsam: Floating space debris jettisoned from a ship.

Leyden rounds: First posited by Jules Verne, are essentially capacitor projectiles which discharge electricity upon striking the target. Can be thrown, or launched via compressed air or chemical cartridges.

Lift: "Elevator" to some is called "Lift" to most.

Lum: Pronounced "loom." Light. From root "illumination."

Marauder: The flagship of the Void Vikings pirate gang.

Marina: Orbiting space station for garaging private spacecraft and starcraft while their owners pop down to the planet below.

Marines: The heavy troops of the Navy, tasked with shipboard and space combat, and orbital insertion operations. They wear heavily armed and armored Exoframes supported by Mechs.

Mechs: Giant walking tanks, mechs have heavy armor, massive heat sinks, and any weaponry they can power. 5 to 25 meters tall.

Medibay: Sick bay aboard a ship.

Merchant Marine: The professional officer corps of the private fleet of commercial starships operating in the Galactic. Large ships are required to have at least one qualified officer on the bridge at all times.

MeTR: Modem/Transceiver/Router in one. Includes petabytes of data storage and access trays for inserting further data modules called 'pins.'

Navy: Space going ships of military grade are "naval," in honor of the long history and tradition of their Earth-analogue navies. Various Navy ships carry Marines to fight from the ship, operate as troop carriers to move the Army to new planets, and project their own fighters, bombers, missiles, and guns for waging war between the planets and stars.

Patriarch Stars: After the 3rd Great Awakening initiated the Grand Reunification, the original colony of the Modern Exodus was led by the new Orthodox Church. Millions were inspired to follow, and so, mankind survived Earth. Those presiding over implementing the Galactic Homestead Act rewarded the entire Orion Arm of the Galaxy to the Orthodox Church.

PBC: Particle Beam Cannon. A neutrally charged beam of atomic elements that flies through space at a fraction of the speed of light, cutting through most starship's shields to shoot out systems or crewmembers within.

Periphery Sector: An independent (wild) sector with over 20 colony planets, all 3rd generation. The Void Vikings preys upon these worlds.

Peyote: Tribal herbal medicine, which gives hallucinogenic daydreams.

Popper: See: Telepod.

Pub: The ubiquitous public houses aboard Arcs and space stations owe their popularity to cramped personal quarters with no open living spaces.

Ravens: Nine-meter long black spaceships with forward-swept atmospheric wings. The wing shape makes them naturally unstable, which gives them excellent maneuverability.

Reflectin: Organic compound from the flesh of the alien jellyfish/squid race Tenublians, which allows materials to change colors.

Ripfast: Hook and loop fabric tape.

Rokkled: Pronounced "Rock-led." Silicon based sentient life that lives in space on asteroids. They appear to be tall living statues.

Ryanite: Exotic matter that absorbs all known radiations, emitting gravity waves in return. By reversing magnetic polarity, this lightweight matter can also emit anti-gravity waves, repelling normal matter.

Sealing Strip: Life support emergency sealing strip, known for centuries as "duct tape."

Skycar: Common personal hovercraft, commuters carry this transportation to and from their telepod stations at either end of their travels. Unfolds into full operational size and shape in seconds. Their repulsor pods mitigate weight when folded into the compact, carry case shape.

Skycycle: Super-light bicycle with small wings, made for low gravity, man-powered flying. They fold up into a pocket-sized case.

Sol: Latin name for "the sun."

Solman: Sol + Man denotes the sentient race of Man from Sol star system.

SOP: Standard Operating Procedure. Standing orders for handling regularly occurring operations following a pre-formatted plan.

Spaceship: A relatively small ship designed to operate in both the vacuum of space and inside a planetary atmosphere. Mid-sized ships might also equip space-rated drives but do not use them in atmospheres.

Starlag: Like jetlag but when travelling through wormholes. The body feels out of synch with the new local time on the other side of the hole.

Starship: A larger ship designed for space only. Rarely streamlined, many are built completely freeform, balanced over the center of thrust. They do not have benign propulsion systems of use in an atmosphere.

Telepod: Nicknamed "poppers" due to the sound of air slamming in to fill the vacuum when the telepod is used. Using wormhole technology, poppers allow instantaneous teleportation across a planet or up to its satellites and space stations.

Tenublians: These xenomorphic sentients look to humans like a genetic hybrid merging a giant jellyfish with a squid.

Thermocaster: Infrared heater.

Tritanium: Stronger, heavier titanium alloy.

Vac: Vacuum. Slang: Vac head, meaning one with "space for brains."

Viewer: A person transmitting their visual input via MeTR for others to view remotely. Newscasters usually employ a viewer so the Holo-news personality can appear on holo-cam in front of the subject scene.

Vocasters: Speakers, arrayed around a holo-display system.

Void Vikings: A vicious band of pirates based on an asteroid in the Periphery Sector. Tyrian Tauri founded the gang with a Viking theme.

Wormhole: See Jumpship. Space stations and large starships use rings of exotic ryanite to open wormholes. Transit is instantaneous.

Xardyons: The bigheaded, grey skinned, almond-eyed aliens of Old Earth 1.0 conspiracy theories, such as those surrounding Area 51.

Addendum
Robotic Housekeeping

Acknowledgments:

Mom, it all started with you. Thanks for nurturing my love of reading, especially Science and Fiction. You fed my mind just the right stuff to stretch, to learn what is and to stretch that into what can possibly be.

To Mrs. Burdge I send extreme thanks for encouraging my first serious creative writings. You were my High School Honors English teacher. I have never forgotten some of the creative stories I wrote with your positive encouragement. It is true that teachers give many kinds of lessons that can affect your entire life.

TCON is forever The CONSORTIUM. Formed by Spiglord to be a community of like-minded MMO gamers, we became friends from around the world. Especially notable here are Bhin'der, Kilgore, Shariela, Harper, and Arsenic. Also Drekkin, Nibroc, Tymme, Bodrake and Spiglord, for helping me visualize Ceres alive within SWG and SWTOR. The list could go on and on but I will just say, thank you to all of TCON. Carynne's crate of [F12] will drop on time! Guaranteed!

Creative Contributors:

Mentors & Gurus: Drew Bridges, Gale Buck, Stefan Duncan, Jon Batson, K.M.Weiland, Steven King, William Gibson, and Orson Scott Card.
Edited by: Dineane Whitaker.
Cover Designer & Military Advisor: Bill Frisbee.
Character Designer/Graphic Artist: Jason Farmer.
Author's Critic Circle: Lauren Bridges, Christiana Buck, Robin Kitson.
Fellow Authors: Terry R. Hill and Steven Lyle Jordon.
Proofreader: Donna Campbell Smith.
Beta Readers: Sammy Young, Clellie Allen, Jeremy Dimmitt.
Assistance from: Page 158 Books, The Storyteller's Bookstore, The Book Bar, Scuppernong Books, and Highland Book Cavern.
-Thank you all for your advice and assistance!

About the Author:

Micheal Lee Nelson resides in Wake Forest, NC with his redhead fiancée, a pair of sugar gliders, and a pair of convertible cars with matching payments!

He was born in Oregon, adopted by a hard working Heavy Equipment Operator and a harder working Schoolteacher in Charleston, OR. He enlisted in the United States Marine Corps from 1989 to 1995, carrying a toolbox and an M60 in the 6th ESB, 4th MarDiv.

Today Micheal enjoys creative cooking, gardening, photography and exploring the East Coast, especially the warm beaches of North Carolina, and wielding his creative super powers for the entertainment of mankind.

He sits on the Writer's Guild for the Franklin County Arts Council, and had two entries accepted into their 2015 literary journal, County Lines. He has also written articles for local newspapers, including Wake Weekly.

Micheal is currently being held captive by his characters, forced to transcribe "CERES 2526" as you read these very words…. Pray that he survives to tell you Ceres' next sordid tale.

Find us online at MichealLeeNelson.net. Micheal blogs about his books, the writing process, and stays in touch with his readers there.

Connect on Facebook at Micheal's author page, Twitter too!

Type: Micheal Lee Nelson —and look for his face!

FAQ's:

1) How do you spell your name?
   a) Mich-e-a-l is correct, "E-A" the Viking way. My father's side of the family is from Scandinavia, where e-a is the norm and a-e is rare, the opposite as in America.
2) How do you pronounce "Ceres?"
   a) "Series," as in "World Series!"
3) "How do I get more Ceres stories?"
   a) Ask for Ceres 2525 to stock in your local bookstores.
   b) Write a good review for me on Amazon.com, etc. Thank you!
   c) Share your review, my website link, my YouTube book trailers, and/or my Amazon links to your social media friends & groups. Thank you!!

d) Interact with Ceres and me on all of our social media (found under my name), with likes, comments, and questions. I will update you there as Ceres tells me more of his exploits over the best Scotch in the Galaxy!

Reader Feedback about CERES 2525:

"Now *that* is some great writing! Do a lot more of *that*!! Good work!"
    -Terry R. Hill, NASA engineer, author of "Third Exodus"

"Great work! I really enjoyed the read!"
    -Sammy Young, Rolesville, NC

"Action, Action, Action!"
    -Clark Anderson

"Ceres is a one man army!"
    -Author Gale Buck, a champion North Carolina Storyteller

"I didn't want to put it down."
    -Robby Culbreath

"It's a blend of technology, action, and character!"
    -Drew Bridges, prolific NC Author

"A James Bond crossed with Mad Max? Just that combination reveals a gifted, born with extraordinary juiced imagination. Can't wait for Book 2!"
    -Stefan Duncan, impressionist, "America's Van Gogh"

Readers:

Thank you, dear reader, for taking the time to read CERES 2525. If you enjoyed it, please consider telling your friends, sharing on social media, or posting a short review. Word of mouth is an author's best friend and much appreciated. Thank you!
    -Micheal Lee Nelson.

Reviews of CERES 2525:

* * * * * 5 out of 5 stars <u>Martial arts, pirates and pretty women</u>

"This was a great story. One of those hard to find Space Opera stories where the good guy is really good, the bad guys are bad, women are beautiful and competent and did I mention the bad guys are bad?

The story is about a hero named Ceres, how he grows up and goes after the guy who had his mother kidnapped.

I particularly like the way the author weaves together the past and present, culminating at the end of the novel.

An excellent read and I look forward to the sequel."
-By William S. Frisbee, 2016, Amazon Verified Purchase

"In his first book, Micheal Lee Nelson tells the story of Ceres Tauri, a 25-year-old playboy superstar of the zero gravity league, as he desperately searches for his parents, long held captive among the Galactic's 500 worlds.

The author even has a YouTube roster of "mood music" he listened to while writing the scifi piece. Among the music videos: R.Kelly's "I Believe I Can Fly."
-27587 magazine's 2016 "Books for the Beach" reading list

99624102R00178

Made in the USA
Columbia, SC
11 July 2018